Colin Butts is a direct descendant of the former Russian royal family and his childhood was spent between Iceland, Kenya and Bermondsey.

After Cambridge he joined the RAF, where he was selected by NASA in 1984 to join their space programme. Six months into his training it was discovered that he suffered from horizontal vertigo, a rare complaint that affects the inner ear and balance. This curtailed his career and on his return to the UK he resumed his studies.

After gaining a degree in marine biology he spent a number of years working with dolphins at the now closed Windsor Safari Park. He specialized in monitoring the emotional stress and psychological traumas that these mammals undergo, brought about by their tendency to mate for life.

Since the closure of Windsor Safari Park, Colin has divided his time between Formula Two race driving and lollipop man duties near a school in Peckham.

is harry on
the boat?

COLIN BUTTS

ORION

An Orion paperback
First published in Great Britain by Tuesday Morning Publishing in 1997
This paperback edition published in 2000 by Orion Books Ltd,
Orion House, 5 Upper St Martin's Lane, London WC2H 9EA

A CIP catalogue record for this book is available
from the British Library.

ISBN: 0 75283 458 4

Typeset by Deltatype Ltd, Birkenhead
Printed and bound in Great Britain by
Clays Ltd, St Ives plc
Cover photograph by Kevin Martin, London
telephone: 0207 622 4556

Cover design of original paperback edition by Deep Creative, London
telephone: 0207 721 8738

Tuesday Morning Publishing can be contacted at:
telephone: 0208 244 0000
email: tuesdaymorning@cwcom.net

foreword and thanks

As you read this novel, you may find yourself wondering if any of the events described are based upon even a molecule of truth. The Young Free and Single reps whose journey we follow find themselves in some far-fetched situations, yet many of these are probably not quite as bizarre as those that real-life reps deal with on a daily basis. Although this is a work of fiction, many of the anecdotes are based upon actual events and experiences. The general rule of thumb should be that the more unbelievable the story, the more likely it is to be based upon such an experience.

To give the story a contemporary feel and to allow for the development of the dance scene, which is so important to the Ibiza backdrop, the action takes place in the present day. Some of the bars mentioned (Madhouse, Charleston) no longer exist. Other places have changed their names. For anybody who has been on such a holiday (even to a different resort) the names are academic – most will recognise or be able to imagine the types of establishment described.

In the same way that the reps are a composite of different characters I came into contact with, so some of the bars/clubs are an amalgam of different watering-holes it was my pleasure to (over) frequent. If you think therefore that you recognise yourself or one of the venues that I'm less than complimentary about, rest assured that you/it may have been only partly responsible for the inspiration. As an example of this, I have probably had at least a dozen different nominations from ex-reps convinced that it is their own resort manager that the Alison character is based upon. Like the other characters, she is a combination of several.

Certain ex-reps have helped either directly or indirectly and I would like to take this opportunity to thank and acknowledge them: Carl Verges, Tony Grant, Mark Hurst, Angie Bland, Michelle, Gresty, Babs Pearson, Des Ball, Debbie Bailey and Martin Morgan.

Thanks are also due to Dominic James (Deep Design), Harry Ritchie, Garry Bushell, Rodney Cooper, Dorise Mensah, Steve Bergin, David Hurst, Andrew Menzies, Dave White, Alan Jones, Bartolo Escandell and Steve Woods.

The story of how this novel got to this stage is almost another book in itself. I am indebted to Bren McKnight of WH Smith, Manchester Airport, for having the maverick vision to put the original pre-Orion edition on the shelves. Similarly, to everyone else at selected Smith's and Waterstone's airport branches for not being far behind (David Atherton, David Jefferies, Catherine, Andrew Thomas, Steve Moxon and Cliff Long). Also, respect is due to Rita Schreyer of Books Etc. for displaying professionalism and a total lack of pig-headedness by changing her original opinion and stocking it. A shout is due to John Newton of the same company for his exceptional support.

Within the publishing industry I must give a special thank you to Alan Wherry of Bloomsbury Publishing. Unconditional help coming from a total stranger in such a senior position helped change my belief that publishers were full of people as in touch with the real world as high court judges.

Most definitely in touch with the real world are Jane Wood and Susan Lamb of Orion. Thanks for bucking the trend and having the *cojones* to go with a book that isn't about a self-effacing nineties man or an overweight PR girl who can't get a shag. Thanks also to Viv Redman, Hazel Orme and everyone else at Orion involved in this project.

Finally, a special thank you to Mick Crowley for his unique combination of honesty, dishonesty, intellect, streetwise savvy and for being the first person whose opinion on the book I really trusted.

To Giuseppe and Biley
... not forgotten

Young Free and Single Staff

Resort Reps *IBIZA*

Alison	Resort Manager
Brad	First Year Rep
Mikey	First Year Rep
Mario	First Year Rep
Lorraine	First Year Rep
Greg	Third Year Rep
Heather	Second Year Rep
Natalie	Replacement Rep
Kirstie	Resort Manager (previous season)

Head Office Staff

Adam Hawthorne-Blythe	Chairman
Felipe Gomez	Contracts Director
Sebastian Hunter	Financial Director
Jane Ward	Overseas Manager
Tom Ortega	Overseas Control

pre-departure

'Ow.'

'What's up?'

'You've got your elbow on my hair,' said Alison. She tried to pull her head away, tutting impatiently.

'Sorry.' Jonathan transferred his weight onto his hands, slipping out as he did so. 'Is that better?'

Alison grunted.

Jonathan guided himself in again and continued. He rested his head on the pillow, but looked out of the window. Parked directly outside his Hampstead flat was the red Alfa Romeo he had collected from Follet's in St John's Wood the previous week. The engine was gleaming and the car purred like a cat. A pussy. Red and inviting. Pistons going up and down. In and out, up and down. Shit. Desperately, his eyes scanned the room. In the corner was a TV and video. That was no good – it made him think of pornos. Then, in a flash of inspiration, he leap-frogged to computer games – Mortal Kombat. The tightening in his loins subsided.

Alison looked at her watch over Jonathan's shoulder. Nine fifteen a.m. She would need to leave within twenty minutes to be sure of getting home in time.

A droplet of sweat trickled off the end of his nose, landing on Alison's left cheekbone. It was quickly followed by his tongue. His breathing quickened, and his thrusts were slower. The two computer-generated characters had been replaced with images of yielding female flesh.

Alison knew what was coming next. Sure enough, Jonathan withdrew his bursting member and replaced it

1

with the middle and third finger of his right hand. At the same time he shifted position and started working his tongue down to her stomach, stopping to give each of her nipples exactly the same amount of attention.

'No, Jonathan, I want it now,' breathed Alison. Her meeting with Kirstie was so important that she grabbed the opportunity to end proceedings prematurely with both hands. With one cupped beneath his bulging ball bag, she used the other to rub the length of Jonathan's circumcised phallus. In less than thirty seconds she felt the first hot spurt land on her forehead. Jonathan groaned, then watched the rest fall between her breasts. Alison was relieved that none had gone into her frizzy blonde hair.

After a few minutes, she looked at her watch again. Good, she thought. Not even nine thirty.

She got back to her parents' house just before ten, had a shower and got ready. Kirstie was due to arrive at eleven thirty.

Kirstie and Alison were fairly similar and, probably because of this, not close, but they always went through the motions of liking each other.

Kirstie had completed her final season as resort manager for Young Free & Single (YF&S) Ibiza the previous summer. Largely funded by the money she had made there, she was now opening a travel agency in her native Brecon. She was visiting her boyfriend's relations in Kent and had agreed to make a detour to see Alison, who would replace her in Ibiza. She knew that Alison was desperate for advice on how to gain maximum financial benefit. Alison wanted to clean up.

Alison's parents' home was a typical suburban semi. At the front was a large bay window with Laura Ashley curtains; at the back, a patio door opened from the dining room on to the neatly bordered garden. The room was dominated by a seldom used mahogany dining table, now covered with a number of holiday brochures, an open briefcase and a passport.

The crunch of gravel in the drive heralded Kirstie's arrival. Alison scooped the brochures into her briefcase. She waited until the doorbell chimed then went to greet Kirstie. She flung open the door theatrically. 'Daaahling!' she shrieked, and kissed her on both cheeks.

'How are you? All right?' smiled Kirstie politely.

'You look a bit wet. Don't you just loathe the British weather? God, I can't wait to get away again.'

Kirstie grunted. 'Living room, dining room, bedroom or study?'

'Well, the drinks cabinet is in the dining room and seeing as you're such an old alkie I think that'll be our best bet. I've poured you a drink. Unless you want coffee?'

'No, that'll do fine.'

They sat at the table and smiled at each other. Alison lit a cigarette. 'So, any regrets?'

'No,' Kirstie replied flatly.

'Oh, come on, dahling, you're not telling me that after four summers abroad you're not going to miss it?' Alison tossed back her frizzy mane and laughed. 'Still, I suppose we've all got to settle down some time?'

She paused and looked across the table. Kirstie's inside knowledge of Ibiza and in-depth knowledge of the fiddles and local contacts could save her a lot of time and make her a lot of money. However, although they both knew why Kirstie was there, Alison didn't want to blow things by being too blunt in her questioning.

Kirstie was flicking through the YF&S brochure. She recognised most of the people smiling out from it – the company nearly always used its reps as models. She stabbed her finger at a picture of a good-looking lad, with two nubile holidaymakers clinging to his legs. He had short, very blond hair, dark eyebrows and green eyes framed by eyelashes so thick and long that had he been a woman he would have had little use for eyeliner or mascara. Even though he was only just over five and a half feet tall, he was almost certainly the closest thing you could get to most

3

people's pre-conceived idea of a 'typical' rep. 'He's with you this year, isn't he?'

'Who's that?' enquired Alison.

'Scouse Greg.'

'Oh, him? Yeah. What's he like to work with?'

'He's fine. You just have to leave him to it. Shags himself silly, but he's pretty discreet.'

'Is he a good seller?' asked Alison. The resort manager had a vested interest in excursion sales.

'One of the best,' replied Kirstie. 'But you'll have to watch him. If he can make a few quid on the side, he will.'

'Not this year he won't,' replied Alison sharply. 'The only person who's going to make any money is me.'

Kirstie knew Alison meant it. She had seen it before; the determination to have one last year with the sole objective of making as much money as possible, with little regard for anything or anyone else. Kirstie had come home with nearly fourteen thousand pounds and she knew Alison wanted more. Kirstie had never seen anyone so ruthlessly determined to make her mark. It made her feel uneasy. Her instincts told her that it was probably going to be a strange old season in Ibiza.

Alison spent the obligatory period of time making small-talk then started firing questions. She soon got the impression that Kirstie was not telling her everything, which was indeed the case – there were some things she was just going to have to find out for herself. Once she realised that she had leeched everything she could from Kirstie, they started talking about reps, past and present. Eventually, they worked their way around to the new ones, all of whom Kirstie had interviewed. Alison should have been involved too, but she had told everyone at the time that she was ill with 'women's problems'. If an abortion could be defined as such, then she could not have been accused of lying. Only the father knew about it and nobody was going to find out who he was.

'You'll like Mario,' said Kirstie. 'His parents are Italian.

Done a bit of modelling. Very sure of himself. Shouldn't give you any trouble, though – he wants to go all the way.'

'If he's anything like you say he is, I'll let him.' Alison laughed at her own deliberate misinterpretation. 'What about the girls?'

'There's a Brummie called Lorraine. I was surprised she got picked, really. She seemed a bit timid. Quite plain too. Jane liked her, though, and you know what Jane's like when she makes her mind up,' said Kirstie, referring to the overseas manager. 'I suppose you know you've had another honour bestowed on you?'

'What, you mean El Negro?'

Alison spoke surprisingly little Spanish in view of the amount of time she had been repping, but she knew what black was.

'That's right, Mikey Jarvis, Young Free & Single's first ever black rep,' replied Kirstie. 'He's got a brilliant sense of humour, as well as being built like a brick wotsit. And he's a karate black-belt.'

'What about this blue-eyed boy Jane was going on about? Brad, is it?'

Kirstie thought back to Bridlehurst, the country house-cum-hotel setting for the reps' final interview. It had lasted twenty-four hours and every aspect of each potential rep's personality was tested. The panel had agreed that Brad would make a great rep. 'Bit of a natural leader, really,' she said. 'S'pose it's 'cos he's older than the normal first year.'

'How old is he, then?' asked the twenty-five-year-old Alison.

'Twenty-six, I think,' replied Kirstie, homing in on Alison's insecurity. 'Yeah, quite sharp too. Very quick-witted. He finished that McQuaig test in six minutes.'

'The what?'

'McQuaig Institute test.' The company had only just introduced the test so Alison had never heard of it. 'It's like an IQ test. They have to answer fifty questions in fifteen minutes. When she first saw him Jane Ward assumed he'd give up when he realised there wasn't a pair of tits on page three of the question sheet. Mind you, she soon changed her tune when she marked it and found out he'd got them all right. Apparently he has an unusually high IQ.'

'I bet he looks like a right little swot,' said Alison hopefully.

'Hardly!' laughed Kirstie. 'He's a bit wider than Mikey, probably he works out a bit, but not quite as tall. Broken nose, light brown hair . . .'

Alison had stopped listening. She was already worrying that Brad might be a threat to her position.

Kirstie could see that Alison was deep in thought. She made a few unsuccessful attempts at conversation, then finished her drink, made her excuses and set off for Kent.

The sun was playing peek-a-boo through the row of uniform-height poplar trees that lined the straight French country road. Brad had one of his favourite garage tapes playing. He would have liked to have the roof off, but keeping it on allowed him to carry more stuff on the roof rack. He was taking in the scenery and generally feeling pleased with himself. During the first few hours of the journey he had had the occasional pang of guilt when he remembered his girlfriend Charlotte sobbing on the doorstep. It wasn't so much the leaving her that made him feel guilty, more the 'Yeee-haaagh' and punch in the air he had let out as he turned the corner.

Brad didn't realise that there was a problem for quite a while. It might have been the music, it might have been the landscape, but it certainly had not been the Triumph Herald's temperature gauge. Cursing, he pulled into a layby and thumped the dial. The Triumph failed to respond so he got out to see what the problem was.

The Sunday-morning stillness of the Dordogne valley was broken by the gentle hiss coming from underneath the bonnet. When he opened it he saw straight away that the fan-belt was broken. His first thought was not on how to overcome the problem, but retribution on the person from whom he had bought the car.

It had an ill-fitting Ford Sierra engine, which gave it the turning circle of the *QE2* and made it a nightmare to drive. However, he had bought it partly because the tickets were booked and he had no other choice. He was miles from anywhere and it was a Sunday afternoon. The only option was to try to flag someone down.

The first to take pity on him was the driver of a battered Citroën 2CV, who couldn't help. He seemed sympathetic, though, and Brad picked up the French for fan-belt – (*courroire de ventilateur*). Just over two hours later a Ford Sierra approached, with British plates. Unfortunately its occupants also had a British mentality – healthily displayed by their shouts of 'Wanker!' and accompanying hand signals.

Brad sat down on the grass verge and opened the last can of duty-free Kronenburg. There was no way he could leave the car because of all the merchandise on the roof rack. A night spent sleeping in the cramped driver's seat with no blankets was not appealing, but he could see no other option. He sat back, crossed his fingers and scanned the horizon in the forlorn hope that somebody would come to his rescue.

Almost four hours after he had broken down his saviour arrived in the shape of one Samuel T. Zakatek. Sammy seemed fine to start with, especially when Brad discovered that he, too, was on his way to Ibiza, where he had apparently spent the last ten years. He assumed initially that Sammy's idiosyncratic personality traits were due to his being American.

During their search for a fan-belt, they stumbled across a farm that had been given special dispensation by the French government to grow hemp to produce oil for use as a machine lubricant. The laid-back farmer contacted his brother, who would bring up a selection of fan-belts the next morning. Brad and Sammy spent a few hours helping out and in return the farmer arranged for them to stay overnight in a friend's guesthouse.

In the time they spent together Sammy told Brad increasingly bizarre stories. One of these was about how he had taken over a beach bar in Ibiza. It had become so famous that the King of Spain 'dropped in' one day to congratulate him and offered Sammy anything he wanted as a reward for being so successful. With fortune beckoning, the thing Sammy had wanted was the King's tie.

Sammy also told Brad how when he was twelve he had planned to kill his parents because they had sold his grandpa's land, which had been given to him by Navajo Indians.

Brad concluded that Sammy was a psychotic Vietnam veteran. Rather than continue with the games of pool they had started playing in the bar of the guesthouse he made his excuses and went up to the room they were to share. He wanted to re-establish his grip on reality – the strong marijuana and Sammy's intense alternative reality were making his head spin.

He had almost fallen asleep when he felt Sammy shaking him.

'Brad. Wake up, man, wake up.'

'Wassamadder?'

'Sorry to wake y', man, but I've just had a great fuckin' idea.'

'Oh, for fuck's sake.'

'No, listen, man. We ain't gonna get a chance to take any more weed in the mornin' right? So I figure we drive up there now and help ourselves to some.'

'Leave it out. I don't fancy smuggling any gear across the border. Besides, if you think I'm driving up there at . . .' Brad looked at his watch, '. . . three twenty in the morning you must be off your fucking trolley.'

'C'mon, man! Where's your sense of adventure?'

'Somewhere just behind my sense of common. Look. Just

go to sleep. We can probably grab a little personal in the morning.'

'Well, fuck you, man. I'm goin'. Y'can do what you want.'

Now Brad was in a dilemma. Although going to the hemp field held little appeal to him, the thought of allowing psychotic Sammy to drive off into the night with the majority of the YF&S merchandise that Brad had temporarily stored in his jeep held even less. 'All right. Give me a minute to get ready.'

Once in the jeep, Sammy started swigging from a bottle of Jack Daniel's. He was driving faster than normal and had a crazed look in his eyes. Brad was scared, but unable to say any of the thousand and one things racing through his mind.

The road leading to the hemp farm was like one of those you see in James Bond car chases, or old movies when a moustachioed fiend has tampered with a car's brakes – very windy, with steep drops and no railings. A car was dawdling along in front of the jeep. Sammy started to thump the horn. 'C'mon. Get outta the road, y' motherfuckin' French sonofabitch.' With that, he rammed its rear bumper.

'What are you playing at, Sam?'

'Move it, fuckhead.' He rammed the car again.

'Stop the car, Sam.'

'No way, man.' Sammy was almost forcing the car off the road.

Brad had had enough. 'Stop the car, you fucking psycho, or so help me, I'll—'

'That's the difference between us, Brad,' said Sammy, grinning maniacally. 'Two tours of duty. Hah, I've already died twice. But how about you? Are you scared to die, Brad?'

This was sounding like a script from a bad B movie.

'Sit tight. I'm the tour guide, man,' drawled Sammy. 'I haven't been like this in a long time. It feels goooood! Y'know, Brad, when I first saw you standing by the road I thought, Wow! That's my brother, man. That's why I stopped.'

Brad was sure there were tears in Sammy's eyes. They were approaching a sharp bend and he was not slowing down. Brad had another look at him: he seemed to be in a trance. He pushed Sammy against the driver's door, grabbed the steering-wheel and yanked on the handbrake. The car skidded to a halt. Brad got out. The distance between the car and the drop was a matter of feet. Sammy was staring straight ahead. Brad turned round and started walking back to the guesthouse. Some things were more important even than YF&S merchandise.

reps arriving

'On behalf of Captain Reynolds I would like to thank you all for flying with British Caledonian and we hope that you enjoy your stay in Ibiza. Please remain seated until the aircraft comes to a complete standstill. You are reminded not to smoke until you are inside the airport terminal.'

There was a click and some classical music started playing. Mikey looked across the aisle and out of one of the windows at the terminal building, which was distorted by a heat haze rising from the tarmac. As he turned his head back he caught sight of the Idiot's face, grinning at him from two rows in front. He returned a half-smile. Mikey's first impressions of people normally turned out to be correct. On this occasion he hoped he was wrong.

As they got off the plane, the Idiot grabbed the stewardess's hand and kissed it. Mikey shuddered at the thought of spending the next six months with him. When they had first met at the airport, Mikey was put off by the pseudo-black attempt at bonding with the 'Hey, Bro, how's it hanging?' handshake and cocksure attitude. Then the Idiot was endeavouring to chat up the check-in stewardess, the duty-free cashier, and a group of girls in the bar. All of these with his rep's badge unnecessarily emblazoned upon his chest. Mikey had made up his mind that Mario was a complete and utter stain.

They made their way to the baggage carousel. Mikey largely switched off to Mario's self-centred ramblings, especially when Mario tried to tell him how he was sure that the stewardess was going to call and that when she did he was going to 'Fuck her brains out, man!' Mikey wondered if too much wanking had caused Mario's cerebral organ to exit its original habitat for similar reasons. He also offered a prayer of thanks to the inventors of the Walkman and sunglasses, which were saving him from having to acknowledge Mario's waffle.

He sat on the edge of the carousel waiting for it to jerk into life. This was it. He was actually in Ibiza. Unfortunately, so was Mario, fresh from preening himself in front of the mirrors in the toilets.

'Spanish birds are fit, man. That young one over there in the car-hire bit keeps looking over. I bet she knows we're reps.'

'Yeah, I'm sure it's one of the conditions of employment.'

'What is?'

'Being telepathic.'

Mario looked at Mikey, baffled. He changed the subject. 'So who's meeting us, then?'

'The resort manager,' replied Mikey.

'That's Alison, isn't it?'

'Sure is.'

'She wasn't at the training course or the interviews, was she?'

'Sure wasn't.'

'I wonder what she's like,' said Mario. 'Yeah. D'you reckon she shags?'

Mikey looked at Mario over the top of his sunglasses. 'Probably, Mario.'

When Mikey and Mario came through customs the airport was fairly empty. Although they hadn't met her before, the YF&S bag draped over her shoulder ensured that they spotted Alison almost immediately. Mikey felt a sudden sense of anticlimax. He had gone through such mental turmoil, such challenging interviews to become a rep that Alison seemed somehow inadequate.

'*Ciao, bella,*' smarmed Mario, and kissed her on both cheeks. 'Nice to meet you.'

'You too,' said Alison, thinking Kirstie had been right about how drop-dead gorgeous Mario was. 'And you must be Mikey.'

'Don't tell me – my sunglasses gave me away.'

Alison laughed politely. 'There aren't too many black reps here.'

Clumsy, thought Mikey.

They kissed each other's cheek. It was the first time she had been kissed by a black man.

'How are you two getting on? All right?' enquired Alison.

'Yeah, man, great,' replied Mario offering Mikey his hand for another handshake. Mikey had no choice but to take it and to go through the motions.

They put their luggage into the white estate car Alison had hired. YF&S supplied her with a moped, but on special occasions she was allowed a car. Mario sat next to her in the front, whilst Mikey clambered into the back with his Head sports bag. He took out his ghetto-blaster unit and looked for a cassette to put in his Walkman.

'Hey, great wog box, man.' Mario realised his *faux pas* almost before the words were out of his mouth. 'Shit. Sorry, man, I didn't mean . . .'

Mikey put him out of his misery. 'It's all right, Mario. That's what I call it.' A relieved Mario laughed. 'You can do me one favour, though,' added Mikey.

'Yeah, man, whaddya want?' replied Mario, eager to please.

'Stop calling me man. I'm from London and we're in Ibiza, not New York. My friends call me Mikey.' He paused before adding, 'You can call me Mr Jarvis.'

'Oh, uh, right. So that's your full name then, is it? Mike Jarvis?'

'No.'

Michael Jarvis chuckled to himself. His dry humour and flat delivery were lost on Mario.

Most reps never bothered to research much more than the prospective nightlife of their chosen destination, but

Mikey had found out a little about the history of the island. He guessed that Mario, and probably Alison, would have no interest in it, so he thought it would be fun to share his knowledge with them on the journey into San Antonio. As they drove away from the airport, he saw a sign pointing towards Las Salinas, the salt flats.

'See those salt flats, Mario?'

'Yeah.'

'Well, it's mainly because of those that this little island has been invaded through the years.'

'Yeah?'

'Yeah. Well, that and its location, of course.'

'And now it's being invaded by Young Free & Single,' chipped in Alison.

'And loads of Krauts,' added Mario.

'Funnily enough, a Germanic tribe called the Vandals invaded Ibiza in the fifth century.' As Mikey had expected, there was no reaction from either Mario or Alison. 'Then the Byzantines.' He soaked up the disinterested silence. 'Then, of course, there were the Saracens.' He smiled to himself and paused for nearly a minute. 'I think it was the Moors next – or was it the Normans?' He took some chewing-gum out of a wrapper and popped it into his mouth. 'No, I'm sure it was the Normans.'

After nearly half an hour they arrived in San Antonio. Mikey remembered reading that it used to be a small fishing port until tourists started arriving in the sixties. It had really taken off however, during the tourist boom that followed Franco's death in 1975 and the advent of the 'specialist holiday', in particular those catering for young people. The 'West End' of San Antonio had grown to service the demand for pub crawls, with a huge variety of theme bars and night-clubs. In the mid-eighties, the island had given birth to the rave scene. Although there was still a strong demand for 'ere-we-go type bars, it was the stylish clubs and more laid-back, drug-dominated places that came into vogue. Places like Café del Mar, which until the mid-eighties

14

had been the domain of locals and a few backgammon-playing workers, were overrun with Moschino-clad ravers and wannabes.

It was quite close to Café del Mar that the majority of YF&S's accommodation was based, including their principal unit, the Bon Tiempo apartments, which was where Mikey was to stay. The area around the Bon was undeveloped and the building stood there, a solitary white block like a lone tooth in a mouth of decay.

As the car pulled up outside Mikey saw that its white paintwork and brown shutters rose five storeys; all of the shutters were closed and the only towel draped over a balcony was on the top floor.

As he walked into Reception he was struck by the contrast with outside in brightness and temperature. He shivered slightly and draped his sweatshirt over his shoulders. His and Mario's rooms were not quite ready, so they left their bags in Reception and went into the bar, where Alison got them all a drink. Mario dominated the conversation, trying to impress Alison, so Mikey refused another drink – he was in far greater need of a spliff.

He told Alison he was going exploring and walked out of the apartments, tapping his balls lightly with his fingertips to confirm that the small lump of solid he had smuggled over was still there.

The apartments overlooked the man-made beach called Calo des Moro. It was evening and there was a slight breeze, but it was still warm enough for just a T-shirt. From the beach, Mikey could see an island. He squinted at it in the evening light and its shape reminded him of an oil tanker. About four hundred metres out from the beach was a boat: it seemed to be pumping out or sucking up something from the sea. Mikey sat down at a white plastic table outside the beach bar and ordered himself a coffee. He grew curious as to what the boat was doing. He spoke reasonably good Spanish – unusual for a YF&S rep – and when the waiter came back he decided to ask him what was going on. *'Que pasa, alli con el barco?'*

The waiter informed him that the boat was pumping sand into the sea so that it would be washed up on the beach. He also told him that over the next few days, lorries would come and dump tons more ready for the season. He was intrigued to know why Mikey spoke Spanish and why he was in Ibiza already. When Mikey told him he was a rep at the local apartments, the waiter wouldn't let him pay for his coffee, then brought over a bottle of San Miguel and a schnapps. He showed Mikey the menu, saying that the food there was second to none, and that if any of Mikey's clients ever came in they would be given a ten per cent discount. Mikey thanked him, shook his hand and walked further round the bay.

When he got to a rocky outcrop, he sat down and pulled out of his pocket a packet of red Rizlas. He turned his back to the wind, put the necessary ingredients together and settled down to his first joint in Ibiza. Between the island and the mainland, a red sun sank into the gently rippling sea. There were no sounds apart from the steady chug of the sand boat, and the call of three seagulls circling overhead. Mikey was in his element.

He had decided to become a rep after splitting with his girlfriend of four years. No amount of persuasion had won her back, and he couldn't stand the thought of seeing her with someone else. A friend had suggested repping for YF&S and almost before he knew what was happening he had found himself at Gatwick.

When he got back to the apartments, Alison was waiting for him.

'Where have you been? I've just been going through some of the paperwork with Mario.'

'Sorry. I didn't realise you wanted me. I've just been having a look round. The guy at the beach café said he'd give our clients a ten per cent discount. Even said he'd give me free food,' offered Mikey helpfully.

Alison looked stern. She puffed out her thirty-four B chest and sat upright in the chair. 'There's something very important that you must understand. The only places we take clients and the only places we go for free food are where I tell you. Is that clear?'

'Sure. It's just that—'

'There are no just thats. You are a first-year rep and that kind of thing is left to the resort manager to look after.'

Mikey could see that discussion was futile. 'Okay. No problem.'

'Good. Now, if I can attract that fat dago's attention, I'll get us all a drink,' she said.

'Oi-yaay. See-nyor. *Dos* San Miguels and a gin tonic.'

Mikey winced.

The next morning all the reps, apart from Brad, had arrived on resort and were gathered in the bar area of the Bon. Alison was sitting at the bar looking at the flight manifests that had arrived that morning. Mikey was practising his Spanish on Frank, the waiter and Greg was telling Mario about a Danish girl he'd got a wank off on the beach the night before. Mario was looking across at Heather, thinking that he wouldn't mind getting a wank off her.

Heather was a petite and pretty second-year rep from Heald Green, not far from Manchester airport, who had only recently become aware of the effect her looks had on men. Working in Spain, she had learned how to use them to her advantage, and her confidence had grown tenfold during her first season as a rep. She was whispering to the Brummie, Lorraine. Every minute or so they exploded into fits of giggles. Although Heather was blessed with Barbie-doll looks, she was cursed with a laugh that sounded like a cross between a hyena sitting on a stinging nettle and a kookaburra with whooping cough. In the background the TV in the bar was showing an old dubbed episode of *Knight Rider*.

Alison looked up from her papers and caught sight of

an over-burdened Triumph Herald turning the corner.
Mikey saw it too.

'Brad's here.'

Lorraine jumped up and ran out to meet him. Greg,
Heather and Mario had not met him before – Greg and
Heather because they were second-year reps and Mario
because he had been on a different training course. These
three went to stand by the doorway, curious to see what he
was like.

Mikey, Lorraine and Brad embraced each other. They had
shared the experience of the Bridlehurst twenty-four-hour
interview and then a one-week training course in Warwick.
Reps who went through these two stages together and who
ended up on the same resort nearly always formed a special
bond.

Brad put his things into a room on the second floor,
where Alison had told him he would live until the first
clients arrived.

When he got back downstairs a row of chairs faced
Alison. He sat next to Mikey and told him about his
encounter with Samuel Zakatek and how he had left him
trying to stuff a bin-liner full of weed into the boot of his
jeep.

Mario was in the middle of a story, of which Brad caught
the tail end. '. . . so I said to her, "What's wrong?" and she
said, "You called me stupid," and I said, "No, I didn't, I said
I was going to fuck you stupid"!' He burst out laughing, but
the story only elicited polite smiles from the rest of the
group.

Lorraine decided to be a little more verbal in her
appreciation of the story. 'Well, she would've 'ad to be
bloody stupid to shag you, wouldn't she?' This got a better
response. She turned her attentions to Mikey, putting on
the thickest of Brummie accents. 'So coom on, then, Mikey,
is it true what they all say about black men?'

'What? That we make great lawyers, accountants, politi-
cians?'

'No, yer pillock, that you've all got cowin' big dadgers.' She was blunt too.

'Even if he was hung like King Dong, Lorraine,' said Brad, 'he'd be able to put it in that trap of yours and you'd still be able to hold a conversation. Could probably get mine in there too.'

'The only way yem'll be putting that thing of yours near me gob is if I need a tooth-pick.'

Lorraine's retort started Heather off on another hyena impression.

'Jesus, could you imagine shagging that?' said Mario, pointing at Heather. 'Is she always like this?'

'No,' said Lorraine, 'only when she sees Italian dicks.'

Heather now had tears rolling down her cheeks, not because Lorraine's remark had been particularly funny but because she was prone to giggling fits.

'Aye, well, you've seen enough of those, eh, Heather?' Scouse Greg joined in.

'Oh, you can talk,' said Heather. 'You were down the clap clinic so many times last season you were on first-name terms with all the doctors. How many did you shag last year? Eighty? Ninety?'

'Fuck off. Be serious, you daft ol' bag.'

'Well, how many was it then?'

'Sixty-four.'

'What! In a season?' exclaimed Mario, convinced that if Greg could do that many then he should be able to do at least the same, if not more.

'Jesus,' said Mikey. 'Did you take any precautions?'

'Aye. I didn't give 'em me fuckin' phone number.'

'For Christ's sake!' screamed Alison. 'Can't you lot talk about anything other than sex?'

There was a general mumbling of 'Sorry' then silence.

'See, we can't think of anythin' else to talk about,' said Greg.

'Don't give me that,' said Alison. 'There must be something else you've all got in common.'

'Like what?'

'Oh I don't know. Anything! Talk about the weather, for all I care.'

Greg looked out of the window, then back at Alison. His face broke into a grin.

'Nice day for a fuck,' he said.

After the meeting and some coach-microphone training, Alison took everyone to a bar called the Cockney Pride. Its small window-panes were surrounded by dark panelled wood in an attempt to make it look Englishly rustic. By the door a board informed potential customers that they sold draught Guinness and English sausages.

Once inside, Alison sat on a stool and introduced the reps to Trevor, the ex-pat professional Cockney turned bar-owner, whose shock of grey hair emphasised his deep tan.

He asked everyone what they wanted to drink. He had a gruff East End voice, and his Rs sounded like Ws. Although Mikey knew it would taste disgusting, he ordered a bwandy and owange and some dwy-woasted peanuts. Reading between the lines, he got the impression that Trevor wasn't too keen on black people – he certainly wasn't too keen on Asians ('Bloody Pakis evewywhere back 'ome. Wunning the off licence, newsagent's – even the wuddy gweengwocer's').

Brad went to the toilet. When he got back Greg was explaining something to Mario and Mikey. 'So, are you sure you've got it?'

'I think so,' replied Mario.

'What about you, Mikey?'

'Nah, dread. I don't want to get involved.'

'Well, you're in the wrong job, mate,' said Mario. 'Just run it by me one more time, Greg, to see if I've got it. It's one point for a wank . . .'

'That's it. One point for a wank, two for a blow-job and three for a shag.' Greg took a swig of his San Miguel.

'And what sexist mother invented this game?' asked Mikey.

20

'You'll soon change your tune, lad,' laughed Greg. 'Within two months, you'll be so bored with shaggin' you'll be desperate for anything to liven it up. No object in your room'll be safe unless it's bolted down. It's just a bit of harmless fun.'

'Yeah. Come on, Mikey, it'll be a crack,' implored Mario.

'So who exactly is the Competition between?' asked Brad, trying to catch Trevor's eye so he could order some more drinks.

'Well, primarily, like, it's between us reps. But some of the other lads join in – y'know, DJs, props, guys on the beach party.'

'Props?' asked Mario.

'People who persuade punters to go into a bar.'

'What about bonus points, then?' asked Brad, finally catching Trevor's eye and mouthing, 'Same again.'

'Bonus points?'

'Yeah, y'know, threesomes, missing the pink and potting the brown . . .'

'Fucking hell, we're not playing snooker,' said Mario. 'What's all this pink and brown nonsense?'

'I think young Bradley is referring to the rusty bullet-hole,' said Mikey.

'The what?' Mario was still struggling.

'The chocolate starfish.'

'Backdooring.'

'Uphill gardening.'

'What the fuck are you all on about?'

'What we're on about, Mario lad, is 'ow many points you score if you gerrit up the dirt box.'

'What, you mean shoving it up their arse?' exclaimed Mario.

'Delicately put,' said Mikey.

'Are you all queer or something?'

'Um, we're talking about women, Mario.' Greg could feel a wind-up coming on. He looked over at Brad and winked.

'So we'll say four points for a bit of backdooring, but only three if you do it to a bloke. Whaddyer reckon, Brad?'

'Sounds fair. But what about if a bloke does it to you?'

'Depends how big his dick is.' Mikey decided to join in, since it was Mario they were taking the piss out of. 'I mean, it's only fair that you get more points if a baby's arm goes up there. If someone's got a dick like Mario's, then . . . .'

'Well, if it's as small as Mario's you should lose points.' Brad was having trouble keeping a straight face. Greg had already cracked.

'What are you all laughing at?' asked Heather, as she passed the group on her way to the toilet.

'Old Mario was just telling us how much he loves anal sex and how he's always felt he's had homosexual tendencies,' said Mikey, straight-faced.

'Oooh, what a waste,' said Heather.

I'm not a fucking queer! screamed Mario.

Alison looked over.

'It's all right, Al,' said Brad. 'Just sorting out who the homophobic reps are.'

Alison smiled and nodded. He could tell she didn't have a clue what he'd just said.

'Well, that's a shame,' teased Heather. 'I like effeminate men.'

'No, what it was, Heath' darlin', was old Mario here was getting a bit queasy over the thought of anal sex,' explained Greg.

'Quite right too. It's bloody painful.'

'You mean you've tried it?' asked a horrified Mario.

'It's every bloke's obsession to stick it up there. Why do you all do it?'

'Yeah, why?' echoed Mario.

'The reason we do it,' said Greg, 'is the reason we do most things – 'cos it's there and 'cos we're not s'posed to.' He finished his drink and got the conversation back to the serious topic of the Competition. 'So. Let's make sure everybody knows the points system. One point for a wank, two for a blow-job, three for a shag, four for a bit of backdooring and two bonus points for a threesome. That means eight points if it's two new people.'

'Is that two blokes or two girls?' enquired Brad.

'Either,' replied Greg. 'Youse girls can join in too, if y'like.'

'I'd love to,' said Heather. She nodded over to Alison who was cooing into Trevor's ear. 'But I think there'd be only one winner.'

The male reps finished their drinks and walked down the road into the West End. *En route*, Greg left the group to try and find whether a girl he had been shagging the previous season was still working in a bar called the OK Corral. The other three went into Sgt Pepper's, where a talented mixed-race piano-player/singer was belting out soul songs. After one drink Brad decided to leave them to it – the drive over had finally caught up with him. Mikey and Mario moved towards the stage to introduce themselves to the singer: they would use the place on bar-crawl nights and Alison had told them they would be expected to get up on stage occasionally. Mario had noticed a really fit blonde standing on her own near him. He swooped upon her with the enthusiasm of a malnourished golden eagle spotting a paraplegic field mouse.

When the singer finished, he came over to where they were all standing, nodded acknowledgement and touched fists with Mikey. Then he tapped Mario on the shoulder. Mario swung round, his face broke into a smile and his voice back into a Brooklyn accent. 'Wicked set man, wicked.'

'Cheers, la'.'

'Yeah, man, wicked.' He looked at the blonde and then at the singer. 'Sorry, I don't know your name,' he said.

'Ray.'

'Ray, this is Cheryl.'

'All right,' said Ray, nodding at her and winking. 'Are youse two an item, then, like?'

'Not yet,' said Mario. 'I've got to wine and dine her first. Then if she plays her cards right she'll see why Italian men are the world's best lovers. What d'you think of that, Cheryl?'

Cheryl Pitt, thought Mikey.

'Well,' said Cheryl thoughtfully, 'as tempting as your offer sounds, I've always found black Scousers the best lovers and Italians all mouth and no – well, you know.'

'Hang on. What do you mean, black Scousers? You mean like—'

'Like Ray,' offered Mikey helpfully.

'You and Ray, you're . . .' Mario's voice trailed off as he saw his first opportunity disappearing.

'Fucking 'ell, la', you Italians may be gash in the sack, but yer fucking quick when it comes to catching on. Cheryl is me girl. So, I'm afraid t' say you've spent the last ten minutes tryin' to chat up me bird. But I tell yer what, gerrin a round o' Jägermeisters an' I won't get me minder to come over and do yer.'

Mario went to the bar and, for once, ended up paying for a drink. Ray turned to Mikey.

'I 'aven't really gorra minder. Still, seems to 'ave done the trick.' Mario was scurrying back with four small glasses of a black liqueur.

'Anyway, what's yer name?'

'Mikey.'

'Well, Mikey, as long as yer don't try and chat 'er up as well, meet me girl Cheryl—'

'Cheryl Pitt,' interrupted Mikey. 'Haven't seen you on page three for a while.'

'Oh, you recognised her, then,' laughed Ray.

Mario had just got back with the drinks.

'I'd recognise those cheekbones anywhere,' said Mikey.

Mario, who had now realised who Cheryl was, had no such tact. 'Fuck. I thought I recognised those tits.'

''Ey, steady on.' Ray was trying to keep calm.

Mario carried on. The only way he could have surpassed

his lack of sensitivity to the situation would have been if he had entered an animal rights meeting and started giving out tickets for a bullfight.

'Jeez, what I wouldn't like to do to you.' Mario fumbled in his jacket pocket for his camera. 'Here, Ray. Take a picture of me and Cheryl. No open-leg shots, but you can get your tits out if you like, ha, ha, ha, ha!'

Ray hadn't grown up in Kirkby without being able to take care of himself. He also hadn't grown up in Kirkby without being able to recognise a prize dickhead when he saw one. He decided he was seeing one. 'Mikey, do us a favour and take your dick of a mate out of this bar before I break this bottle over 'is thick 'ead.'

'C'mon, Mario, let's go.'

'Nah, wait, wait. There's no need for this, Ray. I didn't mean to offend you or your woman. Fuck, man. I respect you, y'know, the way you sing and everything. "Do you like good music . . ."' Mario broke into song.

'All right, all right. Just forget it.' Ray decided that anything would be better than hearing Mario demolish one of his favourite songs.

Unfortunately, Mario always said the wrong thing.

'Yeah, man, no hard feelings. Listen, just because your girlfriend takes her clothes off and loads of blokes wank over her, it don't mean a thing. I mean, shit, even I've wanked over her. Fuck, it doesn't mean she's a filthy slut or anything.'

Ray picked up a bottle just as Mikey grabbed Mario's arm. 'It's all right, Ray. I've got him. C'mon, Mario, we're leaving.'

When they got outside Mikey asked, 'Mario, how much have you had to drink?'

'Same as you.'

'What about in the bar at the Bon while I was getting ready?'

'Oh, just a few aniseed type drinks with Frank.'

'It wasn't called *hierbas*, was it?'

25

'Yeah, sounds about right.'

Mikey realised that Mario was seriously pissed so he walked him down to the harbour, stuck him in a taxi and told the driver to take him to the *apartmentos* Bon Tiempo.

Mikey needed to unwind. He couldn't have a late one because of the meeting with Alison next morning. He walked past the restaurants and fountains that line the bay in San Antonio, and ended up at a small bar near the Es Paradis and the Star night-clubs. Next to the serving-hatch four chickens were sizzling on a spit. He ordered a coffee and sat watching people pour in and out of the two clubs. He noticed that most of the stylish clubbers went into Es Paradis, whereas the ''ere we go' brigade seemed to favour the Star.

It was almost two o'clock when he got up to walk back to the apartments. As he got to the top of the road, he heard a commotion behind him. He looked back but couldn't see what was going on, so decided not to get involved. He walked along the sea front and up through the still busy West End. A very pink-looking girl was throwing up outside Joe Spoon's Irish Bar. Various sun-tanned boys and girls tried to get him to go into different watering-holes as he walked up the hill, and it was not until he had passed a bar called the Highlander that he felt he could relax. He turned left and started walking down a hill that took him to a road with wasteland on either side. It was the road that led to the apartments.

He had only just turned into it when a police car drove past him, lights flashing. Police cars always made Mikey feel uneasy, but he was in Spain now, and he was sure that the Spanish police didn't assume that every black face belonged to a drug-dealer, a mugger or a car thief. The police car got about fifty yards down the road before it swung round and screeched to a halt in front of Mikey.

This doesn't look too promising, he thought.

He was right.

Three policemen got out of the car, started yelling at him

in Spanish and prodding him with their batons. Then they bundled him into the car. Mikey's first thought was to tell them that he was a rep, but he remembered that Alison had said that there might be a problem with some of the work permits. The car sped through San Antonio, and Mikey assumed that they would go on to the police station. Instead, they turned down the busy road where Mikey had enjoyed a coffee ten minutes earlier.

'What the fuck is going on?' Mikey mumbled to himself.

Once outside the bar, the police dragged him from the car and paraded him in front of the owner.

'Is this the boy?' said the burliest policeman.

'*No*,' replied the bar-owner.

'But you said he was black.'

'*Verdad*. But that's not him. He speaks Spanish. I think he's a rep.'

The burliest policeman turned to Mikey, took off his cap and scratched his head.

'We are very sorry. The owner, he say that a boy eat chicken and drink wine but no pay. The boy is negro like you. But now the man say that you are no he. He also say that he think you might be *guia* – how you say? – a rep. *Tu hablas Espanol?*'

'*Si, un poquito*. But I think your English is better than my Spanish,' said Mikey, trying to win him over.

The policeman turned to the other two and said something Mikey couldn't hear. They all laughed.

'Come. Where you stay? We take you home.'

On the short journey back Mikey got on well with the policemen. He discovered that the smallest shared his interest in karate. When they arrived at the apartments, all three got out and shook his hand. As they were leaving, the little one aimed a karate kick at Mikey's ribs, pulling back just before he connected. They all laughed, in a male-bonding type of way.

From the bar, all that the inebriated Alison could see was Mikey having a 'fight' with some police. She had arranged to meet Trev when the Cockney Pride closed, so she had popped back to the Bon to grab a few bits and pieces. Now she ran outside. 'What's happening?' she demanded.

Mikey explained that this was his boss. The burly policeman asked her if she spoke Spanish.

'*Si*,' lied Alison. The policeman told her what had happened in his native tongue. Mikey noticed that she was shaking her head in all the wrong places. When the policeman had finished, she invited them all in for a drink, which they accepted. She made sure they were all comfortable then walked over to Mikey. As she moved towards him, the policemen all raised their glasses to him and mouthed, '*Salud*.' He smiled back at them. Alison saw only the smile.

'This is no laughing matter,' she said.

'What do you mean?'

'What I mean is that tomorrow I am going to get you on the first flight back to London. You're fired!'

'*What?*'

'You heard. Thank God I was able to calm them down or I dread to think what might have happened.'

Mikey thought he was hearing things. 'What have I done?'

'You know what you've done and by tomorrow so will Jane Ward.'

'What exactly did they tell you, Alison?'

This was probably a silly question because Mikey had heard virtually the whole conversation.

'Everything. Don't you care what that poor girl must have thought?'

'*What poor girl?*' Mikey was exasperated.

'The white girl. The one you got your – your – oh, do you really want me to say it?'

'*Yes!*'

'All right, then. The white girl who you made look at your cock outside the Star club.'

'*What?*'

'There's no point in denying it. The police told me everything.'

'So, your Spanish is good enough to understand all they said is it?'

'I understood most of it.'

'So what's Spanish for cock?'

'*Pollo*,' replied Alison matter-of-factly.

'I think you'll find that's chicken. *Polla* is cock,' said Mikey, emphasising the last syllable.

'Well, that's as maybe. But I know that white is *blanco*.'

'Yeah, but they were referring to white wine – *vino blanco* – not a white girl.'

'So you didn't expose yourself in an alleyway then?'

The policemen were leaving and waved at Mikey.

'*Hasta luego*, Mikey.'

'*Adios, amigos*,' replied Mikey, before continuing the conversation with Alison. 'No, I did not expose myself in an alley or anywhere else. Believe it or not, Alison, I have progressed from clubbing girls over the head and dragging them back to my cave. I've actually got my own flat at home with running water and electricity. I've even learned how to use a knife and fork.'

'There's no need to be sarcastic. They must have been speaking a local dialect,' said Alison tartly.

Mikey felt like saying it wouldn't have mattered if they had been speaking in Klingon.

'Anyway, I've still a good mind to sack you. Stealing isn't what we expect from our reps either. Or I suppose because you were wearing your rep's badge you thought you'd found somewhere else you could get free food?'

Mikey didn't want to waste his breath on her, but if he was to have the summer he'd planned, this situation had to be dealt with. It was time tactfully, slowly and deliberately to extricate himself without making an enemy of his resort manager.

'Alison, like you said, the police were speaking Ibicenco so it was hard to follow what they were saying.'

'I know. But I got the gist of it.'

'Well, you did and you didn't. What happened was, another black guy ran off without paying for his food. At this time of year there aren't too many black guys over here and they picked me up. It was a case of mistaken identity so, believe me, there isn't a problem. I'm not a thief, I'm not a flasher, and I wasn't poncing food.'

'All right, then.' Alison lit a cigarette. 'I'll go down to the police station tomorrow and smooth things over.' She took a long, self-important drag on her Marlboro. 'I just hope that tonight has taught you something.'

It had. Mikey had learned that his resort manager couldn't speak Spanish, couldn't hold her drink and couldn't give a toss about anyone other than herself.

Although she was pissed, Alison drove back to the Cockney Pride and picked up Trevor and took him back to his neat, spacious one-bedroomed apartment on the bay at Port des Torrent.

Her original plan had been to go round some of the bars they would be visiting on the Sunday-night bar crawl to finalise the payments and the length of time she would keep the clients in each bar. During her first few days on resort she had introduced herself to all of the owners of the bars YF&S were to be using. She felt that, of them all, Trevor would be the most receptive to a little womanly persuasion, so for this reason she had decided to invest the whole evening in making sure he agreed to what she wanted.

By the end of June there would be several hundred clients on resort so she had to be sure that the whole thing would go like clockwork. YF&S nearly always chose bars that were not particularly busy. The reason that they were normally as popular as a beach at Sellafield was because they were, on the whole, crap. Most of the bars in the West End didn't need the business. Many didn't want the business: when YF&S went into a bar they normally took it over. This scared off the other customers, so that when YF&S left, after

30

forty minutes, the bar was empty. A lot of bars liked 'small' groups of up to about twenty, but the only way they could get these was through individual reps. It was made clear to all reps from day one that if any of them were caught taking money from bars they would be dismissed.

The only backhanders allowed were those officially sanctioned by the company. This 'black' money was organised on every resort through the resort manager, which presented him or her with an ideal opportunity to do some creative accounting to their own benefit. It was with this in mind that Alison had visited the Cockney Pride.

Kirstie had told her that, the previous year, Trevor had paid her seventy-five pesetas a head for each client they brought in on the bar crawl. Alison knew that he was a lecherous old sod, so had decided to pay him a visit with as much flesh on show as possible: she wanted to get the payment up to a hundred and fifty. It would certainly be worth her while: she would tell head office that she was being paid fifty a head. Every week she would admit to a third less clients on the crawl than there had been. This one bar alone might be worth between three and five thousand pounds to her during the season. And there were four bars on the crawl. Plus two night-clubs. Then there were the excursions, restaurants, car and bike hire . . . The list was gloriously endless!

Now Alison kissed Trevor's cheek, kicked off her shoes and flopped giggling on to the cream leather settee.

'Awight, then, luv, what's it ter be? Whisky ter make yer fwisky, or bwandy ter make yer wandy? Ha! ha! ha! ha!'

'What about some wine to make me pine,' teased Alison, in a sexy drawl.

'And what's me little tweasure pining for exactly?'

Alison licked her lips. 'Well, it depends what you're offering, Trevor.'

He put down his bottle of Jack Daniel's, walked across to the settee and leant over to kiss her. Alison knelt up, feeling him start to grow hard against her ribcage. He grabbed her hair and roughly pulled it back, gently biting her neck and shoulder. Alison stretched up so that her right breast brushed against his bursting zip. Trevor slipped his hand down her shirt, flicked her left nipple then undid the remaining three buttons. She started rubbing the front of his trousers, taking her hand away, then putting it back again. Now she was in control and could start playing games. Trevor was getting worked up. Alison kept touching him, then taking her hand away as if she was doing something she shouldn't.

'Oh, Trev, I really want to, but—'

'But what? Come on, darlin'. We're both gwown-ups.'

'I know we are, Trev.'

'So what's the pwoblem?'

'Look, Trev, you're a very horny man. I've only ever slept with three men and I've never done it on the first night,' lied Alison. 'Come and sit down. Anyway, where's that drink?'

Reluctantly Trevor walked over to the breakfast bar and poured Alison some wine.

'Wine, wine, it makes me pine.' Alison giggled and snuggled up against Trevor's chest, squeezing her arms into her sides and crossing her legs so that the only way he could have groped her would have been if his arms grew by a metre and had at least another two joints. It took him two minutes of clumsy fumbling to realise this, after which he resignedly kissed the top of Alison's head and gave up.

'I'm sorry, Trev. You don't mind, do you?'

'No, luv. There'll be uvver times,' replied Trevor optimistically.

Alison purred. 'That's why I like older men – they understand women so much better. I'm sure we will soon. Mind you, all of this worry about hitting black-money targets doesn't help me relax.'

'What's that, then, Al baby?'

'Well, we have to draw a certain amount of money from

the bars and we're not expecting as many clients on resort as last season. That's why I'm trying to get more from the bars this year.'

'You're kidding! I fought you was being a gweedy cah.'

'Trevor! How could you think such a thing?'

'I know, I know. I'm sowwy. I fought most of the money went to you.'

'No, that's all changed. All of the money goes to the company.' Alison truly was an excellent liar. 'So,' she paused, and looked directly into Trev's eyes, 'are we going to be all right at one fifty a head?'

'We'll see.' Trevor still wanted to play games.

Alison decided to go in for the kill. 'There's no time for we'll-sees, Trevor dearest. I need to let head office know what bars we're using by tomorrow.' The lies were coming thick and fast now. 'So, are we going to be using you this year or not?'

Trevor stood up and walked over to the kitchen. He positioned himself behind the breakfast bar and poured himself a drink. His face looked stern. Alison wondered if she'd blown it. He took a sip from his glass. Then, as she held her breath, the ex-cabby's face broke into a grin. 'Go on, then. Do us a favour, though?'

'Of course, darling. Anything.'

'Show us yer tits before you go!'

'Oh, Trevor!' Alison got up and gave him a kiss on the cheek, assuming he was joking but guessing he probably wasn't.

Five minutes after leaving, she lit a cigarette and heaved a huge sigh of relief at a job well done.

Five minutes after Alison had left, and he had discarded a sticky, crumpled piece of tissue paper in the bin, Trevor did the same.

chapter one

clients on resort

Alison eventually walked into the bar at ten o'clock – half an hour late. She didn't apologise but proceeded to open the meeting. 'Right, then, you lot. Good morning.'

'Good morning, Alison,' they replied, like a group of six-year-olds.

'It's good to see that none of you appear to be too rough. I'm sure you won't need reminding that today is the day our first clients arrive. I've got all of the flight manifests here.' Alison gave them out. 'We have thirty-seven arrivals – two couples, fifteen males and eighteen females.'

'*Reeeeesult!*' yelled Greg, punching the air at the news.

'Thought you'd be pleased, Greg.' She smiled. 'The majority of the clients will be staying here at the Bon Tiempo, although two will be at the Delfin. You'll be bringing the flight in, Greg, and, Brad, I want you to be at the Delfin. When Greg has checked his lot into the Bon Tiempo he'll walk down to see that everything's all right. Clear?' Brad looked at Greg, who gave him a reassuring wink.

'Tomorrow night we'll be taking them out on a bar crawl. Thursdays won't normally be bar-crawl nights, but things are always a bit up in the air at the beginning of the season and we need to improvise. The official beach party doesn't start until next week, so on Friday we'll be doing our own down on the man-made beach.' Alison waved towards Calo des Moro, just a hundred yards from the apartments. 'Included in the five-thousand-peseta price of the beach party will be a barbecue back here at the apartments, where we will also be doing a pop quiz. Everyone got that?' There was a general mumbling of agreement. 'Good. That takes us through to Saturday. Everyone needs to be in the office in Ibiza Town no later than midday. Heather and Greg know where it is and there's a map in your information pack. There's another two flights in from Gatwick on Saturday night. Heather and Mikey will be doing the bigger one, and Brad will bring in the smaller one – I think there are eighteen arrivals, Brad – in a minibus. Also, Brad, if you could be up to meet two arrivals who are being stuck in a taxi from the Bristol flight. Should be here at about eight o'clock Sunday morning. Lorraine and Mario, you'll be bringing in the Manchester lot.'

Alison noticed the colour drain from Lorraine's face. Lorraine had not been too good on the microphone and so far Alison had been unimpressed with her performance. The quality that Jane Ward had seen in Lorraine, which Alison had not, was that although she was not an entertainer, she was good with small groups. Girls, in particular, warmed to her quickly. The secret to having a good team was balance. Jane understood this, which was one of the reasons why she was overseas manager, and Alison did not. She gave Lorraine a look of contempt and continued, 'That flight is due to land at eight thirty-five Sunday morning. Unfortunately the flights are all over the place this weekend. Another three clients staying at Las Huertas are turning up Sunday evening, so I'm sorry to have to do this to you, Brad, but you'll have to go and pick them up. You'll be sharing a coach with a rep from a company called Summerplan, so she'll probably do the microphone.'

Most of this went over Brad's head. He had no experience of airport nights and the whole thing seemed quite exciting. He was trying to work out when he would get a chance to sleep.

'Okay then,' she said, bringing the meeting to a close. 'The rest of today should be spent getting your information books and posters ready. You'll be moving to your respective hotels on Saturday, but I'll speak to you all individually about that on Friday. If any of you needs help I'll be up in my room, but only come up if it's absolutely necessary because I've got a mound of paperwork to get through. Any questions?'

There was no reply, so Alison got into the lift up to her apartment on the fifth floor, where she took off her shoes and fell on the bed to catch up on some much-needed sleep.

Downstairs, Greg started examining the flight manifests. He explained to the new reps that the beginning of the season was a great time to score points because a lot of places were not yet open and most of the girls would stay within the group. Also, it was the cheapest time of year so a lot of nurses were here – a group with which Greg claimed to have had particular success.

Looking down the manifest he explained the difference between 'single shares' and 'single rooms'. 'Single shares' were clients who would share a room with a stranger. Although they might be quite normal, in Greg's experience they were usually weirdos, slappers or both. 'Single rooms' were likely to be clients who had booked at the last minute and were prepared to go anywhere to get a tan. They were normally horrified when they discovered what YF&S was all about.

Apart from pulling women, Greg's other main talent was selling. He had never had any official sales training, but he had the gift of the gab and a razor-sharp mind when it came to a scam. His selling skills were what made YF&S turn a blind eye to his 'indiscretions' with clients of the opposite sex.

Excursion sales were important to YF&S. Apart from allowing them to keep control of clients on resort they produced a valuable source of revenue. Reps were targeted to get at least sixty per cent of their clients to buy *all* of the excursions. To encourage this they were paid a small basic salary and a commission structure was geared towards them achieving and exceeding their sales targets. Part of the reason why YF&S holidays were so cheap was because they counted on excursion sales to maintain profitability.

Because the excursion-sales targets were so high, any large groups who decided not to join in decimated the figures. The strategy in this situation was to identify the natural leader and home in on him or her. As a team, Heather and Greg were brilliant. It took a strong individual to resist their combined pressure.

Because he had to be at the Delfin by six in the morning, Brad didn't go into town with the others. Mikey decided to stay in too so the pair took a few bottles of San Miguel up to Brad's room. They sat on the balcony listening to music and putting the world to rights. In the distance they could hear a singer/guitarist ruining Eric Clapton's 'Wonderful Tonight' and the occasional drunken shriek. After an hour or so Mikey could tell that Brad was tired, so he left and popped into town to try to score some puff.

Five thirty came a lot quicker than Brad would have liked. Had he been on holiday he would probably still have been in a club. Instead he showered himself into life, put on his uniform and went down to Reception to wait for Greg's coach. It was a strange feeling, the thought of meeting 'clients'. All of the training had been geared towards looking after *clients*, entertaining *clients*, selling to *clients*, disciplining *clients* – Brad was almost expecting supernatural beings rather than ordinary people.

A little after six thirty he heard the rumble of a diesel engine. He looked up to see the newly risen sun reflecting off the dewy blue and red paintwork that was the livery of the San José coach that had just pulled up outside. Through the closed door he could just about make out Greg's voice on the microphone giving the new arrivals instructions before he led them off the coach. As they all walked past Brad he tried to look as relaxed and experienced as he could, but inside he felt hopeless. A group of three girls looked at him and giggled.

'All right, girls?' He smiled. They giggled some more

which made him feel like a grinning banana in his bright yellow uniform. He sought refuge in Greg, who was busy checking people in and didn't even notice him for almost a minute. When he did see him he was quite impatient. 'You should be on the coach taking the other two to the Delfin. Get a move on. I'll be there in five minutes.'

Brad shuffled off. He got on the coach and glanced at the clients, raised his eyebrows and mouthed, 'All right?' then sat down in the front seat with his back to them. Two minutes later they were at the hotel. Brad got off the coach and walked through to Reception. The clients were girls who had come away together. He checked them in and stood at the desk as they went up to their room.

A few moments later they returned. 'Any chance of a drink?' one asked.

Brad sat with a coffee while the two girls knocked back vodkas and orange. They already seemed a bit tipsy. Both were about five foot two. The blonde one introduced herself as Emma. She started asking questions about Greg. 'He's a northerner, isn't he? I don't normally like northerners but he seems really sweet. He's ever so good-looking, isn't he? I was talking to him on the coach. He's a right laugh. Has he got a girlfriend?'

'No, I 'aven't, and I don't want one,' said Greg, walking in suddenly.

Emma blushed.

Brad noticed that the dark-haired girl was staring directly at him. He smiled at her, a little uncomfortably. 'What's your name?'

'Linda. And you're . . . Brad,' she replied, looking at his badge. 'What about you, Brad, have you got a girlfriend?'

'Course he 'asn't,' butted in Greg. 'He's too fucking ugly.'

'Well, I don't think he's ugly,' said Linda. 'I bet you get loads of girls, don't you?'

Brad started to relax. It dawned on him that just because these were clients he didn't have to watch everything he said. He could just be himself and have a laugh. Greg was already whispering into the giggling Emma's ear. He caught his eye. Greg winked and nodded towards Linda mouthing, 'Go on.' The penny dropped.

'Actually, I've not been with a girl for over a year now,' lied Brad. 'That's why I became a rep. I was seeing this girl who dumped me for a rugby player. I tried to win her back but him and two of his mates from the team beat me up.' Emma and Greg started listening. 'I was in hospital for ten weeks. They kicked me in the – well, you know.' Brad indicated his groin. 'The specialist was worried that I'd never be able to make love again. I couldn't get a decent hard-on so they put this thing in my wotsit. It just means it's hard all the time and when I want to use it I just have to bend it from the side to the front. I'm really embarrassed about it. I've not let anyone see it until now – God knows how anyone will ever fancy me.' Brad looked at the floor, convinced the girls knew he was bullshitting. He caught Greg's eye and winked.

'You'd show it to us, though, Brad, wouldn't you?' asked Greg.

'Well, if I do it'll have to be one at a time and you've got to promise not to laugh.'

'All right, then,' answered Greg, on everyone's behalf. 'Let's go upstairs.'

Brad led the way wearing a huge grin. The two girls followed, giggling. Greg kept telling them to ssh so as not to embarrass Brad. When they got to the room Brad said, 'Okay, Greg first.'

Greg walked into the room and shut the door. The two reps burst out laughing. 'Fuckin' brilliant. Right. You get Linda in 'ere and I'll ger' Emma next door. They're definitely up for it. Emma was making a serious play for me on the coach. Remember, we've got the welcome meeting at eleven so don't be too long.'

'There's no danger of that, the way my bollocks feel at the moment. I just hope she comes across otherwise they'll probably explode – very messy.'

'Yeah, well, don't fall asleep either. I'll see you back at the Bon later. Good luck.'

Greg walked out and ushered Linda in. Brad and she stood facing each other. 'Look, Brad, if you're embarrassed I underst—'

'No. It's fine,' said Brad solemnly. 'It's something I've got to do. Give me your hand.' He took Linda's hand and rested it against his 'injury'. It was already rock hard and pointing to the left. 'Right. All I have to do is to undo my zip and bend it forward.' He undid his trousers and lifted his member over the top of his pants. 'There you go.' He put her hand on it. 'Does it feel any different?'

'I'm not sure. Maybe. It's hard to tell.'

'Linda, can I ask you to do me a huge favour. You see, I've not come since the operation and—' Brad burst out laughing, falling on to the bed with Linda on top of him.

'You bastard. I *knew* you were lying.' With that she bent down and bit his dick before taking the majority of it in her mouth. After a minute or two Brad put his hands on either side of her head and pulled her up so that they were face to face. As he kissed her she slipped off her panties then pulled off her blue and white striped dress. She straddled his thigh and started to rub herself up and down it. Brad raised his knee and pushed two fingers inside her. She let out a low moan and rammed herself against his hand. Brad turned her over without taking his fingers out, so that she was lying on her back. He worked his tongue down her body until his tongue was flicking her clitoris, while his fingers probed her.

'Have you got a condom?' he asked.

'No. Haven't you?'

'Yeah. A hundred and eighty quid's worth, but not here. *Shit!*'

'Never mind. Here.' With that Linda slid down the bed so that she was underneath the kneeling Brad. She licked then sucked his balls whilst deftly rubbing his member. Just as Brad was about to come she raised her head and put her

41

mouth around his helmet just in time to receive Brad's first ejaculation on Spanish soil. He looked down at her, grinning from ear to ear. 'What a fine woman! God, I definitely owe you one.'

'Actually you don't,' replied Linda. 'I've never been much of a screamer but, believe me, we're quits.'

When Brad got back to the Bon the only person in the bar was Greg, who was getting the flipchart ready for the welcome meeting. As he walked in, Greg wrote '3 POINTS' in big red letters on the flipchart. He looked at Brad, who lifted up two fingers.

'*What!* You didn't shag 'er.' Brad shook his head. 'Why not?'

'No dunkies, mate.'

'I thought you brought two 'undred quid's worth with you to sell.'

'I did, only some bastard's apparently supplied all the bars with condom machines. I'll have to try and sell them to our clients.'

'Knowing our lot you'll probably 'ave more chance of using 'em. Anyway, I'd've still shagged 'er. She seemed clean enough to me.'

'Well, Dr Greg, I'm taking no chances this season.'

'Fair enough. Still, good early points, eh? I've gorra 'and it to you, Brad, that was a great story. What a fuckin' team. Almost fuckin' telepathic.'

The bar crawl started at seven thirty. Linda and Emma both turned up and Brad was pleasantly surprised at how nice they looked compared to when they had arrived that morning. There was also a redhead he hadn't noticed at the welcome meeting. Mario clocked her too.

'Cor! What would I do with that?' he whistled.

'Come too quickly?' replied Mikey.

'I can go for ever, mate. Everything you've ever heard about Italians, it's all true.' He continued, 'You watch, by the end of tonight she'll be putty in my hands.'

'The only thing that'll be in your hands at the end of tonight will be your dick, soft lad,' said Greg, as he walked past.

'Oh, I don't know Greg,' added Mikey. 'Let's face it, Mario is a good-looking lad. All right, so he dresses a bit strange . . .' Mikey looked him up and down. As they were going on a bar crawl the reps had to wear YF&S T-shirts. Apart from Mario all of them were wearing either jeans or tracksuit bottoms. Mario had on a pair of baggy black trousers held up with wide black braces, tucked into ankle-high buckled boots. 'Actually, Mario, you're not going anywhere for a few minutes, are you?'

'No. Why?'

'I thought I'd pop upstairs and get you a little red nose to complete the outfit.'

'Fuck off! Do you know how much these trousers cost? A hundred and twenty quid!'

'They might have cost that much when the original owner bought them, but how much did they cost you?'

'What do you mean?'

'Mario, it's obvious that some ex-New Romantic has donated them to a charity shop where they no doubt caught your sartorially inelegant eye. So what were they? A fiver? A tenner?'

'What the fuck do you know about fashion?' said the now agitated Mario, before proudly adding, 'My cousin runs one of the best clothes shops in the King's Road.'

'So why don't you shop there, then?' Mikey was finding this too easy.

'I suppose you could always go and get changed.' Brad had sensed it was getting nasty so he thought he'd try to deflect Mario's rage away from Mikey.

It was too late. Mario's face contorted into a scowl. 'Well, at least I can change my clothes. What are you going to do about your skin?' With that he turned on his heel and went to the bar.

Brad looked at Mikey, worried that the next stage of the

confrontation would be physical. Mikey sensed his concern. 'Brad, I've learnt how to deal with idiots like him. I'm just glad he's shown his colours so early in the season.'

'Well, I admire your control. If he can't stand having the piss taken out of him, what's he doing in this job?'

'Apparently he was outstanding at Bridlehurst – one of the best candidates. All the girls loved him and he comes across as pretty confident. Mind you, a little birdie told me he knew one of the reps from last year who gave him the lowdown on what to expect during the twenty-four-hour interview.'

'So he knew all about being woken up in the middle of the night and dumped in the wilds of Hereford?'

'Guess so. He also knew what kind of five-minute sketch would go down well, and all about that two-minute after-dinner speech.'

'I reckon that was the scariest part of the whole interview.'

'Yeah. One minute you're relaxed, eating, the next they're telling you you've got two minutes to prepare a two-minute speech on a subject they give you. I had to talk about dolphins. What about you?'

'Eating a Cadbury's Creme Egg under water. They spring it on you to see how good you are at waffling and how you react under stress. I s'pose if Mario knew all about it it made it a bit easier.'

'For sure. The other thing that I heard is that his brother's a bit of a "face" back home, sorts out someone in head office with coke or something. By all accounts he pulled a few strings for him.'

'That figures.'

They both looked over at Mario, who had knocked back two quick glasses of Hierbas. He stared at Mikey and Brad, then made a bee-line for the redhead.

Just at that moment Alison came in. She walked over to Greg, who was standing a few feet away from Brad and Mikey. As she passed them she said, 'Come on, you two, you should be mingling with the clients like Mario.' She turned to Greg. 'Right. Shall we get this show on the road?'

The first bar they visited was the Cockney Pride. Brad was conscious of Alison sitting at the top of the bar watching their every move. She seemed to be on Lorraine's case, going up to her and telling her to do things every few minutes. After about half an hour when he was near Lorraine he said, 'Alison keeps pulling you over. Anything up?'

'Oh, she's always telling me not to spend too long speaking to one group of people but some of them are really interesting to talk to.'

'Mmmm. Still, she's the boss.'

'I know. It's just that – Oh, what the hell!' Lorraine changed the subject. 'Old Mario seems to be getting pissed. He's spent the whole night trying to chat up Patricia, the redhead, but Alison hasn't said anything to him.'

'Where's Patricia from?' enquired Brad.

'Nottingham, I think.'

'What does she do?'

'She's an economics student. Don't tell me you're after her too.'

'All right, I won't. What does she drink?'

'Malibu and pineapple, I think.'

Brad smiled at Lorraine, ordered a Malibu and pineapple from Trevor and walked over to Patricia. Mario had left her alone to get himself another drink.

'Patricia, isn't it?'

'That's right. And which one are you?' She looked at his badge. 'Well, hello, Brad.'

'Well, hello, Patricia.' He smiled. 'Enjoying yourself?'

Patricia looked over at Mario. 'Hardly.'

'Oh, don't worry about him. He's just a bit pissed.'

'A bit!'

'All right, *very* pissed.'

There were a few seconds' awkward silence, which Patricia broke. 'So, Brad, have you come over here to tell me

45

how wonderful you are and how three thousand people applied for thirty jobs and how thrilled any girl should be if a rep tries to chat her up and—'

'*Whoa*! Steady on. It would seem my fellow rep has been giving you a bit of an ear-bashing.'

'Oh, come off it, it's not just him. All of you think all you have to do is snap your fingers and we'll just fall into bed.'

'Hang on, hang on. I have a job to do and part of it is to talk to our clients to make sure they're enjoying themselves. Now, if you're saying to me that you'd enjoy yourself more if I made myself scarce then that's fine, but please, do me a favour and don't tar me with the same brush as that cretin. He's got the brains—'

'Brains!' interrupted Patricia. 'You're not going to tell me you need brains to do this job? I thought all you needed was the ability to ponce drinks and a mirror to look at yourself in. You'll be telling me next that you need two A levels to be a rep.'

'It's not a prerequisite but it does help.'

Patricia was laughing, in a semi-mocking way. 'So what are your A levels in, Brad? Sunbathing and chatting up girls?'

'No, I only got O levels in those.' Brad thought that now would be an opportune moment to use the information Lorraine had just given him. 'So, judging by the way you put such emphasis on intellect, I assume you're in the middle of doing a degree.'

'I am, actually.'

'Mmm.' Brad looked thoughtful. 'Not a cop-out subject like sociology or economics.'

'Economics isn't a cop-out. Anyway, how did you know I'm studying economics?' She looked at him quizzically.

Brad knew he was in danger of becoming a little too smug so he brought the conversation to a close. 'Anyway, Patricia, just to show we're not all vainglorious drink ponces obsessed with acquiring notches for our bedposts I'm going to carry on doing my job by talking to other clients, and whilst I'm sure they won't be as interesting as you . . .' he put on a voice of mock sincerity '. . . I've just gotta do what I've gotta do.' He gave her the glass he had in his hand. 'There you go. You look like you drink Malibu and pineapple.' He moved across to Greg, who was talking to Emma and Linda.

Greg looked at his watch, then said to Brad, 'Right. We've been in here forty minutes. Time to move on.' With that he looked at Alison and pointed at his watch. She nodded, so Greg went over to the tape deck, turned the music down and switched on the microphone. 'Okay. Have we got anyone here from Young Free & Single?' A smallish cheer went up. 'That was *pathetic*! I said, *do we have anyone here from young free & single?*' The Cockney Pride erupted in a unified drunken yell. 'That's more like it! Right, then, it's time to knock back yer drinks 'cos we're moving on to the Anglers where your reps will be DJing and gerrin' you into the party mood.' Greg switched off the microphone and came back to Brad. 'Right. Lead them round to the Anglers. Me, Lorraine and Mario will make sure there aren't any stragglers. When you get there start playing some records and gerrem all going. I'll take over as soon as we've cleared this place.'

'Any idea how long you'll be?' asked Brad.

'I don't know. Ten, fifteen minutes. Why?'

'I've never DJed before.'

'Well, now's your chance to learn. Come on, gerra move on.'

Brad and Heather led the majority of the singing holiday-makers to the Anglers. It was empty, and the owner seemed flustered. 'What time do you call this? You're ten minutes late. You'd better stay an extra ten or you won't get—' The bar owner checked himself just before he revealed his 'arrangement' with Alison.

'Would you mind showing me how to work the decks? I've never DJed before,' said Brad.

'Fucking great! They send me round a rep who's never

47

DJed before.' The man shook his head. 'Follow me. I'm Russell. Who are you?'

'Brad.'

They shook hands. Russell's tone mellowed. 'I'm not having a go at you, it's just that I get a bit stressed at the beginning of the season. Ironic, really. I came out here to avoid stress. Tried everything back home. Even took up fishing.'

'Is that why you called your bar the Anglers?' asked Brad.

'Couldn't think of anything else. I had a shoe-repair shop back home. Hasn't got the same ring to it, has it?' Russell laughed. 'I think it's good to call a bar after something that relates to the owner, so I thought the Anglers was quite appropriate.'

Brad thought that the Manic Depressive Paranoid Schizophrenic would have been more like it, but he kept that suggestion to himself.

'Right, Brad. There's the speed select, thirty-three or forty-five. These are your fade controls . . .' He droned on.

Brad nodded, trying to take everything in. He looked through the record collection, which wasn't awe-inspiring. He managed to put on three records before Greg arrived. When Greg took over, Brad was amazed at how easy he made it seem. He was on the microphone getting everybody going and although 'Happy Hour' and 'Shout' were not the sort of records Brad would have chosen to listen to, they were right for the occasion. Every time Emma and Linda walked past the DJ booth Greg caught his eye, held up three fingers and mouthed, 'Three points.' When Brad brushed past them they both pinched his bum. Just before they were all due to leave, Emma cornered him as he came out of the toilets.

'This is great, isn't it?'

'I'm glad you're enjoying yourself,' he said. Emma put her arm through his, which made him look round to check that Alison wasn't watching. He also found himself checking that Patricia wasn't either.

'Brad, I've got some good news and some bad news,' slurred Emma.

'And what's that, then?'

'Well, the bad news is that Linda wants to sleep with Greg.'

'Oh. Oh, well, that sounds more like the good news to me,' replied Brad, his ego-defence mechanism kicking in.

'The good news is that I want to sleep with you.' Emma giggled.

'Well, that's all right, then. You do know that we don't finish this bar crawl until gone midnight, don't you? Do you think you can last that long?'

Emma stood on tiptoe and whispered in his ear, 'I can last for ever.'

Brad smiled, then rushed over to Greg, who had just started playing an Edwin Starr record. 'Greg, you'll never guess what's just happened.'

'Go on.'

'Emma just came up to me and said that they want to swap – y'know, me with her and you with Linda.'

'Oh, that.' Greg put another record on the turntable and cued it up. 'Yeah, I know all about that. It was my idea.'

'Your idea?' Brad looked bewildered.

'Yeah, I sorted it out in the Cockney Pride. Hang on a minute.' Greg started Gary Glitter's 'Leader Of The Gang'. 'It's obvious they'll shag anything with a badge.'

'How can you tell?'

'I just can,' replied Greg. 'Anyway, I've already got maximum points out of Emma 'cos she won't take it up the shit box.'

Ten minutes later the bar crawl proceeded to Sgt Pepper's. Somewhere on the way Patricia got lost, denying Brad the opportunity to speak to her again. Once finished in Pepper's, Mikey and the other reps were going to the Star club to round things off and Greg was going to the apartments to increase his points tally. As Brad was feeling pissed, tired and randy he opted to join him. Linda and

Emma went on ahead and were waiting for them in the bar. Brad sat down with the girls and got himself a toasted sandwich and a coffee, while Greg went to see the receptionist to check that there were no problems.

When he got back Brad yawned. 'Well, I don't know about anyone else, but I'm knackered.'

'That's a shame,' said Greg, slipping his arms around the girls' shoulders. 'Guess I'll just 'ave to take these lovely young ladies upstairs an' look after 'em on me own.'

'You must be joking. It's bad enough that the love of my life has dumped me for you,' Brad said, looking at Linda. 'I'm just lucky that this fine specimen of womanhood has got some sense of justice . . .' he tousled Emma's hair '. . . and taste.'

'Aye, well, I've got something for *you* to taste.' Greg grabbed Linda's hand to lead her upstairs. 'See you at the beach party tomorrow.'

'He's a real charmer, isn't he?' said Brad to Emma. 'Such a way with words.' Emma just smiled. She was very drunk. 'Come on, then. Time for bed.'

Emma hiccuped and stumbled to her feet. Her high heels made an embarrassingly loud clip-clop on the marble floor.

Brad didn't enjoy the sex. They were both pissed and it lacked any passion. There was a short period of fumbling, followed by less than ten minutes of the missionary position, after which Brad dribbled into the first of his hundred and eighty pounds' worth of condoms. Throughout Emma asked questions about Mario and said that at least half of the girls on holiday that week fancied him, herself included. She was dead to the world within minutes, so he switched the light on to set his alarm in an attempt to wake her. It failed.

When Brad woke up, Emma had already left, which was fortunate because Alison knocked on his door to give him a list of things to buy for the beach party. It consisted of consumables and accessories, aimed at getting the clients as

drunk and messy as possible (sangria, champagne, eggs . . .).
During desk duty, he noticed that two of the reasonably
attractive holidaymakers were twins.

Towards the end of his shift the bar filled up with the
clients who were going to the beach party. Brad had to go
over to a group of four lads called the Plymouth Possee who
had their ghetto-blaster on full volume playing thrash
metal. This did not go down too well with those who had
more refined musical tastes – or a hangover.

'All right, lads?' No reaction. 'Do you think you could
turn that down a bit?'

'Sorry, mate, can't hear you – the music's too loud.'

Brad wasn't sure what to do. He didn't want to be
confrontational. On the other hand, he couldn't allow
himself to lose respect, and the music was annoying the
rest of the gathering. He decided to be firm but tactful.

At that moment, however, Greg walked past, snatched
the music system from the offender's lap, slammed it on
the table, and pressed the stop/eject button. 'That's enough
of that fuckin' shite,' he said, throwing the cassette out of
the window. The Plymouth Possee's protestations were
abridged by the cheering of everybody else. 'Right, then,
you lot, get your skates on 'cos it's beach-party time.' He
turned to the Plymouth Possee. 'And you four . . .' Greg
bent down, his face stern '. . . are going to get so fucking
pissed on this beach party 'cos I'm going to throw so much
fucking ale down your necks that you won't be able to tell
the difference between Megadeath and Lisa fucking Stans-
field.'

'Yeee-haaaah!' whooped the lads.

Greg gave Brad a 'that's-the-way to-do-it' wink.

As they made their way to the beach, Brad noticed that
there was an imbalance in the sexes. A few of the males
who had booked the excursion block had overdone things
on the bar crawl and had chosen to look on the beach party
as one of the free ones that buying the block gave them.

A dozen steps led down to the semi-circular beach, which

was about a hundred metres across. Rocks rather than sand provided access to the sea, with sand sprinkled over an area of concrete to provide additional 'beach'. Greg chose a deserted spot and drew out a makeshift volleyball court in the sand. Some bottles of cheap champagne were opened, music was switched on and the party slowly got under way.

For the first hour or so the drink flowed freely. Brad went round making sure that everybody was getting into the right mood (i.e. pissed). It proved an ideal opportunity to acquaint himself with the rest of the group. There were four nurses from the Highlands of Scotland, all on holiday abroad for the first time. There was another nurse from Cambridge, called Vanessa, who was with her best friend, a student called Abigail. Vanessa and Abigail seemed dowdy at first with bland faces, but the more he spoke to them the more their personalities came through. Both had lively eyes and exuded warmth. It was this, and not the fact that they had the biggest, roundest tits Brad had yet set eyes upon, that made him spend at least half an hour engaging them in conversation. It also gave him the opportunity to avoid Linda and Emma, who seemed to be competing with the Plymouth Possee to see who could get pissed the quickest.

Brad noticed that Patricia kept looking at him, but in light of the previous night's exchange his game plan now was to treat her no differently from any of the others – at least for the time being. He found it difficult not to glance at her, but this was mainly because Mario was losing any remaining credibility by doing handstands in front of her and displaying feats of 'strength' (trying to pick her up and throw her into the sea).

Later Greg got the games under way, starting with an egg-throwing competition.

Over the course of the next hour the games and the participants got messier and messier. For anyone with indifferent culinary requirements, the eggs and flour cooking in the afternoon sun on various torsos would probably have provided a hearty meal. When the drink ran out

Lorraine had to go to the supermarket to get some more. By the time they got to the final game everybody was sloshed. It is, of course, sod's law that a crisis always happens when those supposed to deal with it are in their least able state. Today was no exception. Just as Brad was in the middle of a laughing fit, one of the Scottish nurses came running over. 'Brad! Brad, help! I can't find Glenda. She went swimming twenty minutes ago and she hasn't come back.'

'Has she been drinking?'

'Of course she's been drinking! We all have.'

'Where did she swim out?' asked Brad, sobering up. The Scottish girl pointed out towards the boat, which was still pumping out sand, and started howling.

The reps and a few clients spread along the coast to begin the search. Brad went to the left with the other three Scottish girls, plus Vanessa and Abigail. Greg, Linda, Emma and the reps went to the right. Brad was becoming concerned because he could see nobody out at sea, and Glenda's sister, Margo, was hysterical. Then he saw Mikey waving his arms in the air and pointing at a short girl in a white swimsuit walking next to him.

'Is that her?' Brad asked Margo, pointing at the girl next to Mikey.

'Aye, oh, thank God,' she replied, and ran towards her sister.

Brad relaxed, and stopped off at the beach bar to get himself a lolly. When he got back, something wasn't right. A group had gathered around the Scottish girls.

'What's up?' asked Brad. 'I thought she was all right.'

'She is!' replied Mikey. 'It's Margo. All the worry about Glenda has brought on an asthma attack.'

'Oh, fuck,' said Brad.

'She needs a Ventolin. She's having a bad one.' Vanessa, as a nurse, had taken charge.

'I've got one back at my apartment,' replied Brad.

'You have?' said a surprised Greg.

'Yeah, I'm allergic to cats.'

'Well, don't just stand there,' yelled Greg, '*Go and get it!*'

Brad sprinted back to his apartment. It was very hot, and he had drunk a hell of a lot. He ran into the building and was suddenly stone cold sober: Alison was sitting in Reception.

'Brad, what are you doing here? You should be at the beach party.' He was so out of breath he could hardly speak.

'Sorry – emergency – explain – can't stop – move – get past – fuck—' he panted.

'Right. Calm down and tell me what you're doing back here.'

Brad was unable to utter a word.

'Brad, get your breath because I'm not moving until you tell me exactly what's going on.'

Brad shook his head, mouthed, 'Can't,' and barged past her. He could hear her shouting after him, but he felt like a man possessed. Once in his room he found the Ventolin and ran for the door. As he opened it a flustered Alison was walking in. He crashed into her, sending her sprawling across the corridor.

'*Streeter!*' she screamed. 'If you don't come back here now I'll—'

But Brad ran on, out of the apartments and towards the beach. He felt as though his lungs were about to explode. Margo's life might depend on him. He'd had one bad asthma attack himself and he remembered how petrified he had been. As he approached the beach, though, everybody seemed to be behaving normally. There was even a volley-ball game going on. He had been expecting to see a group huddled around Margo, but as he got closer he saw her sitting with her friends, smiling. He stopped next to Vanessa and Abigail.

'What – why – Margo—'

'It's all right, Brad,' said Vanessa. 'Just after you left I found a paper bag and got her to breathe into that, and she was fine two minutes later. You were bloody quick, though.

I'd better look in your trunks to make sure you're not really Linford Christie.'

Brad flopped on to the sand. All of a sudden he felt dizzy, and couldn't breathe. At first Vanessa and Abigail thought he was messing about, but when they realised he wasn't, Vanessa yelled to Greg to get some water. She gave Brad his own Ventolin and poured the cold water over him. After about five minutes the panic was over and Brad got his breath back.

'Fuck me. What happened there?'

'I don't know,' replied Mikey. 'But if you can run like that I can probably get you a game with the London Monarchs.'

'No, thanks. Jesus, I'm shagged.'

'Well, after that performance you should be,' said Lorraine. 'I think the lovely Patricia was impressed. Oh, Brad, you're such a hero,' she added, ironically.

Brad glanced towards Patricia, who smiled at him. He picked himself up and walked over to her.

'Are you all right?' she asked.

'Yeah, I am now. Pretty pathetic, eh? Nothing like nearly passing out on a beach full of people – guaranteed to impress.'

'Oh, and who were you trying to impress exactly?'

Brad cursed himself for letting that one slip. He laughed. 'It's a shame you hate reps so much. Just think, if I'd died then you'd have never known how horrible I really am.'

'Oh, I think I've a good idea.' She was smiling. 'Anyway, you would probably have come back to haunt me.'

'I wouldn't have haunted you, Patricia. I would have been your guardian angel, making sure that no horrible reps made a pass at you.'

'And what about nice reps? Would you have stopped them too?'

'There are no nice reps. We're all egomaniacs who think we can sleep with anyone we want. Remember?'

'Mmmm,' replied Patricia thoughtfully. 'And do you think that you can sleep with anyone you want, Brad?'

'Let's just say that sometimes you meet someone where sleeping with them isn't the main priority.' He looked directly into her eyes. Should he just tell her he fancied the hell out of her?

The decision was made for him. Greg yelled at him to give him a hand with clearing up. 'Saved by the yell. I'll speak to you later.'

Brad never did catch up with Patricia that evening. After the beach party there was a barbecue and a pop quiz, but Patricia did not attend either. Later, he found himself propping up the bar in Sgt Pepper's. He had ignored all messages that Alison wanted to speak to him urgently. He preferred to face her after a good night's sleep. Sgt Pepper's was the fourth bar he had visited with the male members of the group, and he now felt qualified to conclude that they were all dickheads. He no longer wanted to be in their company.

He went and stood by the door to talk to Danny, one of the props. After about five minutes he saw the rather tipsy twins walk past giggling. He chased after them and the first five minutes of the walk back were fine. Brad felt pleased with himself for having a twin on either arm. However, he was so tired that he kept falling asleep momentarily while he was walking. When they got back to the apartments he invited them up to his room for coffee. It was not a well-thought-out idea as he had no coffee. Anyway, the twins couldn't understand his incoherent mumblings, so alone, Brad flopped on to his bed, snoring and dribbling himself into an exhausted sleep.

chapter two

The first thing that struck Brad was the noise: coaches revving, Tannoys blaring, kids screaming, adults laughing or yelling – and so many people. Ibiza airport on a Saturday night was no place for an agoraphobic. Brad felt that everybody was looking at him in his bright yellow uniform. In truth, the majority probably were. Brad remembered the mystique that had surrounded the reps when he had been on holiday: they seemed so calm and in control, so familiar with their surroundings, confident and unflappable. But he was holding things together well.

He, Mikey and Heather were sitting outside the airport doors where they could see the flight arrivals board. Brad was having trouble keeping still, though, partly through nerves and partly because he had seen a vision of beauty in a Thomson's uniform by the agency desk in Arrivals. He stood up to wander into the airport.

'I'd stay here if I were you, Brad,' said Heather. 'You know what Alison told us.'

'Yeah. What was all that about?'

'Oh, I don't know,' replied Heather. 'But she thinks that until our work permits are sorted out we'd better keep a low profile at the airport. In theory, I suppose, they could arrest us and deport us if they find we're working without them.'

'Well, that's bloody sensible,' joined in Mikey. 'Spend all that time training us, let us all leave our jobs, girlfriends or whatever back home and then, after a few days on resort, we end up back in Blighty because some dumb bitch hasn't filled in the right forms. Brilliant.'

'We don't know that it's Alison's fault, Mikey.' Heather defended her half-heartedly.

'I didn't say it was. All I said was "some dumb bitch".' Mikey changed the subject. 'I see that Greg scored another three points last night.'

This was the first Brad had heard of it. 'Who with? It can't have been either of the twins 'cos I walked them home.' He cringed as he remembered the embarrassing end to the previous night.

'No, it was Vanessa.'

'Oh, you're fucking joking! Jammy bastard. You mean he's had his hand round those lovely—'

'More than just his hands from what he was telling me.'

Heather started telling them stories about Greg from the previous season. She was half-way through one about him and the hotel owner's fifteen-year-old daughter when Brad interrupted her. 'My flight's just arrived.' He sounded nervous.

'You'll be fine,' said Heather reassuringly.

Brad picked up his briefcase and clipboard and drifted into the airport like a condemned man. There were reps everywhere, all laughing together as if they belonged to an exclusive club. Brad tried to appear confident, but he didn't know where to look or how to act. He stood at Arrivals staring at the luggage of everyone who came through in case it had a YF&S label on it. He was so engrossed in this that he didn't notice her walk up behind him. There was a tap on his shoulder. 'Hello,' she said.

It was the Vision. She had curly black hair that cascaded down her shoulders, framing a perfectly symmetrical face dominated by a pair of gorgeous green eyes. Her full red lips matched the colour of her uniform.

'First time at the airport then?' she went on.

'No – well, actually, yes.'

'I thought so.' She laughed.

'That obvious, is it?'

'Afraid so. I'm Kelly.'

'Brad.'

They shook hands. Her smile was so captivating that he forgot to let go of her hand. Then she slipped it out of his, and said, 'Well, I'll leave you to it, then. Good luck,' and was gone.

Brad, could have kicked himself. When he had first seen her from outside the airport he had rehearsed at least half a dozen witty lines but he had forgotten all of them.

'Lovely, isn't she?' said a deepish voice with an Irish lilt. Brad turned around. The voice belonged to another Thomson's rep, whose badge showed that his name was Leo. 'You know what gave the game away, don't you?'

'Tell me?'

'Easy. It's normally at least fifteen minutes after a flight lands, before the first passengers come through and you've been standing here since its arrival was announced.'

Brad felt a little silly, but not for long. At that moment, Leo caught sight of some English-looking tourists coming through the door.

'Here they are now. See you later.'

Brad's stomach knotted. He marvelled at how easily all of the reps around him just switched on.

It took ages for the first person to come through with a YF&S sticker, but then there was a flurry of activity and before he had time to blink it was all over. He checked his manifest and, thankfully, all eighteen had arrived.

He found Heather and Mikey.

'Everything all right?' asked Heather.

'Yep.'

'Good. Off you go, then. We'll see you at tomorrow's welcome meeting.'

Brad approached the minibus as slowly as he could, knowing that the clients were waiting for their experienced, know-everything rep. He felt as if he should have a green L-plate around his neck. As he stepped on to the coach, eighteen faces looked at him with tired expectancy. Brad smiled, turned his back and sat down to compose himself.

The coach driver said something to him in Spanish, which sounded like a question. Brad had no intention of letting the new arrivals know that he couldn't speak the lingo, so he mumbled, '*Si*.' It was a lucky guess – the driver had asked if everybody was on board and now closed the doors. They were off. Brad was painfully aware of the silence behind him, so to make it appear that he was doing something, he kept putting exaggerated ticks on his clipboard. He hoped the clients would think he was important and professional.

Eventually, he made himself switch on the microphone. There was a mind-numbing squeal of feedback. Mercifully, the driver fixed it and Brad read shakily through the 'dos and don'ts' at least five times faster than he had originally planned. His audience gave only a minimal reaction, so he looked for salvage in one of his tapes. *Aaaaaarrrrgghh!* He had left his briefcase, which contained all of his tapes, at the airport. The sweat pores on his scalp were working overtime.

He noticed that there was already a tape in the cassette player, and pushed it in. What followed was an aural assault of the magnitude that only a Spanish coach driver's musical taste could inflict. Gingerly, Brad switched the microphone back on and asked if anyone had any decent tapes. A girl sitting half-way back gave him a Madonna album, and although under normal circumstances Brad would have asked her to define the word 'decent', under these circumstances Madonna was just fine. Feeling slightly better, Brad had a go at pointing out some of the local landmarks and telling some jokes. The response was not dissimilar to that normally reserved for Jim Bowen, so he sheepishly pushed the tape back in and began to add another couple of hundred ticks to his clipboard.

Brad only managed an hour's sleep before his alarm woke him in time to greet the two from the Bristol flight. He spent a little while talking to them, and advised them to try to stay up for the welcome meeting. They took their bags up to their rooms just as Mikey came down. 'What are those two like?' he asked.

'Both single shares. He's been on holiday with Young Free & Single for the last five years and thinks he knows more about repping than we do.'

'He probably does. What about the girl?'

'Well, you saw her. She's not about to be the next pageant queen of San An, is she? Maybe there were some decent fillies on your flight.'

'Well, they must have missed the plane. Mind you, I was shitting myself so much that a gaggle of nude page-three girls could have walked through and I wouldn't have noticed.'

'I know what you mean,' agreed Brad. 'At least there's the Manchester lot.'

At that moment, Lorraine's coach pulled up outside with them. As the clients noisily filtered off it, Brad and Mikey looked out for any specimens of glorious womanhood. As the final girl collected her case, they glanced at each other. Mikey said it: 'Never mind. There's still the Birmingham flight.'

By ten thirty, the Bon Tiempo bar contained over a hundred boisterous holidaymakers, all waiting for the welcome meeting. The reps were pouring out complimentary Bucks Fizz (the roughest of sparkling wine with a plastic screw-in bung and orange juice). Brad was quite excited. He was to run through the information at the meeting and the performer in him was looking forward to being up in front of all of these people. First, though, he had to get everyone to settle down and listen to him.

Greg came and stood next to him. 'Nervous?'

'A little,' replied Brad honestly.

'You'll do fine and you know it. You're one of the best new reps I've seen.'

Brad didn't know if Greg was trying to make him feel better or if he meant it. In the first few days on resort he had grown to admire Greg. There was no doubting that he was an absolute hound where women were concerned, but he nearly always had clients eating out of his hand.

'All right, then, off you go.'

Brad had brought a whistle, which he blew now to attract everyone's attention. 'Right, you lot, if you could all shut up for ten minutes.'

After thirty seconds or so the noise and chatter diminished to the odd whisper.

'Thank you,' said Brad.

Everybody was looking at him, including the other reps. He was walking around with a soda siphon in his hand.

'What's that for?' Heather whispered to Greg, who shrugged his shoulders.

'Okay, everyone. Good morning,' said Brad.

There was a general cry of 'Good morning' in return.

'Right, I'd like to thank you all for turning up to this welcome meeting. If you've all got a full glass I'll teach you the Spanish for cheers.' Brad raised his glass. '*Salud.*' The whole room took a drink and responded. 'That was the first of the free drinks you'll be getting on this holiday. Believe me, there'll be plenty more, but we'll tell you about that later. Before we start, I'm going to introduce you to everyone.'

And he proceeded to do just that – Lorraine, Greg, Mario, Mikey and Heather. He had noticed Alison standing at the back of the room and wasn't sure that she would appreciate being pointed out, so he moved on. 'Last but not least is Sid.' The reps looked at him quizzically. Brad raised the soda siphon. 'This is Sid, and he's here to make sure that you pay attention and that nobody heckles. If Sid doesn't like you he has a tendency to spit, so you have been warned.

'Okay. I'm going to spend five to ten minutes telling you a bit about where you're staying, a few dos and don'ts and the best way to keep out of trouble. Then Heather is going to spend about the same amount of time telling you all about the brilliant things we've got lined up for you. If you need us, we have allocated times when we'll be in the bar to answer questions or have a chat, normally between nine thirty and ten thirty in the morning and six and seven in the evening.

'Right. We'll start off with the hotels. Try to get to know the people who work there, because contrary to what you might think they are not all called Mañuel and none of them respond well to being whacked around the head. They all speak English, even a few swear words.' Brad turned to Frank, who was standing a couple of feet away, as he had previously arranged. 'Isn't that right, Frank?'

'Yes, you bloody wanker,' he replied, in his best English.

This brought the house down. Greg mouthed, 'Nice one', and Brad felt more confident.

'You can buy most things at reception. They sell postcards, stamps, sweets.'

'What about condoms?' shouted one of the lads Brad had brought in the previous night.

'I'm glad you asked me that.' He might have been glad, but he certainly wasn't surprised: he had spent five minutes earlier with the question-asker, promising him a free drink if he asked about condoms. 'You might find machines in some bars, but as this is a Roman Catholic country our little rubber friends aren't as easy to get hold of as back home. But luckily I've *come* prepared – arf! arf! – with six different varieties which I'll be happy to let you have for a modest fee. Obviously used ones will be slightly cheaper.

'If you don't want your money to run through your hands like water, or you don't have shares in Spanish Telecom, then I suggest that you use the phone boxes rather than the ridiculously expensive phone in Las Huertas. Isn't that right, Lorraine?' Lorraine nodded. The previous night she had rung home to speak to her mother because just prior to leaving England her eleven-year-old dog had not been well, and she was naturally concerned. She had made the call from Las Huertas, and the owner had charged her a fortune for doing so. Greg and Heather had both agreed that it was bang out of order, but Alison had simply said it was her own stupid fault and that she would know better next time.

'One last thing about the hotels. Whilst we're not asking you to tiptoe around, do spare a thought for people who have come away to relax, as opposed to chucking alcohol down their necks. On the subject of drugs – and this is very important,' Brad looked at everybody sternly, 'if anyone is found with any kind of narcotic,' he paused and looked round, 'then you will, of course, be made to share it with all of us. Seriously, though, do not risk getting into trouble with the police over here . . .'

Sales at the meeting were good, and by the time they had got round everybody it was nearly three p.m. Brad sat in the corner of the bar and ordered himself a coffee. He was joined by Heather and Greg. 'How do you feel?' asked Heather.

'Bloody knackered.'

'You've got to go back to the airport at six o'clock, haven't you?'

'Yeah. I didn't realise I wouldn't get any sleep.'

'You'll get used to it,' said Greg. 'Mind you, it is a bit hard for yer first time.'

Silence fell, during which they each took a sip of their drinks.

'Did you enjoy the welcome meeting?' Heather said to Brad, changing the subject.

'Well, I was a bit nervous to start with, but once I got a bit of feedback I settled down a bit. Seeing this Scouse git giving me the thumbs-up really helped.'

'Aye, well, y' deserved it,' said Greg enthusiastically. 'That bit where you got Frank to call you a wanker was brilliant, wasn't it, Heath?'

'Yeah, really good. I thought that thing with the soda siphon was a great way of setting the tone – firm but still having a laugh.'

Brad was a little embarrassed by the praise, but relieved

too. To be respected by his peers was important to him, especially as they were going to be so close to each other all season.

Alison appeared in the bar. 'How were sales?' she asked.

'I've not worked it out exactly,' said Greg, 'but I think it's over eighty per cent, and I'm sure we'll get a few more when we do the bar crawl tonight.'

'Excellent,' said Alison. 'You did really well explaining the excursions, Heather – I knew sales would be good.'

'Thanks. Brad did well, didn't he?'

'Not bad for a first time,' replied Alison. 'Actually, if you could leave Brad and me alone I've got a few things to go through with him.'

'Aye, well, I'm gonna hit the sack,' said Greg. 'Come on, Heath', I'm sure you're good for five points.'

'You must be joking,' she laughed. 'Frank's got more chance than you. Anyway, you'd probably need a splint to keep it up.'

'There's not a splint big enough, darlin'.'

Grey and Heather said their goodbyes, and left Brad with Alison. He felt as if he was beginning to belong; almost like an apprentice being accepted as a grown-up member of a team. Greg and Heather had given him a real feeling of warmth.

'How did you think your part of the welcome meeting went, Brad?' asked Alison.

Although his self-doubts had been quelled somewhat by Greg and Heather, Brad didn't want to come across to Alison as negative or deliberately self-effacing, so he gave her an honest self-appraisal. 'I was a bit nervous to start with, but once some of the jokes got a laugh I felt happier. I'm sure I can do better, though.'

'By "jokes", did you mean that thing with the soda siphon?'

Brad failed to hear the inflection in Alison's voice. He replied naïvely, 'Oh, that. I only thought of it on the way back from the airport. It worked quite well, didn't it?'

'So what would have happened if someone had started heckling?'

Brad picked up on her tone, but he could see nothing wrong in what he had done so he continued to be honest and light-hearted. 'Well, someone would have got wet, I suppose.'

'Someone would have got wet,' she repeated slowly. 'And after you'd had your fun, do you not think that all hell would have broken loose – drinks being thrown over everyone, maybe?'

Brad thought carefully before replying. 'No, I don't. If someone had started heckling I would have warned them a couple of times and gauged whether or not they were annoying everyone else. If they were, I would have put it to a shall-I-shan't-I vote. That way if I'd had to squirt someone all of the group would have been on my side.'

Alison was not expecting such a well-thought-out answer. He was right, of course, but she could not concede to Brad.

'Well, I'm sure with your vast experience you know best, but let me tell you that you're wrong and I don't want to see it again.' Alison moved on before he had a chance to argue. 'Another thing I don't want to see again is that nonsense with the condoms. Most of these kids come away on a tight budget and we want them to spend as much as possible on excursions, T-shirts and products associated with Young Free & Single. We don't want their money going into your pocket. You should know that head office takes a very dim view on any illegal earnings.'

'Hang on a minute, I'm not trying to make a profit. For all I care Young Free & Single can keep any profit, as long as I get back what they cost me. Like you said, most of them *are* kids and being here will probably be the first chance that many of them have had to be promiscuous. What do you want them to do? Have unprotected sex?'

'What I want is a hundred per cent excursion sales.'

'Oh, come on, Alison. Buying a packet of condoms for a couple of quid is hardly going to affect excursion sales.'

'Well, I disagree. You should not have done that without first asking my permission—'

'Okay,' interrupted Brad. 'I should have asked you first and I apologise for not doing so. But surely you can see the logic in why I did it. Apart from anything else it was entertaining.'

'Well that's a matter of opinion and I don't want to see it again. Understood?'

'Yes, but—'

'I said, *understood*?'

Brad knew that he should shut up, but he was sure that Alison would be able to see the flaws in her argument, thereby allowing them to agree on what was best for the clients. What he had yet to discover was that for Alison to see the flaws in her argument and admit them to Brad was as likely as Ayatollah Khomeini confiding that he liked nothing better than a mug of cocoa and a nice read of *The Satanic Verses* before going to bed.

'Just do as you're fucking told for once. Jesus . . .' said Alison, and slammed her clipboard on the table. 'Who's the manager here, eh? You?'

'No, of course not, but—'

'Oh, good. I'm glad we've got that sorted out. Is that why you didn't introduce me during the welcome meeting? Didn't you want the clients to know I'm your manager? Because I'm a woman? Because I'm younger than you?'

'No, of course not. I just thought—'

'Well, don't think. You're paid to do as you're told, not to think. You've got a lot to learn, Brad – a lot to learn.' Alison picked her things up, and calmed down. 'You should remember that you've got two ears and one mouth, so learn to use them in that ratio. I don't say the things I do to be awkward or to win arguments. I say them because I've got six years' experience.' Brad bit his lip. 'I know you're keen and ambitious. Listen to what I can teach you and one day you might be in this position. All right?'

Brad just grunted. He was drained.

'Don't forget you've got to be at the airport in a couple of hours. If I were you I'd go up to your room and freshen up. Providing the plane's not delayed I'll see you on the bar crawl. Okay?'

Brad gathered up his things. When he got to his room he slumped on his bed. Any enthusiasm for the trip to the airport had gone, along with his little remaining energy. He put his shorts on and walked round to the Tanit apartments where Danny, the prop from Sgt Pepper's, lived. He shared with a Kiwi called Robbo who taught windsurfing. They both supplemented their incomes by selling speed, dope and most other narcotic substances. Robbo answered the door wearing a sarong, his blond hair matted and his eyes as red as the Moroccan sun.

'Yo, man. What's happening? Hey, Danny, it's Rod.'

'Brad.'

'Sorry, man. D'ya wanna skin up?'

'No, thanks, I've got to go to the airport and I'm fucked enough as it is.'

He walked into the main living area. Danny was lying on a settee surrounded by empty Coke bottles, cigarette butts and overflowing ashtrays. The apartment looked like the *Enola Gay* had recently deposited her payload on it. Although the balcony door was open, the room smelt of rancid feet mixed with recently smoked hash. Brad bought a gram of whizz (he couldn't afford coke), exchanged pleasantries then made his way back to his own apartment. When he got there Alison had left a note instructing him to move his things over to Las Huertas. There was just time to have a shower, get ready for the airport, and pack his things as best he could. He would be ready to move first thing in the morning.

The airport was a lot quieter than it had been on his previous visit. The flight was delayed by forty-five minutes so he got himself a coffee, dabbed some speed and sat on a wall outside the airport next to where the coaches lined up.

It was a lovely warm evening, and Brad felt like lying on the grass and falling asleep. After another coffee and a slightly stale cheese roll, he heard his flight announced. He made a point of waiting ten minutes before going through.

The only other English rep in Arrivals had short black hair and a horrendous uniform. Brad walked up to her, looked at her badge and introduced himself. 'I believe we're sharing a coach back to San Antonio.'

'Yes. Oh, am I glad you're here. It's my first time at the airport and my manager hasn't turned up.' She paused. 'Sorry, my name's Stella.' They shook hands. 'So you work for Young Free & Single, then, do you? I applied for a job with your lot – got through to Bridlehurst, you know, the final interview, but . . .' Her voice trailed off. 'Still, never mind. How long have you been with them?'

'Actually this is my first season too.'

'You're joking! Oh, shit, I was hoping you'd do the microphone bit on the transfer for me. I know it's a bit of a cheek, seeing as they're mostly going to be my clients, but I thought you'd be an experienced rep.'

'Well, it depends what you mean by experienced,' offered Brad suggestively.

She blushed.

'Oh, well, I don't suppose I could possibly cock it up any more than I did the last one. Are you sure you want me to do it?'

'Positive!'

Brad's clients were first to come through so he showed them on to the coach, then went back into the airport. It struck him that the speed had started to work.

He got to Arrivals to find Stella surrounded by about a dozen black Cockney teenage males, giving her a good-natured hard time. She was handling them more than adequately.

The coach transfer went infinitely better than Brad's first attempt. He spoke on the microphone for at least half the journey and established an excellent rapport.

The black Cockneys were a British Rail football team who came away together every year. Brad arranged to meet them at the football stadium in San Antonio so that YF&S could give them a game. He thought it would be a good idea to get them all on the bar crawl, so he arranged to meet everyone at a small bar in town called the Charleston. He had briefly met its London owners during the winter and it was central enough for everyone to find easily. He could have chosen Sgt Pepper's, but he felt he needed to score some Brownie points with Alison, and what better way to do so than to walk in with a group of holidaymakers from another tour company?

Brad found himself therefore at ten o'clock with thirty newly arrived, non-YF&S clients and one increasingly pissed Stella, on full throttle in the Charleston, which was quite small, long and narrow. The bar itself was almost the length of the premises and faced a mirror that ran along the opposite side, giving the illusion that the place was bigger than it actually was. Its colour scheme was pink and grey and the ultra-violet-type lights picked out white clothes, teeth and dandruff. The owners were in their early twenties so the music was good and nobody wanted to leave. It was ten thirty before Brad persuaded them to follow him to Sgt Pepper's. He couldn't believe he was still going strong. As he left, the co-owner, whom everybody called Duffy, came over to him and shook his hand. 'Cheers, Brad. If you can keep them here a bit longer next time it'll be more.'

Brad opened his hand to find a crumpled two-mill note. Then he was swept along with the crowd towards Sgt Pepper's. He knew that taking backhanders was a dismissable offence, and his first thought was to give the money to Alison and explain what had happened. However, the way she had been lately he did not want to put himself at her idiosyncratic mercy. Brad guessed that Greg would tell him to keep it, but there was no way of knowing what Greg's relationship with Alison really was, or how his own relationship with Greg would change. In the end the solution was obvious. 'Stella, you got a minute?'

Stella was fairly drunk. She was wearing a lacy white halter-neck which pushed her ample breasts together to produce a glorious cleavage. With her black hair spiked up Brad thought that she looked quite dirty. He could not help ogling her as she bounced her way to him.

'Enjoying yourself?' she said, as she put her arm through his.

'Yeah.' Brad snatched another sneaky look. 'Stella, I've got a bit of a problem.'

'Don't worry, Brad,' she giggled. 'It happens to men of your age.'

'Very funny. It's nothing like that.' He pulled out the bank note.

Stella took it and looked at it. 'Oh, I see,' she said slowly. 'You can only have sex with women if you pay them first.'

'If that was the case, Stella dearest, then I would be expecting at least one thousand nine hundred and ninety-five pesetas' change.' They both laughed. 'Duffy gave it to me for taking all of this lot into his bar and, seeing as they're mainly your clients, it's only fair that you should have it.'

'Don't be silly,' said Stella. 'You persuaded them to come along.'

'Stella, you take it. It's only eight quid. Besides, It'll make me feel better.'

'Oh, you are a cutie.'

She stretched up and kissed his cheek. He felt her right breast yield to his elbow. Stella was becoming more attractive as the night wore on.

Sgt Pepper's was in full swing. Greg and Lorraine were on stage singing with Ray, Mario was talking to Alison, and Mikey was with a group of three girls Brad didn't recognise.

Mikey was the first to see him and the BR football team. He came over to Brad, offering one of his elongated handshakes. 'So where did you pick up all the brothers, then?'

The BR boys were there to party, and as soon as they were in the bar, whistles and horns were going and the place took off. Alison looked over to see what all of the commotion was about and spotted Brad in the centre of the mêlée and realised immediately that the BR group were not YF&S clients. She turned to Mario. 'Who are that bunch of troublemakers with Brad?'

Mario shrugged his shoulders. Alison craned her neck to get a better look at what was going on. Her gut reaction was to give Brad a dressing-down, based on the paranoid assumption that everything he did was aimed at undermining her authority.

She was preparing herself to ask him to step outside when Noel, the Irish owner of Sgt Pepper's, gestured for her to come behind the bar. When Alison was next to him he slipped her a brown A5 envelope. 'There y'go, me darling. I already had it counted up for yeh when that big rep o' yours brought in all them dark fellas. I've stuck in another six mill, which should cover it. I know he brought more than t'irty in with him, but they didn't get here until a good half-hour after all the others. What was the problem? Could yis not persuade them t'leave the Anglers?'

It dawned on Alison that Noel had assumed that Brad's crowd were with YF&S and as a result he had paid her on the previously agreed per head arrangement. She slipped the envelope into her handbag. All she had to do now was make sure they all went down to the Star and another bulging brown envelope would be hers. She went over to Brad.

'Brad.' He could barely hear her over the music. She gestured for him to come up to the bar where it was slightly less noisy. 'That's better. How did the transfer go?'

'Yeah, good. I ended up doing the microphone – that's where I got this lot from. You don't mind, do you? I just thought that if I showed them what a good time we all have then they might book with Young Free & Single next year.'

Alison was glad she hadn't reprimanded him – apart from the money he had just made her, he had a good point.

'No, it's not a problem, Brad. Just be careful with large gangs of lads that they don't disrupt things and ruin it for the rest of the group. This lot seem all right, though.'

She looked over at one of the loudest of the BR group. Rayon had his shirt off and was sliding his lean, muscular torso up and down the twins as he danced on one side of them, while Mikey did the same on the other. Alison reached into her bag, pulled out a handful of tickets and handed them to Brad. 'Here. Give these to them.'

'What is it?' asked Brad.

'Free entry into the Star. I shouldn't really do it but you've done well tonight and, as you say, they might come on holiday with us next time.'

She watched him go over to the group and give them the tickets, pointing to her. In a flash, Rayon had leapt over the railing and was at her side. He took her hand and kissed it, then looked up at her and smiled, his gold tooth glistening as he did so. 'Until the Star.'

An hour after the BR football team's arrival, Greg got on the microphone to tell everyone that YF&S were off to the Star club. Normally only about half of the group would have had sufficient energy to make it there, but the atmosphere was so good that not only did the whole of the YF&S crowd leave but also virtually everyone else in the bar. When Alison saw this she ran outside and jumped on her moped. She got to the club five minutes before everybody else.

The owner of the Star was a suave Spaniard called Jimmy, with a near-perfect English accent. He always looked immaculate and he always made a point of being on the door when a tour company was expected. When he saw Alison he held out his arms to welcome her. He had not yet made up his mind whether or not he liked her. He preferred to deal with men, but Kirstie had been tolerable the previous year so for the time being he put his prejudices to one side. 'Alison, *guapa*. How are you tonight? You look adorable.'

Alison blushed slightly. She fancied Jimmy. He was in his late thirties, exuded a debonair charm and effortlessly commanded respect.

'I'm fine, thanks, Jimmy. We've got quite a few coming down tonight.'

'This is good – how many you have?'

'A lot more than we normally have for this time of year so I'm here to help you count them in.'

'Oh, don't worry. Javier will do that. Come, you have a drink with me. A nice *chupito*, perhaps.'

Outside, the first clients had arrived. Although the bar crawl had finished and the reps could have gone home, most would stay for a few drinks. It was expected of them – another of the unwritten rules that made it a twenty-four-hours-a-day job.

Brad and Stella were at the front of the group. The club consisted of two rooms, and they walked through to the larger, brighter one, which was totally rammed. There was a small bar in every corner and a large rectangular one towards the back but Brad and Stella went to the bar furthest from the entrance, known as bar five. This was where all the reps congregated because here they were given free drinks.

Brad got the feeling that Stella had made up her mind to sleep with him, but that as she had quite a strong character she probably wanted to tease him a little.

'Which hotel are you staying at in San An?' asked Brad.

'I'm not.'

'What – have you got an apartment?'

'No, I'm in a hotel.' She took a sip of her drink.

Brad was a little confused. He thought, optimistically, that maybe she meant she wasn't staying in *her* hotel because she was intending to stay at *his*.

'So where *are* you staying?' asked Brad.

'I told you – in a hotel.'

'All right, all right. What's it called? How many syllables?' He was losing patience.

'You won't have heard of it.'

'Oh, and why's that?'

'Because it's in Playa d'en Bossa.'

'*What?* That's the other side of the island.'

'Very good, Brad. Ten out of ten for your geographical knowledge of Ibiza.'

Brad was not sure whether to be pleased or disappointed. There was no way he could go to her place because he had to move his things to Las Huertas first thing in the morning. It was time to test the water.

'You can stay at my place if you don't want to do the journey home tonight,' he said.

'Can I?' she replied, looking directly ahead whilst sucking her drink through her straw.

Brad still wasn't sure if she was being sarcastic so he watered down his offer. 'Well, you know, it's late and there are no more buses. Anyway, I've got a spare bed if you're worried about my intentions . . .'

'Ooooh, you've got a spare bed, have you?' Now she *was* being sarcastic. 'Well, if you've got a spare bed then there's not much point in me coming back.' She put down her drink and picked up her bag. 'Best I go and get a taxi. 'Bye!' Stella started walking towards the door, grinning over her shoulder.

Right, thought Brad. Two can play at this game. 'Yeah, okay, I'll walk you to the rank.'

Rather than taking the main road, they went around the dark alleyway at the back of the Star. Half-way down, Brad spoke. 'Stella.'

'Mmmm?'

He spun her round, stretched out her arms and pinned her against the cold white wall. He looked into her eyes. She lifted up her right knee, flicking it from side to side against his crotch. Brad let go of her left wrist and, with his right hand undid the top two buttons of her halter-neck whilst their mouths passionately engulfed each other. He cupped his hand under her right breast and lifted it so that he could move his head down slightly to roll her huge brown nipple between his tongue and top lip. Stella's breathing became heavier, and she started squeezing Brad's cock through his shorts. Just at that moment, the emergency exit at the back of the Star club opened. It was less than twenty feet away so Brad and Stella froze. First of all, they heard a man's voice with a slightly Spanish accent.

'I don't know. It's more than we paid per head last year . . . and I think you should not say to your head office that you only have a quarter of the real figure. Last year Kirstie told them sixty or seventy per cent.' There was a pause. 'Oh, well. As long as you keep bringing the people in like you did tonight I don't care where the money goes.' The man laughed. 'Anyway, you be careful on that moped. I would have thought you got a car.'

'So would I, Jimmy.'

It was Alison! Brad dragged Stella to the wall where they couldn't be seen.

'What's up?' she asked, slightly spooked.

'Ssshhh!' hissed Brad. 'That's my boss.'

'What was she doing?'

'I'm not sure.' Brad was silent for a few seconds. 'So that's why she gave me those free tickets . . .'

He waited until Alison had driven past. His erection had subsided and, although he still wanted to do rude things to Stella, he was deep in thought as they walked to the taxi rank.

After a couple of minutes Stella spoke. 'Are you all right, Brad?'

'Yeah, fine. Do you know anything about backhanders?'

'Payments to reps and tour companies?'

'That sort of thing, yeah.'

'Well, only that it goes on and that the higher up you are the more money you get.'

'Do you think my boss would have been paid by the owner of the Star for taking all of our lot in?'

'Yes, of course.' They had arrived at the taxi rank. 'Do you still want me to come back?' asked Stella.

Brad opened the taxi door. 'Get in.'

When they got to the Bon, a few clients were in the bar. Brad told Stella to leave it a couple of minutes before coming up so the clients wouldn't know what was going on, then went to his room. He took a pot of yoghurt out of the fridge and put it next to the bed.

Two minutes later Stella knocked on the door. As soon as he had closed it they were pulling each other's clothes off. Within a short time Brad's shorts were round his ankles and Stella had her back to the wall with her legs around his waist and his cock inside her. Still in this position, Brad carried her through to the bedroom, hampered by his shorts, which he was unable to kick off. His intention had been to cover her in yoghurt, but events overtook him, so the only thing Stella ended up covered in was Brad's spunk. It wasn't until he had got his breath back and saw the thick white stream trickling down her chin that he cursed himself. He hadn't worn a condom. It was only the first week and already he had broken his promise to himself not to have unprotected sex.

Stella went to the bathroom and, within the four minutes it took her to clean herself up, Brad had sunk into a long-overdue sleep. Although she was prepared to stay the night she was none too keen on walking into her hotel the next morning wearing last night's clothes. She wanted to see Brad again, so made an unsuccessful attempt to wake him. As she got dressed, she found a felt pen and wrote her name, hotel and phone number on her panties. Smiling, she slid them up his leg and quietly left the room.

chapter three

Felipe Gomez walked up to his wife, who was at the kitchen sink cutting the stems off some flowers. 'Another week beckons,' he said, kissing her.

'Are you off then?' she said, drying her hands. 'Will you be overseas this week?'

'I don't think so. Nothing planned anyway. I was expecting to hear from Luís in Ibiza. If he calls get him to ring me at the office.'

'When's Luís coming over again? He hasn't been here since before Christmas.'

'It's a busy time of year, my darling, but I'll ask him when we speak.' Felipe looked at his watch. 'Anyway, I must go if I'm going to miss the traffic. I'll call you later.'

He walked over to his new Range Rover to get a packet of Ducados cigarettes. When he had first smoked them he had not liked them, but countless trips to Spain as contracts director for YF&S meant that he had grown used to their harsh taste. They were always readily available and cheap. Not that cost was a primary concern to Felipe: over the years his position had allowed him to accrue a good deal of wealth, many times more than any other contracts director had ever earned. He now had a beautiful house in Dulwich Village, which none of his workmates had ever visited . . . apart from one – and she had only spent one night there when his wife was away.

He had enjoyed spending the weekend at his luxurious home and driving his new car. During the week he stayed in the company flat near their offices in Teddington and drove the company Audi. That was the way he liked it.

Nobody at YF&S knew his private business. A few colleagues knew where he lived, but as far as they were concerned the house had been left to him by a relative. They would have been shocked to know that the small loan he had taken to buy the property would be fully paid off within eighteen months.

Felipe Gomez was in his late forties, swarthy and Mediterranean. He liked the good things in life and he was always immaculately turned out – suits from Savile Row, shirts and ties from Jermyn Street, shoes by Church or occasionally Lobb. His hair was longer than it should have been, always greased back, only slightly greying at the temples but receding significantly on top. He was not dissimilar to Asil Nadir, the exiled Polly Peck chairman whom he admired.

He was a little annoyed with himself for leaving the invoice in his briefcase. If his wife had seen it she might have put two and two together and the game would have been up. He could not pay it out of their joint account because she took pride in managing the home with stoic efficiency. Her stoicism, however, would soon have changed to rage at any hint of infidelity. Felipe could have paid it out of their Spanish account, but he wanted YF&S to pay it. Three and a half years had passed since Felipe had applied to be financial director with the attendant share options. He remembered all too vividly the day he had been called into the chairman's office.

'Good morning, Felipe. Please take a seat.'

Adam Hawthorne-Blythe had a luxurious Oxbridge-educated voice and a grey handlebar moustache, the legacy of his ten years in the RAF. He had the sort of presence that would have had the populace of a bygone era tugging their forelocks and saying, 'Gawd bless yer, guv'nor.'

'I'll come straight to the point.' Felipe recalled the excitement that this statement had caused him. 'As you know, we have been looking for a new FD and you were put forward as a suitable candidate. Whilst there is no doubting your integrity and commitment, the board felt you possessed insufficient relevant experience for this post. The man coming in is Sebastian Hunter, the financial director of our rivals . . .'

Felipe heard little else. The board limited his disappointment by promoting him from contracts manager to contracts director, but the job was just the same. Otherwise, he received a few shares, a slightly bigger office, a slightly larger salary and the new title.

It was inevitable that Felipe would not like Sebastian Hunter, who was a good fifteen years his junior. Moreover, Sebastian rapidly brought about numerous sweeping changes, so Felipe and he had locked horns on a number of occasions. This was why Felipe wanted YF&S to pay the invoice – because he liked the idea of tricking Sebastian into paying for something unconnected with YF&S.

If Sebastian asked why he had been to a private hospital Felipe would tell him that it was for corrective laser surgery to his eyes. He half suspected that Sebastian would pay it without saying anything: because he had been passed over for promotion, Felipe was allowed the occasional privilege, and for such a small amount, he was curious to discover whether or not Sebastian would want a big showdown.

The black company Audi swept on to the road and within ten minutes he was stuck in traffic in Brixton. It was eight thirty in the morning but already nearly 20°C – a 'mid-May mini heat-wave', the forecaster had called it. Felipe just called it bloody hot. It was a different kind of heat from the Med, more industrial and dirty. How he wished he was driving his air-conditioned Range Rover. He stopped the car outside a newsagent in Clapham High Street just past La Rueda, the Spanish tapas bar, to get a bottle of water. He also bought the *Daily Mail* and the *Financial Times* to see what his stars were saying and how his shares were doing. Both looked good.

As he came off the A3, London threw off its grey overcoat

of uniformity, gradually turning into the manicured hedge-rows and detached individuality of suburbia. The traffic queues seemed to get smaller as the cars got bigger, and all around the colours were richer. Felipe relaxed and made a slight detour to look at the houses next to the river. If he did not eventually move to Spain, this was where he would put down his roots.

Felipe had a position in YF&S senior enough to warrant his own parking space. As he locked the Audi he heard a chirpy Scottish female voice behind him. 'Morning, Felipe.'

Felipe looked up. It was Jane Ward, the overseas manager.

'Good morning, Jane. And how are we on this beautiful morning?'

'Very well, thanks. Not too sure if I like this heat, though.'

It never failed to amaze Felipe how the British always complained about the weather. It was either too hot, too cold, too windy, too humid, too wet or too dry.

'Well, I'm sure it's hotter in Spain.'

'Aye, you're probably right there. When are you off again?' Felipe held open the door to the reception area for her.

'I'm not sure. I'll probably be off to Ibiza shortly. I was in Tenerife last week.'

'What was that like?'

'Oh, give me Ibiza any day.' Felipe looked at the receptionist. 'Any messages for me, Amanda?'

'Only to call Luís at Viajes Diamanté in Ibiza,' she replied.

'Well, Felipe,' said Jane, 'looks like there's no way you'll be getting away from Ibiza! I'll see you later.'

'Yes. Goodbye, Jane.'

Felipe turned and walked to his office. What had Jane meant by that comment? It was probably innocent, but was his association with Ibiza becoming a little too high-profile? He never knew how to take Jane Ward. She was one of those people who always gave the impression that she knew something you did not. Rumours were going round that she had been secretly seeing Sebastian Hunter, which added to the mystique that surrounded her. Certainly, all the reps were in awe of her, but Felipe was not happy that she had the same effect on him. He was certainly higher up the company ladder than her, but Sebastian Hunter was considerably more powerful than him, and if Sebastian and Jane were lovers . . .

Felipe opened his office door. He liked dark wood and traditional English furnishings. An executive leather chair stood behind a leather-inlaid desk, on which was placed a neat pile of various leatherbound diaries and reference books. Next to the window a leather two-seater chesterfield jostled for space with a small table upon which was a fax machine. The window had wooden Venetian blinds, the desk a gold and green lamp and the floor boasted an expensive Lahore rug. There was even a drinks cabinet with crystal glasses and a range of spirits purchased duty free on the way back from his constant trips abroad. A few executive toys stood on various surfaces and in the corner was a grandfather clock. Although the room was not large it had a well-ordered opulence, obviously dictated by a neat man. Felipe was the only director who had gone to the expense of furnishing his own office. Its splendour surpassed even the chairman's, and he had justified the extravagance with the same excuse he had used for acquiring the house in Dulwich – that the furnishings had been left to him by a rich relative.

Felipe closed his door, then rang Luís at Viajes Diamanté, the local agents in Ibiza for YF&S. Amongst other things, they were the link through which Felipe contracted all the YF&S accommodation on the island. He conducted his conversation with Luís in Spanish. Nobody else was aware that Felipe had known him for more than thirty years. Luís was a native Ibicenco, unlike Felipe who was from Seville, but they had met at college in Madrid and had remained in touch.

Felipe had been in the UK for more than twenty years,

and married to his English wife Rosemary for eighteen. His English was near perfect and he had adopted what he considered the best of English manners. Adjectives such as 'polite' and 'charming' were often used to describe Felipe. However, his English associates would have been surprised to realise that Felipe spoke Spanish with a regional dialect from which most Spaniards would deduce that he was from the lower end of the social scale.

When he finished his call he looked at his Gucci watch. He had a game of golf arranged near Liphook at two thirty. He made a couple more calls then took the invoice out of his jacket pocket. It was from the Chamberlain Clinic. It did not specify what the treatment had been. Felipe stubbed out his half-smoked Ducados and headed for Sebastian Hunter's office. When he got there the door was ajar. Sebastian wasn't in. Just at that moment, Jane Ward walked by. 'Ah, Jane, have you seen Sebastian this morning?'

'Not in the office,' she replied truthfully.

'Have you any idea where he is or what time he'll be in?'

'I think he had a meeting with the bank or something. Amanda said he's expected in about lunchtime.'

'Okay. Thanks.'

Felipe went into the office and put the invoice on a pile of papers on Sebastian's desk. He attached to it a yellow Post-it note, with 'Sebastian, please speak to me about this' written on it. As he left the office he accidentally slammed the door. He did not see the invoice float under the desk, causing the Post-it note to separate and tumble on to the floor next to the wastepaper basket.

Sebastian arrived a little after one o'clock. He put his head round the door to say hello to Jane, but her assistant Tom Ortega was at his desk in their shared office and Jane was engrossed in a telephone conversation. He mouthed, 'Talk to you later', and left.

Jane was on the phone for another ten minutes. When she finally hung up she slumped in her chair and sighed.

'What was all that about?' Tom asked.

'It was a distressed young Zena ringing from Crete.'

'What's up with her? She's only been out there a week.'

'Mmm, I know. Poor wee girl! Her first week in her first season and she has that to deal with.' Jane shook her head.

Tom looked at her quizzically.

Jane sat forward in her chair. 'Zena was guiding a coach back from the beach party – it was the first time she'd done a coach on her own as well. Anyway, a couple of girl clients had met up with a couple of local Greek guys and decided to take a lift back in their jeeps rather than getting the coach. One of the Greek guys was obviously giving it the big macho bit and tried to overtake the coach but there was a car coming in the other direction so he had to pull in sharply, and you know how unstable those jeeps are.'

'So what happened?'

'Well, the jeep flipped over and landed in a ditch.'

'Were they all right?' asked Tom.

'Hardly. Zena stopped the coach and went over to them. The Greek guy just had some cuts and grazes, but when Zena looked at the girl – oh, God, it's so horrible – her nose and lips were gone. The metal rim of the jeep had sliced away half of her face. Apart from that her legs were all twisted, an eye was missing and the top of her skull had flipped open.'

'*What?* So was she still alive?'

'That's the worst part. She was wriggling and moving around.'

'Oh, my God. What did Zena do? Call an ambulance?'

'They were miles from anywhere so she got the other Greek guy to put the girl in the back of the other jeep. She told the coach driver to take the rest of the clients back to the hotel, and she sat in the back of the jeep with the girl, who was gurgling and mumbling all the way to the hospital. Apparently it took nearly fifteen minutes for some fat-bellied, fag-smoking mess of a doctor to saunter in. He told Zena to leave her there, and when she rang back later to find out what had happened the girl was dead.'

'Jesus. So who tells the parents? It's got to be your turn, Jane,' Tom said.

'I'll wait until I've got all the info together first. Christ! What a start to the season.' Jane stood up. 'I'm just going to pop up to Sebastian's office. If anyone from Crete calls get it transferred to his extension, will you?'

'Sure,' replied Tom.

When Jane had left he smiled to himself. It was so obvious that Jane and Sebastian were having an affair but he wished Jane would confide in him.

When Jane got to Sebastian's office he was on the phone. She closed the door behind her and sat down opposite him. His window was open, allowing the murmur of traffic to sweep in with the gentle early summer breeze. Every so often this inoffensive noise was punctuated with the roar of a bus or lorry revving its engine. This caused Sebastian to screw up his face and put his finger in his left ear so he could hear what the person on the other end of the phone was saying. Eventually he hung up. 'You look a bit stressed, darling.'

'Aye, well, I've just been speaking to a poor wee lassie in Crete who's had to deal with the first death of the season – a particularly gruesome one as well.'

'What happened?' asked Sebastian.

'I'll tell you tonight,' said Jane. 'What's the problem with Majorca?'

'Our agent out there says no excursion money has been banked. Majorca's been live two weeks longer than all of the other resorts and I'm concerned. What's the resort manager . . .' Sebastian looked at his notes '. . . Jason Barnes, like?'

'Barnesy? Loads of experience, shrewd. Popular with all of the other reps. In fact I think Kirstie Davies has just gone out to see him.'

'Isn't that the Welsh girl who ran Ibiza last year?'

'Aye, and she worked in Majorca the year before. She's got her own travel agency in Brecon now.'

'Is Barnes loyal?'

'Was. Not sure about now, though. One of his first-year reps was on the phone last week in tears, moaning about the way he was treating her and the fact that she'd not received any commission. Also, there were a few rumours going around before the season started that it was going to be his last season and that he was going to try and make as much as he could.'

'Why didn't you do anything about it?' snapped Sebastian.

Jane was proud of the way she did her job and would not tolerate invalid criticism, even from Sebastian. 'Because every year I get phone calls from first-year reps who suddenly realise they're not on holiday and who didn't fully appreciate what was expected of them. Also, every year there are rumours going around about resort managers who are intending to rip us off and scarper. If I listened to every rumour and whimper then we'd have no resort managers and no reps.' Jane looked at Sebastian. 'Of course an element of fiddling goes on, but we've eliminated most of it. We know through historical analysis what a resort should be producing and if there are any major discrepancies we start fishing. We talk to the reps and it's very easy for them to unwittingly give the game away. Sometimes they're so fed up with a manager they do the investigating for us.'

'Well, you obviously know your stuff,' said Sebastian. 'What do you propose doing about Barnes?'

'I'll get Tom on a flight out there tomorrow and if there's any hint of foul play Barnes's feet won't touch the ground.'

'You'll make sure you get the excursion money first, won't you?' said Sebastian. Jane glared at him. 'Yes, of course you will.' He changed the subject. 'What about the other resorts? Any other dodgy managers?'

'Only Alison Shand.'

Sebastian looked down his list. 'Ibiza? Isn't she the one Felipe Gomez recommended?'

'He virtually insisted on her going out there. We had her earmarked for Benidorm. She's very good at entertaining and her paperwork's superb, but we didn't think her people skills were strong enough to manage one of the big two,' said Jane, referring to Majorca and Ibiza. 'Anyway, Felipe spoke to our beloved chairman and that was that.'

'Why was Felipe so keen for Alison to get the job?'

'Beats me,' said Jane. 'He does seem to take a special interest in Ibiza, though.'

'All the more reason why Alison wouldn't dare to be on the fiddle,' said Sebastian. 'Come on, let's nip over the road and have a quick pint.'

Jane picked up her things. She was not as convinced as Sebastian of either Alison's or Felipe's loyalty. She knew somehow that something was not quite right.

chapter four

The room was pitifully dingy. Moreover, because Las Huertas was a hotel rather than apartments there were no cooking facilities. This was to be Brad's 'home' for the next six months and he was not impressed. The most depressing thing was the lack of natural light: there was just a window that opened on to the adjoining building with only a three-foot wide gap between them. Brad started to unpack his case. At the top were Stella's panties, which he threw into the bottom of the wardrobe.

He remembered Alison outside the Star club. What a bitch! She had made out that she was being so magnanimous by giving the BR football team free tickets to the Star when all the time she was lining her own pocket. He decided to have a quiet word with Greg to try to find out the implications of Alison's conversation outside the club.

Greg did not turn up at the Las Huertas pool until early afternoon. Every other Monday was a free day (no official excursions), so the reps were supposed to keep the clients amused as best they could. The Bon did not have a pool, so the majority of the YF&S holidaymakers who were not in a bar or on the beach gravitated to the one at Las Huertas. Even though Greg looked a little the worse for wear, most of the girls looked up when he arrived. He slumped on a sunbed next to Brad.

'Fuck me, was I caning last night.'

'Three more points?' asked Brad.

'Two bonus points.'

'What? A threesome?'

'Fuckin' right.'

'Who with?' demanded an envious Brad, already guessing the answer.

'Linda and Emma.'

'You're kidding.'

'I wish I was. My dick is so fucking sore . . . Still, puts me on eleven points, wha-hey. Wharabout you – any luck last night?'

'Yeah, that spiky-haired rep I brought back from the airport.'

'Nice one. Was she as dirty as she looked?'

'Can't really remember. Plenty of Harry on the boat, though.'

'Plenty of *what*?'

'It's Cockney rhyming slang. Harry Monk, spunk, on the boat race, face.'

Greg started laughing. 'Fucking brilliant. I'll have to start using that one.'

Mario had been sitting on the other side of the pool and came over to join them. 'What's so funny?' he asked.

'Have you ever 'eard the expression "'Arry on the boat"?' asked Greg.

'Yeah. Spunk on the face.'

Greg went into apoplexy again. When he stopped laughing he turned to Brad. 'Sold many condoms yet?'

'Have I fuck,' said Brad. 'No one seems bothered. The only reason any of the stupid bastards want one is to blow it up over their head or use it as a water bomb.'

The peace and quiet that had descended upon the pool was interrupted by the four members of the Plymouth Possee with their ghetto-blaster. Mario stood up, 'It's all right, I'll deal with this. I saw how you dealt with them last time, Greg,' and walked over to them.

'Oh dear,' said Greg. 'This should be interesting.'

The Plymouth Possee had just sat down when a grinning Mario approached them. 'Turn that fucking shit off,' he said, pressed the eject button and threw the tape into the pool. He looked round to Greg and Brad for approval, which meant that he did not see the biggest of the Plymouth Possee come up behind and half punch, half push him into the water. 'And don't come out till you've got our cassette!'

Mario surfaced to be greeted with universal mocking laughter.

'Shouldn't we do something?' asked Brad.

'No. 'E'll learn from 'is mistakes – 'opefully,' replied Greg.

Mario was about to get out when a crescendo of yelling came from the bar. Everyone looked up, just as Mikey and half a dozen of the BR football team ran into the pool and bombed Mario. Mikey sprang out of the shallow end, beat his chest and let out a Tarzan-type call, 'Me Masambula, King of the Reps.' 'Me no let this white oppressor out of pool to torture me more with bad clothes and bad chat-up lines. Me have tribe who make sure he no escape.' All the clients loved this, and joined in to make sure Mario stayed in the pool for at least another quarter of an hour, by which time even the Plymouth Possee had tired of the new game.

Eventually Mikey came over and sat with Brad and Greg.

'You seem full of beans,' said Brad. 'What did you get up to last night?'

'More like who did 'e get up to,' corrected Greg.

Mikey smiled. 'One of the twins. Rayon did the other one.'

'Any good?' asked Greg.

'Oh, it gets better,' said Mikey. 'Tell me, Greg – not that I'm joining in this points thing, you understand – but if I was, how many for a pair of twins?'

'Oh, you didn't,' said Brad.

Mikey looked at him grinning.

'At the same time?' asked Greg, worried that his points lead would be threatened.

'Not exactly,' said Mikey. 'They changed half-way through without telling us.'

'So 'ow d'ya know for sure they changed?' asked Greg.

'Believe me, man, I know. Rayon reckons that their biffs are shaved differently, though to be honest I didn't notice.'

'You lucky bastard,' said Brad. 'I walked them home the other night as well.'

'Yeah, I know.' Mikey laughed. 'They said you kept falling asleep and talking crap.'

Brad hid his head in his hands and groaned.

'So, six points to you last night, five points to me and three points to Brad,' said Greg. 'That puts me in the lead on eleven, Mikey on six, Mario on zilch and Brad on nine – no, hang on a minute, you didn't shag Linda 'cos you didn't have a condom so that means you've only got eight.'

'So I don't get any points for sleepwalking and talking crap then?' said Brad.

'You're lucky we don't deduct any.'

Brad was sitting next to Lorraine at the front of the coach, while Heather was explaining the evening's proceedings to the holidaymakers.

'And after the bucking bronco you'll have a chance to show what you think of your reps!'

The inevitable chorus of 'Get your tits out' followed. Lorraine leaned across Brad to Greg. 'What exactly happens tonight, then, Greg?' she asked.

'First of all we give them their own raw meat to cook over the barbecue. While they're eating they can drink as much wine and draught beer as they want. Then we take 'em on the bucking broncos. After that we all go up to the amphitheatre. The venue used to be a zoo an' the amphitheatre used t' be where the seals performed. All it is is a small stage with a titchy moat between it an' the audience. They've got some nutter compering and singing called Woodsy and 'e warms everyone up first with a ten-minute singalong. Then we go on one by one and start singing. 'Alfway through the song Woodsy stops playing and gets this lot to give you the thumbs-up or the thumbs-down. If you get the thumbs-up you walk away, if you get the thumbs-down, in you go. Simple, really.'

'Did you ever stay dry last year?' asked Brad.

'Well, I got the thumbs-up once, but the bastard still pushed me in.'

'Woodsy sounds mad,' said Lorraine.

'Yeah, that's a fair assessment. He's the funniest bloke I've ever met, though,' said Greg.

'Can't wait to meet him,' said Lorraine foolishly.

Once they had completed the five-minute journey to the excursion, the reps led the hundred or so clients to the front gate. There to greet them were two men dressed as cowboys, one Spanish and the other English. The Englishman had what looked suspiciously like a spliff in one hand and a bottle of beer in the other. He caught sight of Greg. 'Ah, Greg, you short-arsed little twat. How's the dose? Cleared up yet?' The owner of the Wigan accent turned his attentions to Lorraine.

'And who's this, your mother? Well, she's certainly ugly enough for me.' He put his arm around her. 'Don't worry, darling, you're not fat enough.'

Mikey made the mistake of trying to talk.

'Oh, hang on a minute,' Woodsy said. 'I'll just go and get me drums so you can understand. Hold on.' He turned to shout up to where they were giving out meat for the barbecue. 'Juanito, grab a couple of missionaries for the barbie.' Mikey was not smiling. 'Oh, fuck me,' said Woodsy, 'I hope he hasn't got one of those effigy things or I've had it. Oi, you,' he said, grabbing Brad and hiding behind him, 'you look big enough to look after me. Fuck me, you've even got a broken nose.' Woodsy pushed his own nose flat against his face. 'Der, my name's Brad, and my specialist subject is—'

'Flattening northern comedians,' interrupted Brad.

'Oh, it fucking is, is it?' Woodsy tweaked Brad's nipple, which made him yelp. 'Well, you'd better come up to the bar so I can get you all a drink before you do me any serious damage.'

As they walked up the hill to the bar, Woodsy had his arm around Lorraine's shoulder. Brad was between Greg and Mikey. 'Christ,' said Brad, 'he's like a human tornado.'

'I did warn you,' said Greg.

'I don't know how he gets away with it.'

'Well, he doesn't always, does he, Heath'?' Heather had caught them up.

'No, he doesn't,' she replied. 'Do you remember that time last year?'

'What happened?' asked Mikey.

By now they had reached the bar and Woodsy sent them all some drinks before walking off to have a serious conversation with Alison.

'Well,' said Greg, swigging his beer, 'we 'ad a group of squaddies over. They were real div'eads an' they'd been giving us a few problems. We were at Hoe Down and Woodsy was taking the piss as 'e does, but 'e was really layin' into these squaddies. One of 'em kept trying to come back at Woodsy – fatal mistake. Woodsy spent five minutes just coating 'im until everyone in the place was cryin' with laughter. When it all finished the squaddies surrounded 'im an' at first it seemed pretty good-natured. Then I 'eard Woodsy say something like, "Listen, you've all obviously joined the army 'cos you're too fucking thick to get a proper job. Then you come over 'ere 'opin' to get a shag but you're all too fuckin' ugly, so what do you do? The same as when you're in your barracks – all wank over a biscuit or shag each other." Well, that was it, they all laid into 'im.'

During the evening Brad couldn't take his eyes off Patricia. He hadn't seen her since the beach party and tonight was her penultimate night. Nearly a week's exposure to the sun had made her look even more gorgeous. When Brad went on stage for his turn in the amphitheatre he was conscious of her in particular sitting in the audience.

He had chosen to sing Stevie Wonder's 'I Just Called'. To assist him in his task he had a black stocking over his head with some sunglasses, a red, yellow and green hat with dreadlocks hanging out of the back and a telephone. Before he got to the first chorus Woodsy had stopped playing the guitar and Brad found himself jettisoned into the water. As he went under, the stocking over his head filled up with water. He came up for air, but all he got was more water and an earful of laughter.

When he came up coughing and spluttering for the third time, a strong pair of arms dragged him out and ripped off the stocking. Mikey was crouching over him and Woodsy had started playing 'Hey Big Spender' for Lorraine.

'Jesus, I thought I'd had it then,' he said.

When they got backstage, Mikey reached into his bag and pulled out a spliff. 'Do you think this will help your recovery?'

'Probably.' Brad lit it, inhaled deeply then let out a satisfied groan. 'I know what would really help, though.'

'What's that?' Mikey took the joint.

'Patricia.'

'Yeah, man, she's looking badly fit. I thought you were getting on all right with her.'

'Mmm, I was,' said Brad reflectively. 'The problem is, Mikey, if I really like someone I've got this real bad habit of putting them on to a pedestal and then I can't talk to them.'

'What a load of bollocks. She's the same person she was when you were talking to her on the beach the other day. If you approach her what's the worst thing that's going to happen? She's not going to poke your eye out or put a curse on you. The worst that's going to happen is that you'll get rejected and if you can't handle that with all the ego boosts this job gives you then you're not the bloke I thought you was.' Mikey paused. 'Any chance of some of that spliff?'

Later when Brad was standing near the pool, wondering what to say to Patricia and pondering Mikey's advice, he felt a tap on his shoulder. 'Not talking to me, then?' It was Patricia.

'Oh, hi.'

'I thought I'd done something to upset you. You haven't said a word to me all night.'

'No, don't be silly,' said Brad.

He cursed himself for not being able to think of anything to say. But he could tell by the way she was breathing and the look on her face that she was interested. After a thirty-second eternity of silence Patricia spoke. 'Oh, well, I'd better go and see my friends. I might catch you later.'

She started walking away. Brad had a rush of blood. 'Patricia.' He skipped a couple of paces to catch her up. 'Look, I know I'm in danger of making a berk of myself here, but I can't think of anything to say to you that doesn't sound corny – but you've only got a couple of days left and I'd like to get to know you better.' Patricia's face lit up. Brad continued, 'That doesn't mean getting you into bed is at the top of my agenda – although I'd be lying if I said it wasn't on the agenda at all. It's just that—'

'Ssh!' Patricia put her index finger to his lips. 'I'm not stupid, Brad. I've known you liked me ever since the beach party, probably before that, actually. I just don't want to be another three points.'

'Oh, that,' said Brad. 'Mikey and me don't get involved in it. And even if we did, there really is something special about you that—' Brad saw Alison walking towards him. 'Shit, here comes my boss. Look, we're all going down Bugala's after this. Will you come along?' Patricia nodded. Brad blew her a kiss and ran off to join one of the larger groups before Alison had a chance to have a go at him.

After leaving Bugala's they went to a little Spanish bar that no English used, and ordered two *carajillos*, espresso coffee with brandy. The conversation flowed freely, and gradually they showed a little more of themselves to each other.

Patricia admitted that she had a boyfriend back in Nottingham, but told Brad that things were not going too well.

As Brad was staying at Las Huertas and Patricia at the apartments, he realised that during the walk home the topic of sleeping together would have to be aired. He was hoping it would come up naturally, but they became embroiled in discussing Mario, so that by the time they were fifty yards from the apartments, it had still not been broached. They arrived at the corner of the road that led down to the block. Brad took Patricia's other hand so that they were facing each other. He softly kissed her lips. Patricia slipped her hands from his and encircled him with her arms. Brad began to kiss her more passionately, pushing his right thigh between her legs. Patricia rubbed herself against him, but Brad noticed that she didn't let herself get too carried away. He wanted her badly, and he suspected that he could have persuaded her to consummate their friendship. However, his instincts told him that she still did not trust him entirely: it would be a battle and she might feel a little uncomfortable the next day. If Brad was going to have her he wanted her totally.

'Patricia.'

She was kissing his neck and moaning. This was going to be hard.

'Patricia, stop.' She looked at him, confused. 'Come on, let's get you home. I'll walk you to Reception. I've had a wonderful, special evening and I don't want to ruin it by making a clumsy lunge. If this is going to happen let's make sure it happens properly, yeah?'

Patricia smiled and snuggled up to him. He kissed the top of her head and they walked over to the door of the apartments, where he pressed his lips softly against hers then looked her in the eyes. 'I'll see you tomorrow. You're coming to the match, aren't you?'

'I wouldn't miss it for the world.'

Brad watched her float up the stairs. As she disappeared

from view he started the walk back. 'Well, Bradley Streeter,' he muttered, 'I hope you know what you're doing.'

Alison woke up feeling unhappy about the events of the previous night. Manny, the Spanish owner of the excursion, had made her feel awkward by not picking up on any of the hints she had dropped about payment for taking customers to him. Kirstie had told her that Manny never gave backhanders, and he was so well liked by the bosses of YF&S that any blatant attempt at getting money out of him would mean treading on thin ice. She felt that maybe she had overstepped the mark and was worried that Manny might speak to someone in head office.

She had also tried to tap Woodsy, but all she had got out of him, other than the piss taken at the size of her nose, was a small cut from raffling the video of the evening's proceedings. And Alison was none too pleased with the bond that had formed between Brad and Mikey.

With all of this playing on her mind Alison went down to reception. Mikey was there on desk duty. Ignoring his cheery 'Morning', Alison grabbed a coffee and went to the desk to call head office. When she got through to Jane Ward's office, a male voice answered the phone.

'Good morning, Overseas.'

'Hello, who's that? Tom?'

'Speaking.' Tom recognised the voice. 'Are those the dulcet tones of Alison Shand?'

'Is Jane there?' Alison did not like Tom and did not want to indulge in polite conversation.'

''Fraid not, Ali.' Alison hated her name being abbreviated. 'Can I help?'

'When's she due back?'

'Don't know. She's in a meeting with Sebastian. Anything wrong?'

Although Alison did not want to deal with Tom, she knew she needed to make contact with head office in case

Manny called and mentioned that she had asked for money.

'No, nothing wrong. If you see Jane tell her that I tried to get some money out of one of the excursion owners but he wouldn't play ball. I did my best.' She did not add that it was her pocket she had been trying to line, not the company's.

'I'll pass the message on. How are the new reps getting on?'

'Oh, not bad. Mario's getting on really well. Lorraine's a bit timid but I should be able to knock her into shape.'

'What about Brad? How's he doing?'

'Well, to be honest,' Alison cleared her throat, 'he's a bit arrogant, thinks he knows it all. He spends a lot of time chasing girl clients and loadsa time sleeping so he's always late. I can probably sort him out. I just hope he doesn't lead Mikey astray.'

Tom was surprised. He had been on Brad's panel at the twenty-four-hour interview and on the training course at Warwick. He had even been out with Brad socially a couple of times. Brad had excelled at both the interview and the training course, and Tom was ninety per cent sure that he was going to be a first-class rep. He knew, however, that Brad was a bit of a womaniser and that his dry sense of humour and quick wit might be mistaken for arrogance. He had to accept that Alison's comments might have some substance.

When Alison put the phone down she smiled to herself, happy that she had avoided any trouble over Manny, and that she had weakened the position of one she saw as a potential threat.

After Brad finished his desk duty at Las Huertas he walked over to the Bon to join Mikey and the others who were playing in the football match against the British Rail mob. He found Mikey standing on a chair changing the channels on the TV. Mikey flicked on the local news, which was running a story about a Vietnam veteran who had rammed his jeep into a police car near Las Salinas.

'How did you get on last night?' asked Mikey.

'With Patricia? Yeah, we had a good night.'

'And?'

'And what? If you mean did I score any points, the answer's no. I want to do things properly. I think it might have been on the cards but it didn't seem right.'

'Jesus. You sound almost human. Go on, she wouldn't let you, would she?'

'To be honest, mate, I don't know. I didn't try.'

'What, you mean if you shagged her she'd fall off of that pedestal of yours?'

Brad winced a bit as Mikey scored a home truth, then said, 'What about you? Much happen?'

'No. I had a fairly early night. Alison was in a foul mood this morning, though.'

Alison! Brad had been so wrapped up in Patricia that he had almost forgotten the events of the night before last. He still had not spoken to Greg about it. He changed the subject. 'Actually, I had a few problems myself last night. You know the tallest one of the Plymouth Possee?'

'Yeah, Peter, isn't it?' replied Mikey.

'That's the one. Well, he came down this morning with a black eye. Reckons that the hotel-owner's son stormed in last night and whacked him for virtually no reason.'

'Do you believe him?' asked Mikey.

'As it happens, I do.' Frank the waiter put a pot of tea on the table in front of him. '*Gracias*, Frank.' Brad poured the tea out of the stainless-steel teapot, and got half of it over the table. He dabbed at the table with a couple of serviettes before resuming. 'It's funny, I know that the four of them come across as dickheads but they're pretty harmless, really. I wouldn't say they were troublemakers, would you?'

'Do you know what they do for a living?' asked Mikey.

Brad shook his head. 'Peter and Timmy are both ambulancemen.'

'Really?' Brad took a sip of his tea. 'I suppose I'd better speak to Alison.'

'Well, now's your chance.'

At that moment Alison had walked in. She could scarcely disguise her displeasure at seeing Brad and Mikey together again. 'What are you doing here, Brad?' she asked.

Brad looked at Mikey and raised his eyebrows. 'Two reasons, actually. First of all, you probably remember that we arranged a football match with that British Rail mob.' Alison nodded. 'Also, I wanted to talk to you about something that happened in the hotel last night.'

'What was that, then?'

'One of my clients got battered by the hotel-owner's son.'

'Who was it?'

'Peter Turner, the tall, ginger lad with the Plymouth Possee.'

'They're that bunch of wankers, aren't they? No doubt he deserved it.'

'Actually they're not bad lads when you get to know them,' contradicted Mikey.

'That's right,' agreed Brad. 'Besides, you should see the state of his face. All he did was have the stereo on a bit loud and I wouldn't say that warranted what was dished out.'

'How do you know? Were you there?'

'No, I wasn't but—'

'Well, if you weren't there how do you know what happened?'

'Because he told me and I believe him. Well, that's my judgement, anyway,' replied Brad.

'Yes. We all saw how good your "judgement" was when you came out with all that nonsense at the welcome meeting,' said Alison tartly. 'Look, if you're that concerned, do a report. Now if you'll both excuse me I've got important things to be getting on with.' Alison headed for the lift.

'Slut!' muttered Mikey.

'Mmmm.' Brad nodded. He badly needed to talk to somebody.

The turnout for the football match was low. Apart from Brad, Greg, Mikey and Mario, the only clients willing to play were two of the Plymouth Possee. A few ringers were roped in, but the British Rail team still thrashed YF&S 6–2.

Four of British Rail's goals were scored in the first half when Mario was in goal. Brad took over as keeper for the second half, and although he had assumed that Mario had not wanted to dive for fear of getting dirty, his own first dive on the hard surface resulted in a badly grazed knee. He thought that maybe Mario wasn't so stupid after all.

The girl reps and a handful of female clients watched the match. At the start Brad was disappointed that Patricia wasn't there. However, she turned up near the beginning of the second half, which unfortunately coincided with Brad letting in his first goal.

After the match, he sidled up to her as discreetly as he could and squeezed her hand.

'You're all sweaty,' she said. Then she glanced down. 'And you're bleeding.'

'It's all right, Patricia, I'm hard.'

'Not yet you're not.' She lowered her voice. 'But you will be.'

Brad felt a tingling in his loins. He felt randy as hell. He had fallen asleep with his dick in his hand thinking about Patricia and awoken in similar fashion.

'You look as though you need a shower,' she said as they walked along. She looked at Brad with a gaze that made him melt and ran her fingernails along the inside of his wrist. 'Have you tried the showers in the Bon? They're really good. I'd let you use ours but I'd have to ask the girls. Oh, hang on a minute.' Patricia put her hand to her mouth in mock surprise. 'I've just remembered. They're out for the whole afternoon and aren't going to be back until gone six.'

She looked at her watch. 'Well, that's another four hours. Now what can I do until they get back?'

Brad took off his shirt and tucked it into the front of his shorts in an attempt to conceal his fast-growing excitement. Patricia looked over her shoulder to make sure that nobody was watching and slowly pulled the shirt out of his shorts, allowing the back of her knuckles to brush against his cock. Brad was now rock hard. He snatched at his shirt and pushed it back into his shorts.

'Any ideas, Brad? What would you like to do for the next four hours?'

'The way I feel right now,' he said, slipping his right hand underneath her mane of red hair and squeezing the back of her neck, 'you'll be lucky to get four minutes out of me.'

When they got back to the apartments hardly anybody was around. They got into the lift and as soon as it started its ascent they were all over each other. As they got out and opened Patricia's door, which was directly opposite, their mouths barely disengaged. Once inside, Brad tried to pull Patricia's vest over her shoulders.

'Whoa there,' she said, panting. Brad ignored her, his fingers pulling aside her bikini bottoms. He put one finger inside her, slowly, rhythmically exploring her warm flesh. As she became moist, he gently circled her clitoris with his middle finger before plunging first one, then two fingers back inside her. As she started writhing, Brad curled back his two fingers and began pulling them towards him more and more vigorously, at the same time letting his palm brush against the top of her lips and her magic button. After a few minutes Brad felt her contract around his hand, after which she let out a scream and released a torrent that ran down Brad's arm.

'Jesus, what was that?' she said, as she slumped against the wall. Brad put his hands on her hips and kissed her.

'God, what did you just do to me?' Patricia looked down at her leg. 'Oh, shit, I'm bleeding.' Brad started laughing. 'What's so funny?'

'You're not bleeding. That's blood from my knee.'

Patricia looked at herself a little more closely.

'So it is. Phew!' She started laughing. Brad joined in and they hugged each other, rocking back and forth. 'Come on, let me show you our bathroom.'

They both stepped into the bath and switched on the shower. Patricia looked up at Brad and, without losing his gaze, ran her tongue down his body. When she reached his groin she licked around his thighs then slid her tongue up the inside of his leg. Eventually she ran her tongue lightly along the length of Brad's cock, barely touching it as she did so. Then she squeezed his balls and pulled them towards her mouth, flicking them every so often with her tongue. Brad was desperate. 'Please, Patricia, put it in your mouth.'

Patricia engulfed his cock with her mouth, managing to barely touch it as she did so. When it was two-thirds of the way in, she closed her lips around it and sucked hard as she pulled away from him. This time it was Brad's turn to let out a loud moan. As she released him she lay down in the bath, supporting herself with one hand. With the other she started probing her womanhood, staring directly at Brad. Brad looked at his throbbing, plum-coloured helmet.

'Don't just look at it, Bradley.' She stood up, turned her back to him and bent over. She put one hand between her legs and opened herself up, then looked back at him over her shoulder. 'This is where I want it.'

Brad could hardly believe that she was talking and being so dirty. He took hold of his cock in his left hand and looked skyward. 'There is a God.' With that he brushed his bell end up and down her lips before ramming himself inside her. They moaned in harmony. After a while Patricia reached back and started squeezing Brad's aching balls. It was too much.

'Oh, shit,' said Brad, as he pulled out. He stood there for a second or two hoping he'd managed to stop himself. But he felt his balls tighten and, sure enough, a string of cum shot up Patricia's back. But Brad did not feel as if he had come properly. It was as if somebody had been shaking a bottle and opened it, but only the froth had come out. The rest of the contents were still in the bottle.

'Quick, get out of the bath.'

Patricia did as he said and they went into the bedroom. Brad got on top of her, surprised and relieved to find that his erection had not subsided. Not only that, he also felt more in control and was able to be less frenetic in his lovemaking. The whole thing felt very special to Brad. At one point, Patricia was on top of him, slowly circling and grinding her hips to take him as deeply into her as she could. Her hair tumbled over her shoulders and she gurgled with delight, her tongue slowly sliding between her lips. Behind her, the balcony door was open and the setting sun made the sky seem as though it were veiled in blood. The diminishing heat touched their skin and, as she twisted, impaled on him, Brad felt pure emotion. As he rolled her over, the synchronised rhythm and shuddering, simultaneous climax that followed made him realise he had badly underestimated the power of foreign climes.

He had not expected to fall in love so early in the season.

chapter five

'Fuck, fuck, shit, shit, shit, shit, FUCK! Bitch, whore, slut, slag-bag!'

Brad was not a happy man. He picked the phone off the receiver and slammed it back again twice, yelling, 'Bollocks,' as he did so. It had been only ten days since Patricia had kissed him at the airport and, with tears rolling down her cheeks, promised that she would come out to see him again within the next two months. There had been one letter, written as soon as she had got back. Then there had been a phone call every other day. But for the last four days Brad had sensed that something was wrong and, sure enough, it was. He recalled parts of the just-finished conversation in his head.

'The time we had together *was* special, Brad ... You did things to me that no one has ever done before ... I don't know how I feel ... You're so far away ... Things seem so different now ... It's just that he's here and you're there ... I know I said I couldn't stand him ... He's changed ... He really loves me ... We can still be friends.'

'We can still be *bollocks*!' said Brad.

He walked back to the hotel from the phone box, his hands thrust into the pockets of his tracksuit bottoms.

The brown and white hotel mongrel ran up to him yapping.

'Fuck off.'

The dog ignored him and ran around Brad barking even louder. In the end Brad sat on a wall and tickled the dog behind the ear. 'I don't know. Women, eh?' The dog sat down, tilted his head and wagged his tail. 'You don't know how lucky you are. It's easy for you. All you've got to do is find someone you like, sniff her bits and jump on her back. You don't have to worry about whether or not she's got a boyfriend, do you, eh?' The dog barked. 'One minute I'm the best thing since sliced bread and her boyfriend's a stain, next minute I'm last year's model and she's getting him his pipe, slippers and cardboard cut-out of *Match of the Day*.' The dog ambled over to a tree and squatted beside it. 'My sentiments exactly.'

Brad got back to the Bon half an hour before the pre-airport meeting. Greg was in Reception. 'All right, mate?'

'Is that a pleasantry or are you genuinely interested?' asked Brad.

'Oh, fuck me. What's up with you? No, don't tell me, let me guess. Women problems.'

'Spot on, Einstein.'

'That redhead you've been going on about for the last week and a 'alf 'as dumped you and gone back with 'er boyfriend.'

'Hmmm. How did you work that one out?'

'Didn't 'ave to. It 'appens all the time. It's obvious if you think about it. Because we work 'ere we get blasé about the place. But to the majority of Brits it's a million miles away from their real world. That means *you*'re a million miles away from their real world. Sure, while they're 'ere it seems as if love will find a way, but at the end of the day they go 'ome, back to their normal lives. When some of 'em think of what they've done or the people they've turned into on 'oliday it scares the fuckin' shite out of 'em. All they want to do is scurry back to their comfort zones, and if that includes an old boyfriend then tough titty.'

'Yeah, but surely it must work out sometimes,' insisted Brad.

'The only time it ever works out is if you gerra girl over at the end of the season who doesn't live too far away from

106

you back 'ome an' who isn't settled. Either that, or start seeing someone who works 'ere.'

'That's really sad,' said Brad sipping his drink.

'Is it fuck,' said Greg. 'I'm afraid that due to your misplaced loyalty to whatever 'er name was, you've slipped down the old league table.'

'Don't worry, I'll catch up.'

They were both silent for a moment. Then Brad said, 'Greg, you've surprised me a bit. I didn't realise you thought about things so deeply.'

'Only certain things. The way I look at it is that these years are probably gonna be the most enjoyable of my life and I'm gonna make the most of 'em. My advice to you is to do the same.'

'And seeing as we're on this male bonding trip there's something I want to ask you,' Brad went on.

'No, y'can't sniff me fingers.'

'Don't worry, mate, I wouldn't want to, the amount of time you spend scratching your balls. No, it's about Alison.'

'Oh, y'can't wanna shag 'er surely. That'd be minus ten straight away.'

'No. It's something quite serious.' Brad looked around to make sure that nobody else was listening. 'Greg, do you think she's taking backhanders?' Greg went very quiet. 'It's just that I saw her outside the Star and—'

'Stop,' Greg interrupted. 'Listen to me. I just told you that all I'm concerned with is 'avin' a good time. What she gets up to is 'er business as long as it doesn't affect me. Yes, she probably is at it but, to be honest, I don't give a flyin' fuck. I've got ways of supplementin' me income and maybe when I get t' know yer better I might tell yer what they are. As far as Alison's concerned I'd keep out of 'er face. She's the manager and that's that.'

At that moment Lorraine walked into the bar.

'Hello, darling. You all right?' asked Brad.

'No, I'm not.'

'What's up?'

'Nothing and everything.' Lorraine pulled out a chair, ordered a cider and sat at the table. 'It's that cow Alison.'

Brad turned to Greg with a now-will-you-listen look.

Greg got up. 'I'm goin' for a dump,' he said.

'What's up with him?' asked Lorraine. Brad shrugged his shoulders and Lorraine continued. 'I don't know, Brad, I'm doing the best I can but it never seems good enough for her. She's always on my case. Lorraine, do this, get up and dance, stop talking to this person, learn to put your makeup on properly, don't drink so much, talk more clearly on the microphone. Every time I see her she's got something to say and it's doing my head in. I'm not that useless, am I?'

Brad looked at her and saw her eyes welling up. He put his arm around her shoulder. 'Come on,' he said, 'don't let it get to you.'

Working so close together and being a bit older, he had already begun to feel like a big brother to Lorraine. He had noticed that Alison had been giving her a hard time and, as far as he could see, the only reason for it was that Lorraine allowed her to. Although Lorraine could be foul-mouthed and come across as sure of herself, Brad knew she was timid and sensitive. This was what made her so popular with the girl clients. She was not glamorous, she was down-to-earth, always took time to talk to clients and be genuinely interested in what they had to say, unlike ninety per cent of the other reps. She was certainly the antithesis of Alison, which was probably why Alison picked on her.

'I'm sorry,' said Lorraine, wiping her eyes. 'Maybe I'm just homesick.'

'Well, if it's any consolation, Lorraine, I don't think she likes me either.'

'What *is* her problem? I sometimes wonder how she got the job in the first place.' Lorraine got up to get her drink. As she did so, Alison walked in with Mario.

'Where is everyone?' snapped Alison.

'Greg's answering the call of nature. Lorraine's at the bar

and Heather and Mikey are just coming out of the supermarket.'

Alison lit a cigarette and sat down in the chair Lorraine had just vacated. Mario pulled up a stool and sat next to her. Greg came back from the toilet as Heather and Mikey walked into the bar. They all swooped for the last remaining chair. Mikey was there first, but he gave it to Heather and grabbed a couple more from outside. Lorraine joined the group, carrying her glass.

'Not drinking again, are we, Lorraine?' said Alison. She looked her up and down and focused on her sunburnt nose. 'No wonder you've got a red nose, you'll be on the meths next.' Lorraine forced a smile. 'On the subject of looking like a down-and-out, I saw you when you left for your airport transfer on Wednesday. Make sure you iron your shirt tonight.'

'I ironed it on Wednesday,' protested Lorraine.

'Well, if you did,' said Alison, 'you either didn't have the iron switched on or your skin's creased.' She looked round the table for an appreciative response to her 'joke'. Mario guffawed. 'Anyway,' she continued, 'tonight's transfers. I can't believe it's the third Saturday of the season, can you?' All of the reps, apart from Mario, mumbled, 'No.'

Mario said, *'Unbelievable,'* in a loud voice.

'Right, before we start, any problems?'

Lorraine whispered to Brad, 'Yeah, you, you bitch.'

'What was that Lorraine?' Alison pounced.

'Lorraine just reminded me,' said Brad, thinking quickly, 'that the hotel-owner's nutty son Rafael decked another of our clients the night before last.'

'Why?'

'No reason.'

'Don't give me that, Brad,' said Alison. 'He wouldn't hit someone without reason unless he was a total psycho.'

'Well, there you go. He *is* a total psycho.'

'I doubt it. At the end of the day, Brad, it's the responsibility of you and Lorraine to keep your clients in

109

order. If you can't do it, we'll have to think about moving either one or both of you.' She flapped open a file. 'Now, then, tonight's transfers.'

The Triumph Herald had proved both a blessing and a curse. It had given Brad status of sorts, but it had already cost him nearly a hundred pounds in repair bills.

Tonight the car had started making funny noises just after the roundabout and was soon spluttering badly. Brad stopped outside the hotel Es Puchet, where it stalled and refused to start again. He got out and had a cursory look under the bonnet but could see nothing untoward. He disconnected the battery – it was the only way to make the ignition light go off – and started to push it towards a side road. As he was doing so he heard a girl's voice. 'Do you need a hand?'

He looked round. It was Kelly, 'the Vision', coming out of the Es Puchet.

'Oh, hi. Yeah, if you wouldn't mind.' He saw that she was wearing her red uniform. 'Actually, you'd better get in and steer while I push.' Kelly jumped into the car exposing a tanned thigh. Brad pushed the car in the most dignified way he knew and Kelly turned it down the dusty side road. Then she got out, once more exposing her perfectly formed thigh.

'Thanks,' said Brad. 'Are you at the airport tonight?'

'Yeah, you?'

'Providing I get this bloody thing sorted out and back in time. I'm bringing in a Gatwick flight at about one.'

'Good, I'll see you there then.'

'Which way are you going?'

'Well, I live about a hundred yards up there,' said Kelly, pointing in the direction of Port des Torrent.

'That's the way I'm going.'

They walked up the road together. Kelly did not say much but she smiled a lot. Brad was confused because her body language suggested she might be interested in him, but his attempts at conversation were greeted with monosyllabic responses. They parted company at her apartments and Brad went to find a garage.

Brad woke up to find Greg in his room. 'So, what's your new arrivals like?'

'There's a group of half a dozen or so lads from Hammersmith who seem like a good laugh. A bit OTT but definitely away for the crack. Oh, and there was another group of eight pissed blokes from Orpington all wearing Molson Dry T-shirts. Seemed harmless enough.'

'Fanny?'

'Yeah, a few bits and pieces. Some girl turned up who reckons she's just had a pacemaker fitted.'

'*What!*'

'Seriously. She reckons this could be her last holiday,' said Brad.

'What's she like? You know, points potential.'

Brad started laughing.

'What you laughing at? I'm serious. Suppose I manage to get her palpitating. That's gorra be worth a couple of bonus points!'

'You're sick,' said Brad, still laughing. 'Go on, piss off back to your own hotel.'

'Why's that? Do you need to knock one out 'cos you've not 'ad a shag for so long?' said Greg as he opened the door to leave. 'I'll see you in an hour or so.'

After Greg left, Brad recalled a particularly rude session he had been involved in with his ex-girlfriend, Charlotte, back in London. The memory had brought him quite close to ejaculating, but he pulled up his shorts, sorted out some hundred-peseta coins and headed for the phone box.

As he made his way down the stairs he knew he shouldn't be ringing Charlotte but, as often happens, when the male member fills with blood the brain empties of logic and reason.

Charlotte's mother answered the phone. Brad heard Charlotte come running down the stairs.

'Hi. Brad?'

'Yeah. How y'doing?'

'Oh, not bad. I'm missing you.' Brad winced.

'I knew you'd call.' Brad winced some more and contemplated abandoning the idea of inviting her over.

'I was just wondering,' he said hesitantly, 'how you'd feel about coming over for a long weekend.'

'Really!' replied Charlotte, just a little too excitedly.

'Yeah, well, I can probably sort you out a flight through the company.'

'Oh, that'd be brilliant!'

Brad realised that he might have underestimated the strength of Charlotte's feelings. 'Look, my money's running out. I tell you what, Charlotte, let me see what I can arrange out here and I'll give you a call as soon as I've got something sorted?'

'Yeah, brill,' replied a still obviously excited Charlotte. 'Miss you.'

'Yeah, er, miss you too,' he mumbled.

Brad went up to his room, took off his shorts and finished off his wank. As soon as the first shot hit his hairy stomach he started to curse himself for making the phone call. He grabbed a dirty T-shirt to wipe away the majority of his sperm, then had a shower before getting his clothes ready for the bar crawl. After a few minutes' deliberation he pulled on a pair of tracksuit bottoms, made sure that he had some more hundred-peseta coins and headed for the phone box again. This time Charlotte answered the phone, which was hardly surprising as she had been virtually sitting on it for the last hour.

'Hi, Charlotte.'

'Hiya. I managed to get in touch with my boss—'

'Charlotte . . . .' Charlotte would not listen.

'I got in touch with her at home—'

'Oh.' Brad sighed. 'Look, Charlotte, I don't know how to say this but . . .' He paused to find the right way to put it. The truth? Sorry, Charlotte, I only wanted to get you out here because I've not had sex for over a week but now I've finished my wank I've changed my mind. No. An outright porkie . . .

'I was really looking forward to you coming over but my boss has said that we can't have girlfriends out here. I'm really pissed off. Obviously I did my best but – Charlotte?'

When Brad got to the Anglers, Greg was DJing and the bar crawl was already in full swing. After a while it became clear to him that the Molson Boys' sole mission in life was to get him as drunk as possible. Although other reps would often let clients buy them drinks, Brad always refused. He couldn't see the point – he got all of his drinks for nothing anyway. But the Molson Boys did not give him a chance to refuse and, in truth, Brad offered only token resistance.

Within the first half-hour the six lads from Hammersmith had tried it on with every girl in the bar, and Brad noticed that they had also had quite a lot of luck with the fruit machine. The constant stream of Snakebites that they had been pouring down his neck had made him feel a little light-headed, so he went outside for some fresh air. He was joined by a surprisingly pissed Greg, who had just finished his DJ stint.

'All righ', lad?'

'Yeah. Bit pissed, though,' replied Brad.

'Fuck me, you're not the only one. I'm caned. Those bloody La Mumbas. What about you?'

'Snakebites – cider and lager. The Molson Boys have been getting them for me.' They both took a swig from their glasses. 'Who's DJing?'

'Mario. Can't believe 'ow good 'e is for someone who's never done it before. Where's that girl with the pacemaker?'

'I'm not sure,' said Brad, looking around. 'There she is,' he added, spotting her by the DJ stand. 'I feel a bit responsible for her, to be honest. She's a single share so she hasn't come away with anybody. I'll try to catch up with her later.' He noticed Greg eyeing her up. 'Keep your grubby little hands off, you perv. She doesn't want corrupting by you, she's a nice girl.'

'There's no such thing,' said Greg, emptying his glass.

Brad was about to turn around and go back into the bar when he noticed Robbo, the Kiwi windsurfer and dealer, sauntering down the road, oblivious to his surroundings. He was wearing a ripped pair of jeans, flip-flops, a brightly coloured waistcoat and about a dozen sets of beads around his neck. Brad interrupted his daydream. 'Robbo, just the man.'

'Uh,' Robbo looked up, startled. 'Yo, Rod. What's happening?'

'Brad, not Rod, you knob.' He ushered Robbo out of earshot of everyone else. 'I might need to pay you a visit.'

'Yeah, man, no problem. Whaddya need?'

'I wouldn't mind some Charles but I'm a bit skint. What about the fast stuff?' asked Brad.

'I've got some more powder turning up tomorrow, but all I've got for now are speed pills called Red Devils.'

'How much are they?'

'Five hundred pesetas to you.' Robbo saw one of Brad's clients walking over. 'Look out.' It was one of the Molson Boys, carrying yet another Snakebite.

'Hang on a minute, Robbo.' Brad turned round.

'All right Brad,' said the Molson Boy. 'There you go.'

'Cheers,' said Brad.

'Can I have a quick word?' said the Molson Boy.

'Yeah, sure. What's up?'

'Oh, nothing's wrong. I just wondered if you knew where we could score some pills.'

'It just so happens that the man you need to speak to is standing right here.' Brad turned back to Robbo. 'Meet Robbo. Robbo this is . . .'

'Kieran,' said the Molson Boy.

'What do you need, man?' asked Robbo.

'Depends. What have you got?'

'Doves.'

'What are they like?'

'Oh, wicked, man. Seriously,' added Robbo sincerely.

'How much?' asked Kieran.

'About fifteen quid each.'

'Oh, come on, mate,' said Kieran. 'You must be able to do better than that.'

'How many do you want?' asked Robbo.

Kieran started counting under his breath. 'Twenty, for now.'

'Twenty,' repeated Robbo, his eyes lighting up. 'I'll tell you what, make it twenty-five and you can have them for two mill each.'

'Done,' said Kieran. 'Give me a minute and I'll go and get the money.' He disappeared back into the bar.

Robbo reached into his trousers and pulled out a bag of pills. He counted out twenty-five and put them into a smaller bag. Then he took out another one, reached into his pocket and pulled out two red capsules. 'There you go,' he said, giving the three pills to Brad. 'A dove and two Red Devils.'

'But I don't know if I want them yet,' said Brad. 'I was going to come down the Star later and see you then.'

'No worries, mate,' said Robbo. 'I don't want anything for them. Put the odd bit of business my way when your clients ask you and I'll always sort you out.'

'Oh, right. Nice one,' said Brad.

Kieran came back with the money. 'There you go mate.'

'Cheers, man,' said Robbo. 'Listen. I'll catch you guys later.'

As he disappeared down the road Kieran turned to Brad and handed him a pill. 'There you go, Brad. Cheers.'

'Don't be silly,' said Brad, giving it back.

'No it's yours. From the boys. And I almost forgot. Lorraine wanted you in the bar. Apparently a group of lads have upset the owner or something.'

Just then Brad heard the sound of breaking glass. He ran into the bar where he saw the owner, Russell, squaring up to one of the Hammersmith crew whom the others called Pit Bull. Pit Bull was very calm but Russell was prodding him and yelling. Brad had to question the wisdom of this as Russell was middle-aged, fat and about five foot seven, while Pit Bull was five foot ten with a Tysonesque neck and in training to be a competing body-builder. He seemed to find the whole thing amusing, which was irritating Russell even more.

Brad stepped between them. 'What's up?'

'I dunno,' said Pit Bull dismissively. 'Ask this silly old sod.'

'I'll give you silly old sod, you bloody troublemaker. First you clear out my fruit machine—'

'We won fair and square,' said Pit Bull calmly.

'Then you come in here breaking up my bar.'

'What you on about?'

'You and your bloody mates,' sprayed Russell.

'Oh, get a life,' said Pit Bull, turning away.

'Get a life? It's 'cos of scum like you I left England in the first place.'

'Steady on, Russell,' intervened Brad, surprised at the self-control Pit Bull had thus far displayed.

'Steady on? I've a good mind to—'

'You've a good mind to what?' Pit Bull was losing his temper now.

'If you think you can come in here and wreck my bar—'

'Wreck your bar?' Pit Bull picked up a bar stool by one leg. 'I'll show you wreck your bar, you fucking mug.'

'Hang on a minute, mate,' said Brad grabbing the stool. He turned to Russell. 'What's he done exactly?'

'They came in here and didn't let anybody else use the fruit machine,' said Russell.

'Bollocks,' said Pit Bull. 'Nobody else wanted to use it. You're just pissed off 'cos we kept winning.'

This was true. But Russell was also surprised: he had rigged the machine so that it never paid out a jackpot.

'And then they start to wreck my bar. Look,' he said,

pointing at the floor, on which lay a broken mirror and a picture frame.

'Is that it?' asked Brad, a little surprised. 'How did it happen?'

'We were just mucking about and I fell against the wall and accidentally knocked them off,' said Pit Bull.

'Accident, my arse,' said Russell.

'Did anybody else see what happened?' enquired Brad, looking around the group.

'I did.' A girl in a tight white top with large conical breasts stepped forward. 'The bloke with the crew-cut fell against the wall and the mirror and the picture fell off. Simple as that.' There was a general mumbling of agreement.

'Bloody yobs. That mirror and picture cost a fortune.'

'Fucking liar!' yelled one of Pit Bull's mates, a blond lad called Kempy. 'The mirror was one of those shitty old Jim Beam ones – you probably got it from the brewery for nothing.'

'And what about the picture?' demanded Russell.

'It's just a cheap old Ferrari print,' said Kempy.

'Who asked you to poke your nose in anyway, you Cockney bastard?' said Russell. It crossed Brad's mind that maybe Russell had a death wish. 'Someone's going to be made to pay for this.'

'You want paying, do you, eh? You want fucking paying, you fat *cunt*!' Kempy was getting riled. He put his hand in his pocket, and pulled out a huge handful of change, freshly won from Russell's fruit machine. 'There you go,' he said, throwing it at him. 'That should be more than enough to cover the shit that's just fallen off your wall. There should even be enough left over for you to buy some breath freshener, you smelly bastard.'

Things had gone far enough and Brad decided that although they were not due to leave for another five minutes, a slightly shorter visit would be to everyone's advantage. He turned to the DJ stand to get the microphone, but Greg was obviously of the same opinion and had already taken it from Mario.

'Right, then, Young Free & Single. If you want to drink up we're going to make our way round to our next port of call, the Cockney Pride.'

As they got outside Heather came up to Brad. 'Well done, Brad. That could've got quite nasty – you handled it well.'

'Thanks, Heath'. Is it just me or is Russell off his trolley?'

'He's definitely not the full shilling. I'm surprised those lads didn't do him.'

They had not been in the Cockney Pride long before the party mood had returned. Brad slowed down on the drinking, but for the first time since he had been away he was genuinely enjoying the company of the clients. He was getting loads of female attention: the girl with the conical breasts, the girl with the pacemaker, a girl from Hounslow, a blonde from Stafford, a freckly Scot; all were giving the right signals. The Molson Boys were proving to be a great crack, and Brad realised that Pit Bull and Kempy were not dissimilar to the friends he knocked about with in the UK. They were more or less his age and shared his enthusiasm for a wind-up and taking the piss.

Also, Heather and Greg were no longer treating him as a novice; Lorraine and Mikey sometimes asked his advice. Greg had even said that later in the evening he would tell Brad how to make money out of the cruise. Brad looked at his badge and suddenly saw that it was more valuable than any gold card: it was getting him respect, popularity, women, free entry into everywhere, free drinks – even free drugs. It all seemed a little too good to be true.

It was.

Alison just missed YF&S leaving the Anglers. She was greeted by Russell's wife, Jean, whose leathery skin had not responded particularly well to the Spanish sun. She also insisted on applying the type of makeup that teenage models in the sixties had favoured. Her strongly bright red hair often had people guessing whether or not it was a wig. She smoked constantly, and loved to poke her nose into other people's affairs. She would have looked more at home behind a pair of net curtains than a bar.

Alison did not like either Jean or Russell – not many people did. She spent as little time as possible in the Anglers. It was a horrible bar, which was normally empty. The only reason she used it was because they paid fifty pesetas a head more than anywhere else. Alison had told head office that it was a great little bar with its own DJ booth and that although they didn't pay as much as some of the other bars it was perfect for YF&S. This meant that the Anglers provided Alison with a healthy personal weekly income. She therefore did her PR bit and shared a glass of wine with the owners whenever she went in to pick up her money after the bar crawl. As Jean caught sight of Alison walking towards her, she poured her usual and said hello.

'Thanks, Jean.' Alison took the drink. 'How are you tonight?'

'Ooh, can't complain.'

'Where's Russell? Many in tonight?' Alison wanted to get her money and get out.

'I think he's out the back. Hang on.'

Jean turned and yelled for her husband. Alison looked across the bar and forced a smile at the two remaining customers. A minute later, a flustered Russell came into the bar.

'Good night tonight, then, Russell?' Alison asked politely.

'You must be joking,' he said, pouring himself a large Jack Daniel's.

'What do you mean?' asked Alison. 'There was nearly a couple of hundred, wasn't there?'

'Oh, yeah, there were, but they wrecked my bloody bar.'

Alison looked around for signs of damage, but could see none. 'What do you mean?'

'I've cleared it all up now, haven't I, Jean?' Jean nodded.

'Bloody hooligans. If I hadn't stood up to them I don't know what they would have done, eh, Jean?'

'No knowing what they would've done,' repeated Jean, lighting another cigarette from her existing one.

'Fat lot of good your bloody reps were.'

'Fat lot of good,' said Jean, nodding and folding her arms.

'There was about ten of them, wasn't there, Jean?'

'Oh, definitely. At least ten.'

'Are you sure they were our clients?' asked Alison.

'Course I'm sure,' said Russell. 'They were with that big rep.'

'Yeah, that's it. The big one.' Jean nodded furiously.

'Brad?' asked Alison.

'Yeah, that's the one,' said Russell.

'Brad,' said Jean.

'All him and the others did was wait until it was all over then leave early.'

'Who made them leave early?' asked Alison.

'I think it was that Brad.' Russell scratched his head. 'And I tell you something else, Alison. I'm not giving you any money tonight 'cos I've got to pay for the breakages.'

Alison was furious. Brad had just cost her her usual brown envelope. As she walked round to the Cockney Pride and began to calm down she realised that Russell was making a mountain out of a molehill. However, she had been looking for an excuse to pull Brad up and this presented her with the perfect opportunity.

By the time she got to the Cockney Pride, YF&S had just finished taking their weekly group photograph, which was subsequently to be sold to the clients. Brad was standing outside the bar when he caught sight of Alison. He went to say hello – but he didn't get a chance.

'*Streeter!*' yelled Alison, in front of all the clients. 'Get over here. *Now!*'

Brad walked over to her, annoyed at the way she had just embarrassed him. 'What's up?'

'I've just come from the Anglers,' said Alison. 'It's bad

enough that your clients wrecked the bar, but how dare you leave before the agreed time? *How dare you?'*

'Would you rather Russell got his head kicked in?'

'Of course not. Which lads did it? Because I'm telling you now, they're on the next flight home.'

'No, they're not,' snapped Brad.

'I beg your pardon?' said Alison, unable to believe her ears.

'I said, no, they're not,' repeated Brad slowly.

'If you're not careful you'll be on the flight with them.'

At that moment Greg walked up to join them, closely followed by the other reps.

'What's up?' he asked.

'Nothing,' said Alison sharply. 'Go back to the bar. That goes for the rest of you too. This is between me and Brad.'

'Is this all about what just 'appened in the Anglers?' persisted Greg.

'Yeah,' interjected Brad, before Alison had a chance to reply.

'Look, I've already said I'm dealing with it,' said Alison.

'Do you know whar 'appened?' asked Greg.

'No, she doesn't,' Brad jumped in again. Alison was getting very wound up. 'She wants to send the Hammersmith lot back home.'

'You must be joking,' said Heather, who had spent the last hour getting to like them.

'It wasn't their fault,' added Greg. 'It was that fuckin' idiot Russell – 'e was lucky 'e didn't get a clump. In fact, if it weren't for Brad 'e probably would 'ave.'

'Yeah,' said Heather. 'Brad was brilliant.'

'Well, that's as may be. But you still left early and things were broken,' insisted Alison.

'Yeah, but the reason we left early was to stop Russell getting killed,' said Greg. 'Anyway, it was only five minutes, an' it was only a poxy mirror an' a picture frame that got broken.'

'And the boys paid for it,' said Brad.

'Mmmm,' grunted Alison. 'Well, I can't claim to be happy about this, but for the time being I'll leave it until after I've spoken to Russell again.' She placed her bag on the floor, then added, 'Right, you lot, get back to work, I want to have a quick word alone with Brad.'

After they had gone she turned to Brad. He was half expecting an apology. He should have known better.

'Right,' said Alison. 'I'm going to go back and sort this out with Russell. God help you if I find out that there's more to it.'

Brad tutted, raising his eyes skyward. 'Is that it?'

'No, that's not it,' said Alison. 'I was going to speak to you anyway, even before all this happened. I've been watching you closely over the last few weeks and I don't think you're pulling your weight.'

'*What!*' exclaimed Brad.

'This isn't a holiday, Brad. Every time I see you you're chatting up some girl or doing your own thing. You were late for desk the other day—'

'Hang on a minute, I'm not taking this. Do you know how much sleep I've had in the last week? Twenty hours. And do you know why? Because you keep giving me all the poxy flights.'

'Everyone gets the same airport duties,' contradicted Alison.

'That's bullshit and you know it,' said Brad. 'I've only been doing the job a few weeks and already even I know that there are good flights and bad flights. And, as for the desk duty, I missed one and that was only because you changed the rota without telling anyone. Don't you *dare* say I'm not pulling my weight.'

'Well, if I compare you to Mario—'

'Hold on, Alison,' interrupted Brad. 'You've obviously got some kind of problem with me.'

'I haven't, it's just that—'

'Yes, you have. I don't know why and I'm getting to the stage where I don't care. I enjoy this job, and I think I'm pretty good at it. I'll listen to constructive criticism, but I'm not going to be your whipping-boy.'

Alison was not sure what to say. She could not admit that she disliked Brad as she did not want a major confrontation. If she was going to get rid of him she was going to have to do it more deviously. She would have to compromise – for now.

'Well, I'm sorry if that's how you feel, Brad. I think you're very able but, as I've said before, you've got a lot to learn and it's up to you whether or not you do so. I'm here to help, but I've got a resort to run and, believe me, it's not an easy job.' Alison knew she was on thin ice. 'Right, then, I'm going to see Russell. I'll see you tomorrow.'

When Brad walked back into the Cockney Pride, Greg could tell he wasn't very happy. He leaned over and had a quiet word in Heather's ear, then joined Brad. 'Come on, mate, we're going for a drink,' he said.

'But we're in the middle of a bar crawl,' said Brad.

'Fuck it, lad. It can wait. I've spoken to Heather and there's more than enough reps to look after the clients.'

'What about Alison?'

'Don't worry about 'er. She'll get down 'ere just after we've gone an' she'll be propping up the bar with dear old Trevor until gone midnight. She won't get down the Star until at least one, if at all.'

'What about Pepper's?' asked Brad.

'She 'ates it in there. Old Wotsisface won't be there tonight so there's nothing for 'er to pick up an—'

'So you *admit* she's taking backhanders?' said Brad, swooping on what Greg had said.

'We'll talk about that later, eh, lad? Finish your drink an' let's leave all these giddies an' go an' 'ave a proper night out.'

'Giddies?'

'Tourists. Come on, drink up.'

The first hour was spent having a laugh together, going into bars they would not normally visit, and they ended up in the Charleston. Duffy's partner Jake gave them a drink and refused payment. They were silent for a bit, then Greg said, 'Come on, let's 'ave it.'

'What?'

'You've obviously gorra lot you wanna geroff your chest.'

'Not really. I'm just having trouble understanding how she got the job. She never stops to think before she opens her mouth. She's definitely got a problem with me and she gives poor old Lorraine a hard time. Mikey hasn't said as much but I know he hates her. She treats him like a performing seal: "Oh, go on, Mikey, do your impressions – show so-and-so how you dance, do that Jamaican talking." The only rep she's got any time for is Mario and he's probably the worst on the island.'

'Aye, lad, you're right abou' that one,' agreed Greg.

'She knows as much about motivation as Tracy Lords does about chastity.'

'Who's Tracy Lords?' asked a baffled Greg.

'Oh, er, some porn star.' Brad hurried on before Greg had a chance to question him further. 'I mean, look at me. I was on top of the world tonight, really enjoying the job. Now look what she's done. That Russell is a fucking fruit cake. But does she bother listening to what really happened? No. She engages her mouth before her brain as usual and has a go at me. I feel like telling her to poke the fucking job.' Greg said nothing. Brad continued, 'I appreciate that you don't want to get involved, Greg, but I *know* she's on the fiddle. I'm not sure how exactly, but I'm going to find out.'

'What's the point?' said Greg.

'The point?' repeated Brad. 'The point is that I don't feel safe, and if she's going to try and get shot of me I'm going to make sure I've got something on her. I know she's taking money from bars—'

'Of course she's takin' money from bars.'

'What?'

'Of course she's takin' money from bars,' repeated Greg.

'So why doesn't somebody tell head office?' asked a bewildered Brad.

'Because 'ead office already knows.' Brad looked at him aghast. 'Oh, come on, Brad, you're not telling me you didn't know the company gets paid by the bars for us taking our clients into 'em?' Brad shook his head. 'Why do you think we go into shit 'oles like the Anglers?'

'I did wonder.'

'It's not just the money. Look around you.' Greg gestured to Capone's and Tropic's, two of the most popular bars in the heart of the West End of San Antonio. 'Why do you think we don't bring our mob to these places?'

'Probably because they wouldn't pay us,' said Brad.

'That's one reason,' conceded Greg.

'But the whole thing sucks. I mean, apart from a few exceptions we take them to the crap bars and march them past all the good ones that they really want to go into.'

'You're missing the point,' said Greg. 'The reason a lot of them come away with Young Free & Single is to be part of a group, all doing summink together.' Greg took a swig of his drink. 'Of course these bigger bars won't pay us for bringin' our clients in – they don't need the business. But by the same token our lot would get lost in here. There'd be no, no . . .' Greg struggled to find the word.

'Corporate identity?' offered Brad.

'Nearly but not quite.'

'Camaraderie? Team spirit?'

'No, but it'll do. Okay, so bars like the Anglers are shit, but when we go in there it becomes a Young Free & Single bar. They feel they belong, they feel part of it all. We do the DJing an' wherever we want an' the clients love it.'

'Fair enough,' said Brad. 'But we herd them around like sheep. It's worse than being at fucking school.'

'Some of 'em still *are* at school. What you've gorra remember, lad, is that a lor'of 'em are coming away for the first time—'

'I know that, but—'

'—an' because they're on 'oliday,' steamrollered Greg, 'they don't wanna make decisions. It's a lot easier if we do it for 'em.'

Brad sipped his drink, thinking through what Greg had said. Brad was not pig-headed and if an argument was well presented, logical and made sense, he would take it on board.

'Don't get me wrong, Brad, I'm not saying we always choose the right bars, just that in principle the philosophy is right.'

It was a few moments before Brad spoke. 'Bit of a smart-arsed little Scouser on the quiet, aren't we?'

Greg smiled.

Just at that moment Duffy brought them two bottles of San Miguel. 'There you go, lads.' They thanked him and clinked the bottles together.

'Well,' said Brad, 'it all makes sense. But why didn't Alison tell me all this?'

'Yeah,' said Greg, running his fingers through his spiky blond hair. 'I was wonderin' that too. It's not as if it's a big secret or anythin'.'

'Maybe she *has* got something to hide.'

'Mmmm.' Greg looked deep in thought. After a minute or so he asked, 'What exactly did you 'ear 'er say outside the Star that night?'

Brad seemed preoccupied. 'Hang on a minute,' he said. Then he sat up in his chair clicking his fingers. 'It's just beginning to make sense.'

'What is?'

'That night Jimmy the owner said something about it not being a good idea to tell head office that only a quarter of the actual figure had been in—'

'A quarter!' Greg was incredulous. 'Greedy bitch.'

'So what's she doing? Only declaring part of the amount she should to head office?' asked Brad.

'Exactly that. But a quarter? Phew.' He whistled. 'That's stronging it a bit. I wouldn't mind bettin' she's lyin' about 'ow much the bars are payin' too. All resort managers do it a bit, but it sounds like she's takin' the piss.'

'So how do we get shot of her?' said Brad, matter-of-factly.

'*We?*' yelled Greg. 'Oh, no, mate, you're on your own with this one. I've already told yer I don't give a toss what she's up to.'

'Even if she's shit at her job?'

'Like I've already said, I do my own thing and that's it. I'd advise you to do the same,' Greg said firmly.

'I *would* do my own thing,' protested Brad, 'and I wouldn't care how much she makes, if it wasn't that her money-grabbing is affecting the way she does her job, and even if it doesn't affect you, it's affecting me, Mikey and Lorraine.' He purposefully put his near-empty bottle down on the table. 'First thing tomorrow I'm going to ring head office and tell them what's going on.'

'Ha,' said Greg mockingly. 'An' I 'eard you were meant to be intelligent.'

'What's wrong with doing that?' said Brad.

'You've just said she's shit at the job. 'Ow d'yer think she gorrit in the first place?'

'I don't follow.'

'Use your loaf, lad.' Brad still looked baffled. 'Well, put it this way,' continued Greg, 'if you do ring 'ead office, make sure you've got loads of firm evidence and be careful who you talk to.'

'What, you mean . . .'

'What I mean, Brad, is that she's got friends in 'igh places – 'igh enough for 'er to be given the job when she probably didn't deserve it.'

'Who?'

'I don't know for sure and if I did I wouldn't say. Just be careful.'

'Oh, come on,' insisted Brad. 'You must have some idea.'

'Look, just fucking leave it. I'm sayin' zilch.'

An uncomfortable silence followed. Brad was still trying

to take it all in, and Greg was trying not to cause a rift between himself and Brad. He eventually broke the gap in conversation. 'I tell you what, though, providin' you drink up and come down the Star right now I'll let you in on summink else.'

'What's that?'

''Ow to make money on the cruise.'

The dog-end was perched precariously on a broken lavatory disinfectant block. Greg tried to blast it off first, but his aim was not true, which was hardly surprising considering the amount of alcohol he had consumed. Brad was closer and his subsequent torrent dislodged the butt and he chased it down towards the plug-hole. Unfortunately, he too had had far too much to drink and, as he swung his hips to complete his task, he caught the bottom of Greg's white jeans and shoes.

'Oi, watch where you're pissing, you clumsy bastard.'

They rolled back into the Star club where the rest of YF&S had just arrived. Heather was at the front of the group. She took one look at Brad and Greg, with their arms wrapped round each other and started laughing. 'Had one too many, have we, boys?'

They stopped and looked up at her, trying to focus.

'The lovely Heather,' said Brad, burping.

'All right, 'Eath?' said Greg.

'Is that cow Alison with you?' asked Brad, forgetting himself.

'No, she's having an early night,' replied Heather. Brad punched the air. 'And in that state you two had better make yourselves scarce. Bar five wouldn't be a bad idea.'

As they made their way through the club Brad bumped into the girl with the conical breasts. 'Sorry,' he slurred. 'Oh, it's you. How the devil are you?'

'Not as pissed as you,' she replied.

'Ah,' said Brad, pulling himself upright. 'I may be pissed, but in the morning I will be sober. Whereas you, madam,' he looked at her chest, 'will still have massive tits. If I thought that there was the—' Greg pulled him away. As he went, Brad called, 'What's your name?'

'Veronica.'

'Well, Veronica, I owe you one for helping out in the Anglers.' By now he was at least six feet away. 'And if I catch up with you later I'll give you one. Weh-hey!'

Veronica gave Brad an embarrassed smile then carried on dancing with her friend.

Brad and Greg positioned themselves on two bar stools in the corner of bar five. On the walk down to the club, Greg had started to tell Brad how to fiddle money on the cruise. Brad was keen to resume the conversation. 'So before you get too pissed go over the cruise thing again. I still don't get the accounting bit.'

'It's easy. If anyone turns up in the morning who 'asn't already booked the cruise, you take their money an' keep it.'

'But surely those people will show up on the figures as extras,' said Brad.

'Yeah, but only if everyone turns up. Say you've got three people who turn up wanting to come on the cruise who didn't book it earlier. Now let's say that three people don't turn up who 'ad booked it. Bingo. The figures balance an' you pocket the money.'

'Yeah, but why would someone pay for an excursion and not turn up?'

'Think about the welcome meetings. What do we say during the sales pitch? We tell 'em that by booking a two-week block they're basically gerrin' three trips for nothing. They'll always miss one or two, so that's when you do it.'

'So it doesn't have to be the cruise, it could be any excursion?' asked Brad.

'Course it can. But the cruise is the best because it starts so early in the morning. Plus you can help things along a little,' added Greg, with a twinkle in his eye.

'What do you mean?'

'If we weren't so pissed tonight, then this bar crawl would have been the perfect opportunity. All you do is go round some of the clients who've booked the block an' get 'em as pissed as possible. As you're doing that you tell 'em that the cruise is a crock of shit an' not worth getting up for. Chances are, in the morning they'll have such a hangover they won't wanna get up anyway.'

'Looks like we'll know how they feel tomorrow, then.'

'Oh, don't remind me,' said Greg. 'Where was I? Oh, yeah. So the other thing you do is go round all of those who ain't booked the cruise an' tell 'em 'ow good it is, an' if they're only gonna book one excursion it should be that one. In the morning you make a point of knocking on the doors of those you think will come along, an' leave the ones you put off the idea the night before. Another little thing I do is bung Frank a bit of wonga to put the clock forward in Reception so that we can leave early. That's it, really.'

'Brilliant,' said Brad. 'I can't wait to get stuck in.'

'You've changed your tune, lad,' said Greg. 'A couple of hours ago you were all for grassing up Alison, now you're thinking of doing the same.'

'There's no comparison,' protested Brad. 'What she's doing affects the way the resort is run, her attitude to us and the clients' enjoyment. All we're doing is supplementing our meagre income.'

Greg slapped his shoulder and started to order another two drinks, but Brad said, 'Not for me, mate. I'm leaving. Aren't you coming?'

'I'll stay another 'alf-'our.' He was only just able to get the words out.

When Brad got to the hotel he ordered himself a coffee and bought a litre bottle of water to fend off the inevitable hangover. He had been sitting there for five minutes when Veronica and her friend came in. Brad called Veronica over. The friend marched upstairs, saying, 'See you in a couple of minutes,' in a very loud voice.

'Do you want a coffee?' asked Brad.

'No, thanks.'

'Look, I'm sorry about that comment earlier on.'

'I get comments about them all the time,' she said. 'At least yours was nearly funny.'

'What's up with your friend? I get the impression she doesn't like me very much,' said Brad.

Although he was pissed, he was instinctively beginning to steer the conversation. He knew that if he was going to get Veronica upstairs he would have to keep things brief, mainly because he was having trouble talking.

'Oh, she just gets a bit moody sometimes.'

'Yeah, that often happens,' said Brad slyly. 'You get one friend who gets all the male attention and the other one doesn't like it.'

'What, me? Male attention? You must be joking.'

'Oh, come off it. Blokes have been coming on to you all night. I've been watching,' lied Brad.

'They were just silly little boys,' said Veronica, blushing.

'You make it sound like you're ancient. How old are you?'

'Twenty-one,' she replied. 'I just can't be bothered with kids.'

'So you prefer older men,' said Brad grinning. 'Is twenty-six too young?'

'No, that's about right. How old are you?'

'Funnily enough, twenty-six,' he said.

'I thought you were younger than that.'

'Well, I've got my passport upstairs. You can come up and have a look at it if you like. Then you'll know I'm not lying.'

'Uh, I don't know,' said Veronica hesitantly. 'I don't want you getting the wrong idea.'

'Look. I'm enjoying talking to you and I'd like to carry on the conversation, but if we stay down here and someone tells my boss I've been spending loads of time with one client then I could get into serious trouble. I've got some

Southern Comfort upstairs so we'll just have a nightcap and take it from there.'

Veronica followed Brad upstairs. Once they got to his room he poured her a drink and they made polite conversation for a few minutes before they started kissing. Brad undid her bra, releasing the two mounds of flesh that had been struggling to escape all night. He rolled on top of her, and as she spread her legs wide open, he started rubbing himself against her while he buried his head in her chest. Things were going well, so he put his hand down her panties and got himself ready to enter her. At that moment Veronica pushed him off and jumped up.

'Stop it. I knew you'd get the wrong idea.'

'Well I must admit, having your tit in my mouth while you had your legs wide open maybe did give me slightly the wrong impression, yes.'

'I'm not like that. I never sleep with anyone on the first night.'

'Well, can't we just pretend we've already been out?' asked Brad lamely.

'I'm not saying I don't want to, just not tonight.'

'Are you going on the cruise tomorrow?' he asked.

'Yes. That's another reason why I want to go back. I'll never get up in time otherwise.' Veronica straightened her clothes and did up her bra. 'I'll see you tomorrow,' she said.

'Yeah, see you tomorrow,' he replied, defeated.

He was feeling as randy as hell now so he lurched back downstairs to see if there were any more stragglers. He ordered himself another coffee and sat down. He was almost asleep when the girl from Hounslow came in on her own. 'Hello,' said Brad. 'Where are your friends?'

'Fu'in' bitches lef' me.' She was very drunk.

'Come upstairs. I'll look after you,' he said, in desperation.

To his surprise she followed him. Saying barely a word, they both got undressed. The next thing Brad remembered was hearing a door slam. He awoke with a start and stumbled out of his room to see the Hounslow girl disappearing down the corridor. 'Oi, where are you going?'

'Y' fell 'sleep with y' tongue out.'

'Sorry, come back.'

Within a couple of minutes he was on top of her and a couple of minutes after that he came in her mouth without warning. She ran out to the bathroom and spat it out. When she came back in she glared at him. 'You bastard.'

'You only had to say.'

'You di'n' give me a chance.'

'Sorry.'

'You don' even know m' name.'

'Yes, I do,' protested Brad.

'Wha'issit, then?'

'I'll tell you in the morning.'

With that Brad fell asleep, in the knowledge that another three points were in the bag.

'Oh, God,' moaned Brad. 'I knew it would be a rough crossing.'

Greg said nothing. He just leaned over the back of the boat staring at the sea.

'Do you want some sangria?' asked Mario.

At that, Greg threw up over the side, which caused Brad to follow suit. When they had finished they looked at each other, faces crimson, eyes streaming, and started to laugh.

'Fuckin' hell, lad. We sank some ale last night.'

'You're not wrong, Greg. Give me class A drugs any time.'

They went back to the front of the boat where the small flat island of Espalmador was growing larger.

'So you got three points last night, did yer?' Greg asked.

'Yeah. I tried with that girl over there,' Brad said, pointing towards Veronica, 'but she wouldn't have it – mind you, I've got a plan for later. Anyway, I went back down to Reception and that girl from Hounslow came in totally pissed so I chanced my arm and propositioned her and she didn't say no.'

'Is she 'ere today?'

'No,' replied Brad, 'which makes it even better. She booked a block and didn't turn up, so I got someone else to take her place. Brilliant, eh? Not only did I get three points out of her but I also made the best part of twenty quid.'

'That's it, Bradley lad, you're learning.'

Espalmador is small enough to walk around within an hour and is predominantly made up of sand dunes with sporadic clumps of coarse grass. It is almost totally flat and offers little protection from the sun, although the shallow bay is perfect for sprinting in to cool off. There are nearly always a number of yachts moored within swimming distance of the beach, gently bobbing and loosely pulling against their anchors. The island also contains a mud bath, which is basically a pool of sewage that a previous YF&S resort manager had thought would be fun for clients to cover themselves in and then to take pictures. Brad and Mikey did not share this view so they stayed with half of the clients while Mario, Heather, Greg and Lorraine shepherded the others to the mud.

Apart from YF&S, another two largish boats were moored on Espalmador, one carrying Italian families, the other Germans. Mikey had brought his American football with him. He got a few clients together and started to throw the ball around. Because it was such a hot day, this was the only real activity taking place on the beach so most eyes were on them. There is a certain knack to throwing an American football correctly and, apart from Mikey, only an Asian lad called Rashid, one of the Molson Boys, came anywhere close to achieving this. As those in the group tired of trying to make the ball spin through the air and gave up, only Mikey and Rashid were left to play. Mikey had shown Brad how to throw the ball early in the season so now he decided to get him involved.

'Brad! Get up off your backside and catch this,' he yelled.

Brad jumped up and caught it on the half volley. He positioned his fingers towards the back of the ball, with the first joints over the laces as Mikey had shown him. 'Ready?' he shouted to Mikey.

'When you are.'

Brad launched the ball. As soon as it left his hand he knew it was a bad throw. He started willing the ball to change direction in the same way that a cricketer does when he knows he is about to be caught out, or a tennis player when they are trying to make the ball stay in. It was heading for an adorable-looking child of about three, naked apart from a white sun-hat, who was happily running towards his parents, oblivious of the projectile descending from the clear blue Mediterranean sky.

'Look out!' yelled Brad.

There was a loud *thud*! followed by the whole beach collectively going '*Ooohhhh*,' and then howling.

Brad watched a crowd of people running towards the prostrate infant. His first thought was to run in the opposite direction, but his conscience got the better of him so he went over to face the music. The father was an overweight six foot plus blond man in his mid-thirties. He ran at Brad, swearing in German. Mikey intercepted him and managed to calm him down, while Brad mumbled his apologies and slid off to the other end of the beach, convinced that he was the most unpopular man on Espalmador.

His self-imposed solitary confinement was broken by Veronica. He had seen her coming but had pretended he was asleep so that he could perve at her topless form as her magnificent breasts appeared to defy all the principles of modern physics. She spread out her towel and sat down next to him. Brad groaned as if he had just been woken from a deep sleep.

'What time is it?' he asked, rubbing his eyes.

'I don't know.' She rolled on to her front, much to Brad's disappointment. 'I heard about your baby-bashing.'

'Don't. I feel really bad about it. I'm scared to go back down there.'

'I wouldn't worry. The kid's OK, and most of our lot thought it was hilarious.'

'Even so, I don't think I'll bother for a while.' Suddenly Brad realised that he had the perfect opportunity to put into action his plan for getting off with Veronica. 'I'm going to get a pedalo out. Fancy coming along for the ride?'

They made their way down to the pedaloes, which were just out of sight of most of the YF&S sunbathers. When they were a hundred metres out to sea Brad pulled out a bottle of sun oil. 'We'll have to be careful out here, Veronica. The sun reflects off the sea so we'll burn easily. Here, I'll rub this in for you.' She turned her back and Brad started massaging in the oil. 'Now the front.' Brad poured some over her reddening breasts. As he smoothed it in he could feel himself getting hard. He moved down to the inside of her thighs and tried to slip a finger inside her. Veronica groaned, but the angle at which he was sitting was such that he could not move his hand in the way he wanted. He stopped and handed her the bottle. 'Your turn.'

Veronica poured liberal amounts over his chest and legs. She spent barely a minute on his chest before working her way down to his tummy and legs. Brad was straining to be released from his swimming trunks and Veronica obliged. The sun oil enhanced the sensation as she ran her hand up and down his length.

'Come on,' he said, 'let's head for that deserted bit of sand over there.'

At the back of the beach was a crudely constructed stone wall. What little clothing they both had on was soon discarded. Veronica was sitting on the wall with her arms around Brad's neck as he stood between her legs. She reached down and grabbed him, deftly slipping on a condom.

'Where did that come from?' he asked, surprised.

'You men think we're so stupid. Don't imagine this was all your idea, Brad. Like I said, not on the first night. But it's not the first night now, is it?' Veronica squeezed his manhood so hard he almost winced. 'So, come on, then – fuck me.'

After the initial shock Brad grabbed her hair and pulled her head back sharply. He sensed that she wanted some aggressive role play. He started biting her neck and then, quite roughly, put a hand on her right breast. He withdrew and started teasing her, each time ramming himself in as hard as he could, waiting until she was almost crying with frustration. On the fifth thrust she let out a bloodcurdling scream. Brad pulled out again, holding her tightly and kissing her as she writhed frantically and carried on screaming. He quickened his thrusts and Veronica scratched and wriggled almost as though she was trying to get free. Brad had been kissing her all this time, so he stopped and said, 'What's up? Am I too big for you?'

'No, get off, you pillock! There's a lizard running up my leg.'

With that she pushed him away and, in so doing, fell backwards over the wall with her legs splayed in the air. The lizard scurried into a hole under the wall. Brad started laughing but he was close to coming, so while she was on the ground he leapt on to the wall, threw off the condom and finished himself off, showering her with his hot semen, laughing maniacally as he did so.

When she regained her composure she ran her fingers over her breasts and realised what he had done. He looked at her sheepishly, expecting an earful. He was therefore surprised when she just lay there and looked at him. 'Come on, then. You've had yours. Where's mine?'

'What do you mean?'

'If you think you're going to walk away without making me come, you've got another think coming.'

'Sorry, darling. I'm a one-shot wonder. You're not going to get any life out of this for a while,' he said, flicking his shrinking dick from side to side.

'Well, you'd better use something else, then.'

Brad picked up his T-shirt, placed it underneath her and

started to drip sun oil up her legs. He moved his middle finger around the outside of her clit and then ran his other fingers up and down her lips before plunging the middle finger inside her. As he slowly moved his fingers in and out of her, he flicked her clit with his tongue. The first time she came quickly, but she grabbed hold of his hair and wouldn't let him stop until her body had shuddered twice more.

'Bloody hell!' said Brad. 'We're going to have some filthy sex this week.' Veronica smiled at him, still breathless and unable to speak. 'Come on. Let's get ourselves cleaned up.' He helped her to her feet and kissed her. Then they put on their swimsuits and ran into the sea.

As they pedaloed back, they passed close to the beach where YF&S were gathered. Veronica was sitting on the side of the boat closest to the beach, so she did not see Brad raise three fingers behind her head as he caught sight of Greg and Mikey. Seventeen points. He was catching up.

chapter six

Mario was wound up. He was getting on well with Alison; Greg didn't seem too bad; Lorraine and Heather probably fancied him. It was Brad and that bastard Mikey who were annoying him. He had shagged seven girls and he was sure it was because of Brad and Mikey's shit-stirring that he had been banned from the Competition. They were always trying to take the piss out of him. They thought they were so funny but Mario never understood their humour. He wasn't too bothered about them, though, because he had made his own friends, two bouncers and a couple of scallies, all Anglo-Italian. He had started to hang around with them when he wasn't working.

He had bought the stolen video camera from one of the bouncers and had already filmed his last three conquests, none of whom had had any idea that there was a hidden camera in the room. Also, his father had sent him enough money to buy a similarly knocked-off portable TV and video-recorder. It was his intention to get Greg, Brad and Mikey round to his apartment to watch a video of him in action so that they would no longer be able to ban him from the Competition.

Mario made the five-minute walk to Las Huertas, but Brad was nowhere to be seen. When he got to the Bon Mikey had gone into town and Greg was at the bar, talking to a girl with short dark hair. Mario nodded at him, mouthing, 'Got a minute?' Greg held up five fingers so Mario went and sat with a group of three lads, where the conversation quickly got round to sex. They all agreed that they would give one to Alison and Heather, but then they started discussing Lorraine.

'Wouldn't shag her with yours,' said Lester.

'Nah, man, she's a pig,' agreed Ryan.

'I'd have to be really pissed,' said Paul. 'You'd have to give me at least fifty quid.'

'Me too,' agreed Ryan again.

'I'd do her for fifty,' said Lester.

'You should get Mario to knob her,' said Paul. 'I've seen him in action. He could pull anything.'

'Is that right, Mario? Are you a bit of a stud?' asked Lester.

'Yeah, man. I reckon I can pull just about anything,' said Mario, without a hint of modesty.

'Go on, then,' taunted Ryan. 'Pull Lorraine.'

'Yeah, come on, superstud,' Paul said. 'We'll make it a hundred quid to shag Lorraine.'

'What if I don't?' asked Mario. 'What's the bet?'

'You'll have to keep us in drinks all night at one of the excursions next week and give us some YF&S T-shirts,' said Paul. 'We'll need some proof, though.'

Mario grinned. 'Will a video do?'

When Greg walked into Mario's room he was surprised at how tidy it was and how many home comforts there were. He was still wondering why Mario had insisted on dragging him away from the bar – something really important, he had said.

'Right. Sit down.'

Greg sat on the bed and watched as Mario switched on the television and put in a video. 'If you've dragged me down 'ere just to watch a porno when I 'ad the real thing waiting for me I'll not be an 'appy man.'

'Just wait,' said Mario. 'You won't be disappointed.' He pressed the play button.

As the screen flickered into life, Greg let out a sigh of disappointment as a porn star he half recognised lay on a bed with her legs apart. He was on the point of getting up to go back to the girl with the short dark hair at the Bon when, to his astonishment, a naked Mario walked on to the screen. 'That's you!' was all he could say. Mario grinned. 'And that's not a porn star, that's the girl who was 'ere last week.'

'Theresa,' said Mario smugly. He bent down and fast-forwarded to his next conquest. 'And that's Ruth,' he said, stopping the video briefly when the night-time action in his hotel room changed to daylight on the screen. 'You'll probably recognise the next one.' On came the girl with short dark hair whom Greg had been trying to pull. 'Letitia.' He let the video continue playing. 'I only got the camera last week so I didn't record the first four.'

Greg wasn't listening. He was engrossed in what was happening on screen, his opinion of Mario reluctantly going up every time Mario did. 'Good show, Mario lad. Good show.'

'Thanks,' said Mario beaming. 'So, are you going to stop listening to those two wankers and put me back in the Competition?'

'Mario, me old mate, if it means that much to you, you're back in.' Mario punched the air. 'I'll even give you a bonus point for filming it. How many d'you say you've bonked?'

'Seven,' said Mario.

'Seven times three, that's twenty-one, plus one for the filming puts you on to a grand total of twenty-two.'

'Am I in the lead, then?' asked a freshly enthused Mario.

'No. I'm on twenty-three – probably twenty-six after tonight. Mikey's on nineteen—'

'He can't be,' exclaimed Mario. 'He must be lying.'

'Don't think so,' said Greg. 'Anyway, he's on nineteen and Brad's on seventeen.'

'So I'm in second place!' Mario punched the air again.

'Right. Well, unless you've gorra wench 'iding in the wardrobe for me, I'm off.'

After Greg left, Mario lay on his bed feeling pleased with himself. He had achieved his first goal of getting back into the Competition. Now he was going to concentrate on the next: earning that hundred quid.

Greg walked into Las Huertas to find Brad talking to a sunburnt blonde girl. Greg beckoned him over.

Brad excused himself and crossed the bar. 'All right, mate,' said Brad. 'Fuck me, am I on a roll.'

'I thought you were going to see that Veronica again tonight. Brilliant sex and all that.'

'I am,' replied Brad, 'but she's had to go out with her miserable mate. She's going to come up to my room when she gets back.'

'What time's that, then?'

'She reckons about three. The thing is,' said Brad, nodding towards the blonde girl, 'I started making improper suggestions to that one over there during the bar night and she seems well game.'

'And you need the points if you're gonna catch up with Mario.'

'What do you mean?'

'He's back in the Competition.'

'How come?' asked Brad. 'I thought you said he was bullshitting.'

'Yeah, I thought 'e was. But our Mario's gor'imself a video camera and it seems 'e fancies himself as a bit of a porn star.'

'Have you seen it?'

'That's where I've just come from. And I've got some more bad news.'

'What's that?'

''E's 'ung like a fucking donkey.'

'Oh, please, tell me you're joking.' Brad groaned.

'Nope. Wish I was. I reckon it's gorra be 'eading for a niner. Maybe a bit more. And 'e's got a massive bell end.'

'Is there no justice? As if he isn't conceited enough.' Brad sighed. 'Oh well. I suppose he was at the back of the line when brains and personality were dished out so he had to make up for it somewhere. It's just a shame he's been over-compensated in the tadger department. God could have just made him good at badminton or something instead.' He sat on the edge of a table, smiled reassuringly at the blonde girl and folded his arms. 'So how many points is he on?'

'Twenty-two. Seven shags and a bonus point for filming. You're in last place so you'd better get your finger out.'

'I intend to. What's the time?'

'Quarter to one,' said Greg, looking at his YF&S watch.

'Shit, that only gives me a couple of hours before Veronica gets back. I'd better get a move on. You out anywhere later?'

'Well, I've been blagging that girl with short dark 'air all day. She's meant to be waiting for me back at the Bon, but I've just seen her in action. Letitia's her name – cellulite on celluloid, co-starring Mario. If she can manage that thing of his without yelping then mine'll be like a dick in a bucket.' Brad laughed. 'Mind you,' continued Greg, 'Mario didn't stick it up the rusty bullet-'ole, so I should be all right there – extra points as well.'

The hand-dryer in the men's toilets at the Hillbilly Hoe Down excursion didn't swivel upwards, which meant that Mario was unable to blow-dry his hair. He looked at himself in the mirror, and smoothed it with the palms of his hands. He straightened the badge on his blue denim shirt and drew his gun on his own reflection. He felt he would make a good Wild West hero. He gave himself a smouldering look and tried spinning the gun from one hand to the other. Unfortunately it spun straight out of his hand into the urinal. As he picked it out Mikey walked in.

'Ah, Mario, dear boy. Searching for dog-ends or are you hoping to find a personality down there?'

'Is that meant to be funny?'

'Mmmmm,' said Mikey. 'I daresay that in some quarters it would be considered humorous, yes.'

'You really think you're so smart. Why don't you just fuck off.'

Mikey walked over to the urinal and unzipped his fly. He looked at Mario and smiled, which irritated Mario even more.

'Why do you keep having a go at me? What *is* your problem?'

Mikey zipped up his flies and walked over to the sink to wash his hands.

'Come on, man. What's your problem?' Still Mikey said nothing. 'Okay, I'll tell you what your problem is, shall I? You've got one almighty big fucking chip on your shoulder. You can throw an American football around better than me, you can probably dance better than me, but other than that you're as jealous as fuck. You'd give anything to be able to change this,' said Mario pointing at his skin.

'Is that right?' said Mikey wearily.

'Fucking right it is, man. I'm not racist – I've got lots of black friends – but I tell you what, most of them are the same as you. A fucking big chip on their shoulders.'

'Well, Mario,' said Mikey calmly, 'why don't you just put a white hood on, wipe the piss off that toy gun of yours and do the world a favour. Shoot me, if that's how you feel.'

'What the fuck are you on about?'

'What I'm on about,' said Mikey, raising his voice, 'is that you have not got a clue. You go on about me wanting to change the colour of my skin. Have you listened to the way you talk, looked at the way you dress, seen the way you try to shake hands? If anyone wants to change the colour of their skin it's you. You're so desperate to be a brother it's sickening.'

'Bollocks, I—'

'And as for not being racist, bullshit,' continued Mikey, almost singing the last word. 'All the time there are people like you around, we'll carry on having doors slammed in our faces, unless we're wearing boxing gloves, running shoes or carrying a microphone. As soon as we don't conform to type, then people feel threatened. You, Mario, feel threatened by me.'

'I ain't scared of you,' said Mario, defiantly pulling himself up to his full height. 'I could fucking do you any day.'

'QED, Mario. You're too stupid even to understand what I'm saying, aren't you? You're threatened by me because you know I'm smarter than you. And I don't give you any more stick than anyone else. Your problem is that you take everything far too seriously, especially yourself.' Mikey turned towards the door, laughing. 'It's a shame, really, because apart from being racist, having a shit personality and no sense of humour, you're not a bad bloke.'

He walked out, leaving Mario trying to make sense of what he had just said. Seconds later, Mickey put his head back round the door. 'Oh, and for the record, if you're going to "do me", make sure you've got a few friends with you.'

As Mikey walked back into the Hoe Down the noise from the hall was deafening, with Woodsy pounding out 'Country Roads' and three hundred drunk holidaymakers swaying and singing along. He focused his attention on a girl from Kent.

Brad was having problems juggling several different women. Two days had passed since he had been supposed to shag Veronica and Melanie, the blonde girl, in the same night. He recalled how Veronica had almost caught him. After Greg left him, he had persuaded Melanie to go up to his room. He had then lost track of time – and Veronica had cut short her night out. When she knocked on the door Brad had not heard her at first because he had a pair of thighs for earmuffs. When she tried the door he told Melanie it was his boss, bundled her into the bathroom, then fell against the unlocked door just as Veronica was opening it, mumbling to her that he was puking up and would come up to her room when he was finished. He rounded off proceedings with Melanie using his first Black

Shadow durex, then went up to Veronica and brought her down to his room. He had not felt ready to perform again right away, but this had validated his story about being sick, because Veronica knew he had been feeling rampant. He had a mammoth session with her the following morning.

Later in the day he had sex with the girl from Hounslow, who he discovered was called Francesca. The following night he had got off with the Scottish redhead, but had not got anywhere because as they had walked into her apartment her friend had been sitting in a chair facing the door and examining her genitals with the same enthusiasm that a baboon examines another's backside. As the friend was five foot two and thirteen stone, Brad's ardour had been somewhat dampened.

Veronica, Francesca, Melanie and the Scottish redhead were all at the Hoe Down and Brad was not sure which way to turn, but Greg had given him a lesson in how to have more than one girl on the go. The standard line was: 'I really like you, but if we get caught getting off with clients then it's instant dismissal. [At this point, page fifty-six of the *Courier's Manual* could be shown as proof.] Obviously, we'll still see each other, but you mustn't get upset if you see me flirting with somebody else 'cos it's just part of the job. It doesn't mean anything. And the reason that sometimes we have to see each other during the day instead of at night is because our boss has a skeleton key and has a habit of checking up on us.'

When Mario emerged from the toilets he went over to Lester and his two friends with whom he had the hundred-pound bet to shag Lorraine. They wound him up sufficiently to goad him into action.

Later in the evening, just after the square dancing, Mario approached her. 'Hi, gorgeous. How's tricks?'

'Not bad. I hate this bloody excursion already, though,' she replied.

'Yeah, me too,' agreed Mario. 'Are you enjoying the job?'

'Loving it. You?'

'Brilliant.' Mario paused. 'Met anyone you like yet?'

'No.' Lorraine looked at him suspiciously. 'Mario, what are you up to?'

'Nothing,' he replied defensively. 'What do you mean?'

'Well, since we've been in Ibiza we've probably only ever had two conversations and I initiated both of those. Even then all you did was talk about yourself. Why this sudden interest in my well-being?'

'It's not a sudden interest,' protested Mario. 'The only reason we haven't spoken much is that we don't work in the same hotel and we've both been busy. You know how it is.'

'Hmmm,' replied an unconvinced Lorraine.

'I see you've caught the sun,' said Mario, trying to keep the conversation going. 'It suits you. Makes you look . . . sexy.'

Lorraine burst out laughing. 'Fuck off, Mario. Since when did a red nose look sexy to anything other than a reindeer? Sexy? Don't make me laugh.'

'I'm serious,' said Mario, as genuinely as he could. 'You shouldn't put yourself down you know. You're a nice-looking girl, you ooze sex appeal.'

'Yeah, well, it must be oozing somewhere else 'cos I've not had a shag since I've been here.'

'You must be getting desperate.'

'No, Mario, I'm not. If I don't meet anyone I like I'll stay celibate until the end of the season.' She took a sip of her wine. 'Anyway, how's your love life going? How many points are you on now?'

'What?' said Mario, a little taken aback that Lorraine knew about the Competition. 'Oh, that. I don't get involved in it. I think it degrades women.'

'Right,' said Lorraine. 'So videoing yourself shagging them and showing it to the other reps doesn't?'

'Who told you about that?'

'I didn't realise it was a secret.'

'You don't understand, Lorraine—'

'Look, I don't know what you're playing at, Mario, but don't try to get me involved.' Lorraine put her drink on the bar. 'Now, if you'll excuse me, I've got to go and dress up as a can-can girl.'

Mario looked over at Lester, who grinned at him. He replied with a thumbs-up. There was no alternative: he was going to have to lie.

Brad walked into Las Huertas at three in the morning. After the Hoe Down he had gone back to the Bon with the Scottish redhead and they had had sex in the shower, a blue Fiesta Durex this time. Brad was exhausted.

He was therefore less than happy to see Melanie waiting in Reception for him. He was less happy still when the night porter ran up to tell him that there was a problem with some clients on the third floor. When Brad got there the first person he saw was Pit Bull in a pair of boxer shorts, with Kempy.

'Oi, Brad, me old mucker,' Pit Bull yelled. 'Over 'ere. I've got something to show you.'

'Keep the noise down, eh, lads.' Brad got on well with the whole group and had even been down the gym a few times with Pit Bull.

'Sorry, Brad,' said Kempy, lowering his voice, 'but you've got to come and see this.'

Brad walked into the room. On the bed on all fours was the girl with the pacemaker. In her mouth she had the tallest of the group, Matt, while preparing to enter her from behind was William, whose severe acne reached down to his buttocks. The girl let Matt's cock spring out of her mouth and turned her head to see what William was doing. When she spotted Brad her face lit up. 'Brad, come over here,' she said, lunging for his belt.

Brad brushed her aside, and briskly ushered Kempy and Pit Bull out. 'What the fuck is going on?'

'We're all shagging her – what does it look like?' said Kempy laughing.

'I can see that. What's she taken?'

'Oh, we gave her some GBH,' said Kempy.

'Oh, Jesus.' Brad knew about GHB – or GBH, as it was more commonly known. It was like a liquid Ecstasy and Brad had witnessed normal girls turn into sex fiends under its influence. He had also witnessed people pass out spectacularly when they had overindulged, especially if they had mixed it with alcohol.

'How much has she had?' asked Brad.

'Only a couple of capfuls,' added Kempy.

'And did she happen to mention any reason why she shouldn't take drugs?' asked Brad.

'No.'

'Did she mention anything that made her different from other girls?' said Brad.

'Like what?' asked Pit Bull. 'Don't tell me she's a sex change.'

'She didn't mention anything about a pacemaker?'

'What?' said Pit Bull.

'Fuck off, you're winding us up,' said Kempy, but he could tell by Brad's face that he wasn't.

'What's 'appening?' said a voice from the top of the stairs. It was Greg.

'This crew have given the girl with the pacemaker some GHB and they're in the process of gang-banging her.'

'Steady on, Brad,' said Pit Bull. 'That makes it sound like rape.'

Brad just looked at the pair of them.

Pit Bull got the message and went into the room. 'Will, Matt, get off her.'

'Bollocks, I haven't finished yet,' said William.

Pit Bull grabbed his mousy pony-tail. 'Yes, you fucking have. She's got a fucking pacemaker and we've given her GHB.'

Brad appeared, to witness Matt jump away from the girl as if she had a highly contagious disease.

'Come on, put some clothes on,' Brad said to her, picking up her dress.

'Spoilsport,' she said, and threw her arms around his neck.

He extricated himself from her grasp. 'Oh, God, I'm so drunk,' she said.

'I don't think you are drunk,' said Brad.

'Yes, I bloody am. I must have had ten tequila slammers. Oh, hell, I'm going to be sick.' She scored a direct hit on Kempy's bed.

'You dirty fucking bitch,' he cried.

'That didn't seem to bother you five minutes ago,' said Brad flatly. He turned to the girl. 'What's your name?'

'Peggy.'

'Are you sure you're only pissed?' asked Brad.

'Of course I'm sure.'

'It's all right,' said Greg. 'I'll take care of it if y'want. I think you're needed downstairs,' he said.

Brad had forgotten about Melanie. Groaning, he made his way back to the bar. Peggy got dressed and left with Greg, whose parting shot was 'Be'ave yerselves, lads.'

He walked her to the top of the stairs. 'Right. What room yer in?' She waved her key at him. Greg looked at it. 'Two one one.'

They walked down the stairs and went into her room, where she flopped on to her bed.

'Why did you have to ruin my fun?' she said without opening her eyes. Greg took off his shoes. 'I've always wanted to do that,' she said. Greg threw his shirt on the floor. 'All those lovely blokes and you two have to bloody stop it.' Greg stepped out of his trousers and pants. 'Spoilsports!' She opened her eyes and was surprised to see a naked Greg walking towards her. 'What are you do—'

Her sentence was cut short by Greg sticking his dick in her mouth. This has gorra be worth a bonus point, he thought.

'Brad, you'll be late for desk.' It was Lorraine knocking on his door.

Brad looked down at Melanie who was in the middle of giving him a blow-job. He was having trouble maintaining an erection. He had woken up with a chronically sore throat and the thought of anybody sticking their tongue down it – especially Melanie – made him feel sick. His knee had still not properly healed from the football match weeks ago and his helmet was getting the hot itch that preceded the onset of thrush. He was starting to realise that morning desk times were a great excuse not to perform.

'Sorry, Melanie, I've got to go down. It's a shame 'cos I was looking forward to a really good session as well,' he lied. 'Do you want me to come?' She nodded, leaving her mouth positioned over his semi-erect cock. Brad brought himself quickly to a poor climax, regretting it almost as soon as the first drop of semen hit the back of Melanie's throat. He could feel himself becoming a complete bastard, but felt unable to stop himself. Maybe it was the way Melanie followed him around like a lap-dog, or because she rarely said anything of any consequence. He was not sure. But he knew he wanted her out of his room.

'Come on, Mel, get up. I've got to go to desk duty.'

'I'll wait here for you – we can carry on when you get back.'

Nothing could have been further from Brad's mind. 'Sorry, darling, but I've got to go and see the boss later. If she finds you here then I'll get the sack and we don't want that, do we?' Melanie reluctantly got out of bed. 'Good girl.' He went into the bathroom.

When he came back Melanie put her arms around his neck and tried to kiss him. 'Melanie, *stop it*! Come on, let's go.'

She walked sulkily down the corridor to her room and Brad went down the stairs, promising himself that no

151

matter how randy he felt he would not sleep with her again.

He decided to call in on Peggy to see how she was. He knocked on the door but there was no answer. It was unlocked so he walked in. There were two people in the bed.

'For fuck's sake. After everything I said . . .' He pulled the sheets back. 'Greg! What the fuck?'

'Told yer I'd shag 'er. Gorra be worth a bonus point – whaddya reckon?'

'You can fuck right off. You're bang out of order.'

'So you wouldn't 'ave shagged 'er then?'

'Of course I wouldn't. I could've done. Mind you, the state she was in anyone could have.'

'So why didn't you?'

'Because she was drugged up and she's got a pacemaker.'

'Well, you didn't miss anything.'

'Shut up, you bastard, she'll hear you.'

'No, she won't; she passed out when I was in the middle of shaggin' 'er. I carried on for about five minutes but she didn't move so I gis'd all over 'er 'air.'

'You shagged her while she was unconscious?'

'Course I did. I tried to gerrit up the rusty bullet-'ole but it wouldn't fit.'

'We'd better wake her up to see if she's alright,' Brad said.

They shook her and called her name but she didn't move. Greg gently slapped her around the face and began to look worried. 'I can't see her chest moving,' he said. 'What about scratching the soles of her feet?'

There was still no response. Greg tried to find a pulse. 'Oh, shit,' he said. 'I can't feel anything.'

'I think we're in trouble,' said Brad.

'Oh, Christ, no,' said Greg, running around the room in a blind panic. 'Oh, fuck, no. She's snuffed it, in't she? Oh, fuck, fuck, fuck. What should I do?' He sat down and stood up again. 'I've gorrit,' he said, clicking his fingers. 'Come on, let's just fuck off an' leave 'er. Then you can come up 'n' discover 'er in an hour or so.'

'Don't be stupid,' said Brad. 'Apart from the fact it's totally out of order she's got all your Harry in her hair.'

'Let's chop 'er 'air off then.'

'Greg, think properly. Pit Bull and all the boys saw you with her.'

'Exactly. They all shagged 'er. One of 'em might 'ave the same kind of 'Arry as me. Anyway, it was them who gave 'er the GHB, not me.'

They stared at the lifeless body. 'Come on,' said Brad finally. 'Let's call an ambulance.'

Greg knew he was right and followed him down the stairs. Brad got through to the medical centre, who said they would send an ambulance as soon as they could. Then they went back up to Peggy's room. When they opened the door and looked at the bed, she wasn't there.

'Is this the right room?' asked a confused Greg.

Peggy came out of the bathroom. 'Hello. What are you two doing here?'

'Are you all right?' asked Brad.

'Never better. I know I was a bit of a naughty girl last night but I can't remember exactly what I did. That GHB is lethal. I can still feel it now. God, it makes you feel as randy as hell.'

'Yeah, you were a bit naughty,' said Greg.

'Well, if you can't be naughty on holiday, when can you be? I suppose I should be embarrassed but ... I can remember being with Pit Bull and his mates. What about you two? Did you both, you know ... ?'

'No. Yes,' said Brad and Greg, simultaneously and respectively.

'What we mean is,' said the scheming Greg, 'that we both started but you passed out before we 'ad a chance to come.'

'That's a shame,' said Peggy.

'Tell y' what though, girl. Do y' fancy wankin' us both off before we go, like? To make up for last night.'

Brad dropped his face into his hands, unable to believe

that she was so rude and Greg so forward.

'All right then.'

He felt as though he had just witnessed two people bartering over the price of a bunch of bananas. However, he still took part in the transaction. Greg already had his cock out and was vigorously wanking himself to an erection. Peggy pulled down Brad's tracksuit bottoms and put his cock into her mouth. Once she had achieved the desired effect, she sat on the bed squeezing their balls.

'Ready to put some 'Arry on the boat, Bradley lad?' asked Greg, after a couple of minutes.

'When you are.'

'On five. One, two, three, four . . . *five!*'

The two reps spurted over Peggy's face at exactly the same time. Greg made a point of aiming for her eye. Brad exploded in a fit of giggles. Peggy shrieked and gurgled with delight.

'Not bad for a corpse,' said Greg.

'Not bad at all,' agreed Brad.

As he said it, he heard the sound of an approaching siren. Brad and Greg looked at each other in horrified recollection.

'The ambulance!'

On his way to the medical centre, Brad was sure he saw the jeep that belonged to Samuel Zakatek driving down the main Ibiza-Town-to-San-Antonio road. Two police motorbikes had been tearing up behind it.

When he went into the surgery and showed his rep's badge, the casually dressed doctor was friendly. He asked him which hotel Brad was in and which other reps were working for YF&S this year. When Brad mentioned Greg's name the doctor chuckled and repeatedly said, 'Penicillin.'

After he had finished examining Brad, he went over to a cabinet and picked out an assortment of medication. 'Okay, this ees for your throat.' He handed him some tablets and something to gargle with. 'This ees for your knee.' He handed him a bottle and some dressing. 'And this ees for your penis.' He handed him a red and white tube of cream.

As Brad walked out of the door the doctor called after him, laughing, 'And welcome to Ibiza.'

chapter seven

The wind that gusted through the open balcony door blew the money off the table and all over the tiled floor of Alison's apartment. She gathered up the notes and put them back into their respective piles, using a glass ashtray, a calculator and a lighter as makeshift paperweights. When she had finished counting, the pile of five-thousand-peseta notes was the largest. She calculated that she had already made the equivalent of four thousand pounds. She gave a satisfied smile and lit a cigarette. At this rate she'd go home with over twenty grand.

A knock at the door interrupted her thoughts, and she swept the money into her YF&S shoulder bag. 'Hang on a minute,' she yelled. 'Who is it?'

'It's me.'

'Hang on, Mario.'

She put the bag under the settee, puffed up her hair and quickly put on some lipstick. When she opened the door she noticed how handsome Mario looked with a suntan.

'All right, Alison. Just got in?'

'No, no. I've had loads of paperwork to do.'

'It must be really hard being resort manager. I don't know if I'd be able to cope.'

'Well, it's not easy.' Alison sat down and beckoned for Mario to do the same. 'What can I do for you? Is anything wrong?'

'No, not really.' Mario looked down at the table. If he was going to make this sound credible Alison would have to drag it out of him. 'No, nothing's wrong. I just popped up

156

to, um, see you.' Mario twiddled his fingers, trying to look sorry for himself.

'Are you sure there's nothing wrong?' asked Alison. 'You seem like something's on your mind.'

'Nothing really,' replied Mario, with rehearsed hesitancy. 'It's just that it's a bit, well, a bit ... delicate. I mean, I'm probably imagining it.'

'Imagining what?' She wondered if she had made it too obvious that she fancied him.

'Oh, well, you'll probably notice it yourself anyway,' said Mario, sighing. 'It's Lorraine.' His voice suggested that the Iraqi secret police had just extracted his teeth one by one to obtain the name.

'Lorraine?' Alison was deflated that Mario was not about to declare his undying lust. 'What's she done now?'

'Oh, nothing,' exclaimed Mario, pretending to jump to her defence. 'Well, nothing yet. It's just that she's been sort of coming on to me. It's making me feel a little bit uncomfortable, that's all, and I'm not sure what to do.'

'Hmmm,' said Alison. 'I'll have a word with her, if you want.'

'Oh, no, don't do that,' said Mario. 'I only wanted to make you aware of it in case it gets out of hand. I'm sure I can deal with it.' Mario stood up. 'I'm a big boy now.' He gave Alison the most suggestive look he could.

Alison blushed and couldn't stop herself glancing down at his groin. 'Well, if you're sure you can deal with it then all right.' She regained her composure. 'But if it carries on come and see me. Okay?'

'Fine,' said Mario. He touched her shoulder. 'Thanks, Alison. You've really put my mind at rest.'

'That's what I'm here for. You'd better get your skates on now or you'll be late for bar night. You've got quite a good crowd this week, haven't you?'

Mario waited until he got into the lift before he started smiling. Five days had passed since the Hoe Down. He had lied to Lester and his friends that he had shagged Lorraine but had not been able to video it. They wanted to see some evidence before they gave Mario the hundred pounds and Ryan had suggested a public display of affection towards Lorraine in front of them. The meeting with Alison had been purely to pre-empt any problems that might arise if Lorraine got upset or if Alison witnessed any contact between them.

Mario grinned at himself in the lift mirror. 'Good-looking *and* clever.'

During the course of one's existence on this planet, it is possible that one will come into contact with someone (normally male), who derives his main source of entertainment from getting other members of the species horrendously drunk. To own a bar would greatly assist such a mission. Monty had his own bar.

Monty's bar was near the hippie market at Es Cana. After the shopping, YF&S would take their clients in and spend the rest of the afternoon there playing drinking games. Along with the hotel bar nights, this was when the reps encouraged their clients to drink more than ever – and Monty was on hand to make sure that the reps got even more drunk than the clients. Because Es Cana was a quieter part of the island, Monty's had only been open a week, so this was the first time this season that YF&S had been there.

Greg had warned Brad and the other reps about Monty and his 'initiation ceremony'. The previous year, one of the first-year reps had ended up in hospital afterwards with alcohol poisoning.

The bar was at the end of a dusty cul-de-sac, at the top of which were scruffy four-storey apartments. The only other two buildings were a yet-to-be opened pub called the White Lion and Monty's. Opposite Monty's was wasteland upon which was a burnt-out Seat, a mountain of bursting bin-bags and an old washing-machine.

As they walked into the near-deserted bar Monty sounded a klaxon and put on a record, a strange version of

'Swing Low Sweet Chariot'. Mikey looked at Brad apprehensively.

All of the new reps were presented with a pint or a half pint of piña colada, pints for men, halves for women. This had to be drunk in one go and anyone failing to do so had to empty the remnants over their head.

Brad helped Monty behind the bar. Monty smoked constantly. It was difficult to tell his age, but he had a full head of shoulder-length mousy hair and his features were ravaged by years of over-indulgence. He would not have looked out of place as a member of the Rolling Stones road crew. He kept Brad supplied with a constant stream of Snakebites. Brad made a point of keeping tabs on which girls were the most drunk.

Veronica had gone home the previous Saturday and he had been glad to see the back of her. Melanie had turned up at his room the previous night, and although Brad ignored her knocking on the door she would not go away. After five minutes he let her in. She had started to kiss him but he turned his back on her and went to sleep, farting loudly. That morning he had started shagging her five minutes before Lorraine arrived to get him for desk duty. She was early, which meant he only had to shag Melanie for a minute before calling a halt. Melanie had all but run out of money, and had dropped numerous hints to get Brad to let her tag along to the hippie market, but he ignored them.

The Molson Boys and Pit Bull and Co. were still there. They had been the life and soul for the first few days of the second week and had helped to persuade virtually all of the new arrivals to book the excursion block. Because of this, Brad slipped them the occasional free drink. Now they were gathered around Monty's fruit machine doing remarkably well out of it. Brad took a break from serving for some fresh air. The fruit machine was by the entrance and as he walked towards them Kempy nudged Will, who was playing it. They stopped putting money in and Pit Bull intercepted Brad. 'Brad, come over 'ere so I can get you a drink.'

Brad looked at him suspiciously. 'No, thanks. You should know by now that I get them for nothing.' He looked back over to the fruit machine. 'What's going on?'

'What do you mean?'

'Pit Bull, you've been here ten days. Every time you go anywhere near a fruit machine it spews out money quicker than you spew out bullshit.'

'I don't know what you're talking about,' said Pit Bull, fidgeting.

'*Crap!*' said Brad, almost laughing. 'I'll find out what you're up to anyway, mate, so you might as well tell me.'

'If I tell you,' said Pit Bull looking around nervously, 'you've got to keep it a secret . . .' He proceeded to tell Brad that they were going home with nearly two thousand pounds more than they had arrived with. They had some kind of device which seemed to revolve around a false coin and a piece of cotton. In the ten days they had been in Ibiza they had done almost twenty machines.

Brad walked out of the bar laughing at their audacity. Sitting on one of the walls that bordered the wasteland was a pale-looking Mario. 'What's up? You don't look too clever.'

'I'm not. That Monty's a fucking nutter. He keeps forcing whisky down my neck.'

'I know how you feel, mate. Even Alison's pissed.'

As if on cue she stumbled out of the bar, gin and tonic in one hand and cigarette in the other. She spotted Mario, headed towards him, and plonked herself on his lap and put her arms round his neck. 'Isn't he lovely?' She squeezed his cheek. 'How long were you a model for?'

'Oh, just a couple of years.'

'I bet you had girls falling at your feet,' she said.

'If you have much more to drink he'll have another one,' said Brad.

'Don't be silly, Brad,' replied Alison. 'I'm not in the least bit pissed. Isn't he just the most gorgeous man you've ever seen?'

'Excuse me, I think I'd rather Monty poisoned me with Snakebites than listen to you gushing all over him.' Brad made his way back to the bar. 'Give me a shout if your guide dog wants a bowl of water.'

Brad joined Mikey and Heather behind the bar. Three different football songs were being sung and the furore was occasionally punctuated with a glass breaking or a girl shrieking. Anarchy was looming. Brad looked at Mikey.

'I am fucking wrecked,' said Mikey. 'Where's Mario?'

'Outside with a very pissed resort manager sitting on his knee.'

'*No way!*' exclaimed Mikey. 'This I must see.' With that, he headed for the door.

During the course of the day Greg had introduced Brad to a new game. It involved going up to a girl, relieving her of her drink, and getting her to raise both arms in the air. She would then be instructed to lean forward, at which point her tits would be given a hearty slap. The male reps would give her marks out of ten for 'wobblability'. At Monty's it had got to the stage where girls were taking off their bras, demanding to be slapped and getting upset if they subsequently received a bad score.

As incredulous as Brad had been when Greg had demonstrated it to him, he had embraced the game as wholeheartedly as if it were his own invention. The two girls on whom Brad had first tried the wobblability test were mammarily challenged, both only scoring four out of ten, but they both had a wicked sense of humour. As they approached the bar now Brad noticed that they were well pissed. The first, who was called Clare, walked behind the bar, lifted up her top and said, 'I'm worth more than four out of ten. I want another go.'

Brad looked at Monty, whose eyes were popping out of his head. 'Sorry,' said Brad. 'The judge's decision is final.' She pulled her top down and started giggling. 'Unfortunately, as your rep, I can't be responsible for ruining friendships and I know if I touch your tits your friend will get jealous.'

'You won't get jealous, will you, Trudi?' said Clare.

'Yes,' said Trudi, laughing.

'See what I mean?' said Brad. 'If I'm going to have any kind of physical contact with you, it's going to have to be with both in even amounts.'

'You're all mouth,' said Trudi.

Brad walked into the kitchen at the back of the bar and beckoned them. Without saying a word, he started kissing Trudi and put his left hand up her T-shirt. Next he pulled Clare towards him. Before he kissed her he looked at Trudi and said. 'Just so I do things evenly, it was the right one I just squeezed wasn't it?' With that he put his hand inside Clare's vest and started kissing her. When he finished he looked at them both and said, 'We'll see who's all mouth.'

Monty had witnessed what Brad had been up to and sidled up to him. 'You're a fucking smooth bastard, and no mistake.'

He gave Brad another Snakebite, then went to announce a yard-of-ale challenge.

Rashid, of the Molson Boys, volunteered to go first. He took twenty-three seconds to finish the yard of San Miguel. Brad turned to Greg. 'Fuck doing that. Just looking at it makes me feel sick.'

'That's a shame,' said Greg. ' 'Cos one of us'll 'ave to do it in a minute.'

'No way,' said Brad. 'I'm close enough to puking as it is.'

'How do you think I feel? One of us *has* to do it.' Greg put his arm around Brad's shoulder and turned him towards the door. 'Come on, let's go an' see Mikey an' Mario outside. Maybe one of them'll fancy giving it a go.'

Outside, Brad put his hand on Mario's arm. 'Mario, me old mate, how would you like to get five bonus points?'

Mario looked at him suspiciously, and Mikey looked at him as if he had lost his marbles.

'What you on about?' asked Mario.

'One of us 'as to drink the yard of ale,' interjected Greg, before adding firmly, 'and there are *no* bonus points on offer.'

'After all we've already drunk you must be joking,' said Mikey.

'So I take it that there are no volunteers?' Greg was greeted with silence. 'That's what I thought. A game of spoof to settle it, then. Loser does the yard. Agreed?'

'If we're all feeling so sick, can I make a suggestion?' asked Brad. 'Something for the, um, unofficial brochure.' He went to his bag, took out his camera and handed it to Clare, who was standing by the door. 'Take a picture of us when I give the signal.' He walked back to the rest of the reps. 'Badges off for a team puke.'

'*What?*' said Mario.

'Have you got a better idea?' he asked. 'We've got another sodding bar crawl tonight and I'm sure Monty hasn't finished with us yet. I can't see that we've got any choice if we're not gonna pass out.'

The other three looked at each other before Greg said, 'He's right y'know.'

The four stood in a semi-circle facing Clare. They all took off their badges and stuck their fingers down their throats. Simultaneously they threw up and Clare took the picture.

A couple of minutes and a bottle of water later, they got down to the game of spoof.

'How do you play it?' asked Mario.

'We've all got three coins to start with,' said Greg. 'We put 'em be'ind our backs or in our pockets an' when we put 'em back in the middle we each 'ave either none, one, two or three. Then we each 'ave to guess 'ow many coins we're all 'olding in total. Got it?' Brad and Mikey nodded. Mario nodded too. 'Right then.' They all put their hands behind their backs then put their clenched fists back into the middle.

'So what do we do now?' asked Mario.

'You have to guess how many coins we've got in total,' said Brad. 'So if I've got two coins in my hand, Mikey's got one, Greg's got none and you've got three then the right answer would be six.'

'But I haven't got any,' said a confused Mario.

The other three groaned.

'You soft twat,' said Greg. 'Right, let's do it again.' Once again they put their fists into the middle.

'Six,' said Greg.

'Five,' said Mikey.

'Eight,' said Brad. They all looked at Mario.

'Seven,' he said.

'Right. Show,' said Greg.

Mario opened his fist to reveal three coins. Greg opened his and showed two, and Mikey had the same amount in his. They all looked at Brad.

'Oh, no,' he moaned, opening his empty hand.

Mikey laughed, and Greg screamed, 'Oh, you jammy, Italian, smarmy, fucking smeg-head. Go on, piss off back into the bar. You've won.'

After another three goes, Brad and Greg faced each other in the decider. Greg called first: 'None.'

'Brave call,' said Pit Bull, who had downed his yard in eighteen seconds and had come outside for some air.

'Why's it brave?' asked Clare.

'Because Brad already knows that Greg hasn't got any coins in his hand, so unless Brad hasn't got any either, then Greg's lost.'

Brad looked at Greg, his hand closed, saying nothing. Greg looked at him nervously. 'Come on, then, you big lump, gerrit over with.'

Slowly, Brad opened his hand. It was empty. Greg leapt into the air, before grabbing Brad by the arm to escort him inside.

Brad went behind the bar and took the empty yard from the previous competitor as soon as he had finished. He had to think quickly.

'I'll just give it a quick rinse,' he said, taking it through to the kitchen. Once out of sight, he got a litre of bottled water and poured it into the yard glass. When he returned to the bar, he put the glass quickly under the San Miguel tap so that it changed colour and looked like beer. By the time it was full, everyone in the bar knew that he was about to undertake the challenge and was rhythmically clapping and cheering. He made his way to the table and stood on it, saluting everyone like a latter-day gladiator, holding the yard aloft in one hand. Monty leapt on the table next to him and gestured for silence.

'Right, then,' said Monty. 'Eighteen seconds to beat. Who thinks he can do it?'

The response was a drunken cheer with a few obscenities thrown in. 'Right, then, Brad. Are you ready? Okay,' said Monty. 'Everybody. Three . . . two . . . *one!*'

Brad put the glass to his lips and started pouring, opening his throat. He had no concept of time and was mainly concerned with completing the task without humiliating himself. The yard emptied, and he put it down. He looked at Monty, who clicked his stopwatch. He grabbed Brad's shoulder and announced slowly, *'Eleven seconds!'*

The place erupted. The Molson Boys with Pit Bull and Co. made their way over to the table and hoisted Brad on to Pit Bull's shoulders. They paraded him around the bar and outside, singing 'We're Proud Of You' to the tune of 'Auld Lang Syne.'

At the end of the afternoon, not one sober person got back on the coach. The drivers hated this excursion and they only agreed to it on the proviso that YF&S supplied a cleaner to mop up the inevitable mess.

Mikey and Brad sat in the seats by the coach door and agreed to do the microphone between them. Mikey had everyone in stitches with his impressions. Brad could tell that he was getting more than a little annoyed with Alison who had once more begun to treat him as if he were a performing seal. 'Do your Richie Benaud . . . Go on, do your John Cole . . . Mikey, Mikey – do that black people talking stuff, what's it called again? Parrot? Pattie? No that's it, Patois. Go on, do that Patois thing.'

Mikey managed to keep his patience and got everyone going with a few singalongs. Brad left him to it. He was really getting into his stride, with fifty or so happy holidaymakers all joining in. After about fifteen minutes, Alison stumbled up the aisle and plonked herself on Brad's lap. 'Ere, Mikey, gi'us mic'phone. Wanna do song,' she slurred.

'Bloody hell, Al. You're pissed.'

'Don' say ahm pissed.' She stopped to belch loudly. Her breath stank of onions. 'C'mon, gi'us bloody mic'phone, I'll show you a song.'

Mikey handed it to her.

'Right, ev'one,' she screamed, then started singing, 'There's a bear that we all know, Yogi, Yogi, there's a bear that we all know Yogi Yogi bear. Yogi's got a little friend . . .' She stopped singing. 'Oh, what's his fu'in frenz name again?'

Although at first it was mildly amusing to see her so pissed, she soon became tiresome and clients at the back started yelling insults. Brad tried a couple of times to prise the microphone from her, but she was having none of it. Then he had a brainwave. 'Al, Mario wants to speak to you.'

Alison made her way unsteadily towards the back of the coach to where Mario was sitting next to a blonde girl, with his rep's bag on his lap.

'Ah, Mario, c'mon, move y' bag so y' resort manager can sit on y' lap.' Mario looked awkward. The girl next to him froze. 'C'mon. Wassup? 'Ere. I'll move it.'

Alison wrestled the bag from his grasp. Then she shrieked. The girl next to him was still grasping Mario's massive cock. Mario closed his eyes and pushed his head back against the seat, in the vain hope that when he opened them he would wake up to find that he had been in the middle of a horrible dream. Alison blustered her way back to her seat, still reeling from shock at the size of what the blonde girl had had in her hand. If she had been in two minds about sleeping with Mario before she certainly wasn't any more. She wanted that thing inside her.

The bar crawl was probably the most subdued of the season. Most of the clients who had been to the hippie market and Monty's did not make it. However, all the reps had to turn out, although Alison did not join them until their last port of call, the Star club.

Brad made a point of seeing Danny, the prop for Sgt Pepper's, to get half a gram of coke, which he shared with Mikey. He also got ten doves for Clare and Trudi. As the evening wore on he continued to wind them up about the threesome, but they didn't seem as keen as they had earlier.

Lester had been goading Mario all night. Mario could say nothing to persuade him that he had shagged Lorraine. In truth, Lester, Ryan and Paul were running out of money so the last thing they wanted was to give Mario a hundred pounds. Mario not only needed the money but did not want to lose face. He was still drunk from earlier in the day and he imagined Lorraine was too. He knew that the only way he could win the bet was to make heavy physical contact with her in front of them. This would mean forcing himself on her. Clearly, Lorraine would hate him afterwards, but Mario could live with that.

He sat at the bar watching her. He knew he'd have to be careful not to grab her anywhere near Brad or Mikey: they would come over to see what was going on and Lester would realise that Lorraine was an unwilling participant.

After careful, if drunken, consideration, Mario got off the bar stool, walked over to Lester and told him to stand about fifteen yards away from the ladies' toilets. He waited for Lorraine to go to the loo.

Nearly half an hour after Lester and his friends had taken up position, Mario almost missed his chance because he had his back to the loos. Lester had to point out that Lorraine was answering the call of nature. Mario walked over to the entrance to the ladies' toilets and waited for her to come out. Eventually she emerged. 'Lorraine.'

'Oh, hello, Mario. Still pissed?'

'Yeah. You?' Mario leant one arm up against the wall, blocking her path.

'Not as bad as I was.' A few seconds' awkward silence followed. 'Anyway, suppose I'd better get back. If you'll 'scuse us . . .'

'I'm sorry about this, Lorraine . . .' Mario grabbed her as tightly as he could and started kissing her. He held her arms so that her wrists hurt then forced one round his back and her hand on to his bum. He did not see Alison walk out of the toilet.

'Look, I've told you before, Lorraine,' he said, at the top of his voice for Lester's benefit, 'I'm not interested. Just leave me alone.' With that he swung on his heels and walked straight into Alison.

'Lorraine, Mario, what the hell is going on?'

'Ask him,' said Lorraine, almost in tears, which were partly born of rage. 'I was minding my own business when he grabbed me.'

'Mario?' said Alison, turning to face him.

'It's like I said before but I don't want to get anyone in trouble,' he said.

'So why did you grab me, you bastard?'

'Oh, come on, Lorraine,' said Mario. 'Alison's not stupid. She probably knows.'

'Knows?' screamed Lorraine. 'Knows what?'

'Calm down, Lorraine,' said Alison. 'Look at the state of you. You're showing yourself up and you're showing up Young Free & Single. Come and see me after desk tomorrow morning.'

Lorraine ran off sobbing.

'Sorry, Alison,' said Mario. 'I warned you. Thank God I did, or you might have thought I was coming on to her.'

'You must be joking,' laughed Alison. 'I'd like to think you had better taste than that.'

'Too right I have.'

'Come on. I'll get you a drink.' She walked away laughing. 'You and Lorraine. Ha, ha.'

As they went past Lester and his friends Mario dragged behind a little so he could whisper, 'Double or quits if I shag Alison. Whaddya reckon?'

'No free drinks. A straight two-hundred-quid bet, and then only if you can prove it beyond doubt,' said Lester.

'And how can I do that?' asked Mario.

'A picture. Or, better still, a video,' replied Lester.

'You're on.'

Brad spent most of his time that evening up at bar five. Kelly the Vision was there briefly, and he found out that Stella had gone back to the UK.

Clare and Trudi kept coming up to him. He could tell by the size of their pupils that they were well and truly up. They had decided to conduct their own wobblability test on Brad's testicles, squeezing or slapping them at every opportunity. Brad contemplated dropping a pill himself, but thought better of it when he remembered how much he had drunk that day and how much Charlie he had put up his nose. Consequently, by two thirty he was more than ready to leave. As he made his way out of the club, Clare and Trudi were dancing near the exit.

'Right, then, ladies. Looks like you've missed your chance 'cos I'm off.'

'Oh, you're not going, are you?' said Clare. 'Stay a bit longer. We're having a brilliant time.'

'Thanks all the same but I'm knackered.'

'Oh, don't go,' joined in Trudi. 'We've got loads of energy left.'

'Yeah, well, if you've got that much energy left you can walk me to the door.'

The two girls went either side of him and put their arms through his. When he got to the door he kissed them both on the lips and in a last-ditch effort said, 'If you change your mind about the threesome, I'm gonna have a quick cup of coffee.'

The two girls went back into the club.

Brad was feeling outrageously horny, and although he had avoided Melanie all day and all night, she suddenly entered his mind. She was going home on a flight at five thirty so if he hurried back he might just catch her for a quickie. He tossed around the idea for a couple of minutes before resigning himself to a night alone. Then as he waved goodnight to the doormen he noticed Clare and Trudi walking out arm in arm.

'Changed your minds, then, have you?' asked Brad, as they came towards him. The girls said nothing but each took hold of one of his arms. 'Oh, I get it,' said Brad, 'you're gonna get your own back by winding up poor old Bradley. Is that it?' Still the girls said nothing. 'Well, I'm getting a cab back, so if you want a lift you'd better be prepared to keep the wind-up going a bit longer.'

Brad hailed a cab and all three got into the back. Brad felt his mouth go dry. The last thing he wanted was to make a play for them and for them to start laughing and blow him out. He knew himself well enough to understand that once the blood started rushing to his groin, he would not have the usual control over his actions. The only thing he could do was carry on tongue-in-cheek.

'Who's going to go first, then? Have you decided yet or am I going to have to do you both at the same time? Oh, and there's one condition. I've got a fucking big spot on my bum, so if either of you start laughing then that's it.' They turned into the road in which the hotel was situated and he tapped the driver's shoulder. 'Here, please.'

They got to the bottom of the stairs. 'My room or yours?' Brad tried to appear indifferent.

'Well, we're going to our room. I don't know about you,' said Clare.

He was not sure what she meant by that. Did she mean that they were going to their room and he wasn't invited, or was it an invitation to a night of hedonistic pleasure? He had to find out.

'Well, I'd rather go to my room, but part of my responsibility as a rep is to make sure you get home safely, so I'll walk you to your door.'

They all went up to the second floor. The girls' room was the first door on the left. Once they were outside it and the moment of truth had arrived, Brad felt a little nervous at both possible outcomes.

'Well, come on, then,' he said finally. 'Invite me in. You know you're dying to.' Clare and Trudi looked at each other. 'Come on. If I'm gonna shag the pair of you I want to be sure before I do that you don't leave dirty underwear lying around.'

Clare opened the door and they walked in. The room was tidy, with two single beds. On the bedside table was a makeup bag with some birth-control pills poking out of it and a small hair-dryer connected to a plug adaptor. The two girls had said barely a word since leaving the Star.

Fuck it, thought Brad. Someone had to make the move. 'Tops off,' he said. 'We're going to have a proper wobblability test.' To his surprise, they both obediently removed their tops. 'Come on, then, you first,' he said, crooking his finger and getting Clare to come over.

He looked her in the eye and told her to bend towards him, which she did, keeping her eyes locked on his. Their noses were a matter of inches apart, so he grabbed her round the back of her neck, pulled her towards him and started kissing her. As he did so she fell on to the bed and he rolled on top of her, his hands exploring her underwear-free body. He stopped and beckoned Trudi over. With one finger still inside Clare, he used his free hand and his mouth to help Trudi remove the rest of her clothes. Once they were all naked, he got Trudi to grab hold of him and guide him into Clare. He was hoping that the two girls would indulge each other, but it soon became clear that their intentions were heterosexual. Brad could find little to

171

complain of, though, as he looked down and saw the two giggling girls swapping his bursting cock from mouth to mouth, with one of them slowly rubbing him as the other took it as deep as she could. They even started having their own competition to see who could get most of it in, the winner getting Brad's cock to herself for five minutes, which the other timed to the second.

One of the girls had a bottle of lubricant called Cyber-glide, with which they covered Brad. They then sat astride one of Brad's legs each, rubbing themselves into an orgasmic frenzy. Brad was grateful for the lubricant, because as they were doing this they were managing his cock and squeezing his balls with such ferocity that without it he would have had friction burns on his dick.

After the best forty-five minutes of Brad's life he had to come. The two girls sat upright on the bed leaning against the wall. Brad stood on the bed astride them both and brought himself to a shuddering climax. He had a habit of laughing as he came, but his orgasm was so strong that his laugh was more of a moaning yelp. He felt his knees shake, and he flopped on to the bed opposite.

'Oh, bloody hell, look,' Clare said suddenly, and pointed at a large dollop of freshly deposited semen. 'Why did he have to come over *my* bed?'

Brad sat quietly as the two girls got into a heated argument over who was going to sleep in which bed.

'Ladies, ladies!' he said eventually, getting up and sitting between the pair. He put his arms around them. 'You've made an old man very happy. If there's any chance of a repeat performance before you go home then I'm available when needed.' He kissed them, then walked out of the room with a spring in his step and a grin on his face. He was amazed at how light-hearted the whole thing had been. He had waited most of his sexually active life for what he had just experienced, and he wanted to tell the world.

For now, though, Greg and Mikey would have to do.

chapter eight

When Lorraine woke up her eyes were hurting, which confirmed that she had not been dreaming. Why had Mario grabbed her? What did he mean by 'she probably knows anyway'? She was confused. Part of her wanted to rush to Alison to discover what it was all about, but she had a horrible fear of facing her – just in case. She really, really did not want to lose her job. It had taken all her courage to apply to be a rep.

The thought of going back to that factory in Sutton Coldfield and folding boxes made her shiver. She loved this job. She was growing in confidence daily. She adored being with people, listening to them, helping them. It was as if her whole life had been leading to this. Another year in a different resort or maybe back to Ibiza. A year or two as a resort manager then a job in head office, maybe on the road or in training. Move to London. Everything had seemed so simple before Mario.

Nine a.m. Half an hour to go. No, Alison couldn't sack her. Once she'd explained . . .

The alarm started beeping. Nine a.m. She tried to ignore it. A nice lie-in. But then she remembered. Just what she bloody needed. She knew she should have arranged it for mid-afternoon. It was all Mario's fault, the bastard. She hadn't got home until nearby six. She had been so close to inviting him in.

She groaned. She had not had enough sleep to be able to make complicated decisions, to arbitrate, absorb facts, punish, reprimand or ignore. Screw being resort manager.

Half an hour to get ready. How the fuck was she going to decide what to do?

Brainwave. She reached on to the bedside cabinet and picked up a twenty-five-peseta coin. 'Heads she stays, tails she goes.' She spun the coin in the air.

Lorraine knocked on the door.

'Come in.'

It was only the second time that she had been in Alison's room. It was lovely and bright with a huge secluded balcony overlooking the beach. The french windows were open and the crisp morning sun filled the room, reflecting off the television with the satellite receiver on top of it. The room smelt feminine, although the clothes scattered everywhere reminded Lorraine more of her old boyfriend's flat. Bastard. Alison was just making some coffee.

'If you want some coffee I've only got black.'

'No thanks. I've already had some downstairs.'

'Suit yourself.' Alison even had a kettle. She poured the hot water into a cup with 'Boss' written on it. 'Sit yourself down.'

Lorraine had butterflies in her stomach.

'Right, then,' said Alison, drawing hard on her first cigarette of the day. It made her cough. 'What's it all about?'

'I haven't got a clue,' replied Lorraine. She was close to crying. 'What did Mario say?'

'Never mind what Mario said. I've already heard his side of the story. I'm more interested in what you've got to say for yourself.'

'I – I don't know, really. I mean, I still don't really know what happened.'

'Do you mean you don't know what came over you? You just felt like grabbing Mario in front of everybody. Is that it?'

'No – no of course not. And what do you mean? I didn't grab Mario.'

'Well, it certainly looked like it to me.'

'You think *I* grabbed *him*?' She started laughing. 'You must be joking! I wouldn't touch him with a barge-pole. He's – he's a creep.'

'A good-looking creep. Anyway, that's not what he says,' said Alison flatly.

'No way!' said Lorraine. 'I came out of the toilets and he just grabbed me. I haven't got a clue why.'

'Neither have I,' snapped Alison.

'Oh, Jesus. I see what this is all about now. You think I've been coming on to Mario. Is that it?'

'Basically, yes.'

'So why would you believe him rather than me?'

'I'd have thought that was obvious.'

'Not to me it isn't.'

Alison became more matronly in tone. 'Look, Lorraine, I can understand how you feel. Mario is good-looking and worldly wise. It's understandable that someone like you would fall for him.'

'I don't believe I'm hearing this.'

'But did you really think he'd see anything in you? Even if he wasn't constrained by the job. Come on, Lorraine, put yourself in my position. Mario even told—' Alison checked herself.

Lorraine pounced. 'Told you what? What's he been saying? Come on, tell me. What's that fucking bastard been saying about me?'

'Lorraine, Mario came and saw me before all this happened and told me you were coming on to him. And that "fucking bastard", as you call him, that creep stuck up for you.'

'I can't believe you've been taken in by all of this. I don't know what he's playing at, but please listen. I do not fancy Mario. Let's get him up here and find out what on earth he's up to.'

'I'm sorry, Lorraine, but that's not possible. Being resort manager is a tough job, and it involves making tough decisions. I've thought about this long and hard. I've carefully weighed up the facts . . .' she looked at the twenty-five-peseta coin that she had taken out of her bedroom '. . . and I'm afraid that on this occasion I believe Mario.'

'Oh, for Christ's sake,' sighed Lorraine. 'Well, I hope you know what you're doing because it's not going to be the best working environment for the next few weeks.'

'I'm aware of that, Lorraine.' Alison stood up and walked towards the balcony. 'That's why I'm sorry to say that we're going to have to let you go.'

'I beg your pardon?'

'I'm sorry, Lorraine. As you implied, one of you has got to go and I'm afraid it's you.'

'*WHAT?*'

'I've got you on a flight this evening. I'll give you all of the details later. Any Young Free & Single property will have to be returned to me by four o'clock or I won't be able to issue you with the ticket.' Lorraine started crying. 'I'm sorry, but you left me with no alternative. You know the rules about fraternising with other reps. As you said yourself, it would be impossible to work as a team. That's the very reason we have that rule.'

'But I *didn't* try to get off with him,' protested the sobbing Lorraine.

'Well . . .' Alison shrugged her shoulders.

'Please,' begged Lorraine, 'please get him up here so we can have this out face to face. *Pleeeease.*' She crumpled into the chair.

'Come on, Lorraine,' said Alison, 'this isn't doing either of us any good. I've got things to do. You don't want to have to pay for your own flight, do you?'

Lorraine looked up at her with red eyes. 'How can you do this to me? I've got nothing to go back to. You can't just sack me on a whim.'

'It's not a whim,' contradicted Alison, looking at the twenty-five-peseta coin again. 'I told you, I've thought about it long and hard.'

'Please, Alison, please give me another chance, I—'

'Oh, for heaven's sake, Lorraine, pull yourself together and stop acting like such a baby. It's only a job – to which you're not suited. Now, are you going to spend the rest of the day here or are you going to go and sort yourself out?'

Lorraine got up and ran for the door, still sobbing.

Alison picked up the coin. 'Tails, she goes.'

It was a beautiful morning and Brad felt as though he had been on a battery charger all night. Full of energy, he swam a few lengths before nine o'clock. Funny, though, he could have sworn he saw Lorraine walking through Reception as he got out of the deserted pool. She wasn't on desk that morning so there was no way she should have been up. Oh, well.

It was all he could do to stop himself standing on the edge of the pool and yelling out to all the balconies at the top of his voice, 'I slept with two women last night.' He dried himself off, had a croissant, and confused the early-risers with his over-enthusiastic good-mornings. He couldn't wait until desk finished so that he could run over to the Bon or the Delfin to tell Greg and Mikey.

Ten o'clock, and apart from the psychotic Rafael behind the bar, he was alone. He was looking through the information book when Lorraine came in crying.

'Lorraine, what's up?'

'Oh, Brad,' she said, running over and burying her head in his shoulder.

'Come on, darling, sit down and tell me what's wrong.'

Lorraine gasped for air between sobs and tried to compose herself. Brad reached over to the next table, took some napkins out of a glass and handed them to her to wipe her eyes. 'Better?' he asked. She nodded. 'So what's happened?'

'I've – I've just been sacked.'

'*What*? Why?'

'Oh, Brad, it's so unfair. I was in the Star last night. I came out of the toilet and Mario started talking to me. Then all of a sudden he grabbed me and started kissing me.'

'He what?'

'I know – I couldn't believe it either. Anyway, Alison sees the whole thing, and says she wants to see me this morning.'

'Hang on a minute.' Brad sat back in his chair. 'I've missed something here. Why have you been sacked?'

'Exactly!' said Lorraine. 'So I go and see the fucking bitch this morning to try and sort it out and she tells me she thinks *I've* been coming on to Mario.'

'No way.'

'Yep. So I'm denying it, but then it comes out that Mario has told her that I've been coming on to him *before* any of this happened.'

'Whoa. Now I am confused. Why would Mario do that?'

'That's what I can't understand.'

'I mean, you definitely didn't give him any indication—'

'No way,' interrupted Lorraine. 'I can't stand him and he knows it. But surely even he wouldn't be that vindictive.'

'I wouldn't have thought so,' agreed Brad. 'And why would he do it?'

'Beats me. He's been acting a bit funny round me this last week but . . .' Lorraine trailed off.

'Fuck it,' said Brad, standing up. 'You stay here. I'm gonna see Alison.'

'Who is it?'

'It's me – Brad.'

'What does he want?' Alison muttered. She opened the door and Brad marched in. 'Shouldn't you be on desk duty?'

Brad ignored her question. 'What's all of this nonsense with Lorraine?'

'And what exactly has it got to do with you?' Alison replied tersely.

Brad realised he'd have to soften his approach. 'Well, I've just had a very distressed Brummie crying her eyes out on my shoulder and I wanted to find out what's upset her. She said something about being sacked, which I found a little hard to believe.'

Alison sat down and lit a cigarette. 'She's been hassling Mario and last night I caught her forcing herself on him in front of clients. It left me with no choice.'

'You must be joking. Lorraine can't stand Mario. In fact none of us can.'

'Oh, I get it,' said Alison. 'That's what this is all about, isn't it? Mario told me that you and Mikey were always picking on him. If the pair of you were half as good at your job as him—'

Brad stood up. 'I don't give a monkey's about Mario. If you think he's super-rep then that's your lookout. All I know is that Lorraine wouldn't hurt a fly. All of the clients love her—'

'There you go again,' said Alison, raising her voice. 'You think you know so much about repping, don't you? How long have you been doing the job now? Four weeks? And you think you know more about what makes a good rep than I do.'

'I don't need to know about repping. What I do know about is people and I'm telling you now that *people* like Lorraine. She takes time to talk to them and isn't wrapped up in herself like some I could mention, and if you get rid of her this team won't be the same.'

'I know it won't be the same, and that's why I'm getting rid of her.' Alison smirked as if she'd just scored a winning point.

'Can't you give her another chance? How about if we get Mario up here and all sit down and discuss it?'

'You must think I was born yesterday,' said Alison. 'You and Mikey will threaten him and get him to say what you want him to say. Oh, no. I've made my mind up and that's it.'

Brad sat back in the chair. He looked Alison directly in the eyes, making her feel uncomfortable. 'What are you up to, Alison?' he asked. 'There's something that just doesn't add up. I can't believe that in your position you misjudge people so – so dramatically.' Brad thought he'd risk playing one of his aces. 'It just makes me wonder if running a happy resort is your main objective, or whether there's some kind of hidden agenda that I'm maybe, well . . . missing.'

'What do you mean by that?' snarled Alison.

'I dunno. You tell me.'

'How dare you! If I were you, I'd watch my step or Lorraine won't be the only one on a flight home.' She walked to the door and opened it. 'Now get out of here while *you*'ve still got a job.'

It was seven thirty in the evening. It was the first extraordinary meeting of the season and the first meeting to be held in Alison's room. By now all of the reps and most of the clients knew that Lorraine had gone.

No one had seen hide or hair of Mario all day, even though Brad had spent most of the day looking for him. The reps' mood was sombre. Brad's morning euphoria was forgotten – he'd not even bothered to tell Greg or Mikey about the eight points he'd scored the night before.

There was a knock on the door and Mario came in. Everybody looked at him, not smiling. He shuffled in and sat down next to Heather.

'Right,' said Alison, 'in case any of you don't already know, I've had to send Lorraine back to the UK today.' There was no reaction. 'It was not something I enjoyed and I had to do a lot of soul-searching, but the smooth running of this resort is the most important thing and for it to run smoothly rules have to be obeyed. One of those rules forbids fraternising between reps of the opposite sex. Lorraine chose to ignore this rule, which left me with no choice other than to terminate her employment.'

'So what did she do exactly?' asked Heather.

'I caught her in a compromising position with another rep.'

'Mario,' offered Brad.

'Brad!' snapped Alison.

'Go on, then, Mario,' Brad continued. 'Tell us what happened.'

Mario looked at Alison feebly for help.

'I don't think this is the time or the place . . .' interjected Alison.

'Oh, I don't know,' said Brad. 'I think we'd all like to know what Lorraine did to Mario that was so bad that she's on her way to the airport.'

There was a hum of agreement from the other three reps, and Alison knew that an explanation was now needed.

'Okay. I caught Lorraine kissing Mario against his will in the Star club last night in front of a load of clients.'

'How do you know it wasn't the other way round?' asked Mikey.

Mario laughed. 'You must be mad if you think I'd fancy that – that – thing.' Heather looked at him with contempt, which Mario noticed. 'What's up with you? You don't think I fancied her, do you? She was a pig.'

Heather looked away, shaking her head. Alison decided to give him some help.

'The thing that Mario isn't telling you is that he came to see me yesterday morning to tell me that Lorraine was coming on to him.' Alison noticed the horror on Heather's face. 'And before any of you say anything I had to drag it out of him and even then he tried to stick up for her.'

'I bet,' mumbled Mikey.

'Anyway, next week we'll have a new rep on resort. I'll tell you more at the weekend. As far as the clients are concerned, if anyone asks you just say she had to go back to the UK, nothing more, nothing less. If I hear anyone saying anything else they'll be joining Lorraine back in the UK. Okay?' There was a subdued murmur. 'Good. We've got the Dickens excursion tonight. There are two coaches – Heather, you guide one, Greg, you do the other. Mario, I want you to stay in San Antonio to do a merchandise stock

181

check. After the others have gone I'd like to have a word with you.'

Dickens was held in a large basement done out to resemble an old workhouse. There were rows of tables, attended by buxom serving wenches. The proceedings were overseen by a Mr Bumble character who was resplendent in town-crier garb, who made the holidaymakers yell for their food and their 'tankards of ale', and organised drinking competitions. The reps' main function during this was to encourage everyone to join in the sing-song and to prevent food fights.

None of the reps was in a particularly buoyant mood, and with no Alison to watch over them, they spent most of the latter part of the evening huddled around the bar talking about Lorraine. Afterwards they all went home apart from Greg, who went down the Star: a young Scandinavian had put him on a promise the night before.

He had been there about half an hour when Lester came up to him. 'Greg. Fucking great club, innit?'

'Yeah, it's all right,' replied Greg, looking around for the Scandinavian.

'I know that this probably isn't the best time to ask you and I know that we're going home on Saturday, but how do I get some money sent over?'

'Oh, it's not that hard.' Greg saw the Scandinavian girl and waved at her to indicate that she should meet him by the door. 'You've all run out of money, have you? You boys just don't know how to budget.'

'Oh, I don't need it yet. It's just that I want to get some pressies before I leave. We'd be all right if we didn't have stupid bets with the reps.'

'Ha.' Greg gave a token laugh, not really taking in what Lester had said. 'Well, that'll teach yer.' The Scandinavian was waiting by the door. 'If you look in the information book it gives details on how to get money sent over.'

'Thanks, mate,' said Lester. 'Probably see you Saturday.'

He went back to Ryan, Paul and the three girls they had been with all day. None of them knew that Lorraine had been sacked.

Alison had told Mario where the T-shirts were and instructed him to take them to his room at the Delfin to count them. She said she would join him later to check that everything was okay. She spent most of the evening in the Cockney Pride, winding up Trevor and getting pissed. At ten thirty she went to Mario's.

Mario had a gut feeling. It was the way she looked at him, some of the things she had said the night before when she was pissed, the way she touched him. He was sure that she was game on. And, for some reason, he thought that tonight might be the night. For the sake of pride and two hundred quid it had better be. He got the camera ready.

Lorraine felt as though she was in a dream. She had rung her mum and cried down the phone. Her mum had said not to worry. She had seen Mr Thomas earlier in the week and there was still a job in the factory for her. The flight was delayed by three hours. Estimated departure time was now just gone midnight.

She said she'd be there between ten thirty and eleven. Mario made sure that he was wet and wearing just a towel. He had prepared his eight-foot-by-ten-foot room. He had a single bed, a bedside cabinet, a chest of drawers and a wardrobe, on top of which was hidden the video camera, all ready to go. There was a knock at the door. He opened it and pretended to be flustered. 'Oh, it's you. I was just having a quick shower. I've finished the stock check.'

Alison feasted her eyes on his bronzed, hairless body. Although he didn't work out a great deal, he had a superb natural shape. Mario had played with himself a little in the shower, and his manhood was obvious through the towel.

Because she was pissed Alison allowed herself to look at him longer than she normally would have done. Mario was not the only one who was wet.

'I feel really bad about what happened today, Alison,' said Mario, rubbing his hair dry with a smaller towel. 'I feel like I put you in an awkward position, especially with Brad and that.' He walked over to the chest of drawers where there was an open wine bottle. 'Drink?'

'Yes, please.'

Mario poured the wine into two glasses. He gave one to Alison. 'Cheers.'

'Cheers,' she replied. 'Don't worry about Brad. It doesn't matter what he thinks. If he's not careful he'll be joining her.' Mario smiled at this comment. 'Anyway, you're enjoying the job, aren't you?'

'Oh, yeah. It's great. You've really helped.'

'Well, that's what I'm here for.'

Alison felt an almost uncontrollable urge to jump on Mario. She knew that she would have to make the first move or, at least, make it obvious how she felt. She didn't think Mario would risk his job by trying it on with her – not without a clear green light. It would have to be a one-off, and Mario would be easy enough to manipulate: one word and she would sack him. She remembered the size of his cock. Any minute now she would have him. She was going to do it! But how?

She didn't have to wait long for her opportunity. Mario brushed past her and as he did so his towel fell to the floor.

'Oh, shit,' said Mario, feigning embarrassment. He saw Alison's eyes head directly for his cock. She couldn't help herself. Slowly, she reached out and took it in her hand, pulling him towards her.

She flicked the end of his fast-growing cock with her tongue. 'If anyone finds out about this, Mario, I'll deny it and sack you.' She took as much of him in her mouth as she could, then rested it against the side of her cheek. 'And this is *not* going on the score sheet. Understood?'

'Loud and clear.'

'Good.' She put him back into her mouth and gave him a playful bite.

Within minutes they were both naked and Alison was on all fours. Mario was ramming her from behind. She reached for the bedside cabinet where there was some baby oil, and poured it between her buttocks.

'Fuck me in the other hole, Mario. See if you can get that gorgeous cock of yours up there.'

'What? Up your arse?'

Before he had a chance even to think about it she grabbed him and guided him in. She screamed with a mixture of pleasure and pain.

'Push, fuck you, *push*! Come on, I want you to ram it into me.'

Mario tried half-heartedly, but it slipped up the small of her back. Alison swung round so that she was lying on her back and Mario started pumping her in a more conventional fashion.

The window was open, and outside the sound of cars and drunken holidaymakers was joined by the roar of a jet as it passed overhead. At that moment, Alison came. Whenever Alison came she started to cry, a whimper that sounded like a dog pleading for its bone, appropriately enough. Mario pulled out and shot all over her stomach. As the jet's roar disappeared into the distance she thought it was a shame that she couldn't allow herself to screw him again. She looked at his travelling clock. Just gone midnight. She smiled at Mario. Maybe she could . . . She wiped a tear from her cheek. It was still a long season.

The plane banked left and roared over the island. The captain informed the passengers that San Antonio was to the right. Lorraine looked out of the window.

'Have you got the time, please?' asked the middle-aged man sitting next to her.

'Just gone midnight.'

She wiped a tear from her cheek. It had been a short season.

Once again Brad was doing the last flight. He had not been able to sleep so he went over to the Bon. It was one o'clock in the morning. Mikey and Greg were sitting at a table both eating pie, chips and beans. Brad had already eaten at Las Huertas, so he just ordered three beers. It was two days since Lorraine had left. Mario had been keeping out of everyone's way, but on the few occasions Brad had seen him he had seemed even more pleased with himself than normal.

When Greg finished his meal he went through the up-to-date scores. Brad had been on a roll and the threesome had helped put him in joint first place with Greg on thirty-four points. Mario was now on twenty-eight, and Mikey had been through a relatively barren period, only increasing his tally to twenty-six.

Brad had been there for about ten minutes when Lester came up to Greg. 'I got that money sorted out.'

'What money was that, then?' asked Greg, on auto-rep.

'Remember I told you I might need to get some money sent over?'

'Oh, yeah, yeah, that's right.' Greg had a distant recollection of the conversation.

'Yeah, popped into the Delfin. Got Mario to sort it out. Then again, I suppose it was in his interest.'

'Yeah, right.'

Lester persisted, 'Where's Lorraine? I haven't seen her about lately.'

'She got the sack,' said Brad, with a hint of anger in his voice.

'Oh, you're joking,' said Lester. 'I really liked her.'

'You're not the only one,' said Brad.

'The boss saw her coming on to Mario down the Star club,' said Mikey.

The colour drained from Lester's face. 'You're joking.'

'I wish he was,' said Brad.

'Oh, shit.' Lester looked skyward. 'Oh, fucking shit. Oh, I don't believe it. That wasn't meant to happen.'

All three reps stared at Lester, suddenly interested in every word he had to say.

'What do you mean, "wasn't meant to happen"?' said Brad, leaning forward.

'It – it was just a bit of harmless fun, a bet. I didn't think it would go that far. Oh, fucking hell . . .'

'What bet?'

'We bet Mario a hundred quid that he couldn't shag Lorraine. We just wanted to shut him up 'cos he was giving it the superstud bit. I've got the money here.' Lester got out an envelope. 'If he'd been here I was going to give it to him, but seeing as he isn't, well . . .'

Brad was speechless with rage.

'What you're saying,' said Mikey, 'is that you had a bet with Mario, and the bet was whether or not he could shag Lorraine. Is that right?'

'Basically, yeah, but—'

'And to prove it, he grabbed Lorraine in front of you?'

'Yeah. He said he'd get a video or something first, but that was the next best thing. Course, when Alison caught him we just assumed . . .' Lester saw the look on Brad's face and decided it would be prudent to say no more.

'So Lorraine got the sack because Mario didn't speak up. Just for a poxy 'undred quid that 'e's not gonna get anyway,' said Greg, summarising the situation.

This was too much for Brad. 'CUNT!' he screamed at the top of his voice, turning the table over and sending glasses flying everywhere. All of the ready-to-depart holidaymakers looked up. 'FUCKING ITALIAN SHIT TOSS WANKING CUNT!' He had lost it. 'I'M GONNA FUCKING KILL HIM!' Brad stormed out of the apartments, heading for the Delfin.

Heather had been sitting outside and heard the commotion. She ran in. 'Heather,' said Mikey, 'look after this lot.' He turned to Greg. 'Come on, mate. We've got to stop him before he does something stupid.'

They both took off after Brad. He was already halfway to the Delfin. Mikey sprinted and overtook him.

'Brad, stop.'

'GET OUTTA MY FUCKING WAY.'

Mikey was in a quandary. He could see in Brad's eyes that he had lost the plot, and Mikey didn't fancy a set-to with him. But he had to stop him. He ran at Brad from about ten yards and used an American football block to pin him against the wall. Before his friend had a chance to react he started talking. 'Brad, listen to me. If you don't agree with what I have to say I'll let you go and I'll even come down there and we'll do the fucker together.'

Brad stopped struggling and looked him in the eye.

'Look. Whatever you do, Lorraine isn't going to get her job back. If we do Mario over, especially after your performance in front of all of the clients, then we'll both get fired. We might even get nicked. You don't want to end up in a Spanish jail, do you? Come on, Brad. Think about this. We won't let him get away with it but let's think our revenge through, let's be clever about this. We don't even have to let him know that we know. Let's just use the information to get back at him and that slag Alison as well if needs be. Yeah? Come on, mate, calm down.'

Greg joined in. 'He's right, Brad. Filling Mario in won't achieve anything. Besides, I can't let you get the sack 'cos I'll 'ave no competition with the ol' scoreboard.'

'Come on, man,' pleaded Mikey. 'He's not worth it.'

Mikey could feel Brad relaxing so he let him go.

Brad turned and punched a solid wood door. The bang echoed around the empty streets and he cut two of his knuckles.

'You all right?' asked Greg.

'Yeah, sorry. Guess I was a bit of a knob.'

'I wouldn't say that,' said Greg. 'But Mikey's right.'

'You better go and see to that hand,' said Mikey.

They were only twenty yards from Las Huertas, so Brad

slipped in to clean himself up. Greg and Mikey continued to walk towards the Bon.

'Fucking 'ell,' said Greg. 'I wouldn't like to gerron the wrong side of 'im.'

'I've seen people go like that before,' said Mikey. 'They don't know what they're doing until it's all finished. Fuck me, if that's what the job does to you maybe Lorraine's the lucky one.'

'No, lad,' said Greg. 'There's a lorra good bits to come yet.'

chapter nine

Jane Ward was stressed. It was always the same at this time of the season. The middle of June and already five new reps had either left or been sacked. Tom Ortega had just got back from Majorca, where he had gone to investigate Jason Barnes. When he had got there Barnes had already left, taking twenty-five thousand pounds of excursion money with him. To top it all, a tabloid journalist had been hassling Jane all week for the story. She had denied all knowledge of it, but now in front of her, on page seven of the *Daily Star*, was the headline '*Majorca's Missing Millions – Young Free & Single Manager disappears with over 5 million pesetas.*'

'I'd love to get my hands on the Judas who leaked this story. I don't suppose you've any idea which reps have been blabbing?'

'To be honest,' said Tom, 'I'm not even sure it was one of our reps. You know what it's like out there. Everyone knows what everyone else is doing. Might have been a rep from another company or even Kirstie.'

'Or Jason himself for that matter, the bastard.'

'Can we prosecute him?' asked Tom. 'Assuming he ever turns up.'

'Not really. We'd have to do it through the Spanish courts, which would take for ever and cost a fortune. Then there's the problem of proving how much he took. You know as well as I do that we don't declare all the money we get from excursions.'

'So basically he's got away with it, then?'

'Basically.'

Tom whistled. 'Twenty-five grand. I wonder where he'll go with that.'

'Well if he's got any sense he'll get out of Majorca,' said Jane.

Tom changed the subject. 'How's Natalie getting on working for the lovely Alison Shand in Ibiza? She's been out there over a week now, hasn't she?'

'As far as I'm aware she seems to be doing fine,' Jane replied. 'Anyway, what do you mean, "the lovely" Alison Shand? Do I detect a note of sarcasm? What's she done to upset my wee laddie?'

'Oh, nothing,' sighed Tom. 'It's just that every time I speak to her on the phone I get the impression that she doesn't like me.'

'You sound a bit paranoid – not been out clubbing again at the weekend, have we? On a bit of a come-down?' She flicked a rubber band at him.

'It's not just me,' continued Tom. 'It seems as though she's none too keen on Brad either.'

'Really?' Jane raised her eyebrows. 'Now, that does surprise me. Mind you, I was disappointed with Lorraine. I thought she'd do really well – such a sweet girl. It just shows you never can tell.'

'Yeah, but come on, Jane. Mario's a good-looking bastard and Lorraine was rather plain.'

'Even so, Tom, she seemed so level-headed. I was sure she'd complement the team perfectly, but there you go.'

She was interrupted by the phone ringing. It was Adam Hawthorne-Blythe, the chairman. 'Yes, I've seen it. No idea – it could've been anyone . . . . Even him, yes. No one seems to know . . . Neither am I, Adam. . . . . No, but I'll be going to see Sebastian in a few minutes . . . Yeah, sure. As soon as I hear anything . . . No, you can if you want . . . Well, that's what I thought. If it doesn't blow over one of us will have to. Okay, Adam, thanks. Yeah, 'bye.'

'Has he heard about the death in Tenerife?'

'Not yet,' said Jane. 'One thing at a time, eh, Tom? Jesus,

what is it with Tenerife? Two deaths in as many weeks. Plus that one in Crete and it's not even July until next week.'

'What was the full story in Tenerife?' asked Tom.

'Apparently when the maid opened the door, the client ran for the balcony and jumped. Splattered himself about ten feet away from a load of our lot lying on their sunbeds.'

'Did he know he was six floors up?'

'I think so.'

'Must've been a fucking ugly maid.'

Brad had made a point of staying out of Mario's way. It was all he could do to stop himself letting Mario know that he was aware of the bet with Lester. But Mikey was right. Lorraine was gone and nothing he could do would get her back. Besides, Natalie had replaced her. Revenge on Mario was about to be meted out surreptitiously.

Natalie was a nice girl, who reminded Brad of a female Greg – not interested in resort politics and just there for a good time. From the day she arrived Brad and she had spent nearly all their time laughing or taking the piss out of each other, which was made easier for Brad by Natalie's penchant for Spanish men. She had been in Ibiza just under two weeks but had slept with one of the waiters at the Rodeo Grill, then the son of the owner of the Bon, who worked in the supermarket, and a barman from Sgt Pepper's. She was a bubbly blonde Geordie, who could laugh at herself.

Brad took the key from behind the desk of the Delfin and crept up the stairs towards Mario's room. When he got there he knocked on the door, just in case. No answer. He put in the key and opened it.

'Mario?' he whispered.

Silence. Brad closed the door. He walked into the bathroom and picked up Mario's green bottle of Wash 'N' Go. Carefully, he removed the top, took a bottle of Immac hair remover out of his pocket and poured the contents into the shampoo bottle. 'Vidal Sassoon – Wash 'N' Gone.'

The invoice had been picked up some weeks before by a cleaner. She had placed it with a pile of other papers. A few minutes later she had picked up the Post-it note and thrown it into the bin.

Sebastian decided to clear his desk. Things had been piling up. It was the first Monday in July – the perfect day for a sort-out. By eleven thirty he had worked his way through most of the clutter. He loosened his tie and ran his fingers through his thick black hair, before picking up the sole remaining A4 sheet of paper on his desk. An invoice. After four and a half hours he was dealing with invoices on auto-pilot.

'Chamberlain Clinic,' he mumbled. 'What on earth is this for?' In the 'Invoice to' box, there was no name, only a customer number. He took off his reading glasses and banged them against his teeth. After a few minutes' deliberation, he dialled the clinic's number.

A well-spoken female voice answered. 'Good morning, Chamberlain Clinic. How can I help you?'

'Oh, hello, I'm just about to settle an invoice, number . . . six, two, one, seven, four, and I was won—'

The receptionist interrupted. 'I'll put you through to the right department.'

Two rings and another female voice answered. 'Accounts.'

'Hello, yes, I'm about to settle an invoice.' He gave her the number.

'Is that Mr Gomez?'

Sebastian was taken aback. 'Uh, yes.'

'How can we help you, Mr Gomez?'

'Well,' said Sebastian, stretching the word out to give himself time to think, 'for my company records I need a more detailed breakdown on the invoice of what the treatment was for. You know, tax deductible and all that.'

Just at that moment Jane walked in. Sebastian beckoned her to a chair.

'That shouldn't be a problem, Mr Gomez. Oh, hang on a minute.' Sebastian heard some murmuring. 'Well, I've heard of creative accounting in my time, but I think the taxman might have something to say about this one.'

'Why?'

'Well, you'd better get yourself an accountant, Mr Gomez. Only make sure he's good – he'll have to be if you want to claim tax back on a termination.'

'A *what*?' Sebastian stood up.

'Hold on a moment, that is Mr Gomez, isn't it?'

'What? Yes, yes. Look I'm sorry, must go. Someone's just come in. 'Bye.' Sebastian hung up.

'What on earth was all that about?' asked Jane.

'Oh, you'll not believe this.' Sebastian sat back in his chair and stared out of the window. 'I've just found this invoice on my desk from a private clinic. Do you know what it's for?' Jane shrugged. 'An abortion.'

'Oh, God, no!' Jane exclaimed.

'It gets better. Guess who put it through?'

'It wasn't Felipe "Leather Office" Gomez, by any chance?' Sebastian looked at her as though she had revealed a psychic talent. Jane looked at him sheepishly. 'Oh dear.'

'How did you . . . ?'

'Oh, Sebastian, I feel so stupid.'

'Don't tell me it's you,' he said.

'No, it bloody wasn't me!' said Jane indignantly.

Sebastian held up his hands. 'Sorry.'

'I got an anonymous call last week telling me Felipe Gomez was having an affair with someone who works for Young Free & Single. She didn't say who, though.'

They sat and looked at each other.

'What I don't understand,' said Sebastian, breaking the silence, 'is why would he try to put it through the company?'

'And more to the point, *who* it was for, now we've established it wasn't me,' Jane added sarcastically.

'I've said I was sorry.'

'Hmph,' said Jane. 'Well, anyway, we know it's not his wife – she's about fifty.'

'Let's find out a bit more, then.' Sebastian picked up his phone and dialled Felipe's extension.

'Felipe. It's Sebastian.' They never exchanged pleasantries, so Sebastian got straight to the point. 'It's about this Chamberlain Clinic invoice.'

'Ah, yes. I'm glad you've called, although I thought you would a couple of weeks ago.'

'Yes, well, I've been very busy.'

'Quite, quite, never mind. Is there a problem?' asked Felipe, spoiling for a fight. 'I thought there might be. That's why I put the Post-it note on it asking you to call me so I could answer any queries.'

So that was it. Sebastian smiled to himself. The Post-it note had obviously become detached from the invoice. He would have to play this by ear – let Felipe do all the talking.

'You see, Sebastian, my eyes have been deteriorating over the last year or so – I guess it's all those contracts I read.' Felipe enjoyed slipping that one in. 'During the winter I had corrective laser eye surgery, and I thought that it would be appropriate for me to put it through the company?'

'So the invoice is for eye surgery?'

'Yes,' lied Felipe. 'Will there be a problem?'

'Um, no. Well, there shouldn't be.' Sebastian was thinking as he spoke. 'I tell you what, Felipe, if there is I'll come back to you.' He hung up.

'What the hell is he up to?' Sebastian stood up and walked round the room. Then he looked at Jane and handed her the phone. 'So much for eye surgery. Do you fancy finding out who the lucky woman was?'

'What shall I say?' said Jane, taking the phone. Sebastian looked at her blankly. Her eyes lit up. 'I know.' She dialled.

'Chamberlain Clinic.'

'I wonder if you can help me. I had a termination last summer but the invoice has been sent to the father's address rather than mine.'

'Oh, no!' said a concerned voice. 'I'm so sorry.'

'No, it's our fault – we should have said at the time. The thing is I've moved since then and I wasn't sure whether or not you had my old address or my new one.'

'Hang on and I'll check for you. What's the invoice number?' Jane gave it. There was a pause. 'The address we've got is the one in Cambridge. Is that right?'

Jane was hoping that the woman would read it out but she didn't. Now what? She couldn't very well ask for her own address. 'No, I've moved.' She gave the address of an old university friend.

'We'll get a copy off to you today.'

'Thanks.' Still no name. Jane had failed. 'Thanks a lot. Goodbye.'

'Goodbye, Miss Shand.'

chapter ten

It had been nearly a year since Tom Ortega had last visited Ibiza. He had been working for YF&S only three months when Jane Ward had sent him over to get a feel for what repping was like on resort. At the time, Jason Barnes was the senior rep, under Kirstie who was resort manager. Tom had been standing in Reception at the Bon when he heard a girl ask Jason if he thought he could manage her *and* her mate. Unable to believe his ears, Tom had turned around. The girl noticed him and spotted his badge. 'Are you a rep too?' she had asked.

'Uh, sort of,' Tom had replied nervously.

'You're not bad-looking, really, are you?' Tom remembered feeling embarrassed. 'Yeah, I think I'll have you by the end of the week.'

She fulfilled her threat that same night.

Since then Tom had made over a dozen resort visits and in that time had realised his potential with the opposite sex. He had inherited his Spanish father's thick black hair, brown eyes, and six-foot frame, his mother's Roman nose and refined English accent. That combined with an easy-going personality meant that every resort visit so far had brought him ample female attention.

Tom was aware that he had changed during the last year. His confidence had improved and he now had no qualms about using this authority to discipline reps. This meant that the reps were pretty much divided as to whether or not they liked him. Most thought he was fine, but the rest decided he was a jumped-up egomaniac from head office with ideas above his station. Brad fell into the former camp, Alison the latter.

About half a mile before coming into San Antonio, both sides of the road are lined by trees only a few feet apart. As well as giving motorcyclists and the odd reckless driver the perfect opportunity to become terminally at one with nature by crashing into them, they also form a natural tunnel. Even in the middle of summer only a flicker of sunlight penetrates their canopy. Tom drove through the tunnel, and squinted as the trees gave way to sunlight and there was San Antonio: some people's idea of heaven, and others' vision of absolute hell. It struck Tom that maybe heaven and hell are indeed the same place; all that is different is the individual's perception and expectations.

Tom drove past the roundabout which had a giant white sculpted egg sitting in the middle of it. Apart from a nightclub called Extasis and a hotel called Piscis Park, this is the first thing visitors see as they come into San Antonio harbour. The harbour boasts a recently renovated promenade that overlooks the departure point for boats taking holidaymakers to local beaches. At the back of the promenade is a row of restaurants, where semi-interested diners watch a fountain-and-lights display between trying to find the English page of their menu, hoping it contains something other than 'bloody foreign muck'.

Tom remembered to be careful driving his hired Renault Clio along the promenade road. Even during the day, drunk or daydreaming jaywalking Brits would forget that the Spanish drive on the right. Most locals were aware of this and drove to accommodate them.

Tom successfully negotiated the promenade and drove a little faster as he came to the back of town. It was just coming up to seven thirty, so most of the people he saw in the bars were families or teenagers who had yet to realise that the bars did not ring last orders before eleven o'clock. He thought about making a detour to Café del Mar to check out the quality of female workers and what type of pills were on offer. Instead, he decided that a shower would probably improve his later social standing.

For once Brad had been given an early flight transfer. The plane was due to arrive at nine p.m. so he was in the coach and ready to go at seven thirty. Once satisfied that everyone was on board he made his way to the front and turned to the coach driver. 'Okay, José, *vamos*.'

José started the engine and closed the door.

Sitting at the front of the coach was a girl from Stoke called Angela. Two nights before, she had come to Brad full of Dutch courage and told him that he had promised to sleep with her. Brad couldn't remember but, chivalrous as ever, obliged her that selfsame night. What he didn't know at the time was that Angela was the type of girl who religiously videoed *Little House on the Prairie* and always made sure that she listened to Simon Bates's Our Tune. A hopeless romantic, happiest with a wet handkerchief, she was now certain that Brad was her Antony and she his Cleopatra. However, the only 'infinite variety' Angela possessed was a huge repertoire of annoying habits that Brad had tired of after one night. She had been pestering him ever since and had told everyone else that he was her boyfriend.

In fact, she had caused him so much grief during the last two days that he wanted to get his own back. Not nastily – in fact, he thought she'd probably enjoy what he had in store for her, in her own perverse way – but she was the perfect candidate for Greg's new competition.

Brad finished his usual spiel about passports, the reunion and how to check in at the airport, switched off the microphone, turned to José and nodded. José started a stopwatch. Brad switched the microphone back on. 'So that's all the information you should need at the airport. All that remains is for me to thank you once again for being such a great crowd and, as we drive out of San Antonio, I hope you've all got some wonderful memories to take home with you.' He gazed out of the window: the harbour looked fantastic as the low sun and the bar lights reflected off the water. He tried to sound as slushy as possible. 'I'm sure you'll all agree that this island can be a magical place. Maybe some of you have met the boy or girl of your dreams and fallen in love, so if you have, I hope it works out for you.' He glanced at Angela. Almost.

'Like I said before, you've been the best crowd ever and I'm going to miss you all and maybe I'll see some of you again one day.' He paused. Surely that would do it? Not quite. 'Anyway, for once in my life I'm going to shut up and let the music do the talking.'

He put in a cassette and 'When Will I See You Again' started playing. If that didn't work he was sure that 'Leaving On A Jet Plane' would do the trick. He hoped so – he'd spent a good couple of hours at the Anglers making up a tape of the slowest, slushiest songs with references to leaving or lost love that he could find. Within the first four bars of the song he heard a sniffle. Sure enough, it was Angela. He turned to José.

'Jose, amigo, how long?'

'Fifty-three seconds,' replied José.

'Yes!'

Brad sat back smiling. Even Greg was going to have to go some to beat that. A blubber in less than a minute – it had to be a record.

Tom had a quick shower and got himself ready to meet Greg in the bar at midnight. Alison had allowed Greg the night off from airport duty so that he could escort Tom around town. She considered Tom's visit a minor irritation – she had no intention of spending any more time with him than necessary.

Tom was in the bar before Greg. Cases were piled in the hallway ready for the arrival of the coach to take their owners to the airport. Twenty or so subdued clients were sitting outside the Bon with the last drink of their holiday in front of them. Most were dressed in shorts and a T-shirt. Before joining YF&S Tom had worked at Gatwick airport and it had never failed to amaze him how holidaymakers returned home dressed in attire more suited to the climate of their place of departure. When Tom had left London this time it had been cold and raining, hardly T-shirt and shorts weather.

He chatted to Frank in English while he was waiting for Greg. From the day he had joined YF&S Jane had told him to keep his linguistic skills to himself. That way she reckoned he might be able to pick things up from hotel staff or resort managers, who assumed he could not speak the language. Tom knew that Alison and the other reps apart from Mikey spoke hardly any Spanish but he kept to English anyway.

Just after midnight Greg walked in. When he saw Tom his face broke into a broad grin. 'All right, mate?' he said, shaking Tom's hand.

'Not bad, thanks. What you been up to?'

'Oh, plenty of caning. Over forty points now.'

Tom had been introduced to the points competition the year before by Jason Barnes. Greg had also been in Ibiza that year, and Tom remembered how vigorously he had pursued first place.

'What have you got in store for us tonight?' Tom asked.

'Well, I thought we could go an' 'ave a look at a rather interesting church near San Augustine, then maybe go to a flamenco recital, per'aps rounding off the evening with a cup of coffee an' a chat about airport procedure. On the other 'and, we could go into town, get pissed for nowt an' try to pull a couple o' slappers. What d'ya reckon?'

'Let's leave the cultural bit till tomorrow, eh?' Tom knocked back his drink.

Sgt Pepper's was where Tom and Greg chose to commence their crawl. When they walked in, Ray the piano-player/singer, remembered Tom instantly. November had seen the YF&S reunion held at what used to be a Butlin's holiday camp, but was now a modernised 'holiday centre' and Ray had been one of the acts booked to play there. On the first night he had shagged a very pissed client in Greg's chalet, at the same time and along with Greg and Tom.

'So you gonna do the reunion again this year?' asked Tom, once they had all toasted each other and downed a Jägermeister in one.

'Aye lad. Mind you, I'm trying to make sure me bird don't come after last year.'

'Of course,' said Tom. 'You're going out with that page-three girl now, aren't you? Cheryl Pitt, isn't it? Or should that be Cheryl Fit?'

Ray laughed. 'Yeah she's certainly that. Definitely better than that monster we all shagged at the reunion.'

'Yer right there,' said Greg. 'The thing that got me, though, was turning round and seeing old Barnesy in the corner wanking 'imself off. Remember? I asked 'im if 'e wanted a go and 'e just said—'

'Carry on, I'm 'appy 'ere,' finished Ray.

They all laughed. 'How is old Jason? He's boss in Majorca this year, in't he?'

Tom shuffled uncomfortably. 'He was. I had to go over there to sack him.'

'Why?' asked Ray.

'Well, as it turned out he beat me to it – already done a bunk. I thought you'd've heard about it,' Tom said. 'He scarpered with about twenty-five grand of company money.'

Ray whistled. 'Dodgy bastard.'

'You can say that again.' He took a swig of beer. 'So what do you think of the new reps? Getting on all right with them?'

'Yeah, not bad. Mikey's safe. Brad's a nice bloke – I let 'im get on the ol' piano sometimes. That new bird . . . Natalie?' Tom nodded. 'She's a fuckin' nutter. I think she's already 'ad one of the barmen.'

'What about Mario?' asked Tom innocently.

'I'm going for a quick slash. Fuck off when we get back?' said Greg.

'Yeah, sure,' said Tom, glancing at his half-empty bottle. 'Yeah, so what about Mario?' he asked again.

'Less said about 'im the better,' said Ray. Tom said nothing, and Ray knew he would have to elaborate. 'Let's just say we didn't gerr off to the best o' starts, an' if it weren't for Mikey I would've probably decked him.'

'What happened?'

'I'll leave it at that,' said Ray, finishing off his drink. 'I've got to get up and do me bit. Good to see you again, Tom. I'll catch up with y' later.' He saw Greg come out of the toilet and mouthed, 'Later,' at him as he got on stage.

As Tom and Greg left the bar, Tom asked, 'What was all that nonsense between Mario and Ray at the start of the season?'

'What did Ray tell you?' asked Greg.

'Not a lot really. Is everything okay now?'

'Mario's not 'is bosom buddy if that's what yer mean. But Ray's too professional to let it affect the way 'e does 'is job so 'e tolerates 'im.'

'So what the fuck did Mario do?'

'What did 'e do?' Greg laughed. 'Let's just say that Mario isn't exactly the most popular rep on the island. Come on, let's go in to Rainbow.'

This season the Rainbow hosted non-stop karaoke and as Tom and Greg walked in, another tour company was in the middle of a bar crawl. It was nowhere near the size of a YF&S bar crawl and the reps were not used to entertaining. It amused Tom how reps from mainstream companies would try to copy YF&S, getting the younger members of the party out on crawls or certain excursions. He often recognised the reps as candidates who had failed YF&S interviews. The result was normally a shoddy, unprofessional imitation of a YF&S night out.

Tom and Greg left the Rainbow after their first drink. 'I

dunno about you, mate, but I've had enough of drinking,' said Tom.

'Leave off. I've only just started,' said Greg.

'What about getting a couple of pills?'

'You mean Es?'

'Yeah, fancy it?'

For once, Greg looked almost bashful.

'Come on,' said Tom. 'You're a rep – you must know where to score some pills.' They stopped in the road outside a Scandinavian bar called Mermaid.

'Yeah, I do. It's just that, well, I've never – you know. It's not that . . .'

'Greg,' said Tom, 'stop waffling. What's the problem?'

Greg shuffled uncomfortably. 'I've never taken Ecstasy before.'

'You're joking!'

'No. I've always been 'appy with the ol'grog.'

'Oh, mate, you don't know what you're missing. You've got to try one.'

'Nah, I'll stick to the beer.'

'Why, Greg? What you scared of?' Tom found it hard to believe that a supposedly streetwise Scouser had never taken an E.

'I just don't fancy it. Come on, let's 'ave a drink in 'ere.'

They went into Gorm's Garage, a long bar with a DJ that held about three hundred people. It was frequented by all the tour companies on their bar-crawl nights. It was a melting-pot of Brits, Germans and Scandinavians. Despite this, there was seldom any trouble, mainly because it had a reputation as a ravey dance bar rather than a drinkas-muchasyoucanandfallover- bar. Greg ordered two beers before Tom had a chance to refuse. Because it was so busy they took them outside.

'I'm not trying to turn you into a junkie, you know, Greg,' Tom said.

'I know you're not. It's just that no one seems to know for sure what they do to you.'

'Maybe not, but I sure as hell know that booze fucks up your brain, liver and kidneys, as well as making you fat and antisocial. Give me Es any day.'

'What about if I 'ad an allergic reaction?' said Greg.

'There's more chance of having one to peanuts or tomatoes.'

'I still don't know . . .'

'Look. Just take a half to start with – I'll keep my eye on you.'

'I'm not sure,' said Greg. 'What was that bit about sex again?'

'It's fucking brilliant. Your whole body is like one big, fucking erogenous zone. It's almost impossible to come, and when you do . . .' Tom made an explosion-type noise.

Greg sat still for a moment or so. Suddenly he stood up and downed his drink in one. 'Fuck it. Let's go an' gerra couple.'

'Attaboy,' smiled Tom.

At the bottom of the main hill in San Antonio's West End is the Night Life club. A pretty girl with sunkissed curly brown hair was herding the constant flow of people inside.

Ninety per cent of the drunk or drugged males she addressed were convinced she fancied them. But Maddy was immune to looks, chat-up lines, pheromones or designer clothes while she was working. She was on auto-pilot. The only time she injected a mild dose of enthusiasm was when the bearded, bespectacled manager came scurrying out to check that the other bars were not doing any better than Night Life. Even if Night Life was full he was on her case: 'Maddy, plenty other girls want to work here.'

And, of course, he was right. Even though it was seven hours a night for little more than the equivalent of fifteen pounds, at least four young people came in every night asking for work. The main thing Maddy had in her favour was that she had worked there the previous season and she knew that Toni (the manager) didn't want to let her go because she was good at her job and had showed resilience and loyalty. Most props lasted only a few nights. It had therefore become Toni and Maddy's nightly ritual to wind each other up.

Greg had taken Tom back to Sgt Pepper's to score from Danny, who had some unusual Es called Mad Bastards. The name alone almost put Greg off, but Danny reassured him that they were 'really rushy' and that he would be really 'loved up'.

Tom and he walked down the bottom road by the Tanit apartments. It was quieter and darker than all of the others that led to Night Life. There were two stalls on opposite sides of the road, both selling ready-made rolls in cling-film, ice-cream, sweets and drinks. Tom bought a bottle of water.

'Right, then, mate,' he said. 'You sure you wanna do this?'

'You fuckin' muppet, you've spent the last 'alf-hour talking me into it and now you ask me if I'm sure,' said Greg. 'Just give us 'alf the thing and let's gerrit over with.'

Tom broke the speckly pill along the line that bisected it. He knocked his back straight away and handed the bottle to Greg. Greg put the pill on his tongue, took a gulp of water and swallowed.

'If I die, you fucking twat, just make sure that Mario doesn't win the Competition.'

At the bottom of the road Greg saw Maddy. There were few people for whom she came out of working-zombie mode but Greg was one of them. He'd shagged her at the end of the previous season and, surprisingly, it had improved their friendship although they had no intention of a repeat perfomance.

'Hello, lover,' said Maddy, kissing him. 'No airport tonight?'

'Nah, night off. I'm showin' Tom around,' he said.

Maddy gave Tom a smile only slightly more genuine than

the one she reserved for passing punters. 'So, you coming in tonight, Greg?'

'Aye. I've just 'ad a fuckin' E.'

'You're joking!' exclaimed Maddy.

'It's this fuckin' twat,' he said, pointing at Tom. 'Caught me in a moment of weakness.'

'I told him he'd be shagging all night,' corrected Tom.

'That figures,' said Maddy. 'What did you take?'

'A Mad Bastard,' said Tom.

'Oh, they're mental,' said Maddy smiling. 'You get flickery eyes and they're rushy as anything. Good luck.' She saw Toni coming up the stairs. 'Gotta go. I might see you later.'

Tom and Greg walked down the five tiled stairs. Each time the swing doors ahead opened they caught a snippet of the beat emerging from the darkness. Inside a wall of sound and a blast of heat like a savannah wind struck them. The club was small and square. It struck the right balance between the 'ere-we-go brigade and the more ravey clientele.

Greg reluctantly accepted the bottle of water Tom gave him – it was odd being in a club without a bottle of beer – and went over to Irish Ben, the bouncer. At five foot nine, slightly overweight with a humorous Desperate Dan type face, he didn't look like a typical bouncer. Moreover, he had a high, fast speaking voice, and stuttered when he was excited. His Eire accent was so strong that most people only caught the gist of what he was saying. He had a sharp sense of humour and often took the piss out of people when they thought they were taking the piss out of him. In his early twenties he had been European karate champion three years running, and one of his students had taken over the title for the following two years. However, he had suffered a number of personal tragedies, which he kept to himself, and which had caused him to leave home for a life in Ibiza when he was twenty-nine, nearly ten years ago.

He teamed up with an American to give karate exhibitions in night-clubs on the island; breaking bricks, splitting melons on volunteers' chests with a Samurai sword, but his partner went off the rails. Then he had taken on door work.

Greg was about to talk to him when a huge, muscle-bound Swedish-looking man entered, closely followed by four mean-looking bodybuilders. Those closest to the door froze, convinced there was going to be trouble, but when the five man-mountains saw Ben their faces broke into grins and there was lots of backslapping. Once they were safely at the other side of the club, Greg went up to him.

'Thought it was going to go off, then,' said Greg. 'I was just about ready to jump in and sort it out for you.'

'T'anks a lot. Oi feel an awful lot safer now yis told me that,' replied Ben, raising his eyebrows.

'Who were they then?'

'Danes. Just a bunch o' eejits. Yer man wi' the big arms is an awful gobshite, so he is. Says they're all bodyguards or something loike that. Oi had to educate them the other noight.'

'Wharabout?'

'Oh, they just got a wee bit boisterous an' one of them t'ought he'd troy and get me in a stranglehold.'

'So what 'appened?'

'Oi just gave him a flip over me shoulder and showed him a couple of little pressure points o' me own. Would y' loike t' see 'em?' asked Ben, as he gently dug the first joint of his finger into the small of Greg's back and then his collarbone.

'Ouch!' yelped Greg.

Ben laughed. 'Will y' be wanting a drink?'

'No, thanks, mate, I've got one.'

'Water,' said Ben, noticing it. 'That's not loike you.'

Greg wasn't sure what Ben's attitude was towards drugs so he said, 'I'll catch you later, Ben – I've got me boss over.'

He had a real urge to go and dance and at last found Tom on the edge of the dance floor, nodding and moving his arms. He went over to him. 'So, what's meant to happen, then?'

'You'll know,' said Tom.

'I can't feel a thing yet,' said Greg, his body unconsciously picking up the beat.

'You will,' said Tom knowingly.

Greg shrugged his shoulders and went to the toilet. He'd made his mind up that when he came back he'd get himself a beer. This E lark was a lot of fuss about nothing.

He felt a little light-headed as he made his way to the loos. The people around him seemed to be moving slower and looking at him more intently. By the time he got to the toilet, he found himself in a cubicle, rather than at the urinal. His stomach had an empty, hollow feeling, almost like he wanted to be sick, although it could have been that he needed a dump. He took his trousers down and sat on the pan just in case. Behind his eyes, a warm sensation travelled across the bridge of his nose. He couldn't focus properly so he shut his eyes, unconsciously swinging his shoulders in time to the music infiltrating from the club.

Slowly, it dawned on him: he was coming up on his first E. He panicked slightly, becoming aware of his shallow breathing and his heart thumping in his chest. Suppose he was one of the unlucky ones? The more he thought about it, the more scared he became. Where was Tom? He couldn't possibly go out to find him – everybody would be looking at him, knowing he was 'on one', or about to die. But he needed someone around.

He stretched his neck, pushing his head back, and felt a tightening in his lower abdomen. Almost before he was aware of it, his bowels opened. It was a great feeling, one of the most wonderful shits he had ever had. His prostate gland sent a message to his groin, and Greg noticed that he had started to get a hard-on. He stroked himself, all thoughts of death or a fatal reaction long since passed. He laughed at how he thought he must have looked – in the middle of a glorious shit, dripping with sweat, his head and eyes rolling whilst he stroked a hard-on. God, this was weird. His erection subsided and he pulled his trousers up, flushed the loo and straight away sat down again, increasingly aware of the music. His thoughts were still racing – conscious, controlled, but mingling randomly with bizarre nano-second daydreams and spurts of shape and colour. Out of one of these daydreams came a voice. 'Greg . . . Greg? Are you in there? Greg, open up.'

He jolted back to his newly discovered reality and opened the door. Standing in front of him was Tom.

'Fuck me. You must've been in here at least ten minutes. What do you think of it, then?' Tom asked.

Greg gave him a soppy smile and gurned. Then he rose slowly to his feet. 'I'm not sure I like it,' he said. 'Can we go outside for some fresh air?'

'Sure. You'll be all right. Just get this first rush out of the way and you won't be able to stay off the dance floor.'

Greg wasn't looking forward to walking through the club. He stuck close to Tom, trying to look at the floor, but finding it difficult to focus.

When Maddy saw him emerge from the club with his chin sticking out and his eyes rolling, she burst out laughing, but Greg was oblivious to everything. Tom ushered him away from the crowd and down to a bench by the harbour. Greg sat down, regained control of his breathing and was at last able to focus properly.

'You all right, mate?' Tom asked.

Greg exhaled, shaking his head. 'I'm still not sure if I like it, lad.'

'Don't worry,' said Tom. 'You'll be fine in a minute.'

'Fuckin' 'ope so.' Greg put his head between his knees, rubbed his neck then stood up. 'I tell you what, la', I don't feel too steady on the ol' pins.' Tom smiled at him reassuringly. 'Fuckin' 'ell, Tom. I'm *really* glad you're here. I don't think I'd've got through this without yer.' Tom nodded. 'Seriously, mate, you're a top bloke. It's a shame you're not 'ere for the season. You 'n' me, we'd 'ave a right laugh – do some serious caning.' Greg was feeling good now. 'So that's a rush, then, is it? I suppose it's not too bad, as long as there's someone like you around, y'know, someone that can be trusted. I suppose Maddy saw me like this. She's a great girl, that Maddy. Maybe tomorrow I'll go and ask 'er out properly, y'know. It's a great island this, innit? I mean, just look at the stars. It's weird, we're seeing those stars like a thousand or a million years after ... y'know, like it's taken a thousand years or whatever to get ... well ... anyway ... fucking amazing. Cor, look at that bird, she's fuckin' 'orny. When should I take the other 'alf, then?'

Chaos. It always was frantic but tonight was worse. It started with the airport police, who wanted to see Brad and Mikey's non-existent work permits. Brad's early flight had been delayed by five hours. The other reps, apart from Mikey, had been and gone. Mikey was doing the perpetually late Manchester flight, so only he and Brad were affected. The airport police decided to arrest them, but thanks, once again, to Mikey's command of Spanish, they had agreed on a compromise. They would allow the YF&S reps to pick up their clients, just this week, but they must not set foot in the airport. If the permits were not ready by the following week they would be thrown off the island.

Mikey and Brad were sitting on the wall outside the airport, both seriously stressed.

'That fucking dozy cow,' said Brad, referring to Alison. 'I can't believe she hasn't got those permits sorted out. What the fuck does she do all day?'

'To be honest I'm beyond caring about her. What goes around comes around. Something'll happen to her one day.'

'I'll believe it when I see it. People like her get away with murder.'

'Don't let it worry you. I know what'll make you feel

better,' said Mikey, reaching into the breast pocket of his airport shirt and pulling out a spliff.

'Oh, you diamond,' said Brad. 'But where can we smoke it?'

'We'll take a walk down there,' said Mikey, pointing to the end of the coach car park.

'Cool. I'll check that our flights haven't landed.'

Brad went to the doorway to look at the Arrivals board. The flights weren't on the display. He caught Kelly the Vision's eye and beckoned her over. She knew of Brad and Mikey's plight and had agreed to direct the YF&S clients out to them. As she approached the door it opened automatically, as if in reverence to her beauty.

'Don't suppose there's any news on the flights yet, is there?' Brad asked.

'There's a rumour that they'll both be arriving in about half an hour.'

'Oh, good,' said Brad. He looked at Kelly, desperate to ask her out without making a prat of himself.

For once, she started a conversation. 'What will you do if you don't get a work permit?'

'I dunno,' said Brad. 'Go home I suppose.'

'Oh, that would be a shame.'

Was that a green light? Or was she just being polite? Fuck it. Without giving it any more thought he blurted, 'Yeah, it would be a shame. I was going to leave asking you out until August, you know, just to give me a chance to check that you weren't a woman of easy virtue. But I guess I'll ask you out now instead and if you *are* a woman of easy virtue, I'll just have to deal with it. What about Wednesday?'

Brad knew it was one of the naffest proposals for a date he had ever made and that he'd fucked it.

'Okay.'

'Huh?'

'Wednesday's fine.'

'What? Oh, great. I mean – oh, shit, I'm working

212

Wednesday. Howzabout . . .' Brad paged through a mental diary '. . . Thursday. Eleven o'clock in the Charleston?'

'Eleven o'clock it is.'

'Great.' They stared at each other for a few seconds. 'Right, I'd better go and see Mikey. Back soon.'

Brad skipped off back to his friend, unable to believe his luck. He'd done it. He'd cracked the Vision.

'Mikey, guess what?'

'Both our planes have collided over the Bon, killing all passengers, holidaymakers and reps apart from Alison.'

Brad gave him a confused look. 'You need fucking therapy, mate. I've just asked Kelly out and she said yes.'

'I think I would've got more pleasure out of the plane crash. Here . . .' He passed Brad the spliff directly after lighting it.

'Have you always had a warped sense of humour or did it take a lot of practice to develop it to its current, sick level?'

'Oh, I'm sure it's partly genetic. When you taking her out?'

'Thursday, after the bar night. She's fucking gorgeous, in't she?'

'I've seen you with worse.' Mikey relit the spliff, which Brad had allowed to go out. 'Was Mario up here earlier?'

'Yeah – jammy bastard. His flight was actually ten minutes early. He can't have been at the airport for more than half an hour. He still winds me up, y'know. Since Lorraine went he's been doing my head in. It's like he knows something we don't, right smug. I wish I could put my finger on it.'

'Fuck him.' Mikey flicked the roach at the kerb. 'Looks like the first lot of people are coming through.'

Brad looked at the glass doors twenty metres away and, sure enough, there was a flurry of people.

'This should be fun.'

Almost an hour later, the 'fun' was just about over. It had been hell. Kelly had been so busy that not all of the YF&S clients knew where to go. Some had been wandering aimlessly around the airport, while the ones who had got on the coaches straight away had been sitting there for the best part of an hour and were understandably getting restless. Mikey and Brad stood by the door and could see no sign of any more clients.

'How's it looking?' Mikey asked Brad.

'Still four missing. Fuck it. I'll have to leave them. What about you?'

'All aboard. Thing is, there's forty-nine blokes and three girls.'

'Oh, you're joking,' said Brad.

'Wish I was. Some fucking week this is going to be.'

Brad got on to his coach. 'Morning, everyone.'

Silence. Mikey was probably right. This was going to be 'some fucking week'.

chapter eleven

His arms were in the air. His jaw was hurting through chewing gum and smiling. He'd talked to numerous people – suddenly feeling as though he was a member now of a special society that previously he had only pretended to belong to.

While he was dancing, a pretty blonde girl kept smiling at him. When he caught her eye again she spoke. 'Hi. You're Greg, aren't you?'

'Yeah.'

'I'm Jacqui. You work for Young Free & Single, don't you?'

'Yeah. How d'ya know?'

This was a stupid question as Greg was wearing his badge. Jacqui didn't seem to notice.

'That's who I've come on holiday with.'

'Really? Where yer staying?'

'At the Bon.'

'How come I 'aven't seen you?' asked Greg. 'Not been on any of the excursions?'

'No. We only came over here for the clubbing and Young Free & Single was the cheapest package on offer.'

'So where you been going?'

'Space, Amnesia, Ku, Pacha. The clubs out here are amazing.'

'Yeah, they are, aren't they?' Greg had only been to Ku.

They carried on dancing. Occasionally Jacqui brushed against Greg. Each time she did he felt his whole body tingle. It wasn't long before they were dancing close to each other and becoming quite tactile.

'What did you say your name was again?'

'Jacqui.'

'Right.' Greg nodded, smiling. 'So what you taken, then?'

'A dove. You?'

'A Mad Bastard.'

'A what?'

'A Mad Bastard. They're really rushy,' said Greg, now an authority. 'What's the dove like?'

'Usual sort of thing, really.'

'Uh-huh.' Greg was none the wiser.

'Yeah,' continued Jacqui. 'Quite lovey.'

'Yeah, these too,' said Greg.

Jacqui turned her back on Greg. 'Do me a favour.'

Greg started massaging her shoulders. After a while he ran his fingers up the nape of her neck then let his fingernails gently scratch her on the way back down. He couldn't believe how erotic it made him feel.

'Mmmm,' moaned Jacqui. 'That feels wonderful. I felt all stiff before.'

'Not as stiff as I'm feeling now,' said Greg.

Jacqui playfully rubbed her backside against his hard-on. She giggled. 'So you are.' She turned round, rested her arms on his shoulders and looked him directly in the eyes. They started kissing and it was all that Greg could do to stop himself from ripping her clothes off.

'Do you wanna leave?' asked Greg.

'I can't. I've got to find my friend.'

'She'll be all right.'

'No, honestly. Look, I might catch up with you later.'

Before Greg had a chance to argue she disappeared into the crowd. He carried on dancing for ten minutes, then went to the bar where Tom was standing. The music didn't seem as captivating as before and the warm sensation had all but disappeared.

'You all right?' asked Tom.

'Nah. I just pulled a blinding bird an' she's fucked off.

Plus the music don't seem so good and, I don't know, it's just not as good as it was a little while ago.'

'Sounds like you're coming down,' said Tom.

'What?' said Greg.

'The pill – it's wearing off. Here,' he said, biting another in half. 'This'll sort you out.'

Greg popped it in his mouth and swigged it back without a second thought.

'Taken like a veteran,' said Tom.

Brad eventually got to sleep at just before five a.m. Despite his attempts at winning them over, they had been the most miserable bunch of clients he had ever brought back from the airport. He always sent himself up as soon as he got on the microphone, aware of the hostility that his bright yellow uniform, bronzed skin and air of confidence could provoke, but on this occasion it hadn't worked – there had even been a few mumbles of 'Cockney bastard.' (Brad had discovered that, to northerners, anyone south of Luton was a Cockney.)

He had been asleep for little more than an hour when a loud bang and screaming woke him. It seemed to be coming from the floor below. He put on his shorts and ran downstairs to see what was going on.

As he walked on to the landing one of the doors was open. From it came a male voice yelling in Spanish. Brad walked into the room where he was confronted by Rafael, the hotel-owner's son, about to punch a small blonde girl. Brad pushed him away. Rafael went into a karate stance. Brad looked in the corner where the blonde girl's friend was sitting. She had a black eye. Brad looked at Rafael, who moved towards the blonde girl. Brad leapt between them.

'Yeah?' Rafael stopped in his tracks. 'Fancy your fucking chances, do you?' He pushed Brad. 'Well, come on, then. Try and give me a black eye, dickhead.' Brad stepped back. 'Come on, what you waiting for? What's up, you fucking wanker?' Rafael glared at Brad, then glanced at the two girls. A moment later, he barged his way out, spitting out Spanish that Brad had no chance of understanding. The two girls huddled together on the bed, sobbing. Brad closed the door and sat on the bed next to them. 'I think it might be a good idea to tell me what happened, don't you?'

'Nothing, he's just mad,' said the blonde.

'So he just came in here for no reason and hit you?'

'Yeah, look at my eye,' said the other girl.

'It's bad, but I need to know why he hit you.'

'These two blokes came back . . .' said Black Eye.

'Nothing in it, though,' interrupted the blonde. 'They just came to chill out for a little while.'

Black Eye continued the story. 'Next thing there's a banging on the door. We opened it and it was that nutter. He started yelling and attacked the boys. They ran off and then he turned on us. God knows what he would've done if you hadn't stopped him.'

'Mmmm.' Brad digested the story. 'You're not meant to have anyone in your room who's not staying in the hotel, so that sounds like the reason he went mad. But, there's no excuse for the way he acted.' He stood up. 'Look, there's not much I can do now. Will you be all right until later? I'll go and have a word with my boss before the welcome meeting.'

The knocking confused Brad. Squinting at the clock he saw that it was five past nine. The knocking was insistent now. It crossed his mind that it might be Rafael, ready for round two. He was in no fit state for a physical confrontation.

'Who is it?'

'Alison. Open up.'

'Give me a minute.'

He put on his tracksuit bottoms and T-shirt, then opened the door. Alison stormed in and stood by the window with her hands on her hips. She was never one for small-talk – shout first, ask questions later.

'You've annoyed me a few times during the season already, Brad, but this time you've really done it.'

Brad had learned through experience that it was almost impossible to interrupt Alison when she ranting.

'First of all the airport. What on earth do you think you were doing letting four clients get a taxi into San Antonio? They've just collared me in the Bon demanding the cab fare and threatening to sue us for the inconvenience. Next thing I'm confronted by the hotel-owner downstairs who tells me that you've been letting clients bring non-residents into the hotel.' She shook her head. 'It makes me laugh. Everyone in head office was going on about how smart you are but I've yet to see any indication of it. You're lucky you've still got a job. I know a lot of resort managers who would have had you off the island by now.'

'Yeah, and I know a lot of resort managers who would've got the work permits sorted out before the middle of July so that the reps were allowed into the airport to do their job.'

'What?'

'Alison, I can't be bothered to talk to you about it now. I've had one hour's sleep, there's a welcome meeting in just over an hour, then that meal with Felipe and the agency, then a bar crawl, then a cruise at eight in the morning. If you're just gonna come in here shouting and screaming, don't expect me to listen to you.'

'What was that you said about the work permits? Mario didn't say anything about not being allowed in the airport and he was there after you.'

'Yeah, but as usual dear Mario got the best flight and was in and out of the airport within half an hour, whereas I was there for over six hours.'

'And what about this stuff with the hotel? I think we're going to have to move you somewhere else.'

'Alison, do what you fucking want,' said Brad, losing his cool. 'But while you're at it go and have a look at that poor girl in room three two two who's nursing a black eye courtesy of that nutter Rafael.' Alison looked bemused.

'Yep, that's right. He's hit a girl. I warned you but you wouldn't listen. And as for the airport, we weren't allowed to set foot in it. It was hell up there. All the clients are totally pissed off so I wouldn't be counting on a very good week for sales if I were you.'

'Well, I still can't claim to be very happy.' She was stuck for anything else to say.

'Yeah? Well, I can't claim to give a fuck. And if you want to put someone else in here then I don't care either because this time next week it'll be academic.'

'What do you mean?'

'The police said if we haven't got permits by then we're all off the island.'

'I don't believe it.'

'Believe it or don't, it's true.' Brad sat on his bed and shut his eyes. 'Yeah, you've done a real good job, Alison. You know what really confuses me, though?' Alison looked at him, hatred growing in her eyes. 'How you got the job in the first place.'

Alison was almost shaking with rage. She said nothing, just flew past Brad and slammed the door behind her.

Within minutes she was back in her room at the Bon. She lit a cigarette. She needed to think and act fast. She went downstairs and rang Jane Ward at home.

'Hello,' said a sleepy voice.

'Hi, Jane. It's Alison Shand in Ibiza.'

'Alison? What on earth's the matter?'

'We've got something of a mini crisis here and I really don't know what to do.'

'What's up?'

'Well, it's two things, really. I sent through all of the reps' details ages ago for the work permits but I've still received nothing.' In fact she had forgotten to post them.

'Hang on a minute,' said Jane. 'What details? I remember asking you for them a few weeks ago but as I didn't receive them I assumed you'd sorted out the permits on resort.'

'God, no,' said Alison. 'I thought they were all going

220

through at your end. Don't tell me they've got lost in the post.'

'They must've done,' said Jane. 'Look, give me a chance to get myself together and call me later with the reps' details. I'll get it sorted out for you first thing in the morning.'

'Oh, Jane, thanks ever so much.'

'That's fine. Now what else?'

'It's Brad and Las Huertas. He's not controlling his clients and they've been antagonising the hotel-owner's son – y' know, parties, music at all hours. Anyway, a couple of times the owner's son has lashed out.'

'What do you mean by lashed out?'

'Hit clients.'

'Jesus, why haven't I heard about it?'

'I managed to contain it to resort.'

'Didn't you get Brad to do a report?'

'Of course I did. I've asked him countless times but he hasn't or won't,' lied Alison.

'That's not good enough. If you tell him to do something he's got to do it. You're the resort manager, after all.'

'That's half the problem, Jane. He thinks he knows it all. I keep telling him but he won't listen. I think he's even turning Mikey against me.'

'Well, there's only one answer to it.'

'What?'

'Sack him. It hurts me to say it because I thought Brad would do well. But I'm not there. Look, I tell you what, Tom's there, isn't he?'

'Yes,' said Alison.

'Have a chat to him about it and get him to call me. We'll have the whole thing resolved by tomorrow one way or another. Is that okay?'

'That's marvellous, Jane. Thank you ever so much. You don't know how helpful you've been.'

Alison let out a sigh of relief. Brad was going to go.

chapter twelve

The welcome meeting was disastrous. For the first time Brad sensed genuine animosity from some of his clients. A group of six lads from Burnley, who had arrived the previous Wednesday and were staying for ten days, had formed an unholy alliance with some of the other large groups he and Mikey had brought in that morning.

A hard core of about thirty northern lads watched Brad's every move, making snide comments or jeering from the safety of the group. He sat with them for a while, trying to find a shared common interest. He wanted to ascertain who the natural leader was so that he could give him some special attention, but no natural leader yet existed. It was an amalgam of three or four different sets of lads who were still jostling to sort out their own hierarchy. Unfortunately their common bond seemed to be a shared hatred of YF&S, its reps and, in particular, Brad. He was glad when Mikey turned up in a taxi to take him down to Es Reguero, the restaurant where the company meal was to be held. He flopped into the back seat.

'Get much sleep?' asked Mikey, swivelling round from the front passenger seat.

'Don't ask,' replied Brad. 'I sometimes wonder if it's all worth it. Everyone thinks this job's all about getting a tan and shagging yourself senseless – if only they knew.'

'You mean if only they knew it was about getting pissed for nothing as well?' Brad was too knackered to bite. Mikey realised this so continued, 'I know what you mean. I worked out that since I've been here I've averaged just over four hours sleep a night. Do you believe that?'

'Mate, I'd've been doing cartwheels if I'd got four hours last night. That fucking nutter beat up another client, only this time it was a girl.'

'No way!'

'Yep. Thought he was gonna have a pop at me as well.'

'Alison would've probably blamed you if he had,' said Mikey.

'You haven't heard the best bit yet. I'd been asleep, for an hour when she banged on my door . . .' Brad proceeded to give his friend a blow-by-blow report on Alison's visit. 'She's gunning for me, mate, and, after this week's arrivals I couldn't give a fuck.'

'Yeah, I thought they'd be a handful. Mind you, two of those girls were quite fit.'

Brad burst out laughing. 'They came up to me this morning, moaning their bloody heads off. It's the first time they've been on a package holiday and they were expecting Holiday-Inn-type accommodation, and a Riviera-type resort.'

'Leave off.'

'Honest. Anyway, next thing they started to get hysterical. One of them says "You don't know how much this holiday means to us, it could be our last one."' Brad was still laughing, unable to believe what the girl had told him. 'She reckons they met each other last year at the Papworth Clinic – after they'd both had organ transplants.'

'You're winding me up.'

'No, as I live and breathe. They're still in the critical period where the organs could get rejected. I just hope Greg doesn't find out.'

'Why's that?'

''Cos he'll wanna shag 'em, of course.'

A long table was set out beneath one of the white canopies that protected Es Reguero's customers from the sun. Although the restaurant was only a five-minute walk from the Star club, few tourists frequented it. However, because

223

the food was so good, it was almost always busy with expats and workers. When Brad and Mikey arrived, everyone was there, apart from Alison. Brad sat next to Tom and Greg, who were with Felipe Gomez from head office, and Luís from Viajes Diamanté. Mikey joined Natalie, Heather and Mario.

Alison arrived just after the wine was placed on the table. She kissed Felipe and Luís politely then turned to Tom. 'Have you got a minute? I need to speak to you.'

'Oh, right.' Tom stood up. 'Excuse me, everyone.'

They walked inside to the cool, dark bar. Alison sat down first and Tom followed suit after he had ordered two beers.

'Don't you even know what beer is in Spanish?' asked Alison.

'I did, but I keep forgetting,' lied Tom.

'You'll have to learn the language if you want to make any progress, you know.'

This puzzled Tom, because his position was already senior to Alison's.

'You speak Spanish, then?' asked Tom, who knew she couldn't.

'Enough to get by.' As if to prove the point she said, '*Gracias*', as the drinks arrived.

'So, what's the problem?' asked Tom.

'I spoke to Jane this morning and she suggested I talked to you,' replied Alison. 'There were two things, really. The first problem was the airport. I don't know if you remember, but I sent all of the reps' details through to you at the beginning of the season.'

'I don't remember receiving them,' said Tom.

'Well, that's what Jane said, so they've got lost in the post or something.' The lie didn't come as easily to Alison now as it had over the phone. 'Anyway, Jane said she would be able to sort that out so hopefully it won't be a problem as long as it's done by the weekend. The other problem,' said Alison, taking a sip of her drink, 'is Brad.'

'Brad?'

'Yeah. It's a shame because, like everyone else, I thought he was going to be really good. But from the day he got here he's been trying to tell me how to do my job. Every time I tell him to do something he questions it. I wasn't going to say anything because I could deal with it. But it's got a little more serious.'

'In what way?'

'Well, for starters, I think he's turning Mikey against me. As you know, Brad's got a strong personality. Before we came out to resort even Kirstie told me he was a bit of a natural leader.' Alison paused. 'The other problem is Las Huertas. He doesn't get on too well with the staff there and he's more into having a good time than controlling the clients.'

'Yeah, but come on, Al, the job's about getting on and joining in with the clients.'

'You don't have to tell me – I've been doing this job for a few years, you know. The thing with Brad is he doesn't know where to draw the line and that causes problems.'

'What sort of problems?'

'The clients get out of hand and someone else has to control them and sometimes that person may not be the best person for that job.' Tom wasn't sure what point she was trying to make. 'On a few occasions Brad's clients in Las Huertas have got a bit lairy and Rafael, the owner's son has hit them.'

'What?' said Tom. 'Why weren't we notified of this in head office?'

'It's probably not as bad as it sounds and as I thought Brad would make a good rep, I didn't want anything bad on his record. But I asked him time and again to do a report . . .' Alison shrugged.

'What did Jane say?'

'That I should sack him, but to talk to you first.'

Tom sat back in his chair. Although everything Alison had said made sense, something didn't seem quite right. After a minute or so, he said, 'I'll need to speak to Jane before I do anything. And I'll also have to hear Brad's side of the story.'

'Of course. I mean, clearly Brad's going to say that he did a report, but he didn't give it to me.'

'Okay, leave it with me and I'll sort it out.'

When they got back to the table Alison went to one end, where Heather was saying she'd never slept with a man with a foreskin, and Tom sat next to Felipe and Greg. Greg had just finished telling Brad about his morning with Tom and the two girls. It reminded Tom that he still hadn't slept.

Tom needed to get the conversation with Alison out of his head so he could act normally towards Brad. He remembered that the husband of a girl who came away at the beginning of the season had rung up head office claiming that Greg had got his wife pregnant. He had forgotten to tell Greg this, so it was with great glee that he relayed the story and added untruthfully that the 'brick shithouse' of a husband was arriving on Wednesday. He enjoyed watching the colour drain from Greg's face.

After the meal, everybody was pleasantly tipsy and in good spirits. Felipe, Luís and Tom were all smoking cigars and talking shop. Alison was quite drunk and had moved to sit very close to Felipe. Tom noticed them exchange a couple of hand squeezes. He tried to imagine them in bed together.

Felipe's voice interrupted his thoughts: 'So, Tomas, do you speak Spanish?'

'Not really.'

'But I would have thought with a name like Ortega . . .'

'My great-grandfather,' lied Tom. 'From Madrid.'

'Ah,' said Felipe. 'And what about the reps, do any of them speak Spanish?'

'Only me and Mikey,' interrupted Alison.

Felipe almost laughed: he knew that Alison was one of those people who, rather than admit that they do not have command of a foreign language, say they understand more than they speak.

'And Mikey,' continued Felipe, 'which one is he again?'

'At the end, wearing the rimmed sunglasses,' said Brad.

'The black bloke,' said Alison.

'Good,' said Felipe, realising that Mikey was out of earshot. 'Well, if you'll all excuse me I need to speak to Luís and it will be easier for us to converse in our native tongue. Please do not think we are being rude.'

'No problem.' Alison answered for everybody.

Tom thought this unusual because they both spoke impeccable English, so he kept one ear on the conversation, which at first was general gossip. Tom laughed to himself at how Alison kept nodding as if she understood what they were saying. When she felt she had sufficiently impressed them she slid off to the other end of the table to sit with Mario, Mikey and the girls. As soon as she had gone, Tom heard Felipe say, in Spanish, 'Fucking nuisance. I wish the whore would just leave me alone. I only fucked her twice and the stupid bitch got pregnant. I don't know how – I spent most of the time with my cock up her arse.'

Both men laughed. They were speaking fast in regional dialect, but Tom understood every word they said.

The next five minutes of conversation left him gob-smacked. It was almost too much to take in.

When they finished, Felipe smiled, in his normal charming way. 'I'm sorry about that. Now, as this is on the company we should order a bottle of champagne. What does everybody think?'

Tom was the only one who didn't reply. If what he had just heard was true, a bottle of champagne wasn't the only thing that Felipe had bought 'on the company'. He stood up and went to the bar. 'Is there a phone I can use to ring England?'

chapter thirteen

'Jane?'

'Tom?'

Tom looked around to check that no one could hear him. 'Yeah.'

'What's up? Have you spoken to Alison?'

'Yes, but—'

'What did she say?'

'She was going on about Brad – but that's not—'

'What did she say about Brad?'

'Just that he doesn't respect her. Look, I need—'

'Do you think we should get rid of him?'

'Jane, *shut up!*' There was a stunned silence at the end of the phone. 'Thank you. Now, if you'll kindly listen, I've just heard something that makes Brad, Alison and everything else seem irrelevant by comparison.'

Tom had never spoken to her like that before, so Jane guessed it had to be pretty serious. 'Go on, I'm listening.'

'Right. You know how you've always gone on at me about not letting anyone know I'm fluent in Spanish?'

'Uh-huh.'

'Well, it's finally paid off.'

'How?'

'Felipe and Luís, the guy from Viajes Diamanté, had a conversation in Spanish, but only after Felipe checked that nobody else spoke the lingo. Oh, and you were right about Alison and him. He did get her up the duff, but it's not an ongoing romance.'

'But he was the father?'

'Definitely.'

228

'Is that why he was so keen for her to be given the resort manager's job?'

'Partly, but there's more to it than you could ever imagine.' He looked round again to check that nobody was listening. It took him nearly ten minutes to tell Jane the whole story.

There were a few seconds' silence before Jane said, 'Oh, Christ, Tom, this is really spooky.'

'Hardly the adjective I'd have chosen. Still . . .'

'No, you don't understand,' she said. 'Just before we found out about Alison's abortion I received an anonymous phone call from a woman to tell me that Felipe was having an affair. That same woman called me a couple of days ago to tell me that Felipe and Alison were on the fiddle.'

'I'll come to Alison in a minute. Any idea who made the calls?' asked Tom.

'I haven't. It's obviously someone who doesn't like Alison – or Felipe, for that matter.'

'Well, now I've seen how popular Alison is out here, that should narrow it down to half of Ibiza.'

'I reckon it's someone over here. The calls didn't sound as if they were from abroad.'

'What about the voice?'

'It's so hard to tell, Tom. It sounded a bit like someone from the West Country trying to put on a posh voice, or a posh voice trying to sound regional. There's no way of knowing.' Jane paused to collect her thoughts. 'Jesus, Tom. Do you realise how much he could have been making each season?'

'Um,' Tom did some quick mental arithmetic, 'over quarter of a million pounds.'

'And the rest! More like half a million. Bugger.'

'It doesn't bear thinking about, does it?'

'So how does Luís fit into all this?' asked Jane.

'He was the first person Felipe started doing it with. Apparently they go way back – met at college or something. Luís put him on to a contact in each Diamanté office and they got a cut. Let's face it, even a small cut of that kind of money's worth their while.'

'Let me just make sure that I've got this absolutely right. Felipe has been contracting a room for, let's say, seven pounds a night. He then gets the agency to invoice us for a tenner. We pay the agency, who pay the hotel and cream off the difference. Right so far?'

'Yep.'

'So Felipe keeps more than half.'

'Nearer two-thirds.'

'Whatever. Then what's left is kept by Luís or the agency on top of their normal commission.'

'That's about it.'

'So Felipe's making about two pounds a night on every room in all of our accommodation. Phew! But how come the boss of the agency doesn't know what's going on?'

'Think about it. The agency invoice us for what they believe to be the correct amount. We pay them and they pay the hotel. Sometimes they pay the hotel in cash so when that happens it's easy – Felipe just takes the money and the hotel isn't any the wiser. But when they pay by cheque, the hotel has to know, so they give Felipe a kickback. That way the boss of the agency doesn't know.'

'But suppose a hotel or apartment block isn't interested?' asked Jane, trying to cover all the permutations.

'Then I guess they don't get contracted. Christ, Jane, you know how competitive it is out here. Most of our accommodation is run by one-man bands desperate for the business.'

'But what about some of the bigger contracts, the stuff the mainstream companies use?' Jane was referring to other companies within the group that YF&S belonged to, which catered for families.

'I don't know. Felipe didn't say anything about that.'

'Do you not think that maybe some accommodation is being contracted legitimately?'

'Probably, yes. Don't forget that it's only happening in Spain.'

'*Only!*' repeated Jane ironically. 'And he's been doing it for at least two seasons?'

'Well, I heard him talking about last season so he was definitely doing it then. I don't know if Kirstie was in on it and, of course, it's always possible that he's been at it longer.' Tom had just thought of something else. 'Who are our agents in Andorra?'

'Diamanté,' replied Jane slowly. 'Oh, no. Not the winter season as well?'

'It's possible, isn't it? And imagine if he's pulled a similar scam in France or Italy – there are affiliated Diamanté agents there. He could be making even more than half a million a year.'

There was silence again as they digested the implications.

'Oh, and there's something else. You know that house in Dulwich and that fancy stuff in his office?'

'Left to him by his relative?'

'Wrong,' sang Tom. 'He was bragging to Luís that the house is almost paid for by his "little" scam. *And* he's bought a new Range Rover.'

Jane was silent. She was too busy thinking what all of this meant. Now she said, 'So if he contracts accommodation on the basis of whether or not they'll give him a back-hander, then surely that means our clients aren't getting the most suitable places to stay? If quality or value for money isn't the main criterion . . .'

'Exactly,' agreed Tom.

'And if, as a company, we're paying more for our hotels and apartments than we should be,' said Jane, 'then we pass that cost on to the holidaymakers, which means that—'

'—the holidays cost more than they otherwise would,' said Tom, finishing her sentence.

'It's fucking scandalous, right enough.' Jane whistled. 'Anything more I should know?'

'Yep. The lovely Alison Shand. He launders all of his

money through Ibiza and she looks after his accounts while he's not here. They're all joint accounts with his wife but from what I can make out she knows hardly anything about them. Of course, the account only needs the one signature so he probably just shoved the application form under her nose to sign or forged her signature.'

'Why would he do that?'

'To emphasise to Alison that he's married. I'm not sure whether the hotel- and apartment-owners know she's in on it, but it wouldn't surprise me. Apparently some of our clients have been friends of Alison's. They get their holiday paid for in return for taking back some of the cash with them, so that's how most of it finds its way to the UK. Felipe was laughing at the minuscule amount he's paying her. She's obviously not stupid and can see how much he's making, but he's told her that Diamanté are taking a lot more than they are. From what I can gather, Alison really wanted to be resort manager in Ibiza, so Felipe's pulled some strings and partly used that as justification for not cutting her in. He told Luís that he's promised her ten grand at the end of the season, but he's even thinking about not giving her that. Mind you, he'd be silly if he didn't 'cos I'm sure his wife wouldn't be too happy to find out that her two sons almost had a half-sibling.'

'Unbelievable,' was all that Jane could say.

'So now what? Shall I sack Alison?'

'God, no!' said Jane, whose sharp mind was well and truly in gear. 'If anything we've got to keep her there, even if she breaks every rule in the Courier's Manual.'

'Why's that?' asked Tom, who was now some way behind her.

'Because Alison is our key to catching Felipe. Don't you see? We can't possibly do anything on the basis of what you've heard. We need proof.'

'Like what?'

'I don't know. A bank statement? Pictures? I'm going to have to give this some serious thought. I'll obviously have to speak to Sebastian and Adam. I think for now we'll just have to sit tight.'

'So what about this stuff with Brad?'

'Puts a different light on it, doesn't it? I don't know about you, Tom, but I find it hard to believe that Brad screwed up. Of all the new reps . . .'

'I know. That's what I thought too. And, from what I've heard so far, he seems to be doing great. The only one out here I've heard anything bad about is Mario.'

'Mmmm. Well, he was borderline. Still, Mario's the least of our problems. The question is, what now?'

'I haven't spoken to Rafael or his father yet, and I haven't spoken to Brad. What should I do?'

Jane paused to think. 'Find out exactly what's going on. I was all for sacking Brad when I spoke to Alison, but after this I'm sure there's more to it than meets the eye. In the unlikely event that she is telling the truth, do what you have to. The most important thing is that she doesn't suspect anything because we *must* keep her there. If that means Brad has to go, then—'

'Oh, come on, Jane, that's hardly fair.'

'Well, what do you suggest? We keep on a first-year rep – albeit potentially a very good one – and let them get away with huge amounts of money? More expensive holidays next year, piss poor accommodation, more—'

'All right, all right, you've made your point.'

'Tom, of course I want you to do everything you can to keep Brad on resort, but it's not the most important thing. Do you understand?' Jane stressed the point. 'It is not the most important thing.'

'All right, Jane, I get the message. Cor, I thought this was gonna be a nice, painless visit. Couldn't've been more wrong, could I?'

'All part of the job, Tom.'

'I know – and I'd better get back to the meal before I'm missed. I'll speak to you later.'

'Okay. I'll call you as soon as there are any developments, assuming that you haven't called me first.'

'Yeah. *Adios*.'

'Oh, and, Tom . . .'

'Yeah?'

'Well done.'

chapter fourteen

'Women problems,' said Tom, to excuse his absence as he returned to the table. He felt shattered. The pills and the adrenaline had worn off, leaving him with all the energy of a sixty-a-day septuagenarian crossing a triathlon finishing line.

Five hours' blissful sleep later, he woke up to make his way over to the bar night at Las Huertas, which was replacing the usual Sunday-night bar crawl.

When he got there Brad had the bar rocking. Although some of the new arrivals had tried to disrupt the beginning of the evening, he had got rid of them. Alison had earlier instructed him to make the clients spend as much money in the hotel bar as possible. The circle of seventy or so people had therefore been led through two hours of drinking games, causing them to pass their year's savings over the bar with unparalleled urgency. It was the first time Brad had seen the hotel-owner smile.

There was a group of three lads from Bradford who were drunk before the games had started. Brad had wanted to stop getting them drinks after only half an hour of games, but Alison had popped in and told him to keep persuading them to buy drinks and pour them down their necks. Two of them had already been sick, one all over the floor. But the one who was undoubtedly the most pissed (skinny, with a black denim shirt and Buddy Holly-style glasses) had so far kept down the contents of his stomach.

He finished off the games with Confessions. This was where they would go around the circle and say something like, 'Take a sip anyone who lost their virginity before they were sixteen.' The questions started out quite tame, but by the time everyone had taken a few sips the questions got nearer and nearer the mark. Brad was particularly interested in a girl in her late twenties, who had so far taken a sip in response to losing her virginity before fifteen, having sex with more than one person at the same time, having a homosexual relationship, shagging on top of a fridge, having something bigger than a finger up her bottom, enjoying having Harry on the boat, and liking water sports – she was one of the few girls who understood that one, let alone admitted to enjoying it.

When the games finished, most of the clients went down to the Star. Tom took Brad to a corner where they sat down for a chat. He told him what Alison had said about the hotel and him not filing a report. Brad pulled out a copy of the report he had written and several more, none of which Tom had seen, which meant they had not found their way to head office. Luckily, the girl with the black eye was in the bar and she validated Brad's story. It was all making sense to Tom. Here was the classic case of an unsuitable hotel being used because the owner was in on Felipe's scam. It was becoming apparent that Alison was lying, and that Brad was in the right, but circumstances had twisted Brad's future. Brad also told him about the airport and, although he didn't say so, Tom's opinion was that Alison had forgotten about the permits – probably because she'd been too busy looking after Felipe's accounts.

Brad was pissed, tired and depressed. He was not the type of person to backstab someone even if they deserved it, but when the conversation got round to Lorraine he couldn't stop himself telling Tom about Mario's involvement.

Tom was left in a quandary. Had things been different, he would have been on the phone to Jane Ward to sack Alison. Instead, his orders were that if anybody had to go it should be Brad. But he could not bring himself to sack Brad after all he had just heard. Instead he told Brad that he would put him and Natalie in the Bon, and bring Mario and Heather into Las Huertas, effective from Wednesday. He left to go down to the Star at ten to one.

Brad had not slept since Alison's intrusion that morning so for once all thoughts of music, dancing, drink, drugs and sex were overtaken by the need to rest his eyes, whose lids felt like they had opposing magnets attached to them. He was asleep by one o'clock.

Greg only just made the coach for the cruise and he looked like shit. After the bar night he had gone down the Star and taken another E with Robbo. They had pulled a girl who was off her head and taken her round the back of the club. Bending over, she had given Greg a blow-job while Robbo shagged her from behind. Greg had a great time, but he couldn't remember when he had last slept.

The Competition was getting out of hand. Each rep was finding it difficult to keep tabs on their own score, let alone everyone else's. Brad knew he'd already been to bed with over twenty girls, but how many had been a full-on consummation, how many had just given him a blow-job, and how many bonus points he'd scored, he didn't have a clue.

The cruise set off from Ibiza Town, so Brad did the coach transfer from San Antonio. It occurred to him that he had finally mastered the art of sounding happy even when he was pissed off. Mario had met a gorgeous-looking girl he was keen to impress, so after five minutes he took over the microphone from Brad. He was actually mildly amusing and when he finished he put on his Derek and Clive tape. Unfortunately, it was the racist sketch about darkies. A black couple from Manchester were on the coach, who took it quite well, but Brad enjoyed watching Mario squirm.

He was surprised that most of the people from the previous night's bar frolic had made the cruise. The three lads from Bradford hadn't turned up, but they had been absolutely legless. The dirty-looking girl in her late twenties, however, who was on holiday by herself, was there.

Half-way through the afternoon Brad started talking to her. The conversation was loaded with innuendo. In the end, Brad could take no more. 'Look,' he said, 'I'm not very good at euphemisms. I really want to fuck you.'

They got a pedalo over to Brad's favourite wall and had filthy, lizard free sex. She was petite, but listening to the noise she made, Brad wondered if she too had visited the Papworth clinic, for her lungs surely belonged to a woman four times her size. Judging by the way his dick barely touched the sides when he was inside her, he thought there was a good chance that another part of her anatomy had been donated by a similar-sized woman.

On the coach back to San Antonio Brad put on his *Thunderbirds* tape. He had got it just for the countdown at the beginning, which he played at full volume from his balcony when he wanted to wake up his clients, but latterly he had taken to playing the whole episode as a respite from the music tapes with which he was growing increasingly bored. He had also started playing *Reader's Digest* Spanish language cassettes, which he put on during excursions. It had got to the stage where clients were asking for the language tapes instead of music.

As the coach pulled up outside Las Huertas, Alison and Tom were both waiting for Brad. They looked serious. Brad stepped off the coach and Alison beckoned him over.

'Brad, can I have a word with you?'

She whispered something to Tom, who nodded and walked away, then led Brad through to the hotel bar. They both sat down. 'Brad, something quite serious has happened.'

Here it comes, thought Brad, looking at his arm and deciding that at least he'd have a decent tan to go home with.

'I've spoken to Tom. After what has happened you should be going home. However, after discussing it we've decided to move you to the Bon on Wednesday. I'm not happy with your performance and if you step out of line

again I think you know what the consequences will be.'
Alison had had to agree to this compromise that Tom had
come up with, but she knew it would be only a matter of
time before she got rid of Brad. 'Anyway, that's not why I
want to talk to you.' Brad looked at her with a mixture of
puzzlement, indifference and relief. 'Something happened
last night, so I need you to have your wits about you.'

'Go on,' said Brad, leaning forward in his chair.

'One of your clients has died.'

'What! Which one?'

'Nick Harland. One of the lads from Bradford – the one
with the Buddy Holly glasses.'

'Oh, God, no. What happened?'

'His two friends got up for breakfast this morning and
gave him a shout but he didn't move. They didn't think
anything of it but when they got back he was still in the
same position. He'd choked on his own vomit.'

'How?'

'Too much to drink.' Alison didn't look Brad in the eyes.
'Hopefully there won't be any repercussions. Apparently
after they left the bar they were in town doing tequila
slammers, so—'

'So we might be off the hook,' said Brad cynically.

'No, that's not what I meant. It's not our policy as a
company to get clients totally pissed, just merry.'

'Like, when I suggested they'd had enough to drink at
nine o'clock last night and you told me to make them carry
on drinking? Is that what you meant?'

'No, that's not what I meant at all. If they hadn't got
drunk in the hotel, they'd have got drunk somewhere else.'

'Maybe. But it's not gonna look very good if the boy's
parents start asking questions and find out that the night
their Nick died, we'd been doing drinking games and
everything we could to make him so drunk he couldn't
stand up.'

'No, Brad,' corrected Alison. '*You* did, not *we*. What each
individual rep does in his or her hotel is down to them. If a

239

rep oversteps the mark and goes outside our stated company policy then only one course of action is open to us.'

'Right, so what you're saying is, if this goes any further then it's yours truly who's gonna carry the can. Whereas if I'd done what I have been wanting to do since the beginning of the season, and moderated the stupid fucking bar night, then you'd've given me the chop anyway for going against you. Does that sound about right?'

Alison leaned forward and, smiling, hissed at him, 'See? You're not as fucking smart as you thought you were. I told you to watch your step. Now we'll see—'

'I don't believe you,' snapped Brad. 'There's a poor guy just died and all you're worried about is using it to get one over on me. You're pathetic.' Brad stood up. 'I'm going upstairs 'cos if I have to listen to your drivel any longer I might do something I regret.'

As he went away Greg walked in. 'Wha's all that about?'

'Just giving Brad a few home truths,' said Alison. 'I suppose you've heard about the death?'

'Yeah, bad news.'

Tom walked over. 'Where's Brad?'

'Gone upstairs,' said Alison.

'I've rung head office,' continued Tom.

'What did they say?' asked Alison.

'Not a lot.'

'So, how many deaths is that so far this season?' asked Alison, gathering her things together.

'Um, two in Tenerife, one in Crete and one in Gran Canaria.'

'Well,' said Alison, 'we'd better get our finger out if we're gonna take the lead.'

Greg stayed in the hotel to cover Brad's desk duty. He'd been there for about ten minutes when Nick's two friends walked in. Greg beckoned them over. 'I'm really sorry to hear whar 'appened to Nick. Are you all right?'

'Aye, still a bit shocked, like.'

'I've just spoken to 'is mum,' said the other. 'That was fucking hard.'

Greg didn't know what to say so he offered them a drink, which they declined. The two boys stood there awkwardly, so Greg brought the conversation to a close. 'Well, if there's anything I can do for you . . .'

'Actually,' said the boy who'd spoken first, 'there is summink you can do.'

'Just name it,' said Greg.

'I let Nick borrow two mill yesterday. Any chance of getting it back for us?'

Greg looked at him, not sure at first if he was serious. He was.

'Uh, I'll see what I can do.'

Brad didn't wake up until just before midnight, but Natalie was doing desk in the morning so he could have a late night if he wanted.

It was, without doubt, the most down he'd been since he'd arrived in Ibiza. It was only a matter of time, he knew, before Alison sacked him. He was always tired, he was drinking too much, he hated this week's clients – he was even bored with sex. Earlier in the season Greg had said this would happen. He remembered, too, Greg's remark about forming relationships. He had been right. It was easy to shag yourself senseless, a different girl every night, if you really put your mind to it. And indeed girls fell in love with you. But Brad had learned that it was always a classic holiday romance. The phone calls and letters stopped; the old boyfriend reappeared, it was the Patricia syndrome time and time again. As for relationships with other reps or workers, well, that was fine for normal reps but YF&S reps had such a bad reputation for womanising that to forge any partnership was a mammoth task, especially with such a small amount of free time. Still, Brad was looking forward to his date on Thursday with Kelly.

Mikey was due round at twelve thirty. At just gone

quarter past, Brad heard a commotion on the stairs. He went down a couple of floors and a scruffy-looking bloke ran past him. Two girls started screaming, so Brad quickened his pace. Suddenly the bloke ran out of a room, with what looked like a wallet in one hand and a knife in the other. Instinctively Brad tripped him up. As he did so, he brushed against the wall, where a protruding nail ripped his shirt and scratched him. The intruder was on the floor and the wallet and knife had skidded along the corridor. Brad skipped over and picked them up. The intruder looked at Brad, and obviously didn't fancy his chances: he raced off down the stairs. The two girls hurtled out of the room. They were both Cockneys.

'Where'd 'e fuckin' go?'

'E's nicked our passports.'

'These?' said Brad, showing them what he had thought to be a wallet.

'Fuckin' 'ell,' said one of the girls, with wavy bleached hair and pretty, freckly face. 'Ow d'ya get that? 'E 'ad a bleedin' knife, did'n'e?'

'This?' said Brad, showing them the knife.

'Look, 'e's striped ya,' said her friend, who had dark hair and battered features that would not have looked out of place in a gritty Channel 4 documentary.

Brad looked down at the graze the nail had inflicted.

'Are you all right?' asked the prettier girl.

'Yeah, it's nothing.'

'Bastard reckoned we owed 'im some wonga. Came up 'ere and took our passports when we told 'im we 'ad nuffink,' said the dark-haired girl. 'You must be a bit tasty to get that knife off 'im.'

Brad liked the thought of being 'tasty'. 'It's what I'm here for.'

'Yeah, but could've bin nasty,' said the pretty one. 'If 'e'd slashed yer face or sumfink . . .'

'No chance. I've done a bit of, uh, karate. Anyway, gotta go.'

He had just changed his shirt when Mikey, Tom and Greg turned up, dressed to the nines and filling his room with the scent of different aftershaves and deodorants. Greg produced a small bag of pills. Tonight they were all going for it.

Brad was rushing his tits off. Robbo had got hold of some Es called Apples, which Greg had bought and were brilliant. All four boys had dropped one in Brad's room, although Tom and Mikey had only done half each.

Brad loved Es Paradis. The spacious white club was designed around a circular dance floor surrounded by sculpted columns. It was quite bright and attracted a posey, cosmopolitan crowd. Looking round at the smiling faces and feeling the great atmosphere, he guessed that Robbo had had a profitable night. Rusty and his mob were there and apparently on the same buzz. None of them had yet surpassed the tree effort although they had all shagged the same girl. Rusty told Brad that to his knowledge she had slept with twenty blokes in her first week. Just then she walked down the stairs leading into the club. Brad had an idea. He waved to her. 'Over here.'

She came across, smiling. She looked really sweet and was a very attractive girl.

'How's young Donna tonight, then?'

'Great. I've had a couple of those Apples. Wicked. What about you?'

'The same,' replied Brad. 'I've got to be a bit careful, though. I've got my boss over from London.'

'Oh, which one's he, then?'

Brad pointed to the bar, which was half-way up towards the balcony. Tom was there with Greg.

'He doesn't look old enough to be your boss,' said Donna. 'He's good-looking, though, isn't he?'

Yes, thought Brad, silently punching the air. 'Funny you should say that, Donna, 'cos he noticed you yesterday and was asking about you.'

'Really?' Donna's face lit up.

'Really,' repeated Brad. 'I'm gonna have a word with him in a minute, so you go and have a dance and I'll see what I can do.'

Brad walked up behind Tom and winked at Greg. They both threw their arms around him and Brad realised they'd consumed more drugs. After general E talk, Brad said, 'See that girl over there, Tom? That really fit blonde in the middle of the dance floor? The one in the short yellow dress with the gorgeous tits?' He thought he might as well lay it on.

'Yeah,' said Tom.

'I don't know why I'm telling you this, 'cos I doubt if you'd do the same for me, but a little birdie tells me she's got the hots for you, which is a real fucker 'cos everyone on resort has been trying to crack her all week without any luck.'

Greg almost choked.

'Really?' said Tom, in Apple-induced innocence and gullibility.

'In't that right, Greg?'

'Oh, aye,' said Greg, composing himself.

Tom put his drink down to make his way over to her.

'But before you go,' said Greg, 'I've gorra new competition.'

'Oh, not another one,' groaned Brad. 'What is it this time?'

'We've all got cassette recorders, 'aven't we?'

Brad nodded. Mikey, who had just joined the group, nodded too.

'I've got a Sony Walkman,' said Tom.

'Does it record?' asked Greg.

'I think so.'

'Perfect,' said Greg. 'What we do is 'ave a word of the week that we 'ave to get whoever we pull to say while we're shagging 'em.'

'What sort of word?' asked Mikey.

'Well, I thought for the first week it should be Fluffy-flops.'

'*What?*' screamed the other three.

'Yeah, Fluffyflops,' repeated Greg. 'So while you're at it you've gorra get 'er to say Fluffyflops. Doesn't matter 'ow yer do it, as long as yer don't tell 'er it's part of a competition.'

Tom headed off towards Donna, and within ten minutes was leaving with her, much to the amusement of the others.

The pretty girl who had had the knife-wielder in her room earlier turned up without her friend, and within an hour Brad had left with her.

Mikey left Greg alone for a while. When he came back, Greg was in a terrible state and all over the place, barely able to stay conscious. 'What's up, mate?' He couldn't understand his reply, and seconds later Greg passed out. Nearby was Vince, who ran the Madhouse.

'Any idea what's up with him?' asked Mikey.

'Dunno. 'E's 'ad a lorra drink.'

'Well, that's why, then,' said Duffy, from the Charleston. 'He had a load of that GHB stuff earlier on. Mixed with alcohol it's fucking lethal. I'd get him down the medical centre, if I were you.'

Mikey tried to wake him up but Greg barely stirred. There was a medical centre less than a hundred yards from Es Paradis, so Mikey got Duffy to help carry Greg up there. Mikey told the doctor what he thought Greg had taken and the doctor gave him an injection.

Fortunately Greg had not had as much GHB or alcohol as everyone thought. However, when he came round just under two hours later he panicked. For a few moments he thought he was dying, and he had a strong desire not to expire – because the last girl he had shagged had been a monster and he did not want the posthumous embarrassment of having her face next to his, plastered all over the *Sun*. Fortunately, by dawn he felt fine and was able to leave.

Brad took the pretty girl to his room because her room-mate had pulled. Her name was Amanda and she had made it clear to Brad that they were not going to have sex. Ten minutes later, with her hand around his weapon, he figured that she'd probably changed her mind. She had. Brad had only taken one E, which had worn off sufficiently for him to have to concentrate on not coming. He was enjoying keeping himself as close to orgasm as possible. Greg had been right. Sex was so abundant that the other participant had almost become irrelevant. Trying to master a new technique or doing something different or outrageous to tell the others the next day had become the most important thing – next to scoring points, of course. He could not for the life of him think of a way of getting her to say 'Fluffyflops', though.

He was considering this when he was aware of something behind him. The hotel mongrel had pushed open the door of Brad's room and was sniffing around. Dogs seem to have a natural affinity with smelly body parts, so it was not long before he was attracted to the two bodies on the bed. His timing could not have been better. Just as Brad was slowing down to stop himself coming, the dog nudged its cold nose up his arse and licked his balls. It finished Brad off. He pulled out and whipped off the condom, aiming for Harry on the boat but ending up with Harry somewhere on Amanda's mid-stomach. He glared at the dog, which slunk out of the room wagging its tail.

chapter fifteen

The slap hurt. Rick's instinctive reaction was to give her a
Glasgow kiss, a knee-jerk reaction to the stinging pain, but
the impulse passed in seconds.

'What did you do that for?' He hoped she hadn't found
out about his visits to Viv in Lochaber, or to Lena in Park
Head.

'I can't trust you to do anything,' said Carmen.

'What are you on about?'

'Sandy,' she said, referring to her Yorkshire terrier.

'What about her?'

'Don't give me the innocent. Alistair told me all about
what happened.'

'Oh,' said Rick sheepishly.

'And what was it that almost killed my poor wee dog?
The same thing that causes us not to see each other every
weekend, the same thing that made you lose your job, the
same reason you're incapable of anything before Wednesday. Bloody drugs.'

'Och, that's hardly fair, hen. It was'nae pills she swallowed.'

'So puff's all right, but?'

'I didn't mean to leave it lying around. The wee bugger'll
eat anything. It didn't do any harm, though, did it?'

'God knows. And what about when you almost garrotted
her with her lead?'

'That was an accident. Anyway, you can't blame that on
drugs.'

'Can't I? When did it happen?'

'Sunday morning.'

'And where had you just got back from?'

'Um, the Arches.'

'And I suppose you were straight.'

'Well, I'd taken a couple, but—'

'But nothing. You were off your head.'

Rick remembered what had happened only too well. He'd got home from the Arches in Glasgow totally nutted. Thinking it would be a good idea to take the dog out for a walk, he had attached the extending lead to Sandy's collar and set off. It was a beautiful sunny morning and he had started running. Sandy, her little legs a blur, had struggled to keep up, so Rick let more of the lead out. All of a sudden, he felt a sharp yank. When he looked behind, the dog was airborne, swinging around a tree. Rick had run past it on one side and the dog on the other.

Carmen had entrusted him with her beloved Sandy for a week while she went to visit her sister in London. The dog was like a Tasmanian devil, zooming around his small flat and yapping incessantly. On the third day of Sandy's residence, she was unusually quiet. Rick remembered the pleasure he'd felt at the respite from stress the dog had been causing him. He decided to reward himself with a spliff. Ten minutes later, still unable to find the eighth he'd bought the day before, he put two and two together and made the correlation between the dog's inactivity and the sudden loss of his hash. Sandy didn't move for six hours and for once Rick was thankful when the dog resumed her previous level of boisterousness.

Like a fool, he'd told his friend Alistair McBride because he thought it made a good story. He should have known better. Alistair never could keep a secret.

For Carmen, the dog's mishaps were the final straw. She'd tired of Rick. He was twenty-nine, divorced and had just discovered clubbing and Ecstasy. For the last six months he had been out on his own or with his friends almost every Saturday and the whole scene for him was an excuse to relive his youth and pull girls barely out of their teens. This was naïve, as Carmen was beautiful and intelligent and way out of his league. She looked a little like Nicole Kidman, but with softer, rounder features, brighter red hair and captivating translucent blue eyes. She was quick-witted, too.

She had met Rick on the rebound from a short, passionate affair. She had known him for a number of years because he had been in the same class at school as her sister, who always spoke highly of him.

However, Carmen had been clubbing for at least six years, since she was seventeen. She was able more or less to control her buzz and was contemptuous of lost-its – guys walking around with gormless, grinning faces, dancing to anything and homing in on any girl who gave them the briefest eye-contact. Rick fell into this category. She was sure he was sleeping around, but she wasn't too bothered, especially as they hadn't had full sex for over a month.

Rick couldn't understand how she could chuck him over something as trivial as the dog. Over the next few weeks he realised the mistake he had made, beat up Alistair, took loads more drugs and constantly rang Carmen to try to get her back.

Carmen knew she would never go back with him. She also knew that she wanted to get out of Scotland and make a fresh start, find a new challenge. Maybe something abroad?

The mood in the boardroom was sombre. Adam Hawthorne-Blythe sat at the head of the table, as calm as ever. Jane Ward was sitting opposite Tom, who wanted the day to end as quickly as possible so he could catch up on some sleep. He had caught a flight in the early hours of Tuesday morning and had gone straight to work from the airport.

Sebastian was pacing up and down, his tie loosened and the sleeves of his blue-striped shirt rolled up to just below his elbows. A pen was behind his ear and a calculator in his hand. 'You're right, you know,' he said. 'It could run into hundreds of thousands – maybe even a million. No wonder we've been struggling to compete with our rivals.'

'What's done is done,' said Hawthorne-Blythe. 'Our main focus should now be on ensuring that we gather sufficient evidence to bring him to justice, so that future accommodation is contracted for our customers' benefit rather than the fiscal gain of a rogue director.'

'Easier said than done,' said Jane, wondering if anything ever ruffled him.

'Why can't we just tell him we know what he's up to, give him the boot and make him pay the money back?' asked Tom.

'Were it only so easy,' replied Hawthorne-Blythe.

'The problem is, Tom,' offered Sebastian, 'that we have to be careful what accusations we throw at him without evidence. He's a devious sod and I would imagine, with the money he's now got behind him, he could hire himself a good lawyer.'

'Unfair dismissal, slander – shoot ourselves in the foot, sure we could,' said Jane.

'Precisely,' agreed Hawthorne-Blythe. 'We need evidence. But the question is, how do we get it?'

'We could always ask Alison,' suggested Jane sarcastically. 'God, if you hadn't found that invoice, Sebastian . . .'

'No wonder he was so keen for her to get the job,' said Tom. 'What about sacking *her*? Don't you think that might ruffle his feathers enough for him to slip up?'

'Possibly,' said Jane. 'But I still think our best bet is to keep her out there. If she's looking after his accounts I reckon we've got much more chance of getting something on him – certainly more than we have back here.'

'Most definitely,' agreed Hawthorne-Blythe. 'He would be foolish indeed to leave evidence in the UK. I could probably find out a little about his affairs over here, but frankly it would prove nothing.'

'Mmmm,' said Sebastian thoughtfully. 'Getting rid of

Alison is the worst thing we could do at the moment. No, she must stay there at all costs.'

'But you should see how she's screwing up the resort, Sebastian. The reps are all demotivated, and no one has a good word to say about her,' said Tom.

'It's unfortunate, but this is so big that even if we have to write off the season out there and change all the reps we must get some evidence,' said Sebastian, sitting down. 'Alison must stay.'

'But *how* are we going to get the evidence?' asked Tom.

'We need someone out there,' said Jane.

Tom had a brainwave. 'What about Brad?'

Jane raised her eyebrows. 'He's certainly bright enough,' she said. 'And, from what you've said, he dislikes her sufficiently to have the right motivation.'

'She's almost certainly gonna sack him,' said Tom, 'and he knows it. Can't think of any better motivation.'

'Sorry, but about whom are we talking?' asked Hawthorne-Blythe, peering over the top of his glasses.

'Bradley Streeter,' said Jane.

'Who is he?' asked Hawthorne-Blythe.

'He's a first-year rep,' said Jane, realising as the words came out of her mouth, how the idea must sound.

'Absolutely not. Preposterous idea,' said Hawthorne-Blythe. 'If you think we can entrust what is tantamount to the future of this company to someone who has been with us for little more than three months and with whom we've had no previous dealings, well . . .' He didn't need to expand any further.

'Apart from anything else,' added Sebastian, 'if there's already animosity between him and Alison it would make it even more difficult for him to get anything worthwhile.'

'I guess you're right,' said Tom, watching Brad's lifeline disappear.

'No, what we need is someone who either has Alison's trust or who isn't known to her. It also needs to be someone we can count on for loyalty one hundred and ten per cent – somebody with the same blood running through their veins as we have,' said Hawthorne-Blythe.

They all looked blankly at each other. 'Maybe Brad'll turn something up,' said Tom lamely.

The bookings for Aguamar, the water-park next to the airport, were abysmal. In fact, the excursion bookings for the whole week were. Brad had been having a terrible time. Five large groups of lads were gunning for him: they had vandalised his information book, defaced his posters and tried to disrupt his bar nights while he was in Las Huertas. He had been in the Bon for one night, sharing a two-bedroom apartment with Natalie. Three groups were staying in Las Huertas, but they had turned two other groups in the Bon against him. Brad had seen Alison laughing and joking with the lads, and judging by the way they looked at him he suspected correctly that she had not been helping him. He couldn't wait until the weekend when all five groups were going home. He only hoped he didn't have to take their coach to the airport because he was fairly certain they were out to do him before they left.

Brad got on the coach Greg was guiding to Aguamar. Greg cracked a few funnies, and got everyone in the right mood. He told everyone it was his birthday the next day. He did this every two weeks to get presents, and as another angle for scoring points. Sitting at the front of the coach was a chubby, mousy-haired girl called Felicity, whom Greg had slept with the previous night.

When he had finished his spiel, Greg burrowed around in his bag. Brad guessed he was looking for the *Thunderbirds* tape, because they had had to leave it half-way through on the coach journey back from Hoe Down the night before. Most of the clients wanted to hear its conclusion.

Greg put a tape in the cassette player, but before pushing it in he switched on the microphone. 'Right, then, everyone. Whoever guesses who this is gets a free bottle of champagne.' He pushed in the cassette.

'Oh, Greg. I'm not sure I want to.'

'Look, I'm not gonna force yer. If yer don't wanna do it, like, just say so and I can get some shut-eye.'

Felicity sank in her chair turning beetroot.

'I bet you get loads of girls. Why me?'

'Cos loadsa girls ain't 'ere and you are.'

Noise of clothes rustling, springs creaking and slurping.

'Oh, Greg. That feels wonderful. Oh, yes. Don't stop. Why are you stopping? No, not up there. Greg, stop it. Ow! Get it away and put it back where it was.'

The coach was howling. Felicity sank further into her chair and her friend won the champagne.

'C'mon, Felicity, talk dirty to me.'

'I can't. I'm too shy.'

'Oh, please. It'll really turn me on.'

'What do you want me to say?'

'Just say "Fuck me, Fluffyflops." I won't be able to come if yer don't.'

Pause.

'All right, then. Fuck me, Fluffyflops.'

Brad got back from his date with Kelly just before four o'clock in the morning. Natalie was in the apartment taking off her makeup when he walked in. He thought she looked a little down.

'You all right, darling?' he said.

'Oh, nothing I won't get over. What about you? How did you go with the lovely Kelly?'

Brad scratched his head and sat down opposite her. 'To be honest, I don't know. It was a bit of a weird night. I mean, we got on all right but there was no . . . I dunno, can't put my finger on it.'

'Oh dear,' said Natalie, reaching behind her for a bottle of Southern Comfort and two glasses. 'Sounds like we'd better have a drink 'cos I've had a shit night too.' She poured out the golden liquid. 'You go first.'

'It wasn't really a shit night. I suppose I was looking

forward to it so much that it all seemed a bit of an anti-climax.'

'In what way?'

'There wasn't any rapport. I mean, all she did was smile sweetly and look lovely. We didn't talk about anything much. She laughed at my jokes. She didn't give me a knockback, but it didn't seem right to make a lunge. I don't know. Like I said, it was weird.'

'So what *did* you talk about?' asked Natalie.

'I asked her about what she did before she came away, what her ambitions were, a bit about relationships . . .'

'Did she ask you anything?'

Brad thought for a moment. 'Actually, I can't remember if she did.'

Natalie chuckled. 'Well, there you go. It sounds to me like she's totally wrapped up in herself. To be honest I've spoken to a few people about her.'

'Why?'

'When a woman looks like she does, Brad, other women want to know about her as much as blokes do – probably more so.' Brad accepted her insight. 'Most people I've spoken to say that she's pleasant but with not a lot to say for herself. You often find good-looking people are so used to using their looks to get what they want that they don't develop their personalities.'

'Were you an ugly child?' asked Brad.

'Was that a compliment or an insult?'

Brad smiled. 'Anyway, enough of my wailing. Suffice to say that I don't think I'll be bothering with her again. I wish there was someone here who was a bit of a challenge, y'know, someone who really flicked my switch.'

'Tell me about it,' said Natalie. 'All I end up with are bastards. I met this bloke at the beginning of the week – a punter – and he's lovely. We've had a couple of really nice nights out and now he's started fucking me about.'

'I don't know,' sighed Brad. 'Maybe we're just waiting for Cupid to shoot us up the arse with his arrow. Don't you think it would be nice to be with someone you were so into that when old Burt Lancaster and whatever-her-name-is are rolling around lovestruck in the waves you could totally relate to it, rather than arguing with someone in Tesco's over skimmed milk?'

'But that's the real world, Brad.'

'Yeah. That's probably why we're all here.'

The five men were squeezed into a corner of the Geordie Lad. The owner was a sarcastic seventeen-stone singer/guitarist from Sunderland called Big Al. The bar was in Port des Torrent, more of a family resort than San Antonio, and as such, it was a bar that YF&S never visited. It was for this reason that Mario had thought it the ideal place to meet his brother's friends.

Two had been based in Ibiza Town for the season. They were mugging, robbing, ducking and diving – anything to avoid working and to sustain a reasonable lifestyle. The other three had just arrived to an indefinite holiday. None of them had much time for Mario but one was his cousin and they were all friends of his small-time-gangster elder brother. It was more out of respect to him that they indulged the white sheep of his family.

Big Al looked suspiciously at the group. He had been around enough criminals to recognise wrong 'uns when he saw them. He tried to eavesdrop on what they were saying but was unable to make out a single word. All of the group, apart from Mario, looked like bruisers; a mixture of broken noses, scars and steroid-filled muscles. Mario's hair had grown to a respectable length so he no longer resembled an escapee from the Foreign Legion. However, his face wore the bitterest scowl. He had not forgotten the humiliation caused by the Immac.

If Big Al's attempts at eavesdropping Mario's conversation had been successful, the word he would most frequently have heard was 'revenge'. Mario was giving them all the information they needed to give a hiding to the perpetrator. Where he stayed, what time he passed the wasteland, what kind of fight he'd put up. Mario had all the information they needed and it was all correct – apart from one crucial element.

The name being mentioned was Mikey, not Brad.

chapter sixteen

When he woke up Brad was still pissed. He couldn't remember who the girl beside him was. She had her back to him, so he lifted her leg up and shagged her anyway. He emptied out within five minutes. She turned round but he still couldn't remember who she was. He didn't respond to her idle chat and a few minutes later she left, suitably unimpressed. Brad wasn't sure if it was her fault, but there were flies everywhere. They had been annoying him all season, but as he tried to get back to sleep they were even more persistent than normal, tickling his skin, buzzing in his ear. One in particular was trying to enter every available orifice. That was it. Brad was declaring war on flies.

Half an hour later he was in the supermarket under the Bon. He bought a fly swat, some spray and a device you put into a plug. Dehydrated, he went to the fridge to get himself some peach juice, which he liked because it was silky smooth on the throat. As he did so, he noticed a suave-looking Clark Gable lookalike – a sort of debonair squaddie – buying fruit. Until then, Brad had forgotten he had given the guy a severe talking to the night before because he had been messing Natalie around. He was trying to remember what he had said to him, when a sunburnt Brummie boy of about eighteen approached.

'Brad, you got a minute?'

'Sure,' he said, wincing at the red outline of a vest on the Brummie's blistered torso. 'What's up?'

'Well, you know during the welcome meeting you said that if we got sunburnt yoghurt was a good cure?'

'Not a cure, but it'll offer some relief.'

'Does it matter what flavour you get?' the boy asked.

'Shouldn't,' said Brad. 'Natural's the best though.'

'Really?' said the Brummie. 'That's a shame.'

'Why?' asked Brad.

'I don't like natural yoghurt.'

Brad realised he wasn't joking. 'Um, you're not meant to eat it.'

'What are you supposed to do with it, then?'

Brad couldn't resist. 'Rub it round your balls and in your hair. See you later.'

When he got back upstairs, Natalie was making tea. 'Two sugars, please.'

'You were wrecked last night,' she said, as she looked for the tea-bags. 'Do you remember the picture?'

'The group one outside the Cockney Pride? Yeah, course I do. Those bloody National Police!'

'That's not what I meant, but they were bastards, weren't they?'

'Too right – don't wanna mess with those guys. I was surprised Alison made us do it when they'd gone. Probably didn't want to lose her commission.'

'So do you remember the picture, then?' repeated Natalie.

'What do you mean?'

'Do you remember *seeing* it?'

'No. Why?'

Natalie fetched it.

Brad looked at it. 'Oh, no,' he groaned. 'I don't believe it,' he said. 'My left bollock's hanging out.'

'That'll teach you to go out not wearing any pants.'

'Oh, fuck. How many have we sold so far?'

'Last count, one hundred and eighty-three, I think.'

'Oh, great,' said Brad. 'So we're going to have all these clients going back saying, "Look, Mum, that's our rep's left testicle." Bloody marvellous.'

They went on to the balcony and sat down to drink their tea in the morning sun.

'I'm a bit worried about Greg, you know,' said Brad.

'Why?' asked Natalie.

'I think he's taken a pill every night since he had that first one when Tom came over. He told me the other day that morning desk duties were a bind – he's missed two in the last week.'

'I'm not surprised,' said Natalie. 'He's not normally in till seven, and then he's usually got some girl with him. God knows how much sleep he's getting.'

They sat quietly, relaxed enough in each other's company for silences not to feel uncomfortable.

'What transfer are you on tonight?' asked Natalie, placing her empty cup on the floor.

'Dunno. As long as it's not those bastards who've been making my life hell all week I don't give a fuck. You? It's your night off, isn't it?'

'Was. I swapped it with Mikey 'cos I was gonna see that bloke but he's stopped messing me about and come clean. He's got a wife back home.' The talking-to had worked, thought Brad. 'So I've swapped it back. Mikey's off tonight.'

Just then, the door burst open and Greg was there, still in the same clothes as the night before. It was clear that he hadn't slept and he still seemed slightly charged.

'Fuckin' 'ell, lad. I've gorra tell yer wha's just 'appened to me.' He flopped on to the settee. 'I've just shagged that girl who's on 'oneymoon.'

'Where was her old man?' said Natalie.

'He'd gone 'ome early, pissed. I did 'er in that spare room on the first floor.'

'Hang on a minute,' said Brad, remembering the couple because he had thought it sad that someone should come on honeymoon with YF&S. 'Correct me if I'm wrong, Greg, but doesn't she look like Olive from that old sitcom *On the Buses*, and . . .' Brad suddenly remembered the worst bit '. . . isn't she eight months pregnant?'

'Yeah,' said Greg enthusiastically. 'Fuckin' great what pills do, innit?'

'You and me are gonna have to talk.'

Alison had made a decision. She was going to get rid of Brad by the end of the following week and at last she had worked out how. From the conversation she had had with Tom, she guessed that it would have to be something pretty drastic to get rid of the blue-eyed boy. God, she hated him. But he wasn't as smart as her. If he was, the fourteen thousand pounds would have been sitting in front of him not her. Of course, there was still the money to come from Felipe for her part in helping him with his 'pension'. All this money and it was only just August. Alison looked at the transfer sheets. She smiled as she put Brad's name next to the Birmingham flight, which had fifty-two other male names on it.

Mikey gave the joint to Brad. They were on the roof of the Bon. Whenever they wanted to get away from it all, this is where they came.

'So what you gonna do?' asked Mikey.

'Well, for starters,' said Brad, reaching into his shirt pocket, 'I've been saving this for a special occasion.' He pulled out a gram of coke. 'And it's either going up my nose or in that spliff.'

'Do you think that's a good idea?'

'Got a better one?'

'I could always come with you.'

'Mmm.' Brad thought about it. He liked that idea – he could certainly do with the back-up. 'Yeah, all right, then. Cool. Still gonna do the Charlie, though.'

Mikey laughed and nodded.

'I just can't believe – after the week I've had – that she'd be stupid enough to give me that transfer. They'll fucking lynch me. I'm getting on that coach tooled up. Old Wotsisface from the Star is gonna get me some gas. I've had enough of all this bollocks.'

By the time the coach arrived, the coke had worn off and Brad was feeling mellow. He was so stoned he didn't give a toss about anything. When he got on, the hostility towards him was almost palpable. He hadn't bothered with the CS gas – he'd got too pissed and stoned. As the coach pulled away there was silence. Brad switched on the microphone. Mikey was sitting next to him, looking out of the window. Brad stood up and looked at all the miserable faces. Fuck it, he thought.

'Right, then, everyone,' he said, in his happiest *Hi-De-Hi* voice. 'Have we all got our passports?'

Silence.

'Have we all had a good time?'

Oh, shit, thought Mikey. He's going to start taking the piss.

'Have any of you little treasures fallen in love this week?'

'Fuck off,' said someone near the back.

'No? Oh, that's a shame. Well, I'm sure you've all had a wonderful time, nevertheless.'

'Sit down, you Cockney bastard,' from half-way down the coach.

'Yes, well, I'll sit down in a moment.' Mikey caught Brad's eye with a please-don't look. Brad ignored it. 'Before I do, I'd just like to say that I hope that, if any of you have somehow managed to score during this last week or two, you wore a condom. Now, please, don't for one moment think that I give a toss about any of you catching Aids. I can't stand the thought of any of you fuckers breeding and populating the planet with your sorry offspring.'

Mikey sank lower in his seat and pulled his baseball cap over his eyes.

'As we drive past San An harbour, I'd like to point out some of the sights for the last time. If you look to the right you can see the boats in the harbour. Take one long last look at them all, lads, ready to go to your favourite beaches tomorrow. Now spare a thought for your poor rep Brad, lying on a beach while you're stuck indoors looking at the situations-vacant column in your local paper – that's for those of you who can read.'

The coach drove passed a group of girls all wearing short skirts.

'Take one last look at all those lovely girls, and think about your poor rep Brad, shagging who he wants – maybe even your girlfriends.'

The coach drove on.

'Take one long last look at the Star and think about your poor rep Brad getting into all the clubs for nothing, when you're getting turned away from clubs back home because you can't afford any decent clothes and are too fucking scruffy to get in.'

Brad continued the barrage of insults for almost five minutes. '. . . and I hope you all have a safe flight home, but if you don't then I hope the plane crashes near Burnley, where I know most of you are from, 'cos, by the look of you lot, they must be used to having shit all over their streets. Hope to see you with Young Free & Single again. Bing-bong.'

Miraculously, the coach was almost totally silent for the rest of the journey. At the airport, Brad sent them all to the wrong gate, just for good measure, and instead of checking them in, he made his way straight to Arrivals.

An hour later, he had his clipboard in his hand and the first client came through. 'Young Free & Single?'

Looking around the group gathered in the bar of Las Huertas, it struck Mikey that YF&S clients had a certain blandness about them. Apart from the three Cockney slappers from Leyton, who had a certain brainlessness about them. The group was probably the most rowdy Mikey had had to control all season. Even before the crawl started a Mancunian lad had had to go to the medical centre because he had been having a bundle with his two friends one of whom had bitten his dick and made it bleed.

Mikey was dividing his duties between Las Huertas, where Mario was now staying, and the Bon. He had started winding Mario up again, which was proving particularly easy as Mario had just placed a food order in Spanish. His self-satisfied smile turned to a scowl when Mikey informed him that the waiter's hysteria had been brought on by Mario's request for a dog on heat instead of a hot dog.

Earlier in the day, the company photographer had been over to take some pictures for the following year's brochure, where he had got Mario to pose on one of the mechanical bulls at the Rodeo Grill. Mikey had started the bull on full speed sending Mario flying off.

The bar crawl was the biggest of the season, and as the massive line of singing, shouting YF&S holidaymakers wound its way through the streets of San Antonio, Mikey could feel the disgust with which other holidaymakers viewed them. Mario was at the front of the group, leading the singing and enjoying the power trip of having more than two hundred people doing more or less exactly what he wanted.

Two girls, both called Mary, were giving Mikey the come-on. He wasn't sure at first which one to make a play for. The choice was narrowed somewhat when the darker-haired of the pair was found in the toilets of the Cockney Pride giving one of the clients a blow-job.

This must have set some kind of precedent, because later Mario and Greg emerged triumphant from the same toilet, having received a wank and a blow-job respectively from a girl called Geraldine. They spent the next hour bragging about it to anyone who would listen. Later, when all of the group were in Sgt Pepper's, Mikey found Geraldine sitting outside crying. She'd been off her face when she had indulged Greg and Mario and was regretting it because almost everyone knew about it. Mikey talked to her for nearly ten minutes, trying to console her, but she would not stop sobbing.

Brad came out to see what was wrong, and as Mikey was telling him what had happened, the girl suddenly stopped crying. She stared directly ahead, then jumped up and ran into the road, into the path of an oncoming van. Luckily it was only doing about thirty miles an hour and Mikey was quick enough to push her out of the way.

Mikey brought her back, took her into a restaurant next to Sgt Pepper's and ordered her a coffee. He beckoned Heather to look after her and marched up to Brad. The two men looked at each other, thinking exactly the same thing.

'Well?' said Mikey.

'Yeah, I know, it's all getting out of hand. Let's go and have a word.'

They walked into the bar to find Greg and Mario.

'It's got to stop,' said Brad.

'Whassamarrer?' said Greg, putting an arm around Brad's shoulders.

'This points thing's getting out of hand,' said Mikey.

'You don't like it 'cos you're in last place,' said Mario mockingly.

'I don't give a toss which place I'm in. Did you see what just happened to Geraldine?'

'Who?'

'The girl in the bogs,' laughed Greg.

'I'm glad you find it funny,' said Brad. 'She just ran out in front of a car 'cos of you two. Thankfully she wasn't hurt.'

'This whole points thing's gotta stop,' said Mikey.

'It was just a bit of fun at first,' said Brad, 'but it's turned into a fucking obsession.'

'Oh, you've changed your tune, soft lad,' said Greg to Brad.

'Yeah, maybe I have. And I'm as guilty as anyone else,' admitted Brad. 'But you've gotta draw the fucking line somewhere. I know a lot of these girls know the score, but it's got to the stage where we don't even treat them like people. And to be honest, I'm bored with it.'

'Well, I'm not,' said Mario belligerently.

'It's just a phase,' said Greg. 'You'll gerrover it.'

'No. I'm all for a laugh but—'

'There's a laugh, and there's a laugh,' completed Mikey. 'You two were bang out of order.'

'Oh, shut up, you wanker,' said Mario.

Almost before Mario had finished the sentence Mikey had him pinned up against the wall. 'No more warnings. No more messing. Cross me again and you'll be the sorriest Italian on this island.'

Mario could tell he was serious and, for all his bravado, there was no way he wanted to fight Mikey – not on his own, at any rate. Mikey let him go and stormed out.

Brad took Greg to one side. 'Listen, mate, these pills you're doing, slow down a bit, eh? There's nothing wrong with them but it's like anything, moderation.'

'But they're fuckin' great. Ten times better than being pissed. And sex!'

'Just be careful. I know it's hard. Fuck me, if I'd started taking pills out here, getting them for nothing, partying every night, then I'd probably be the same. Just make sure you control them rather than the other way round.'

Brad walked away, not convinced that Greg had heeded his advice. He brushed past Mario who looked surprisingly unruffled after his confrontation with Mikey.

Mario looked at his watch. Another couple of hours and Mikey would know all about no warnings.

It was less than a week since Brad had taken Kelly out. Although he had decided not to pursue her further, he was less than happy when he got down to the Star and discovered she had just started seeing someone called Digger. He worked at the go-kart track and was classically tall, dark and handsome. People often said he looked like Eddie Kidd. He drove around in a bright yellow Karmann Ghia, which always drew admiring looks when he was sitting at the wheel.

Brad was at bar five in the Star, surrounded by Thomson's reps, none of whom liked Digger. They thought it quite funny when Brad started calling Digger Noddy Holder and singing Slade songs. However, as Brad got more and more pissed, he eventually found himself alone.

Mikey came up to him. 'Brad, I'm off.'

'Mikey, me old chum, see that twat over there? Noddy fucking Holder. Remember? That geezer from Slade. Come on, feel the noise . . .' Brad was off again.

Mikey laughed. 'See you later, mate.'

Mikey walked back towards the apartments the same way he always did. As he went past the wasteland he was aware of some people lurking in the shadows. He got closer and made out five large male silhouettes, speaking what at first he thought to be Spanish, but then figured was Italian. Something didn't feel right, so he crossed the road. The group sprang into life and, within seconds, were surrounding him. Mikey relaxed on to the balls of his feet, his fists clenched loosely by his sides and tried to position himself so that none of the group was behind him.

'What do you want?' he asked.

'We're here to teach you a lesson.'

Mikey knew there was no point in trying to reason, and all escape routes were cut off. He lashed out with his right foot and his instep connected with a groin. Six foot four and eighteen stone of bully doubled up, and as he was heading for the ground, Mikey swivelled and aimed a karate kick at his head. There was a loud crack as his jaw broke.

Mikey threw out a vicious right fist behind him. It glanced the cheek of another, stunning him temporarily. Then Mikey felt a blow to the back of his head that almost made him sick. He fell face down to the ground. Before he hit it, a foot volleyed him in the face. It was a miracle he stayed conscious. He huddled up in a ball. Fists and boots hammered into him. Occasionally one connected with his groin or his head. He thought it would never stop.

Eventually his assailants ran off. Mikey lay there, drifting in and out of consciousness, unable to move. As the body's natural pain-killers wore off he groaned and tried to look up through swollen eyes. The fight had taken him away from the road and passers-by. Mikey knew he was in trouble.

Brad stumbled out of the Star and into the café next door. He sat in a corner, drinking coffee and throwing food down his neck like a caveman. Half an hour later he wove his way to the taxi rank but there was a massive queue. Cursing under his breath he started the walk back, still singing Slade songs.

Half-way through 'Goodbye To Jane,' his bladder guided him towards the Anglers. By the time he got there he'd sobered up a bit, but the door was locked and the bar was closed. 'Wankers,' he said. Fortunately the wasteland was only yards away, but in case he didn't make it he started pissing as he walked.

A low groan and rustling from about twenty yards away halted him. At first he thought it was a stray dog or cat, but as he got closer he realised it was a man. He approached cautiously. Someone might have been luring him into a trap. But as he got closer . . .

'Mikey!' Brad ran over. He lifted his friend's bloodied head and cradled it in his arms. 'Shit. What happened?' He was sobering up fast.

Mikey just groaned.

'Fuck, you need help. Stay there.'

'I'm hardly going anywhere, you moron,' said Mikey, through broken teeth.

'Oi, any more of your lip and I'll do you myself.' Brad tried to make light of the situation. He took off his shirt and cardigan, placed the shirt under Mikey's head and draped the cardigan over him. 'I won't be long.'

'Hurry up, Brad, I think I'm in a bad way.'

'It's a fucking miracle,' said Brad, as Mikey eased himself upright in bed. 'I thought that was your lot for the season.'

'I thought it was my lot full stop,' said Mikey, wincing as

he rested his bruised kidneys against the wall at the top of his bed.

'So what was the final tally, then?' asked Brad.

'Two teeth, broken nose, concussion, a couple of black eyes and loads and loads of bruises. Otherwise not even a cracked rib. I must admit, I thought it was a lot worse.'

'So did I. I've never sobered up so fast. I can't believe it was me who found you. Wish I hadn't now. You've ruined my clothes, bleeding all over them. It's me who should be getting treatment, coming into contact with your blood without wearing surgical gloves.'

'If you don't watch it you'll be coming into contact with your own blood,' joked Mikey.

Brad went over to the fridge and poured out a couple of glasses of orange juice. When he brought them back and sat down, a wad of money fell out of his tracksuit bottoms.

'What's that?' asked Mikey.

'Er, just some money I had sent over to get the car sorted out. The gearbox has gone. Plus I just picked up some money from the Charleston and the Madhouse for the condoms.' Brad quickly moved on. 'Do you still reckon your little bashing was down to our friend?'

'Who else could it have been? They didn't try to rob me, they were Italian, and they said that they were going to teach me a lesson. No, it was down to Mario, all right.'

'So now what?'

'I dunno. Something will happen to Mario before the end of the season, I know it will. The doctor reckons the bruising will go down in a few days so we'll see then.'

'Yeah, well, taking the advice you gave me when I wanted to do him, I'm gonna get him back in another way.'

'Oh, yeah, and how's that?'

Brad pulled out a bottle of laxative.

It was 45°C. There were going to be a few burnt bodies later on. The official Ibiza beach party was one of the most popular excursions, so six boats were transporting almost three hundred expectant revellers to where it was held. It was well organised, the groups split into two teams for the beach games and competitions. The reps normally took turns to captain the teams, and on this occasion the honours fell upon Brad's and Mario's shoulders. When the games were finished, a meal of chops, salad and spuds was laid on, during which there were a few drinking games. At the end of the competitions, the two teams were neck and neck. Brad had the perfect opportunity.

He went to the bar and got a couple of La Mumbas. Into one he poured almost half a bottle of the powerful laxative. Then he went to the table where Mario was sitting, stood on an empty chair and blew his whistle. Everyone looked up. 'If I could have your attention, please,' he yelled. As he did so, a girl who was sitting next to Mario came back to her seat. Brad didn't see her move the two La Mumba's to make room for her bag. 'Me and Mario are going to settle the competition by seeing who can down a La Mumba first.'

There was lots of cheering, and Mario stood on his chair. Brad bent down to pick up the two drinks, but was horrified to see they had been moved. He froze, but three hundred clients were clapping and egging him on. Whilst he was dithering, Mario grabbed the drink Brad was certain was laxative-free. But he could do nothing for fear of alerting his intended victim. Instead he brought the glass in his hand up to his lips: he was going to have to drink it and hope for the best.

The next half-hour was one of the longest in Brad's life. It was small consolation that he won the drinking race. To try to take his mind off the expected gurgling from his bowels, he picked up a pretty brunette and ran into the sea with her. He threw her into the water when they were knee deep. Unfortunately, she landed on some jagged rocks and gashed her leg. Brad felt about as popular as a hurricane at a wig-makers' convention.

The toilets were round the back of the bar so he sat down near them, waiting for the inevitable. A couple of times he felt his stomach rumble. Here it comes, he thought. He strolled over to the one functioning toilet and sat down on the seatless pan to prepare himself. Nothing happened.

Suddenly there was a desperate banging on the door. 'Open up, open up. Quick!'

I recognise that voice, thought Brad.

The door didn't have a lock on it and flew open to reveal Mario, clutching his stomach, and two girls who had been waiting patiently to use the toilet.

'Let me in, for fuck's sake,' gasped Mario.

Brad pulled up his shorts. Mario barged in and slammed the door.

Once inside, Mario leant forward to hold the door shut, and crouched over the toilet. His bowels exploded with such force, that hardly any of their contents made it into the pan. But the relief was so great that Mario could do nothing to alter the trajectory or stop the expulsion.

It was almost two minutes before he was able to turn around and see the damage he had done. When he saw the mess he was flabbergasted. Throwing water from the sink over the back of the toilet only made it worse. He pulled open the door slightly and peered out. More than half a dozen girls were waiting there now. Brad was rounding up some more.

'Go away,' said Mario. 'You can't come in here.'

'Why not?' said one of the girls. 'We've been waiting here for ages.'

'Just fuck off,' hissed Mario. 'I'm not well.'

'There's no need to talk like that,' said the girl.

'Piss off,' said Mario.

The girl turned to her friend. 'I'm not going to let him speak to me like that.'

She yanked open the door. As she did so, seven mouths dropped open. The girl let go of the door, which swung shut, and puked up. From the toilet came the most ferocious sound of flatulence imaginable. Mario was off again.

The weeks seemed to be getting shorter and Saturday transfer day had arrived yet again. Kevin Roundtree, the training manager from head office was on resort. So was Kirstie Davies. She had had a windfall and wasted no time in telling Alison what a fabulous lifestyle she now enjoyed. Anyone who knew how much they hated each other would have been surprised at what great friends they appeared to be.

Kevin Roundtree was in his mid-forties but his thick grey moustache and thinning grey hair made him seem at least ten years older. He was flying back on Sunday and wanted to assess a couple of reps' microphone work on the incoming and outgoing airport transfer. Everyone was dreading it was going to be them, apart from Mikey. His face still looked battered, and it was felt that he was not the ideal choice to meet the new arrivals. Mario, who had only just recovered from a two-day intimate relationship with the toilets, was chosen to accompany Kevin for the outgoing journey, Natalie the inbound.

It was seven o'clock in the evening and the bar of the Bon was packed. Kevin was having a drink and chatting to Brad and Natalie when Alison burst in. 'Everyone, Reception quick,' she said, addressing the three of them.

Brad looked at Natalie and raised his eyebrows, then, with Kevin, they followed Alison.

She was standing by an open locker. 'See? All gone,' she said.

'What's all gone?' asked Kevin.

'The money.' Nobody knew what she was on about. 'The excursion money. I reckon it must be at least fifteen grand. I was just about to check it so Jaime could collect it for banking.'

'Who's Jaime?' asked Kevin.

'He's from Viajes Diamanté. He collects the money on Saturdays or Sundays.'

'Did anyone else have a key?' asked Natalie.

'Only me. The master key doesn't even fit my locker.'

'When did you last check it?' asked Brad.

'This morning.'

'Where was the key between then and now?' asked Natalie.

'In my room, on the table.'

'So it's possible that someone could have got into your room and taken the key for a while,' said Kevin.

'Yes, but – I don't know. Who would do that? It'd have to be someone . . .' Alison's voice trailed off.

'You two leave this to Alison and me. I – I'm sure you've both got to get things ready for the airport,' Kevin said. Once they had left the room, he turned to Alison. 'Any ideas?'

'Not really. I can't see how it happened.'

'Was the key where you left it?'

'To be honest I can't remember. It's possible.'

'Someone must have been into your room and it must have been someone who knew about the excursion money.'

Kevin paused to let Alison work it out for herself.

'Oh, no,' said Alison, realising what he meant. 'Not one of my reps, surely?'

'Can you think of anyone else?'

'I guess not.'

'I'll ring head office. Put your thinking cap on and see if you can come up with anything.'

'Here we go again,' said Sebastian, walking into Jane's office and slamming the door shut. 'It's already started. Just had Kevin on the phone. Allegedly fifteen thousand pounds of excursion money's been stolen from Alison's locker in Ibiza.'

'Oh, no,' said Jane. 'How?'

'Your guess is as good as mine. I'm waiting for more info, but Kevin reckons it's probably one of the reps.'

'Which one?'

'Don't know.'

'Kevin's not in on what's happening out there with Alison and Felipe, is he?' asked Tom.

'Christ, no,' said Sebastian. 'He gets on too well with the pair of them. The only people who know about what's going on, apart from Hawthorne-Blythe, are in this room.'

'So now what?' asked Jane.

'We sit tight and see what transpires,' said Sebastian.

'Is there any way of putting a tap on Felipe's phone?' asked Tom.

All of the reps, apart from Mikey, had gone to the airport. Mario and Natalie were glad that the locker had been broken into – it meant that Kevin wasn't going to the airport with them. Alison had suggested that, while the reps were at the airport, each of their rooms was checked for any sign of involvement in the theft. Alison was going to look through Mario and Greg's rooms with Jaime from Viajes Diamanté. Mikey was to accompany Kevin, after his room had been given the once-over by Kevin and Alison.

Heather's room was clean. Mikey noticed that Kevin spent a long time going through the drawers next to her bed. When he glanced into them they were full of panties.

When they went into Brad and Natalie's apartment, Mikey looked in Natalie's room and Kevin in Brad's. Mikey was just thinking what a messy bitch Natalie was when Kevin called him. 'Mikey, in here.'

Mikey walked into Brad's room. The mattress was on the floor, the bed base up against the wall and three boxes of condoms were stacked in the corner. Kevin was holding up the bedclothes.

'Look.'

Poorly hidden beneath a sheet were several empty brown envelopes. 'Excursion money' was printed on them and Alison's signature was across the seal. Mikey remembered the wad of money that had fallen out of Brad's pocket. 'Oh, no.'

*

The airport was the busiest Brad had ever seen it. Greg had excelled himself: he had pulled a girl and taken her into the toilets for a shag as soon as he had ticked her name off on the clipboard. Brad had agreed to check in the rest of his flight. Everybody had come through except one male single share, whose surname was Fisher. Greg was in and out of the loos within ten minutes. The girl looked a mess.

'Harry on the boat?' asked Brad.

Greg grinned. 'Thought y'wouldn't approve – y'know, me not respecting women.'

'My attitude might have changed a bit but not that much, mate. Good effort!'

Greg waited another five minutes for the stray client. In the end Brad agreed to look out for him so that Greg could get on his coach. No sooner had Greg gone than Brad was interrupted from checking down his list by a voice. 'Are you the rep for Young Free & Single?'

Brad looked down, at a man who was less than three feet tall. 'Mr Fisher?'

Dennis Fisher sat with Brad for the half-hour it took for Brad's flight to arrive, then next to him on the transfer to San Antonio. Fortunately, Dennis had a wicked sense of humour, and had Brad in stitches for most of the journey. By the time they got to the apartments, he had persuaded Dennis to star in a dwarf-throwing contest on the cruise the next day. If he didn't feel tired, he decided to do a poster to advertise it when he got back to his room.

'I'm shocked,' said Alison.

'Brown envelopes with your signature on them – just like you described putting in the locker. You can even ask Mikey. Good idea, that was, having two of us there. And just as well, seeing as the best part of fifteen grand is missing and with two of us finding it no one else can be suspected,' said Kevin.

'But what was Brad thinking of? How stupid of him. I had such high hopes for him, you know.'

274

'Well, you can forget those,' said Kevin, 'because I'm sure that once I've got in touch with someone else from head office he'll be in a cab to the airport and home.'

Just then a coach pulled up outside. 'Right,' said Kevin. 'That'll be Greg's coach, so Brad will be here soon and I've got to make some calls. I'll be in my room or on the phone if you need me, but try and make sure I'm not interrupted – unless someone finds the rest of the money.'

Brad was surprised to see Kevin in Reception.

'When you've checked them all in, can you come up to my room?' asked Kevin.

'Yeah, sure,' said Brad. 'Five one two, isn't it?'

'That's the one.'

Brad checked the clients in without a hitch. He got himself a coffee, went up to Kevin's room and knocked on the door.

'Come in.' Kevin was sitting at a square table made of a light-coloured wood. He had the chairs positioned opposite each other, as if prepared for an interview. 'Sit down.' He gestured to the empty chair.

Brad made himself comfortable. Smiling, he waited to see what Kevin wanted.

'Brad, I'm afraid we're going to have to let you go.'

It didn't sink in at first. 'I'm sorry,' said Brad, looking at him blankly.

'We're letting you go. As of now you are no longer employed by Young Free & Single. I've managed to get you on the eight-twenty flight this morning, which leaves in around four hours. If you miss that you'll have to make your own way back to England.'

Brad was reeling. He had been sacked. But why? Had someone found out about the money he'd taken from Duffy at the beginning of the season? Was it the free meals he'd had in the Anglers?

'I should warn you also that it would not be in your interests to stay on the island. If need be, we sometimes involve the police in this kind of incident when we consider it relevant. We certainly don't want you having any further contact with any of the reps.'

'Hang on a sec, what's this all about? What am I supposed to have done?'

'I'm sorry, I'm not allowed to say.'

'But this is my future you're talking about.'

'Sorry, Brad, I'm just here to do the dirty work. If you've any questions they should be addressed to head office.'

'Too right I will,' said Brad. 'In fact, I'll ring them now.'

'It's only every other Saturday that they're in the office and even then they leave at eight. By all means give them a call first thing Monday.'

It sank in that he really meant it. 'You can't sack me without telling me what I've done. I haven't done anything wrong. What's that useless slag Alison been saying about me, eh?'

'It's got nothing to do with Alison. As I've said, when you're back in the UK—'

'But what's the point in sending me back?' asked Brad, raising his voice. 'I'm gonna have to pack all my things up only to get home, unpack them and pack them again when this is all sorted out and I come back here on the next flight.'

'Whether you come back or not is clearly something that you will have to discuss with head office. In the meantime I'd get your things together otherwise you'll be paying for your own flight.'

Although Brad knew he could afford his own flight, all he could think of was getting back as soon as possible to see what the hell was going on. Then it dawned on him. 'This is about that money, isn't it?'

'As I've already stated, Brad, I cannot divulge the reason for your dismissal.'

'This is fucking pathetic,' said Brad. 'I'm going to see Mikey and Alison.'

Kevin stood up. 'I should warn you, Brad, that if you

make any attempt to approach any of the other reps, I will call the police. I've sent Natalie to the Delfin so you can get your things from your room.'

Brad looked at Kevin. He could tell that he was serious. For Brad, the season was over.

chapter seventeen

Carmen had put the mattress back on the bed. The three condom boxes were still in the corner, which made her chuckle. She found some group pictures. So that's Brad, she thought. She'd heard a lot about him and he sounded interesting. Now she thought he looked interesting too.

It had all happened rather quickly for her. One minute she was in Glasgow, in a relationship and in a rut, and after a phone call, a meeting and some basic training she was in Ibiza, sharing Brad's old apartment with Greg. Natalie had been moved to Las Huertas, where she was working with Heather and Mario. Mikey was by himself at the phoneless Delfin and, as such, had still not spoken to Brad.

It was the Thursday after Brad's departure. The only person who had spoken to him was Natalie. She had told everybody that, as suspected, Brad had been sacked for stealing fifteen thousand pounds' worth of excursion money. Although none of them wanted to believe it, Greg and she both knew that Brad was quite sharp and not averse to the idea of the odd scam. He had told them both of dealings he'd had back home which had not been exactly on the right side of the law. Even Mikey had his doubts. He had told Greg, in confidence, about the money he had seen Brad with. Greg had told Heather, in confidence, Heather had told Natalie, in confidence, Natalie had told Mario, in confidence, and Mario had told Alison, in confidence. Alison had smiled.

Felipe saw Tom's reflection in the window opposite his slightly open door, so he started to speak louder.

'Yes, I've heard all about it, Alison. He stole fifteen thousand, didn't he? . . . You say he what? My, my. So even Mikey thinks he did it? My, my. It just goes to show. Well, thank you ever so much for calling. You take care now. 'Bye.'

Tom hurried into Sebastian's office without knocking. Jane was there and had been having one of her rare snogs at work with her lover.

'Haven't you heard of knocking?' asked Sebastian.

'I was just standing outside Felipe's office,' said Tom, ignoring the comment. 'I heard him on the phone to Alison. Looks like I was wrong after all. From what he was saying, Brad did do it.'

'What did he say exactly?' asked Jane.

'Just that Mikey thinks Brad did it as well, and you know how close they were. Other than that, he didn't seem to know much about it or be too interested.'

'Well, I'll be . . .' said Jane. 'I'd've put money on it being something to do with Alison.'

'Looks like your famous gut feelings were wrong for once,' said Sebastian. He caught Jane's admonishing look and hurried on. 'Well, it doesn't matter now anyway. Brad's history.'

Just then the phone rang.

'Hunter,' said Sebastian, before handing the phone to Jane.

Jane nodded, said, 'Yes, okay,' a couple of times then hung up. She looked at Tom. 'It's Brad again,' she said. 'He wants to see me.'

'That's the fourth day running, isn't it?' said Sebastian.

Although Brad had explained everything, and although Jane believed most of what he said, she could do nothing.

'Look, I'm sorry, Brad. There really is nothing more to say on the matter. You can deny all knowledge of the money but the fact is that the empty envelopes were found in your room. You can tell me that Alison's on the take, but without any proof there's not much I can do. Anyway, your replacement arrived on resort yesterday.'

Brad had a sick feeling in the pit of his stomach. He had realised that, no matter what happened, he wouldn't be going back as a rep for YF&S.

'I don't believe it,' was all he could say. 'I was so sure I'd be going back out there that I even left my car behind. Admittedly it wouldn't have been worth bringing it back, but . . . I honestly thought that, of all people, you'd believe me, Jane.'

'I'm sorry, Brad, but even if I do believe you – which I'm not saying I do – then I would still be able to do nothing.'

'My replacement, what's he like?' asked Brad.

'It's a she, actually. Her name's Carmen.'

'Oh.' Brad had run out of conversation. 'Well, I guess there's not much left to say, is there?'

'I'm sorry it had to end like this, Brad.'

'So am I.'

'What are your plans?' she asked, standing up to open her office door for him.

'Dunno. Get my head together and sort out what I'm going to do.'

Looking at Brad Jane felt sorry for him. She stretched up and kissed his cheek.

As he left she had another one of her gut feelings.

Alison opened one of the giant boxes of Persil under the sink in her apartment. She reached through the first inch or so of powder and pulled out a plastic bag. The bank statements and documents it contained were quickly spread out over the table, along with the money she had made in the last few days. It gave her considerable pleasure to see it all there. She chuckled to herself. Seeing Brad go had been the highlight of her season – even better than screwing Mario.

A friend of Tom's had got him a plug adaptor that

contained a hidden microphone. Tom had swapped this with the normal adaptor in Felipe's office and spent as much time as he could with his Walkman headset tuned in. He could only hear Felipe's side of any conversation, and two days passed without anything untoward being said. In fact, hardly anything had been said because Felipe was seldom in his office. It was just a hunch Tom had. He knew it was too late to help Brad, but for his own peace of mind he wanted to know what had happened.

It was Friday afternoon and Tom was bored. He tuned in his Walkman. When he heard Felipe talking he was pleasantly surprised. It soon became clear that Alison was at the other end of the line. Tom pressed the record button.

'Yes, I'm sorry about that. Of course I knew what you were on about. It's just that Tom was standing outside my office. Of course he did – hook, line and sinker. Now, don't worry, everything will be fine. Yes, I'll be there in a week or so. I just hope you're happy that Brad has gone. Well, whether he did or whether he didn't doesn't matter now, does it? Look, I must dash. I'll see you soon. You too. Goodbye.'

'Told you so,' said Tom, throwing the cassette on Sebastian's desk.

'Told me what?' asked Sebastian.

'Told you Brad was innocent.'

'How so?' asked Jane.

Tom played them the tape. When it was finished, he turned to Jane. 'Shall I call Brad and offer him his job back?'

'You know we can't, Tom. Carmen's already there. Anyway, he didn't categorically say that Brad didn't do it. All it really tells us is that Felipe made up the conversation you heard the other day because he knew you were standing outside his office.'

'But why would he do that unless he was hiding the fact that Alison set him up?' asked Tom. 'It seems so unfair.'

'Life's unfair,' said Sebastian. 'It's too late. There's always the risk that Alison might smell a rat, which I'm not prepared to take.'

Tom looked at Jane.

'He's right, Tom,' she said. 'It's a terrible shame, I know, but we all understand what's at stake here.'

'Oh, well, that's the end of Brad, then.'

chapter eighteen

A little over two weeks had passed since Brad had arrived back in Ibiza and already he was making Alison's life hell.

He wasn't sure what was going to happen when he first returned to San Antonio. A lot of bar-owners made out that they liked the reps but when the clients were no longer around, they were given the cold shoulder. Brad was glad he had gone out of his way to get on with everyone, so that most of the bar-owners and workers genuinely liked him, rather than his badge. This had been reflected in the number of jobs he had been offered. Ray had got him a job DJing in Sgt Pepper's; Giles, who ran the beach party, had offered him a job taking group photographs and videoing the day; Irish Ben had pulled a few strings so Brad was taken on as a bouncer in the Star, and Woodsy had persuaded Manny to let him work on the excursions. This meant that virtually everywhere Young Free & Single went, Brad was working, and if ever Alison turned up, Brad made his dislike more than evident.

Brad loved not having the pressures of repping. It meant he was able to go out clubbing a lot more and the only days he needed to get up early were when he was due to work on the beach party. He felt sorry for Mikey and the gang when he saw them having to herd the pissheads on bar crawls. He even still got free drinks in most places.

However, he discovered that female clients weren't as interested in him – although other reps and workers were. One of these was Zena, a Dickens wench, who had told him that she had always thought he looked 'dirty'. Brad did his best to fulfil her expectations by shagging her on the roof of the Bon and tying her up with the washing-line.

He had found an apartment not far from the Delfin, sharing with a girl called Sally, who was propping for Koppas Bar, a bloke called Roly, who sometimes worked with him as a bouncer, and another bloke called Hicksy, who wasn't working and had an annoying hissing laugh, like a leaky pressure valve. Some things had gone missing out of the apartment and Brad had heard that one of Hicksy's dodgy friends had gone into the Madhouse to try to sell an Olympus Trip camera, which coincidentally was the same model that had been stolen from Sally's room.

The previous few days, Brad had been staying back at the Bon with Mikey. He had to be careful that Alison or the owners didn't find out, but Raoul, the night porter's son, was cool and always kept a lookout. Mikey had been moved back to the Bon to work with Greg and the new rep, Carmen. This meant that Natalie had replaced him at the Delfin. Mikey was pleased when Brad convinced him that he hadn't stolen the excursion money. They both agreed it must have been Alison because only a resort manager was given a skeleton key and knew where the money was kept.

Before going to the Bronco Bar-B-Q Brad went to the Bon to help Mikey with his paperwork, which was causing him problems. He had been nearly a hundred pounds short on his excursion money the week before, and Alison had made him pay it out of his own pocket.

Mikey filled in his friend on what had been going on for the three weeks Brad had been away. He told him about the massive row Natalie had had with the owner of Las Huertas over yet another client getting beaten up. Alison had actually backed her up, but to avoid further trouble had moved her to the Delfin, which was why there had been another change-round.

As the night wore on, Brad realised he had formed a strong relationship with Mikey and that during the course of the few months on resort they had learned a lot from each other.

He told Mikey of how frustrating it had been trying to clear his name in the UK. News of his dismissal had spread around the other resorts like wildfire, and Brad still couldn't understand why Jane had not backed him up. He had shown her the reports that Alison had not sent on to her. He had explained exactly how Alison was on the fiddle and had even offered to show Jane evidence. But it had all been to no avail. Brad had impulsively flown back to Ibiza the same day – before he had had a chance to change his mind.

It was YF&S's night up at the Hoe Down. Brad normally drove to work in the Triumph Herald, but whenever it was a YF&S night he got a lift up in the coach – just to annoy Alison. Alison had complained to Manny, but as Brad was working for him and it was also Manny's coach company, she had to lump it.

Brad watched the reps running back and forth to get more drink for the clients, pretending they were having the time of their lives. Brad knew the truth: the smiles plastered across most of their faces were as false as the two replacement teeth Mikey had on order.

The most beautiful smile, in Brad's eyes, false or otherwise, was Carmen's, but Mikey had told him that there was something about her that didn't seem right: she spent a lot of time with Alison and he didn't trust her. Despite this, Brad had warmed to her instantly. She was intelligent and quick-witted. She didn't suffer fools gladly, which meant that she gave Mario almost as much stick as Mikey did. Yet there was something deeper than that, though Brad couldn't put his finger on it. Since they had met, he and Carmen had teased and wound each other up, but the pleasure they got out of it was akin to intellectual fencing.

Had it not been for her sister's persuasion, Carmen would not have become a rep. She had decided to take the job feeling that it would provide an experience rather than an education. Before meeting the reps, she had assumed that they would be simple, fun-loving souls with little depth. That was not to say that she considered them her subordinates, but she certainly didn't expect any of them to be smarter than her or to make her have to think hard.

She had first met Brad on a bar crawl at the Star, where he was working as a bouncer. Although she had seen the photographs of him, she didn't recognise him in the flesh, partly because during his return to the UK he had shorn his hair and also because he had facetiously introduced himself to her as Billy Bouncer. They had a brief chat and Carmen found him pleasant enough. He made her laugh a few times and she thought he was reasonably attractive – in a bouncer sort of way.

When she had been there a week, and had seen him working at three other jobs, she asked Natalie who he was. When she realised it was the same Brad she had replaced, she was intrigued. The next time she was down the Star, they spent almost two hours taking the piss out of each other and anyone else unfortunate enough to attempt to join in.

Their second conversation was deeper and Brad really got into her head. When he walked away from the table he knew he had left her thinking. He smiled to himself as he got into his car and drove off. He was pulling out all of the stops for this one.

Luigi Canelli reached under the desk in his office at the back of his Basildon restaurant and pulled out a mirror tile. He placed it on the desk top and sprinkled some of the creamy-coloured powder on it. He used a gold credit card to chop it into a line and a stripy straw transferred it to his nose. He tilted his head back, sniffing vigorously. 'Mmmm. Good gear. It's not a repress, is it?'

'Nah, mate. Pukka Charlie that is. Best I've 'ad for ages.'

'How much for a key?'

'Twenty-eight grand.'

Luigi sucked in through his teeth. 'Bit steep. Sharpen your pencil a little?'

'Nah. Can't be done. You can see the quality. I'm barely getting a drink out of it meself.'

Luigi paused to see if silence would reduce the price. When it was apparent this ploy wasn't going to work he said, 'Okay. I'll get one of my boys to pick it up tomorrow. Usual place?'

'Yeah.'

'And,' said Luigi, standing up, 'don't forget that last lot of pills was eighteen short. What do you wanna do? Knock it off the bill or make it up with the next lot?'

'I'll make it up.'

They shook hands and the dealer left. Luigi chopped out another line, snorted it then checked in the mirror to see if any had fallen into his goatee beard. Out of the inside pocket of his dark blue Armani suit he took a comb, which he ran through his jet black receding hair.

In recent years, drugs had provided Luigi with an income and status that previously he had only dreamt of. He was by no means a major player, but had befriended the head of the local 'family', who had provided him with the muscle to enable him to deal in largish quantities of cocaine and Ecstasy without being ripped off. However, Wilson had been shot and killed, and Luigi had scaled down his operation. Deep down, he knew it was only a matter of time before he was caught by the police, or maybe worse.

The door of his office opened and one of the waiters popped his head round it. 'Luigi, your brother's on the phone.'

Luigi picked it up. 'Mario? How's sunny Ibiza?'

'Wicked,' replied the voice on the phone. 'But I've got a bit of a problem out here.'

Luigi was fiercely protective of his brother. 'What kind of problem?'

'There's a couple of reps who are giving me a lot of stick. I've dealt with one of them already.'

'I'll speak to Don at Young Free & Single,' interrupted Luigi. 'I'm still sorting him out the you-know-what so I can pull a few strings.'

'It's gone past that stage. They've got a little gang together, pulled in some of the other workers,' lied Mario.

'What about Sergio and the other boys? Can't you get them to deal with it?'

'They dealt with one of 'em a few weeks ago, but Sergio got a bust jaw.'

'What?'

'All eighteen stone of him spark out. One of the reps is a black belt or something. The other's about fifteen stone. I mean, I can look after myself but now they've got these others involved I need help.'

There was silence at the other end of the line. Mario pressed on, knowing his brother's Achilles heel. 'A flight's only eighty quid, I could find somewhere cheap for you to stay.'

'Hey, hey, hey! What's all this "cheap" talk? Give me a week or so to tie up things here and I'll be over, okay?'

Mario hung up. It was payback time.

The Bronco Bar-B-Q was rocking. Woodsy was on top form, but determined to get Brad and himself thoroughly pissed. When Brad worked at the Bar-B-Q, one of his jobs was to help set up the amphitheatre for him. Every time he tried to make a start, Woodsy gave him another drink.

By performance time Woodsy was unconscious. It was Heather who discovered him flat out by the pool with his dick in his hand. When word got round, there was a blind panic. The reps stood around not knowing what to do. Brad was leaning against the railings trying to sober up. The crisis unfolding in front of him could not have suited him better. If all else failed, he thought, he would just have to volunteer, but he dearly hoped that Manny or a rep would ask him.

Alison was screaming at Manny. 'We've got three hundred fucking people here, and that useless bastard's unconscious.'

Manny shrugged his shoulders. 'It is bad but it is only one part of the evening. You can still sing without music.'

'No, we can't. The clients expect a show, not just a few reps getting on stage and singing out of tune.'

Carmen walked over to Brad. 'Bit of a disaster, this, isn't it?'

'Guess so,' replied Brad.

'Shame none of us can play guitar. Don't suppose you can, can you? Any more hidden talents?'

Oh, joy, thought Brad. 'What do you mean?' he asked.

'Well, so far I've seen you working as a DJ, a bouncer and a photographer. I thought you might be able to play guitar as well.'

'No,' said Brad.

Carmen smiled. 'Oh, well, never mind.'

'But I play a bit of piano.'

'You are joking, aren't you?'

'Nope. It's what I used to do. I've been playing in bands for years.'

'Well, what are you waiting for?' asked Carmen. By now the clients had started a slow handclap and were singing, 'Why are we waiting?' She rushed over to Alison and Manny, who were still arguing. 'Alison, I've found someone who can play and compère.'

'Who?' asked Manolo.

'Brad,' replied Carmen.

'What?' said Alison. 'Don't be stupid.'

'Brad, you can play?' asked Manny.

'Keyboards.'

'No way!' screamed Alison.

Brad looked at Manny. 'I'll give it a go, if you want. Don't expect me to be as good as Woodsy, though.'

Brad's back was hurting where so many people had slapped

it to congratulate him. He was sitting at the bar in Bronco's, and on the strength of tonight's success Manny had just offered him a job compèring and playing the following season. He was on top of the world. Carmen popped into the bar just before making her way to her coach. 'Is there anything else about you I should know?'

Brad turned round. 'Oh, hi. Not too painful on your ears, then?'

'Och, you were fine, so don't go fishing for compliments. You're a bastard, sure you are, for taking the piss out of my nipples like that after you'd thrown me in.'

'Well, what do you expect if you don't wear anything under your T-shirt?'

'You didn't put a sock over your willy like Woodsy does.'

'Couldn't find one small enough,' said Brad.

'Aye, they don't have a branch of Mothercare here, do they?'

'Do you know what I like about you, Carmen?'

'What?'

'Nothing.'

Carmen giggled. 'See you down the Star later?'

'It's not beyond the realms of probability.'

'Good.' Carmen kissed him softly on the lips.

Brad felt butterflies in his stomach. He knew he fancied Carmen. The question was, did she fancy him?

The smell of burning awoke Brad from his drunken slumber. He stumbled out of bed towards the smell. On the kitchen stove was a saucepan with flames coming out of it. Someone had decided to boil some water then fallen asleep. Brad grabbed a tea-towel, soaked it under the tap and flung it over the pan. Then he went into the living room where three of Hicksy's friends lay comatose. He kicked them. 'Wake up. Come on, you dozy fucks, wake up.' They stirred. 'Which one of you wankers left a saucepan on, eh? Come on, fuck off, the lot of you.' Brad picked up any clothes he didn't recognise as his and threw them out of the front door. 'Come on – move.'

Once they had all gone, he banged on Hicksy's door.

'Fuck off, I'm asleep.'

'If you don't come out here now you'll be sleeping for good.'

'Piss off and leave me alone.'

Then he saw Hicksy's suitcase in the passageway. He opened it. Inside it was a Nick Coleman shirt, which Hicksy wore all the time and never stopped telling people cost ninety pounds. Brad took it and walked out to the garden. On the way, he picked up a white lighter with Ibiza written on it. When he got outside he held the shirt out at arm's length and set fire to it. Once he was sure it was properly alight, he placed it on the concrete and returned to his room where he packed his things. Before leaving he wrote a note:

Roly, Sally.

Can't stand living here any more. I think we're all square on the rent, but if there's anything outstanding let me know.

Hicksy – you're a fucking lowlife. Your Nick Coleman shirt's in the garden. One of your stupid mates almost set fire to the apartment so I guess somehow your shirt caught alight. I tried to wake you up to tell you but you told me to piss off. Shame.

Brad.

chapter nineteen

The beach looked glorious as Brad stopped his car and looked down on the sheltered bay. Today he was doing group photographs, and Young Free & Single were the clients. The boats had just moored and, once everyone had been divided into two teams, Brad gathered them together for the group photographs.

He spent just under an hour collecting orders. Normally he would have left straight away to get the pictures developed – so that they were ready for handing out when the boats brought all of the beach party attendees back to San Antonio – but Carmen was there and he wanted to spend some time with her. They messed around in the sea together, urging each other to say something that was not obfuscated by *double entendre* or intellectual sparring.

Afterwards Brad went and sat with Mikey. 'She's definitely game on, Brad.'

'You reckon?'

'Brad, you're so into each other you can't see past your noses.'

Brad felt a warm glow. 'I dunno, mate. Maybe she's just a friend.'

'Bollocks. Tell me something, how many girls have you got out here who are just friends?'

'Three or four probably.'

'And why don't you sleep with them? Don't you fancy them?'

'I dunno. I suppose half the fun is the chase. I mean, if I was into hunting deer then I guess the fun comes in stalking it, lining it up in your sights. If it suddenly appeared in your telescopic lens with a grin on its face saying, "Go on, then, shoot me," it would all be pretty pointless. It's the same with some women. On top of that, because they all work here, it would be a hassle afterwards. I just enjoy the friendships.'

Brad looked bewildered as he reflected on what he'd just said, that sex was not always at the top of his agenda. He shook his head sharply, as if to exorcize the spirit with a Ph.D. in common sense who had temporarily taken control of him. Normal service was quickly resumed. 'Of course, if we were both off our heads, I s'pose I'd shag 'em.'

'So how's Carmen different?' asked Mikey.

'I didn't say she was,' said Brad.

'I'll tell you what the difference is, then, shall I? You think you could have a long relationship with Carmen. She stimulates this,' said Mikey, pointing to his head, 'as well as *this*.'

Brad looked pensive. 'So what do you reckon then?'

'She's gorgeous-looking, sexy, intelligent and witty. But there's something about her that I'm not sure about. It's as if she's acting or hiding something.'

'Like what?'

'Dunno. It's irrelevant. What's relevant is that you fancy her and you should go over there right now and ask her out.'

Brad sat there for a few seconds. 'Fuck it. You're right.'

He walked across the beach to where she was standing. 'Bikini line needs doing,' said Brad, nodding at her crotch.

'Willy needs extending,' said Carmen, nodding at his.

'Enough of these compliments,' said Brad. 'After we've finished showing the video in Night Life I'm taking you out for a meal.'

'You are, are you?'

'Yeah, I'll book a table at Sa Plana for twelve thirty.'

'Is this your bashful way of asking me out?' teased Carmen.

'No. If we go for a meal your mouth might be full just

293

long enough to stop you coming out with the normal crap you're prone to spouting. Is that a yes, then?'

'Well, seeing as you put it so charmingly . . .'

'This room brings back memories,' said Brad, as he walked into his old bedroom. 'Where's Greg?'

'He's gone to Amnesia. He's heavily into pills and Charlie, you know,' said Carmen.

'I didn't know about the Charlie,' said Brad. 'I'll have to talk to him.'

'I wish someone would. He hardly ever sleeps and he's looking rough.'

Carmen made some coffee and they sat on her bed.

It took a superhuman effort for Brad to keep his hands off her. He was waiting for a signal, but none came. His heart sank. After a while, the conversation was no longer as light as it had been, but neither was it deep and meaningful. It was the verbal equivalent of piped Muzak. In the end Brad could take it no more. 'Carmen. I'm mad about you.'

It was as if someone else had said it. But there it was. Out. All of the innuendo and guessing were over. The possibility of mammoth rejection stared Brad in the face and he wished he'd kept his mouth shut.

Carmen looked at him and smiled. She leant forward and kissed him gently on the lips. 'I was hoping you'd say something like that.'

Brad's heart pounded and he felt a natural rush that made the hairs on the back of his neck stand on end. All of the possible scenarios he had played out in his mind could not have prepared him for the reality he was now experiencing.

They kissed more passionately, but Carmen was reserved. Ten minutes later, Brad wanted her desperately. He tried every trick he could think of. He got her to sit between his legs with her back to him while he massaged her shoulders. He let his hands settle at the top of her chest, then made her boobs rise and ride against her T-shirt by gently pulling up the skin at the top of each breast – her nipples went hard as they brushed against her T-shirt. Brad let his fingers slowly glide over them. He kissed her shoulder, then bit it gently. She moaned. As Carmen got more excited Brad laid her on her back, got on top of her, then began to grind his hard-on between her legs. It had got to the point where he was sure it was going to go all the way when Carmen switched off. 'No, Brad, not tonight.'

Brad said nothing, hoping that physical perseverance would wear down what he hoped was token resistance.

'Please, Brad, stop.'

Brad got off her and retracted his hands with fumbling obedience. He put his arm around her and she snuggled up to his chest. Once his erection had subsided he was happy to be just as they were.

Carmen was special.

'Why do men always do that?' giggled Carmen.

'Do what?' asked a naked Brad, as he walked back into the bedroom with a towel to clean up the mess he had just made. They had spent three nights together before they consummated their relationship, but for the next two days they had been at it at every available opportunity.

'As soon as a bloke comes, he either falls asleep or loses interest. Us girls want a cuddle.'

Brad smiled. He had fallen for Carmen in a big way. In the short time they had been together he had opened up to her about things he never had to anybody else. Yet it had not left him feeling vulnerable. Their growing together seemed the most natural thing in the world. She occupied his every thought, and even though there were some gorgeous girls on holiday with YF&S, Brad did not give them a second glance. The only subject that caused any tension was Alison. Carmen flatly refused to talk about her, and Brad could not understand why she was so friendly towards Alison despite everything that Brad had told her about the woman.

*

The eleven men barely fitted into the room. The Jet Bossa was a hotel near the airport where Luigi and his five travelling companions were staying. With him was Alberto, his main debt collector, while the other four were friends or waiters. Luigi figured that taking care of Mario's tormentors would be simple enough, even though Mikey was a black belt and Brad was big. Part of the reason for assembling all eleven for such a small task was to make it more of a social occasion. It also helped to bolster Luigi's ego.

When Mario came into the room he felt intimidated. He was still looked on by Luigi's friends as the kid brother. This, of course made him try to act as tough and as in the know as he could: he invented at least four people he'd beaten up during the season and claimed to know the main dealers on the island.

It was arranged for Brad and Mikey to be jumped in the car park of Ku the following night. Mario knew that they were going up there in Brad's car at eleven o'clock, because one of Mikey's friends from back home was the first DJ playing. Sergio was going to lead the attack, his jaw a reminder of the previous encounter with Mikey. This time he was determined the outcome would be different.

Brad had taken the photographs and collected the orders at the beach party on autopilot. He was in a daze. He had not been able to get the previous night's conversation with Mikey out of his mind. They hadn't come to blows, but Brad had been angry. He knew that Mikey's comments were not down to petty vying for his friendship but genuine concern for his happiness. That was what made it all the more worrying.

But how could he have been so completely suckered? Brad was experienced with women and could see through most of their wiles, but Carmen had hooked him and reeled him in.

Mikey had told Brad that he was almost certain Carmen

was in cahoots with Alison. As if this wasn't bad enough, during the course of the morning, two different people had told him that they had seen her go into Mario's room after leaving the Star club. The only reason Brad had spent the night in Mikey's apartment rather than Carmen's was because Carmen had said that Alison was visiting her first thing in the morning. The idea of Carmen with Mario made Brad feel sick. The memory of Mario's nine-inch dick didn't help.

Mikey had said that Carmen spent a lot of time with Alison. She was sometimes even in Alison's room when Alison wasn't there, which no other rep ever was. A large amount of the money that had been stolen had never been recovered. Mikey had a theory that Carmen was Alison's friend and was trying to find a way of planting more evidence on Brad to deflect suspicion away from Alison. As their imaginations had run wild, fuelled by Spanish wine and Dutch skunk, they even contemplated the possibility that Alison and Carmen were trying to get Brad arrested by planting drugs on him. As far-fetched as this was, in Brad's current state of mind it seemed plausible.

Brad pulled up at the photo lab, walked in and put the camera on the table.

'What's this?' laughed Mason, the American owner of the lab, opening the back of the camera. 'There's no film in here.'

'Huh?' Brad looked in the camera and, sure enough, he had forgotten to load it. 'Oh, for fuck's sake,' he groaned.

'Heavy night?' asked Mason.

Brad ignored him, grabbed the camera, jumped into the Triumph and sped back to the beach, perversely grateful that he had something other than Carmen to occupy his thoughts.

Once at the beach he assembled the groups again and took more pictures. He got back to San Antonio and managed to get the photos developed just as the boats from the beach party were pulling back into the harbour.

Thankfully Giles, the beach-party owner, had kept it going a little longer than normal so they arrived at six thirty rather than six o'clock. He gave Brad a look that meant 'One more time and you're sacked'.

When he got back to the Bon, Brad went to Mikey's room. Mikey looked serious. 'You better sit down, Brad.'

'What's up?'

Mikey hesitated. 'Someone has *definitely* been snooping through your things and Carmen *definitely* went back to Mario's room last night.'

Brad went cold. He looked at Mikey helplessly. 'Oh, bollocks.'

'I'm sorry, mate. After you left I got a couple of brown envelopes and put money and different bits of paperwork in them. I didn't seal them, but I tucked one flap in and left the other one out. When I looked at them they were both tucked in.'

'It could have been Alison,' said Brad desperately.

Mikey shook his head. 'I asked Raoul to keep an eye on my room and he saw Carmen hovering around, plus Alison was in Ibiza Town all day.' He continued, 'I spoke to Antonio, the new night porter at Las Huertas. Carmen went into Mario's room at two in the morning. He didn't see what time she came out because he fell asleep, but . . .'

Brad flopped back on the settee. 'Now what do I do?' he said.

'I'm really sorry it had to be me who told you, Brad.'

Brad stood up. 'Well, you're my best mate over here, so if anyone was gonna tell me, I suppose I'm glad it's you.' For no particular reason he shook Mikey's hand and they hugged each other.

'Right, then,' said Brad, composing himself. 'Guess I better go and sort this out.'

He walked to Carmen's room as slowly as he could. When he got there, he stood outside for a few moments before knocking. Carmen came to the door dressed in a YF&S white T-shirt and bikini bottoms. She looked surprised when she saw it was Brad. 'Where's your key? Why did you knock?'

'I wasn't sure if you'd have anyone in there with you.'

Carmen searched Brad's face for an explanation as he walked past her and into the room. 'What do you mean?'

'I thought maybe Mario might be in here with you – you know, continuing where you left off last night.'

Carmen looked at him guiltily.

'God. You're not even going to deny it, are you?'

She sat down and put her head in her hands.

'And,' continued Brad, 'I know you've been going through my things.' Carmen looked up in horror. 'Fucking hell, Carmen, if you think nothing else of me, the one thing I would've hoped you wouldn't think I was, was stupid. You must've known I'd find out.'

'Oh, Brad, if only—'

'If only what? If only I hadn't found out that you and Alison were trying to stitch me up even more?'

'No, Brad, that's not—'

'As if being branded a thief and losing my job wasn't enough! What else did you have in store for me, eh? Fucking hell, I can't believe that someone can hate me enough to want to do this.' A tear rolled down Carmen's cheek. 'Why did I have to go and fall for you? God, I really am not as smart as I thought I was, am I?' By now Carmen was crying. 'Save the fucking waterworks.' Brad started to gather up his things.

'Brad, please listen. It's not like you think.'

'All right, then.' Brad dropped the things he had just picked up and stood facing her with his hands on his hips. 'Supposing you tell me what it is like.'

'I'm not trying to stitch you up.'

'Did you or did you not go through my things?'

'Yes, but—'

'And did you or did you not go into Mario's room after the Star last night?'

'I did, but . . .' Her voice trailed off.

'Go on, then, I'm listening.'

'Oh, I can't explain. You'll just have to trust me.'

'Trust you? There's more chance of me trusting Greg to stay drug-free and celibate in a brothel with a jar full of Es than there is of me ever trusting you again. Crawl back to that slag Alison and tell her whatever it was you were plotting against me ain't gonna work. And if you're thinking about grassing me up for staying in Mikey's don't bother 'cos I'm out of here.'

'Where are you going? You're not leaving the island, are you?'

'No, I'm not – not that it's any concern of yours. Do you know what the ironic thing about all this is? Initially I was obsessed with getting revenge on that stupid bitch Alison. But I'd more or less decided she wasn't worth it 'cos I'm enjoying doing my own thing. It's not until you step back from it that you see how wrapped up in themselves reps are and you realise that a couple of years in the job could turn you into a total egomaniac.' Brad opened the door and looked at Carmen. 'Well, at least you've got a head start there. Have a nice life.'

Mario looked everywhere for his three video-tapes, containing footage of twenty-two of the fifty-three girls he had slept with since he had been away – but he couldn't find them. He was sure they would turn up but he was pissed off that he couldn't show them to his brother.

He sat in the bar of Las Huertas doing his desk duty. He had been there for five minutes or so when Antonio came in to tell him that he was wanted on the phone.

It was Luigi.

'Mario, are they still going up to Ku tonight?'

'Yep.'

'You do know that we're gonna give 'em a fucking good hidin', don't you?'

'Yeah, course I do.'

'We won't tell 'em, but they'll probably guess it's from you.'

'Just make sure you do 'em good.'

'Consider it done.'

Alison couldn't find some of Felipe's bank statements. She had got very pissed with Trevor a couple of nights before – so pissed that she'd actually wanked him off. When she'd returned to her apartment, she had drunkenly gone through her finances to see how much money she had made, so she assumed that she had simply misplaced various bits and pieces.

She had made nearly twenty-five thousand pounds. A huge amount of money had gone into Felipe's account, so she had been able quite easily to filter off a couple of thousand pounds to add to her own growing nest egg, without it being noticed.

Her parents and her boyfriend Jonathan were coming over at the weekend and they were going to take back some of her money. The way things were going, Alison was considering doing another season – Jonathan would just have to lump it.

She was pleased with the season so far. Brad was out of the picture and without him Mikey was easier to control. The money had been rolling in and she had shagged all of the people she wanted to, apart from Spanish Jimmy at the Star. Jane Ward thought she was doing a good job, so with Felipe's continued string-pulling, another season as resort manager should be assured. She took out a thousand-peseta note and lit a cigarette with it.

There were less than a dozen other vehicles in the car park. Ku didn't get going until midnight and it was only a quarter to eleven. Brad got out of the Triumph and lifted the bonnet to disconnect the battery. It was still the only way to switch off the ignition light. He heard Mikey say something.

'What did you say, Mikey?'

When he closed the bonnet he saw a group of about a dozen large males getting out of three cars and walking towards them.

'I said, shit,' repeated Mikey.

'Who are they?' asked Brad, fearing that he already knew the answer.

'It's the fuckers who did me over – plus a few.'

Brad remembered the state Mikey had been in after being battered by five of them. Now there were more than twice as many and a couple were carrying what looked suspiciously like pickaxe handles.

'Remember me?' said Sergio, when they were a few metres away.

Mikey looked at him without speaking. Brad reached into the back of the Triumph and grabbed a wheel spanner that was lying on the back seat.

'We're going to teach you two a lesson,' said Luigi.

'Look, I don't know what this is all about,' said Brad, 'but we don't want any trouble.'

'It's too late, boy. You've already got it,' said Luigi, pulling out a flick-knife.

Brad went cold. 'Oh, for fuck's sake.' He dropped the wheel spanner to his side, trying not to look aggressive.

'I'm gonna break more than your jaw,' said Sergio to Mikey.

Brad wondered if his friend was shitting himself as much as he was. 'What's this all about?' he asked.

'What's it all about?' laughed Luigi. 'It's all about you two getting the biggest kicking of your lives – however short they might be. I'll teach you not to fuck with my family.'

Brad looked at him closely. The resemblance suddenly struck him.

'Is this all about Mario? Are you telling me you're related to that prick?'

'Yeah,' swaggered Luigi. 'That "prick" happens to be my kid brother.'

'So, that tosser has to get someone else to fight his battles for him?' Brad shook his head, laughing. He didn't speak for almost fifteen seconds but when he looked up, his eyes were wide and glaring. 'Well, come on, then, you fucking piece of shit.' He brought the wheel spanner back up to chest level. 'I'll take on you and any other members of your stinking, lowlife, wank-stain, shit-for-brains fucking family! Come on!'

This time Mikey was glad Brad had lost it because it was obvious that they were going to have to fight their way out. That being so, he wanted by his side a Brad who had lost the plot, rather than the normal ever-friendly-ever-smiling rep.

'You're gonna regret saying that,' said Luigi.

'And Mario's gonna regret this, 'cos whatever you do to us, we're going to do to him twice as bad,' said Mikey.

Alberto came and stood at the front of the group. When they saw him, both Brad and Mikey lost a little of their bravado. He was just over six foot tall, almost as wide, and had a face of pure evil, with a voice to match. 'I don't think so.'

The detachment in his voice sent a shiver up their spines.

For a moment there was silence, an unnatural calm before a tornado. The mute tension was broken by a car entering the car park. Weapons were held out of sight as it headed towards the group. When it was twenty metres away Brad saw it was a jeep. 'Oh, fuck me, no,' he said.

It pulled up next to them, its headlights shining on them. A man with a bandannaed head got out of the driver's side.

'Brad!'

It was Samuel T. Zakatek.

'Sammy?'

'Shit. I don't believe it. Brad, man, how y'doing?' He came over and hugged him. 'So what you bin up to? Jeez. I bet you never thought you'd see me again.' Sammy seemed oblivious to the situation he'd walked into. 'So what y'doing up here?'

'Who is this clown?' said Luigi.

'Sammy, we've got a bit of a problem. You'd better go.'

'An' what koind o' problem would yis all be havin' exactly?' said the passenger, as he got out of the jeep. It was Irish Ben.

'It's gonna be your problem as well if you don't fuck off, Paddy,' said Sergio.

'Now, tha's no way t'be talkin' t'someone yeh've never met. Did yeh ma never teach y'any manners?'

'Go away, my Irish friend, or it will be you who'll be getting a lesson in manners,' said Alberto.

'Bejaysus, yeh's an ugly-lookin' bloighter, so y'are. I bet y'can eat a few o' them there Shredded Wheat t'ings.'

'I only eat people,' Alberto growled.

'Well, yis wan' t'be careful there, big feller, 'cos us Paddies have an awful habit o' causin' indigestion, so we have.'

Alberto made a lunge at Irish Ben with a knuckle-dustered hand. Ben stepped to one side and, as Alberto's momentum carried him past, the outside of his fist crashed down on the Italian's temple, knocking him out instantly.

Luigi was too busy watching incredulously what was happening to Alberto to see Brad's spanner crash down to break his collar-bone. The knife fell out of his hand and Brad kneed him in the face as he dropped to the floor.

Sammy leapt in the air and, with a Kung Fu kick that Bruce Lee would have been proud of, sent the pickaxe handle flying out of Sergio's hand. Mikey spun round and, with a kick, broke Sergio's nose to match his previously broken jaw. He sank to his knees. Brad connected with the side of his face, booting him into unconsciousness.

Another Italian punched Brad just under his eye, then picked up Luigi's flick-knife. From nowhere, Sammy flew through the air. The Italian crashed against the Renault 19 and dropped the knife. As he did so, Brad caught him with a glorious upper cut, and Mikey swept away his legs for good measure.

Mikey didn't see Luigi's head waiter come up behind and club him on the back of the head. He stumbled towards Brad, who caught him. The head waiter aimed a punch at Brad's head but Brad ducked and swung his elbow into the man's face with a satisfying crunch.

Sammy and Irish Ben were surrounded by the other six members of the gang. Irish Ben's fists were a blur and within a couple of seconds, four of the group were heading for the floor. Sammy was whooping as he kicked one, then punched the other to join the rest.

With the adrenaline pumping, Brad went round kicking the semi-conscious assailants, who were crawling to their cars.

The four sat in the VIP bar of a still relatively empty Ku.

'So, let me get this straight, 'cos I still can't fucking believe it,' said Brad, his eye swelling as he spoke. 'You both arrived in Ibiza at more or less the same time and it was Sammy you used to do the karate exhibitions with?'

'Have yis ever t'ought about apploying fer *University Challenge*?'

'All right, you piss-taking bastard,' laughed Brad. 'I just can't believe it.'

'Tell him Sammy,' said Irish Ben.

'It's true, Brad. I studied martial arts in 'Nam, so when I got here me an' Ben met up an' decided t' make a few bucks doin' exhibitions. That was before I went to the beach. Did I tell y'about when the King of Spain visited—'

'Um, yeah,' interrupted Brad hurriedly.

'What I don't understand is why you were both up here,' said Mikey.

'Well, oi was goin' t' get y'man Sam's car fixed in the mornin'. Tha' meant givin' him a lif' t' work so oi had the car, y' see.'

'So you really do work in Ku, then?' said Brad, still half expecting to wake up.

'Yeah, man. Dontcha remember me tellin' y' in France?'

'Yeah, yeah, of course,' said Brad.

'So, what're yis gonna be doin' about this Mario feller?' asked Irish Ben.

Mikey looked at Brad. 'I think we'll pay him a visit down the Star, don't you?'

Brad nodded in agreement. 'Definitely. But let's make a little detour. There's something I want to pick up first.'

Brad pulled up on the main road outside the Star and Es Paradis. He felt light-headed.

'Don't forget to disconnect the battery,' said Mikey.

'Oh, yeah,' said Brad.

Mikey watched as Brad lifted the bonnet and pulled off the positive terminal. Then they walked into the Star, where one of the first people they bumped into was Carmen.

'Oh, my God,' she said, when she saw Brad's closed eye. 'What's happened?'

'Mario thought he'd get his brother and a few of his friends to show us what he really thinks of us,' said Mikey.

Carmen went to touch Brad's eye. 'Are you all right?'

Brad wanted to say that his injuries were nothing compared to what she had done to him, but he decided it would sound too pathetic, so settled for the more ambiguous, 'All wounds heal with time, Carmen.'

They marched through the club towards bar five. Because of their dishevelled appearance a lot of people stared at them or moved out of their way. Gus, the head bouncer, was standing next to the DJ stand so Brad went up and asked him to turn a blind eye to what they were about to do.

They saw Mario just before Mario saw them. He had a couple of girls around him at bar five and was laughing and joking with them. When he saw Brad and Mikey his face

306

froze. Roughly, they grabbed him and frog-marched him through to the gents' toilets.

'Out,' said Mikey, to the two holidaymakers using the urinals.

Roly, who was working as a bouncer down the Star, stood guard at the entrance to the loos to stop anyone going in. Mikey threw Mario up against the wall. He booted him in the groin and, although he pulled the kick, Mario still doubled up in excruciating pain. 'Right, Mario, I'm going to give you three punches head start and then I'm going to beat the living shit out of you.'

'No, I don't wanna fight you,' Mario wheezed.

'We know that, Mario,' said Brad. 'You'd rather get your brother and his mates to do it for you, wouldn't you?'

'C'mon, then, Mario,' said Mikey, sticking his chin out. 'What are you waiting for?'

'I've already told you,' he said pathetically. 'I don't wanna fight.'

'No?' said Mikey. 'Do you wanna hear an alternative?'

'Yeah,' whispered Mario.

'Can't hear you,' said Mikey.

'I said yes,' repeated Mario, more loudly.

'Right, then. You get your sorry racist ass off this island first thing tomorrow morning.'

'But there aren't any flights home tomorrow,' protested Mario.

'Tough. Get a flight to Majorca. Just get the fuck off Ibiza, and,' continued Mikey, 'you don't tell Alison or anyone else you're going. Understood?'

Mario nodded, defeated.

'Finally,' said Mikey, 'you tell that cardboard gangster brother of yours that if this goes any further not only will it be you who suffers most but you'll also have a whole load of angry niggers to deal with back home and they'll break every bone in your motherfucking bodies. Clear?'

Mario nodded again, glad he had got off so lightly. He hadn't.

'The only other thing, Mario,' said Brad, 'is that I've got this real bad problem. You see, if someone hurts me I've just got to do something back to them.' Brad looked at his swollen eye in the mirror. 'Now, I reckon that this eye is gonna be with me for a week or so. Therefore it's only fair that we give you something a little more permanent to remember us by. What d'you reckon, Mikey?'

'For sure.'

Mikey noticed that a trickle had started running down Mario's shaking leg. 'Oh dear,' he said. 'Mario's peed his pants.'

Mario was almost in tears, worrying about how he was going to be scarred. Mikey grabbed him and bundled him into a cubicle, pushed his head down the pan and flushed the cistern. He yanked him back up and pinned him against the wall.

'If I were you, Mario,' he said, 'I'd keep pretty still.'

Mario looked at Brad with wide-eyed fear as Brad reached for his back pocket. From it he pulled out a flick-knife, one of the two things he'd stopped for on the way to the club.

'Now, don't move, Mario.'

Mario screamed and lost control of all of his bodily functions.

Brad looked at Mikey and they grinned at each other. He handed him the flick-knife and took out of his pocket the other thing he had picked up from his apartment: a Bic razor.

Five minutes later, an eyebrowless, wet-legged, crying Mario went running out of the Star, heading for Las Huertas, his suitcase and the first available flight to Majorca.

chapter twenty

Alison had brought her parents and Jonathan along to the beach party. The older couple spent most of their time at the bar. Jonathan knew nothing about the animosity between Brad and Alison, so made an effort to talk to him when he saw him going around with the video-camera. He even told Brad he was a bit pissed off because Alison was talking about coming back next year. Brad found him a thoroughly nice bloke, and wondered what on earth he was doing with Alison.

He spent the whole day on the beach doing the video. Carmen continually tried to speak to him, but each time she approached he walked away. When they got on to the boats back to San Antonio, she made a point of getting on the same one as Brad, which meant that he was unable to avoid her.

Eventually she cornered him. 'Brad, I really need to speak to you.'

'There's nothing left to say.'

'But things need to be explained.'

'No, they don't, Carmen.'

She looked up at him and all he wanted to do was to take her in his arms. The weeks she had spent in the sun had made her eyes even more striking and had brought out cute freckles across the bridge of her button nose. She was desperate to communicate with him and her normally challenging eyes now had a vulnerable warmth that Brad had to call upon all of his reserves of will-power to resist.

She stretched up and kissed his cheek, then took his hand and squeezed it. 'Things are going to change, Brad – sooner than you think.' She kissed him again and whispered into his ear, 'I love you.'

This made Brad feel as confused as a Dutch lemming. His feelings for Carmen hadn't changed, but as wonderful as it was to hear her say that, there was no way he could trust her after what she had done. He walked away.

When everyone got back to the Bon, they were surprised to see Jane Ward and Tom Ortega, Alison in particular because she had no prior warning of their visit. As resort manager she should have been informed – especially as they were both there, which was unusual. She supposed they were there because of Mario's sudden departure. Alison had heard rumours that Brad and Mikey had been involved and she was looking forward to sharing them with Jane and Tom.

Once all of the reps had said hello, Tom noticed that Brad was leaving. He had moved back in with Sally and Roly as he had already paid the rent and Hicksy had fled the island after being caught with a stolen credit card. Tom caught him just as he was getting into the Triumph. 'Brad.'

'Hi, Tom, thought I'd leave you all to it.'

'Yeah, thanks, but I was wondering if you'd mind hanging around in the bar for half an hour or so.'

Brad looked puzzled. 'Well, I've got to go and edit the beach-party video for tonight.'

'How long will that take?'

'Dunno. Hour or two, I guess.'

'Please, Brad, I'd be grateful if you'd wait. It's quite important.'

'Okay.' Brad could spare the time and he was curious.

In the bar Alison was proudly going through her achievements to Jane Ward, Jonathan and her parents.

'Oh, yes, you've only got to ask people like Trevor. They say that this has been one of the best seasons out here. Obviously I can't take all of the credit. Some of the reps have been a great help. It's such a shame about Mario. Actually, Jane, I wanted to talk to you about that.'

'Yes, well, Alison, perhaps we could go up to your room and talk about it there.' Jane turned to Alison's parents and Jonathan. 'If you'll excuse us.'

Carmen accompanied them upstairs.

'Where are you going?' asked Alison. She added sarcastically, 'Have you suddenly been promoted?'

'I'd like Carmen to come with us, if it's all the same with you, Alison,' said Jane.

Alison shrugged her shoulders. 'Fine.' As the four got into the lift, she wondered what Carmen had been up to. She was surprised she hadn't been consulted but guessed it wasn't anything too serious.

When they got into the room, Alison and Jane sat down, Tom and Carmen remained standing. Alison sensed tension in the air.

Jane looked at Tom, who nodded. Jane broke the silence.

'Right, Alison. The game's up.'

'What?'

'We know exactly what's been going on.'

Jane paused deliberately, to see how Alison would react.

Alison wasn't sure to which particular misdemeanour Jane was referring. 'Sorry, Jane. What are you on about?'

'For the whole season you have been banking money for Felipe, who has been undertaking a massive fraud involving contracting accommodation for an amount different from that for which we have been invoiced. You have been lying about how much the bars have been paying, and how many people have been visiting them. We also strongly suspect that it was you, not Brad, who was responsible for the theft of the excursion money.' Jane leant forward. 'You have run this resort with an unimaginable degree of incompetence. Frankly, you should never have been given the job and had it not been for your liaison with Felipe – and, yes, we know about the Chamberlain Clinic – then I am sure you would never have been appointed. However, they say that if you give someone enough rope they'll hang themselves, and that's exactly what you've done. It's just a tragedy that you have ruined what should have been a great season for so many people. Your selfishness is almost incomprehensible.'

Alison was stunned. 'I don't know what you're talking about. I swear I didn't take the excursion money.'

Tom thought that she sounded genuine, but said nevertheless, 'We've been around to all of the bars threatening to withdraw our custom next year if they failed to co-operate. Russell from the Anglers, Jimmy from the Star, Noel from Sgt Pepper's, even darling Trevor. All of them have told us what you've been up to.'

'I don't believe you. You can't prove a thing.'

Alison turned to Carmen. 'Carmen.'

Carmen went over to the giant boxes of washing-powder and reached inside.

What are you doing?' asked a horrified Alison.

Carmen pulled a plastic bag out of each box. She emptied the contents over the table: millions of pesetas and sheet upon sheet of incriminating documentation.

'Alison,' said Jane, almost smiling, 'I'd like to introduce you to Carmen *Ward*.'

'What?' said Alison slowly. 'Oh, please, tell me you're joking.'

'Afraid not,' said Carmen. 'I've been over here all this time gathering evidence on you. It took me a while to find your hiding place – shame you took laundering money so literally. It beats me how you lie so easily. I've hated having to do it.'

'Anyway, all that aside,' said Jane, 'clearly we want every penny back. We'll take this for starters.' She scooped up the notes on the table. 'We know that your parents and boyfriend are about to take some to the UK for you, so unless you'd rather I did it, I'd suggest you get it off them.'

'I suppose we could arrange for them all to be stopped at Customs,' said Tom.

'All right, all right,' said Alison. 'But I'm telling you, whatever else I have or haven't done, I did not touch that excursion money.'

'Well, that will have to be investigated. We couldn't get you on a flight tonight,' said Tom, 'but you're on a flight tomorrow morning at eleven o'clock. We'll decide whether or not to prosecute you based on how much money we retrieve. The only other thing that will save your bacon is agreeing to testify against Felipe.'

Alison was horrified.

'Right, then,' continued Jane, 'that's about it. I thought you might be interested to know that we're going to ask Heather to take over running the resort. We've also got someone who I suppose will effectively be your replacement. Do you remember Lorraine?'

Alison nodded expressionlessly.

'Poetic justice, don't you think?' said Tom. 'She was so excited when I told her, but I bet she'll be even more pleased when she knows you won't be her manager.'

Jane stood up. 'Alison, if I were you I'd go down and speak to your parents. Tom, get the reps assembled in the empty room down the corridor.' She looked at Carmen. 'And, Tom, you'd better bring a certain young man up here who I think deserves an explanation.'

Felipe had been trying to get through to Luís at Viajes Diamanté in Ibiza all day. He had also tried his contacts at the other Diamanté offices with equal lack of success. He knew something was wrong. Jane and Tom were abroad, Sebastian and Adam Hawthorne-Blythe were in meetings all day. At first he had panicked, but as the day progressed he knew there would be nowhere to run to. With the calmness of a condemned man who had accepted his fate, Felipe left his company flat and sat waiting in his Dulwich home to prepare himself for the inevitable. He could at least keep his dignity.

At seven twenty in the evening an unmarked Vauxhall

Cavalier swept up the gravel drive. Three men with short hair got out, walked up to the front door and rang the bell.

'Are you expecting anybody, Felipe?' yelled his wife, from the kitchen.

'Yes,' said Felipe, smoothing down his clothes. 'I am.'

Brad walked into Alison's room behind Tom, confused as to what was going on, especially when he saw Jane and Carmen in the room.

'Sit down, Brad,' said Jane, gesturing to the seat Alison had just vacated.

'What for?' asked Brad, arrogantly. They weren't his bosses any more, so why should he do what they told him?

'Please,' said Jane. 'We've something to tell you and when you hear it, I think you'll want to sit down.'

Jane and Carmen smiled at each other.

Brad sat. 'Okay – I'm listening.'

'Well,' said Jane, 'where to start?' She paused. 'Our contracts director, Felipe Gomez, has been defrauding the company of hundreds of thousands of pounds. You will appreciate the gravity of such an accusation, so clearly we have had to gather proof to substantiate it. The majority of his illegal gains was being laundered,' Jane, Tom and Carmen all smiled again at this word, 'through Ibiza by one Alison Shand.'

'You what?' said Brad.

'At the time of the incident with the excursion money,' continued Jane, 'we knew what was going on and we more or less knew everything that she was up to – and what a dreadful manager she was. But we could do nothing about your predicament for fear of blowing our investigation into what you must now understand to be a major travel-industry scandal.'

'We felt dreadful at the time,' said Tom, 'but there really was nothing we could do.'

'Thank God you're so bloody-minded,' said Jane. 'When

we found out you were back over here, you don't know how happy it made us.'

Brad sat there taking it all in, but was wondering what Carmen was doing there. Jane sensed what he was thinking. 'Of course,' said Jane, 'we needed to gather evidence to prove what they were up to. We needed someone we could trust, someone intelligent who would blend in and could get Alison's confidence. The only suitable person we could think of was my younger sister, Carmen.'

Carmen looked at Brad, searching his face for a reaction. For the first few seconds all she got was a blank stare.

Then Brad flopped forward on the table. 'No, no no.' He started laughing, banging the table with his forehead each time he said the word. 'Why didn't you . . . couldn't you . . . What was . . . Fucking hell.' He was speechless.

Jane nodded at Tom to join her in leaving the room. 'I daresay you two have a lot to discuss. We'll talk again later, Brad. I just want to say that, if you want it, you've a bright future with Young Free & Single.'

As soon as the door closed behind them, Carmen started speaking. 'All the time you thought I was going through your things I was just trying to see if there was anything I could use against Alison, not you. I went through *all* of the reps' things. I even got this,' she said, throwing Brad a bag with three video-tapes in it. 'I think they're films of Mario's conquests. That's what I was doing in his room that night, looking for anything that would help to incriminate Alison or Felipe. I'll admit I flirted with him a bit to see if he'd any useful information, but I left after an hour, I promise you. I went back into his room the next day when he was out and took the videos. I only took the videos because I saw girls' names written on them – maybe we could see what kind of cameraman he is a bit later.' She felt Brad's mood was softening. 'Oh, Brad, I *hated* Mario. When I heard about what he almost did to you and Mikey I wanted to kill him myself.'

There was a moment of uncertainty before Brad held out

his arms, beckoning her to come and sit on his lap. She sprang over excitedly and kissed him.

'I'm so sorry. I've missed being with you so much. I'm so glad it's all over.' She placed a hand on either side of his face and gave him a lingering kiss. 'How can I make it up to you?'

Brad made out he was thinking. Then, 'How about earning three points?'

She slapped him playfully.

'Actually,' he said, picking her up and carrying her into Alison's bedroom, 'make that four.'

chapter twenty-one

Kirstie was on top of the world. She hadn't seen her boyfriend for more than a week and he was due at any minute. Her travel agent's was looking marvellous, especially since the Reggio low-voltage lighting had been installed. Business had been brisk and she had bought a cottage near Brecon in Talybont-on-Usk, which was ready for moving into that weekend.

She sat by the window and looked at her watch. It was six thirty – he was normally punctual. Sure enough, almost on the dot, his light blue TVR pulled up outside. Kirstie opened the door and let him in.

'Jason!' she squealed, throwing her arms around Jason Barnes's neck. 'Have you missed me?'

'Course I have, you old slapper,' he teased, kissing her fondly. 'This place is looking good.'

'Thanks to Young Free & Single,' laughed Kirstie.

'Nice of them to pay for it,' said Jason. 'And still a bit left over for a few of life's little extravagances,' he said, nodding at the car.

'We could have had a few more if I hadn't screwed up in Ibiza,' said Kirstie, pushing him on to a chair so that she could sit on his lap.

'You didn't screw up, someone just beat you to it. Anyway, let's just be happy with the twenty-seven grand we nicked from Majorca.'

He picked up the two glasses of champagne Kirstie had poured just before he arrived and handed one to her. 'To us,' he said.

When Alison walked into Night Life, Jane Ward could not believe her audacity. All of the YF&S clients were there to watch the beach-party video Brad was late in bringing to show them on the big screen. The reps now knew the full story, so they just stared at her, amazed that she had turned up. She sat in the corner with her parents and Jonathan.

Fuck 'em all, she thought. She had told her parents and Jonathan what had happened. However, she played it down by saying that all managers were 'at it' and that she was just unlucky to have been caught. Taking them to where YF&S were that night would, she thought, help to emphasise that what she had done was not particularly serious.

Jonathan was quite pleased she had been caught because it meant she would not be going back next year. Alison had decided to testify against Felipe, if necessary. She sat back and relaxed a little, consoled in the knowledge that, with Jonathan's earning power, she would still be able to live in the manner she felt was hers by right.

The place was packed with over three hundred YF&S holidaymakers and a hundred or so others. The manager of Night Life was scurrying around even more frantically than normal because Brad was nearly an hour late with the video. Eventually he came running through the door hand in hand with a giggling Carmen. Mikey was standing by the entrance. 'What kept you?' he asked.

'Oh, mate,' replied Brad, 'wait until you see what we've found. Can't stop – gotta go and play the video.'

Brad put the tape in and came back to Mikey, who had been joined by Greg.

After about ten minutes, the video was showing the egg-throwing contest and, through the powerful system, the screams and sounds of the day's entertainment could be heard perfectly. Suddenly, the screen flickered and the picture changed. Brad and Carmen nudged each other like a pair of excited schoolchildren about to see Father Christmas for the first time.

On to the screen came the back of a naked male. After a few seconds the face turned to the camera and winked. It was Mario. As he moved to the side, viewers could make out a girl on all fours pouring oil between her own buttocks. Some dialogue came out of the sound system and spread over the almost hushed room and its agog inhabitants.

'Fuck me in the other hole, Mario. See if you can get that gorgeous cock of yours up there.'

'What? Up your arse?'

When Alison heard the voices she spluttered out the drink she was sipping. She jumped up and looked at the screen. Then as soon as she saw what it was, she sank into her chair, wishing it would stop. It didn't.

'Push, fuck you. PUSH! Come on, I want you to ram it into me.'

Everyone in Night Life was falling about and pointing at Alison. Jonathan glared at her, took off the engagement ring she had given him the previous October and threw it at her. Then he stormed out of the club. Her parents sat there with their mouths open. Alison ran out, chasing after her former boyfriend. As she barged through the reps, a hysterical Greg called after her, 'Well done, Al! Bonus points for that one.'

chapter twenty-two

Luís from Viajes Diamanté sat alone in the yacht club in Ibiza drinking a *carajillo*. The October sky was mottled with orange clouds, which were blowing across the island quicker than in previous months, heralding the onset of winter. Most holidaymakers had gone home and all of the reps had left or were about to go. Everybody in the bar was either Spanish or a resident of Ibiza. He looked at the last of the day's pleasurecraft mooring on the jetty, many of them doing so for the last time that season. The Sunseeker he had just bought was nestled between a speedboat and a small cabin cruiser, the low sun reflecting off her white gleaming hull. He had named her *Rosa*.

The perfume filled his nostrils before he saw her. Her smell was as distinctive as her appearance was distinguished. Even at fifty she was beautiful. Striking features, a well-maintained body, with clothes and makeup that oozed class and style.

Luís stood up and kissed her, then clicked his fingers to the waiter for the champagne he had already ordered. He brought it over and popped it open. They toasted each other. 'What to?' said Luís.

'To us?'

'No.' Luís coughed, then raised his glass. 'To a woman whose masterly plan has brought us together. To a woman who has had to suffer the infidelities of a cheating husband for as long as I can remember. To a woman who has made phone calls, left clues, broken her rivals and finally – I hope – cleared her husband's accounts because he was stupid enough to underestimate her and will now pay the price.'

Luís changed from his grandiose speech-maker's voice to his normal one to add, 'You did clear the accounts, didn't you?'

She nodded at a huge suitcase. 'Of course. Nobody else could touch them and Felipe was hardly going to tell anyone else about them, was he?'

'Excellent.' He resumed his speech. 'To a woman who I hope I can spend the rest of my life with, be it here or in that sceptred isle . . .'

'Oh, Luís,' she giggled, 'you sound almost English.'

'To the woman I have loved from the first day I met her, to the woman who married the wrong man, to the woman who shall soon marry the right man, please, raise your glass to . . . the former Mrs Gomez.'

Rosemary Gomez gave an embarrassed smile and took a sip from her glass.

'Not quite the former,' she said. She took Luís's hand. 'Oh, Luís, this has worked out better than I could have ever imagined. I'm not sure if I would have gone through with it if I hadn't found that invoice. Knowing that Felipe was sleeping with all of those reps and managers was one thing, but getting that dreadful Alison pregnant and then making her have an abortion – well, it really was the last straw. I have done the right thing, haven't I, Luís? I just couldn't stand it any more. I've always known that you and I should be together, but out of loyalty and for the sake of the children—'

'I know, I know,' said Luís, squeezing her hand.

'But now, oh, Luís, I'm so happy.'

They hugged each other.

'So your conscience is clear then?' asked Luís.

'Of course it is,' she replied. 'You know, the only thing I feel a little bad about is that rep getting the sack.'

'Brad?'

'That's the one. Why did you put the empty envelopes in his room?'

'I had to put them somewhere to leave a false trail. That bitch Alison was planning to get rid of him anyway.'

'It seems such a shame.'

'I know. But I wouldn't worry about Brad, if I were you. He's in for a nice surprise.'

'I don't fucking believe it,' said Brad, kicking the hissing Triumph Herald. 'That noise isn't steam, you know. The fucking thing's laughing at me.'

'What's wrong?' asked Carmen.

'The bloody fan-belt again.'

They were just outside Paris on their way back to the UK and it was close to midnight. In the last few weeks of the season Brad and Carmen had been inseparable, so much so that a leisurely drive through France with Brad had appealed to Carmen much more than a rushed two-hour flight into Gatwick.

'Come here and give us a kiss,' said Brad.

Carmen walked around to him and they cuddled each other.

'D'you know what?'

'What?' replied Carmen.

'Getting the sack was the best thing that ever happened to me.'

'Course it was,' said Carmen, squeezing him tightly and tucking her smiling face into his chest. 'Otherwise you wouldn't have met me.'

'Exactly.' Brad kissed her and walked to the front of the car. 'You might as well get in.'

'Okay.'

'All I need now is for a sodding jeep to come trundling up the road,' mumbled Brad.

'What was that?' said Carmen.

'Nothing. I was just thinking about an old friend. I'll check my case to see how much money I've got and we'll have to find a B & B to stay in until the morning.'

Brad went to the back of the car and fumbled around for

his wallet. He found an envelope he didn't remember packing. Curious, he pulled it out. Carmen was sitting in the car so couldn't see what he was doing. He opened the envelope and was startled to see a wad of pesetas. With it was a note.

Brad
I can't explain what this is all about. You should not have been sacked but it was partly my fault that you were. From what I can gather, Alison would have sacked you anyway. Although Alison got her just deserts, she was not in fact responsible for stealing the money and planting the envelopes. I was.

This million pesetas (about £4000, I believe) may seem a lot, but after what you have been through it is probably no more than you deserve. All I ask is that you tell no one about this. Clearly, I cannot reveal my identity.

A shocked Brad stood in silence for a few moments. Once he had composed himself he took the cases out of the car and opened the passenger door. 'Come on, out you get. There's been a change of plan.'

'What do you mean?'

'Sod staying in a B & B, I feel like splashing out. Let's get a taxi into Paris and spend a romantic weekend in a top hotel. I'll get the car sorted out tomorrow.'

'Are you feeling all right?'

'Never better.'

'What are you up to, Streeter?' asked Carmen suspiciously. 'What kind of sexually perverted act are you trying to bribe me into doing now? 'Cos I'm telling you this for nothing. Anything that involves one of those horrible French poodles and we're history.'

'I'll have to give Greg a call and see if there's any bonus points for that. Anyway, we've already done virtually every perverted act possible and *you*'ve come up with half of those.'

Carmen slapped him playfully. 'So what's the catch?'

'No catch. Let's say I've only just realised that I've got more out of this season than I previously thought.'

He locked the door and they made their way back to the road.

'You know what, Brad?' She linked her arm through his.

'What?'

'It's actually been quite a short season.'

'Funny. Everyone says that.'